A Girl Must Live
STORIES *AND* POEMS

NAOMI MITCHISON

A Girl Must Live

STORIES AND POEMS

RICHARD DREW PUBLISHING
GLASGOW

First published 1990 by
Richard Drew Publishing Ltd
6 Clairmont Gardens
Glasgow G3 7LW Scotland

The publisher acknowledges the financial
assistance of the Scottish Arts Council
in the publication of this book.

British Library Cataloguing
in Publication Data

Mitchison, Naomi 1897 —
A girl must live.
I. Title
823.914 (F)

ISBN 0–86267–287–2

270497

Designed by James W. Murray
Set in Bembo by D.J. Clark, Glasgow
Printed and bound in Great Britain
by Butler & Tanner Ltd, Frome and London

Contents

Introduction

A YOUNG SCOTTISH MOTHER ATTEMPTS SUICIDE because her tinker origins become public knowledge; an inexperienced young dragon encounters unexpected difficulties when he sets out in conquest of his first princess; a dolphin from the future relates how humans engineered the third world war; a flying saucer bisects a repressed lady scientist, producing a striking instance of 'split personality'. Four situations picked at random from the extraordinary range of stories in this collection.

But while situations and characters are very different, and the writer employs every mode from realism to fantasy and back again, some qualities recur. Alongside science and logic the stories often celebrate the irrational, the religious, or the magic; frequent consideration is given to ancestral gifts and powers, as well as to future generations, mutant or naturally evolved; the importance of communication and understanding is central. The stories are frequently presented by individual voices: more than half of them have first person narrators, most but not all female, most but not all human. Their voices are all different, urgent or gentle, insistent or comic or informational. All, it seems, talking rather than writing, and to a perceived audience that is definitely present.

The reader will find that variety is a keynote of the collection: the author of these stories and poems is not to be pigeon-holed, nor can they be described by any ready tag such as Comic, Scottish, African, English, Science Fiction. And yet Mitchison has produced such a range of marvellous things that Science Fiction enthusiasts for example proudly claim her as a mistress of that multifarious mode, as indeed she is. But the experience of reading this volume shows how insufficient such labels are. Mitchison has published over eighty books, and uncounted numbers of stories and poems in magazines, journals and anthologies. Her settings can be in Botswana, a Highland fishing village, or deep space, and the time may be in the most distant past, as in her most recent novel, *Early in Orcadia* (1987). Or now, or tomorrow, or the most unthinkable future. Perhaps a collection of stories such as this is the only practicable way of sampling her range. In 1986 I edited a volume of her longer short stories, *Beyond This Limit: Selected Shorter Fiction*. It attempted to indicate her development from 1930 to 1980. This time, only postwar stories have been selected, and the overall impression is different, as we will see.

The commonest tag for Mitchison, the one everyone takes for granted, is 'historical novelist'. For many decades Naomi Mitchison has been regarded as primarily an historical novelist, concerned above all with the ancient civilizations of Greece and Rome. [It was she who inspired Mary Renault to write her novels of ancient history and myth.] And she has certainly written a large number of acclaimed historical novels, from *The Conquered* (1923) and *The Corn King and the Spring Queen* (1931) to *The Blood of the Martyrs* (1939) and *The Bull Calves* (1947). No literary critic in his or her senses would attempt to ignore these achievements or try to play them down. But in the course of the fascinating experience of collecting, selecting and editing these postwar stories, I have been made more conscious that the postwar Mitchison seems to follow on the whole a rather different pattern from the prewar writer. The stories, like her postwar fiction generally, reflect this.

So I shall here outline two phases of her adult fiction, suggesting that the early and the later Mitchison are intriguingly different in some of their interests, settings and modes, although certain central and recurrent themes make her work always recognisable as such. In my Introduction to *Beyond This Limit: Selected Shorter Fiction*, I described her development as a novelist and stressed in particular the integrity of her work, her themes. I do not wish to disown that description in any way, but here the stories under consideration cause me to stress instead the change of perspective that I see in her work, which makes 'historical novelist' a rather misleading label for the later Mitchison.

The pivotal book is her Scottish historical novel, *The Bull Calves* (1947), one of her very finest. Its characters are her own ancestors, the Haldanes (she has a lasting fascination with genes), and it is set in the troubled peace in Scotland after the effective civil war begun by the Jacobite Rising of 1745-6. I think we could say that after this her focus shifted somewhat, and present and future were more directly confronted, while to some extent she turned to history for inspiration less often. She did not give it up, of course: fine novels like *Behold Your King* and *Cleopatra's People* make that very clear, as do many works for younger readers. But the contemporary, the fantastic, the future, are much more often the subjects she chooses, and to some extent this collection of stories reflects this.

If we turn first to what I shall call the prewar Mitchison, for the sake of shorthand, then 'historical novelist' is an obvious and useful tag. She began publishing historical novels in 1923, and only published her first works with contemporary settings, with some difficulties of censorship, in the early Thirties. When Bob Tait and I interviewed Mitchison in 1984, she was candid about her early conversion to ancient history.

IM: Your lively and entertaining memoirs include such remarks as 'history bored me deeply', and 'the choking dullness of any history people tried to turn me on to.' So how does it happen that you started off in particular as a historical novelist?

NM: Well, I was very badly taught, I think. The school in some ways was very good, but at that period, I think history *was* badly taught, and it wasn't until I married that my husband, who was a double first in Greats, was terribly keen that I should wander about the same world as his. First of all he wanted me to learn Greek, and gave me a 'Greek Without Tears' textbook, but I didn't get far with that. And I was always writing these imaginary things. Plays usually at that time. I just put my people anywhere. The first play I did, I put them in a remote part of the Andes, so remote that anything could happen. This was just fairy tales. And then I wrote one of these plays and he read it and I said, 'Well, when could that have been?' 'Well, about the fifth century AD.' And I said, 'Oh, what's happening then?' And he said, 'Would you like to read a bit about it?' So he gave me the appropriate volume of Gibbon [*The Decline and Fall of the Roman Empire*]. Then I thought, this is rather interesting; I wonder what happened before that. So then I read the volume before and I gradually read backwards through Gibbon and then bravely I read Mommsen [*History of Rome*]. By that time I was hooked.

This initiated a decade or so of historical fiction, from *The Conquered* (1923) to the vast and justly acclaimed epic of 1931, *The Corn King and the Spring Queen*. Ancient Greece and a mythical Scythia, the opposition of Athens and Sparta, Caesar's Gallic wars, the Greek island states, all these gripped and held her imagination for the time. And she developed an extraordinary talent for commenting through these fictions on the contemporary world, which has always been a major concern for her. So *The Conquered* is a clear comment on the troubled state of contemporary Ireland, as well as a novel of the Gallic wars, just as *The Blood of the Martyrs* (1939) depicts Christian martyrdom in Nero's Rome while uttering a loud warning about threats to freedom in Europe just before the war.

So a pattern was established. It involved a lot of research, which the writer discovered she loved doing [she was to produce a very long set of notes to *The Bull Calves,* in which she discussed some of the evidence with the reader in a relaxed and leisurely way]. The delight with which she discovered the ancient world is unfeigned and infectious. Oscar Wilde said unkindly of one of George Moore's novels that he was conducting his musical education in public, but I don't think it is at all unkind to suggest that much of the zest and excitement of Mitchison's early work was related to her conducting her classical and political education in public. And these books have initiated a like process in many later readers.

By far the most interesting and voluminous commentator on Mitchison's life and fiction is Mitchison herself. In the last few years a number of volumes of memoirs and the like have been published, which shed all sorts of light on the writer and her work, and I have no room here for condensed appreciation of these. The best introduction is an article by Alison Smith in *Chapman* 50-51, called 'The Lady from the Big House'. I can only make an enthusiastic gesture toward these books. There are three recent autobiographical works, *Small Talk . . . Memories of an Edwardian Childhood* (1973), *All Change Here: Girlhood and Marriage* (1975), and *You May Well Ask: A Memoir, 1920-1940* (1979). During the Second World War, Mitchison was one of those who kept a diary for Mass Observation, and a generous selection of these was made and edited by Dorothy Sheridan in 1985 as *Among You Taking Notes . . . The Wartime Diary of Naomi Mitchison 1939-1945.* One of the most important things that happened to Mitchison — and thus to her work — since the war was the beginning of her relationship with Chief Linchwe of the Bakgatla. The encounter and its ramifications, and all the self-scrutiny it gave rise to are chronicled in a particularly interesting book, *Return to the Fairy Hill* (1966). [Unfortunately, this book is very hard to find.] These books offer invaluable evidence about the fiction, as well as the particular pleasures of memoirs, giving the privileged reader free access to an extraordinary life.

I think we might describe the first phase of Mitchison's prewar fiction writing, from *The Conquered* (1923) to *The Delicate Fire* (1933), as the classical phase. This includes several novels and volumes of stories, some now hard to find, and culminates in *The Corn King and the Spring Queen.* They reveal a deep interest in power as it is exercised between individuals or between, say, city states. In these books shocking situations are explored with sensitivity, as the author, committed feminist and socialist, works out her own ideas of life.

The most permanent of these will remain unchanged in whatever 'phase' of her work we turn to, the bedrock of her faith in human beings and society, and their possibilities. The most explicit statement of this kind comes not from an historical novel but from the overcrowded pages of *We Have Been Warned,* the contemporary and highly autobiographical novel that fell foul of publishers' prejudice and effective censorship and was at last published in 1935. Here the main character Dione Galton works out her idea of 'good will'. She comes to see most ethics as 'commercial ideas'; fair deals, the scales of justice, 'the jealous God of Scotland, the Family Grocer visiting with his wrath those who questioned the price of his sandy sugar or attempted to evade an extortionate bill.' Her 'new idea' is in a sense as old as Aristotle, who said: 'When people are friends there is no need for justice between them.' Her idea of good will or brotherhood is specifically 'non-commercial':

Good will, that curious product of consciousness, of leisure and energy to spare and share. That thing we put out against the forces of interest. That extra thing. Religions and nations and political parties have taken it and used it as coinage, have said that you must only give it in exchange for value. Good will towards other Christians, Moslems, Jews, towards other English, Scots, Allies, Europeans, towards other Monarchists, Republicans, Conservatives, Labour folk, Communists; hatred and cheating towards heathens, non-Moslems, Gentiles, towards the people across the frontier or with a different-coloured skin, towards all the other political parties. We will give you good will, but you must give us in fair exchange your soul, or your body, or your mind. And lately, since good will has been spoken of more freely, since we have given lip-service to universal good will, distributed free as a kind of advertisement for humanity, we have asked instead that we should be given something to show for it, peace, prosperity, happiness even. If we don't get it we are angry about our bargain and say we have been done. But the whole point of good will is that it is a by-product, a thing we can have too much of for our own immediate surroundings and belongings, as a mother can have too much milk for her baby. We have to give it away, not only in place but in time. We have to give even to the future.

This passage has obvious relevance to 'The Wife of Aglaos', but just as much to the science fiction novels and stories of the last thirty years. Another subject of equal importance throughout her work concerns loyalties. Mitchison said to us in 1984:

I'm sure that one of the most interesting things that happens to anyone, is this business of loyalties and how to reconcile them . . . One's got a loyalty — presumably to one's family — to start with, and then it widens out to one's village, one's town, one's country. Perhaps to being European, and finally, I suppose, to being a human being. But one feels *that* loyalty is the one that's got to be cultivated, because at the moment we are *all* threatened, whatever our colour or race or anything.

If I say that she is absorbed in questions of loyalty, in creating loyalties of the widest kind, and in conserving or creating the loyalties that unite smaller groups, this will be a fair start. And if I add that her fiction is often involved with the clash between personal loyalty and group loyalty, or loyalty to an idea, I think she will not disagree.

Mitchison was to go on reminding people of topical issues, however unwelcome — indeed she still does. But as her fiction deepened and widened, her books ceased to be simply applicable on more than one level. All the same, it is clear that *The Blood of the Martyrs* (1939) had much to say about oppressed minorities in the Europe of the time, and it was no accident that *The Bull Calves* (1947), set in 1746, in the aftermath of the Jacobite Rising of Forty-Five, dealt with the end of a damaging and divisive war, and the need for reconstruction and reconciliation. After *The Conquered,* the topical reference is less direct and less obvious, but the fictional world is very much more realised, the characters become more real and complicated, and the issues can be as messy and difficult as we recognise them to be in real life. They also tend to seem 'relevant' in a more permanent way. Mitchison is never one of those writers who turn to history for escape: if she is not in search of direct contemporary lessons or analogies, she tends to be working out on historical canvases issues of crucial importance to human civilization generally. Again and again, in historical and modern novels, in biographies and political or social treatises, in poetry and plays, she writes about what makes people fully human, about values and loyalties, and all manner of relationships involving love, sex, power and slavery.

The exploration of the psychology of both slave and slave owner is a central interest for Mitchison in her prewar books. This is the subject of the sequence of stories in *The Delicate Fire* called 'Lovely Mantinea'. One of these, 'The Wife of Aglaos', can be found in *Beyond This Limit: Selected Shorter Fiction* and is characteristic. In this sequence, Mantinea is destroyed, and Greek citizens are sold into slavery: even from their new perspective some of them find it hard to reject the enormity of slavery as an institution, and only perceive the unnatural injustice of their own particular situations. The evils of slavery and the subjugation of women are interwoven subtly here, along with an often shocking story of people under stress finding pragmatic answers to the evils of life as they occur. It has to be remembered — and the feminist Mitchison does not allow us to forget, although she is rarely strident — that even in the best days of Athens, the best of Greek states, the situation of women was a state of oppression, however kindly.

The early Thirties mark a new phase in Mitchison's prewar fiction, when she abruptly turned away from the Hellenic world, and temporarily abandoned historical fiction altogether. This coincided with darkening clouds in Europe, and increased political commitment by both Mitchison and her husband Dick, who began his apprenticeship as a Labour candidate, at first in a seat where he had little chance. Mitchison supported him loyally and successfully in his political career, turning down an offer in 1945 to be a candidate herself in Dundee. But she *had* stood as Labour candidate for the Scottish Universities in 1935, honourably saving her deposit in another predictably unwinnable seat. The books of the Thirties are more various than before. They now first include the utterly contemporary and personal, and the self-consciously Scottish in *We Have Been Warned* and *Beyond This Limit* (1935). *The Fourth Pig* (1936) is a collection of stories and fables often rather too dominated by socialist intentions for total imaginative success; and the non-fiction *Vienna Diary* (1934), chronicles her own experience of the counter-revolution of Dollfuss in 'Red Vienna' [she came home with her knickers stuffed with compromising documents . . .]. And as the Fascist challenge to European peace grew more insistent, she tried direct warning, in *The Moral Basis of Politics* (1938).

In my Introduction to *Beyond This Limit: Selected Shorter Fiction* I wrote at some length about *We Have Been Warned* (1935), which presents very difficult problems to the literary critic. On the one hand it is a very revelatory personal account of the author, her life and artistic and political interests, and a very urgent warning against the dangers of Fascism; but on the other hand it inevitably lacks objectivity, and is overcrowded in every direction. It reminds the reader forcibly that Mitchison comes from a very distinguished family, accustomed to great houses and public affairs, and generally conscious of their social responsibility. It is people like her own family that she addresses particularly in many novels, what she calls 'the intelligentsia, the people who should be giving a lead'. Mitchison's socialism may be atypical of her family inheritance: her sense of responsibility is not. This is the first book in which the writer — through her two main female characters, sisters — is self-consciously Scottish, and interested in the implications of her Scottishness.

The war caused the longest hiatus in Mitchison's publishing history. During it, she and her family lived mainly in Carradale, Kintyre, which they had bought in 1937, and her developing sense of Scottish identity was confirmed. Her postwar writing is often consciously Scottish. In these years *The Bull Calves* underwent its long gestation period. And at this time she wrote some of the best of the stories published in 1958 as *Five Men and a Swan* (the title story and 'The Hunting of Ian Og' are both in *Beyond This Limit: Selected Shorter Fiction*). Mitchison's postwar writing — and her Scottish writing — has begun and still continues. Ever since 1937 the writer has based herself in Carradale, with however many globe-trotting expeditions and spelis in London. She has been farmer and trawler owner, has served at length in local government and on the Highland Panel, fighting for improvements in transport and education — and farming, fishing and forestry — in the Highlands and Islands. And in her 'Saltire Self-Portrait' (1986) she points out that since *The Bull Calves* she has written nine books with a definitely Scottish background (not all of course are adult fiction).

I shall just point briefly to *Lobsters on the Agenda* (1952). It deals with the contemporary local concerns of a Highland fishing village, the most urgent being the hotly contested question of a new village hall. It is suggested that this may help create a sense of community, and stem the flow of the young to the towns and cities:

... the Village Halls might be the thing we need, the kind of magic thing to keep people together, to make them able to stand up against the cities and all they've got there. Some place where people would come together naturally in friendship, for a common purpose.

The handling of this novel of parochial politics and sectarian differences, gossip and antagonisms is expert and confident, and quite unruffled by the news that among the members of the visiting Highland Panel will be a woman: 'Mrs Mitchison from Carradale; she writes books.' Mrs Mitchison plays only a tiny part, but she does point out in passing a central idea, that there is not only one kind of loyalty: 'there are a dozen! There's family and class and job, as well as nation — and church'. And she adds the possibility of party-political affiliations, which strikes the village company dumb. *Lobsters on the Agenda* is an accomplished and delightful novel in what is very definitely a postwar mode, and should be high on any list of Mitchison novels needing reprinting.

In the postwar Mitchison, writing styles vary and co-exist: she seems to enjoy a new freedom of approach. The Scottish interest certainly persists; the most recent novel, *Early in Orcadia* (1987), goes back in time further than the author has ventured before, and chronicles the lives of very early settlers in Orkney. From now on Mitchison holds to the themes she has made her own, in a fascinating variety of eras and places, with increasing attention to scientific and ecological subjects. And since the war Mitchison has written considerably more books for children and young people than novels for adults. These fall outside the scope of this Introduction, but their concerns are unsurprising, from the writer we have seen so far. They are (always painlessly) educational: they typically take children to other countries, to meet other races, to discover their common humanity. Often they are concerned to link children to a heritage that seems to be slipping away: *The Swan's Road* (1954) and *The Land the Ravens Found* (1955), for example, retell stories from Viking sagas. The Scottish offerings memorably include *The Big House* (1950), a fairytale of childhood in Carradale, in and out of time, which also makes rewarding reading for Mitchison's adult readers.

The adult fiction since *Lobsters on the Agenda* is also more varied than before. It includes several fine novels that do not fit any obvious grouping. *Travel Light* (1952: now available from Virago) is a charming fairytale which lightly and entertainingly incorporates mythic material; and *To The Chapel Perilous* (1955) is a strong novel about the nature of truth and history. We see the Grail story as it happens, in front of two modern-minded newspaper reporters only too conscious of what stories the managements require of them. When *several* knights are seen to emerge from the Chapel Perilous, each bearing his own Grail, it is up to the reporters to decide what the truth of the matter will thereafter be. Clearly the two delightful stories here, 'Nagli's First Princess' and 'Death of a Peculiar Boar', belong to the same world as these last two. History is by no means banished; *Behold Your King* (1957) is a novel of the betrayal and death of Jesus, with thought-provoking political presentation, and *Cleopatra's People* (1972) shifts between different times in Cleopatra's life and the times of the daughter of one of her women, again producing provocative political analysis.

There are only two other identifiable areas of subject matter and style left, the African and the Science Fiction. Both of these are clearly important for the stories here as well as for her fiction as a whole. In her brief 'Saltire Self-Portrait' the author indicates in passing the way in which her sudden but ongoing commitment to the Bakgatla tribe in Botswana connects to the Scottish dimension, and indeed reinforces it:

> By the mid-sixties I was also much involved with Botswana and managed to get back there every year, if only for three or four weeks. The loyalty seemed to parallel rather than erode my feeling for Scotland. There were plenty of likenesses, one being the class relationships, including the Chiefs, in a rapidly moving political situation. Another is the oral tradition of stories and singing, with the importance of certain kinds of tribal songs for special occasions, comparable with the 'great music' of the Highlands. Botswana visitors to Carradale found no problems in making friends with farmers or fishermen.

And her next sentence again testifies to the variousness of the postwar Mitchison: 'I wrote some science fiction at this time, but it was difficult to concentrate on any one thing.' Many books have African elements, including biographies and children's books, but in adult fiction we have *When We Become Men* (1965) and *Images of Africa* (1980). *When We Become Men* strikingly reverses the question of loyalties, so often central. Isaac begins as an urban freedom-fighter, inadequately and superficially self-educated in his aims: he has to learn a more local loyalty, to individuals and to tribe, before he can fully become man. But although these are both strong books, and draw the reader into a new and important intimacy with tribal ways of thinking, I find the non-fictional *Return to the Fairy Hill* even more revealing. In *The Big House,* the fairy hill was a dangerously magic place, 'where they both awfully much wanted to stay and yet knew they had got to go'. In *Return to the Fairy Hill* Mitchison combines an account of her relationship with the chief and his tribe with an examination of it, a re-scrutiny and revaluation of the themes of much of the earlier work, which makes it another book of exceptional interest. And several of the stories here, including the title story, testify in very different ways to Mitchison's knowledge and love of Africa.

The Science Fiction books, *Memoirs of a Spacewoman* (1962), *Solution Three* (1975) and *Not By Bread Alone* (1983), extend Mitchison's central themes in new ways, to other intelligent species, to planet-wide considerations. Science has been an abiding interest to the daughter of an internationally renowned physiologist, the sister to an outstanding geneticist, herself no mere amateur of botany. Threats to human genes, and undue standardisation, or cloning, are one concern, and enormous strides in food production through interference with natural plant structures are another: these can eliminate world hunger, with unguessable consequences, or can go disastrously wrong. *Not By Bread Alone* is the most serious indication of the hazards of too quickly grasping at technological 'improvement', but for me it remains very much a book of ideas, working well as such, but where the characters carry little conviction. I think *Solution Three* manages to combine the message with imaginative fiction more successfully. A number of the stories in this volume belong to the sub-genre of Science Fiction, and they illustrate once again Mitchison's range and inventiveness.

I have tried to illustrate Mitchison's range and inventiveness in the first set of stories here. They range over Africa, South East Asia, India, Japan, Scotland, England and various mythical or fairy tale regions. They are set in a range of times from the early civilization of 'Telling to the Master' or the quasi-Arthurian times of 'Death of a Peculiar Boar', to the topicality of 'Nobody likes a Refugee' or 'The Money They Must Have Spent'.

The present volume also contains a short selection of poems. These illustrate characteristic themes and loyalties, and all tend to some extent towards a narrative mode that makes them congruent to the stories. 'The Talking Oats' is a deliberately Scottish poem, illustrating some sombre bits of Highland history, and 'Siren Night' and 'London Burning' both belong to the Blitz, experienced by the poet in London. She said to us in Carradale: 'When I'm here I feel basically a Scot but in London during the Blitz I felt tremendously a Londoner. Not English but a Londoner. We set our will against yours, the will of London. We won't be bombed out.'

The stories in the third section of the volume particularly illustrate the ways in which the contemporary Mitchison is concerned with the present and the future. They range widely again, but can be contained under a general umbrella of Science Fiction or fantasy. 'Mary and Joe' is a futuristic variation on an old story we will all recognise, while 'Rat-world' is a bizarre account of the future which contains an urgent message for us now.

Many of the stories and poems are here published for the first time. Others have appeared in a wide variety of journals and magazines, and anthologies of fiction. Particular acknowledgement must be made of *Chapman* magazine, which has published many of Mitchison's recent works, and in 1987 devoted a double number (50-51) to the celebration of Mitchison and of Alasdair Gray.

As she explained to us in our interview, Mitchison's earliest writing began with stories, and the subsequent desire to place them. I am inclined to think that *Not By Bread Alone* began with an idea, and the need for a story to illustrate it. And *Early in Orcadia* began with a peculiarly evocative visual image:

It really started off, oh, years and years ago, when I was on the Highland Panel, and we were up on that coast, talking to estate owners about sheep and so on, and going along that road one was always seeing these white shining cliffs of Orkney across ten miles of sea. And that stayed with me and stayed with me, and I did nothing with it.

All three methods produced recognisably Mitchison books, linked together not only by her characteristic use of language but by her fascination with human relationships under the most impossibly varied conditions. Her concentration on 'this business of loyalties and how to reconcile them' is central. The most hopeful of her books show individuals who have found ways of combining personal and local loyalties with larger ones, like 'being a human being'. That last one is the one that's got to be cultivated now, 'because at the moment we are *all* threatened, whatever our colour or race or anything'. People are now, she says, 'in a position where they have just *got* to work together', but in life as in her fiction, it is rarely quite straightforward:

I think it's all terribly difficult because, however much one wants to be a person of good will, one's running into contradictions the whole time. One can only avoid contradictions by shutting one's eyes quite a bit. If you are a good Marxist you can probably avoid certain contradictions, but then other people are outside. There are always people who are outside, and even if America and Russia got on terms and hugged one another, there would be people like the Ayatollah.

Isobel Murray

(The interview frequently quoted here is one of a series funded by the University of Aberdeen Development Trust.)

Stories

A Girl Must Live

LAUREEN HAD STARTED LOOKING OVER HER DRESSES and this always made her a bit gloomy, most of all if she'd happened to have seen something on someone or in a shop window and just knew how it would suit her. But out of reach. She turned over the frilly nylon tops and old Mission overalls she sometimes wore as a kind of tease — but she didn't really like doing it — and there was her old Brit passport, still in date. Before Dad died, and she was always hoping. Her Dad's name. Thompson, real Brit. Fancy never knowing her Mum's name. Only just that one single time with her Dad getting a bit tiddly and speaking about poor Mum, how she'd been a settler's get, but had been thrown back. Back among the blacks, he said. Till he'd picked her out. Didn't want to talk about it, only to tell Laureen that she'd plenty of white blood. Well, she knew that, she felt it, and how could the Mission have believed all those lies about her? Part lies anyway. For of course, well, a girl's a girl, isn't she?

Aunt Cissy had that short African hair under her old scarf and she was her Mum's sister, half sister anyway. But Laureen had lovely long hair, better than Indian hair because it was ever so wavy, and she wore it shoulder length. Yes, that was nice. She brushed it slowly and then looked at herself in the hand mirror; that wasn't so nice, no. There were little lines beginning under her eyes and at the corners of her mouth. Smile please. Yes, they disappeared, almost, but when she was feeling low like she was now, it didn't work. She had a pale complexion, right, and a pink lipstick was all right, but if only she'd been cream and roses! She rearranged the bottles of lotion on the shelf: English Meadow — what's a meadow anyway? Dad always saying he'd take her back one day. And then he'd died and there was nothing but the hospital bill. Not that they hadn't been decent. Him and his grand notions about what a white man could do in Africa! And they got cards from his family at Christmas when she was a kid, but then there were fewer and then they stopped.

She did wish ever-so that she could find somewhere else to live, not this little flat, even though she'd tried to make it look bright. Things had happened here that she didn't want to remember. Well, a girl's got to live, hasn't she? Let alone that there'd been nice things too. That young chap from the University, oh he was sweet, even if he was an African and nothing else. Pity he had to go off to that job. And then there's that nice Indian, always telling me what he'd do if he was rich, the presents he'd give me, not that he'll ever get rich but nice hearing him talk and he brings these Indian take-aways from the curry shop. And there's Mr Chilao, I can count on him. But Monkey's gone off to the mines. So now? Old Bertie Bobs wanting me to feel him up, not nice, and I have to get in that lemon drink he fancies, but it's regular money. And that chum of his, white they may be, but it makes me sick. And that ten kwacha note I thought I had in my evening bag — knew I had — now it's gone and who could it be? You just turn your back to put the kettle on and they think you're nobody!

It couldn't have been any of the girls I know, my set. No. Or could it have been? That Florence, big lump from the Mission School where she'd been Under-Matron in the old days before the big misunderstanding? No. Must have been a client. For a joke maybe. But it's not a joke to me. Oh well, better get dressed and back to the usual. The five notes there anyway, tomorrow must get tea, tin of milk, biscuits if they've got any. Now, was I wearing the blue with the long ear-rings when — ? My lucky colour. Well, we'll see. Lock up, hold that bag tight, you never know. And then the bar and me in my corner, sipping my glass with my little finger out the way Dad showed me, lady-like and looking pensive, that was his word, whatever does it mean. Is anything ever going to come right for me?

And it was then that Mr Chikonki came in. At first glance she could tell he wasn't a regular. An African anyway, but somehow he looked different, very upright, with his white hair and a good, well-pressed suit. She couldn't help looking. White hair looks well over brown eyes and his shirt was snow-white; a nice new tie, not too gaudy. She must have smiled a little, because he came over, sat at her table and offered her a ciggie. And so they got talking. She had a little trouble with his accent at first. But it seemed he came from a long way off, another province, somewhere it took you a day's journey to get to. But in a while he began to tell her about a house he had bought in Lusaka: to be nearer his associates he said. Well, that was certainly a good address! He spoke sharply to the waiter, commandingly. Well, yes, she'd take a tiny brandy, just for company.

He went on talking, as if he needed someone to talk to. She asked more about the house, what the rooms looked like, how many, tried to find out about his family. He spoke of a brother in politics, yes, she thought she'd heard his name, someone going on about corruption, the way they always did. He told the waiter to bring a box of chocolates, gave him a couple of good notes. She looked away delicately, but noted that he'd pushed the change away like a real gentleman.

He opened the box, offered it, touched her hair, ever so gently, then suddenly said: 'My great new house is empty. Woman, will you marry me?'

She said: 'My name is Laureen.' And she was breathing quickly, she could hardly see him.

'Laureen,' he said, 'Laureen,' and he snatched both her hands and held them between his. What does one say? What does one do? 'Answer,' he said.

So what can a girl say but yes.

He took her out and there at the door was a Mercedes and the driver opened the door and it started off and they were in the back seat together and then he turned her way while she was still wondering what to say and then — well, it had been like something in a film almost, all arms and legs and she couldn't do a thing, but if she was really going to get married — oh what a man! She couldn't hardly stand on her feet when they got to the house, but it was real, the big gates, the drive, the Mercedes at the door and her getting out of it and had the driver seen in his mirror? So after a bit he took her up to a room with a big bed and he said, 'For you.' And before she knew he was at it again, but she couldn't help it, she felt wonderful.

When she woke up it was still true, she knew by the way he looked at her. Then he said, 'My Wife.' And after that what a whirl, money, money, money, new clothes, everything. She gave away all she'd had in the old flat, even her nearly new pair of shoes, the other girls saying wasn't she lucky in spite of him being his age and a black — they never thought she'd fall for someone like that! But they didn't know! Well, she was getting ever so fond of him, truly, looked forward to that look on his face that meant — well, she'd get all hot herself. And the things he gave her, a necklace and ear-rings and could they be real emerald? And going shopping in the very best places, new nighties, bras, naughty panties, and then the wedding dress, she just couldn't believe it, but the day came and the church and the funny little priest, so she supposed it was all right and now she was Mrs Chikonki. There hadn't been a real party, but then, could she have asked her friends, wouldn't they have been out of place, saying the wrong things? Some of his friends came in and drank champagne, the real expensive kind, and made jokes in what seemed to be a language of their own.

Mrs Chikonki. She couldn't quite believe in it but there it was and all the rest of her life dropped away and she didn't miss it, not one bit, and him saying he wanted a son and this son would have soft hair like hers. Well, that was a thought and she'd need to stop taking the pill — if she went on someone would find out and tell him, one of those two cheeky maids who were supposed to keep the house clean. He had a man in the kitchen. But what would her Dad have said? His telling her that if ever he caught her so much as looking at one of these bloody stuck-up kaffirs — but oh goodness, that was all past wasn't it and she'd done more than look. Even before getting married to one. Well, a girl has to live, hasn't she? And that nasty letter from the Mission so she couldn't get what some people call respectable employment. Not that it is, always. But being married, black or white, that was respectable, and what a man!

It was a bit of a shock when one of the cheeky maids, a girl called Mutinta who'd at least got to Grade Three, told her that Mr Chikonki had a wife back in his village, perhaps two wives. But did they count? In his position an African has to have wives or they think there's something wrong with him. She remembered that was what her Dad had told her, and he'd ended up with a black chum he used to drink with, told Laureen the old boy was a Chief in his own place otherwise he wouldn't have associated. So it must be all right about these wives and she wouldn't mention it, not to her hubby. Then one morning she heard a great yelling and caterwauling and when she looked out from the window that faced onto the back yard there was Mr Chikonki with a great leather whip, slashing away at a couple of men, and when she asked Mutinta who was looking out with her, what it was all about, the girl giggled and said it was the village wives' brothers, but he had chased them. He looked very grand, standing there staring at the gate with that whip curled round his wrist.

That house, yes, it seemed to her that she was part of the house, the centre round which it was moving, and it was just as expensive as she had guessed. It was fitted up with radio, telly, and an all-electric kitchen, which she found a bit tricky if she just wanted a cup of tea, bathrooms in pink and blue with towels to match, big sofas here and there. And as to the master bedroom, it had everything, mirrors and lights and all these great cupboards, drawers and hangers full of their clothes, Mr and Mrs. The other rooms were only part furnished and when she told him she'd need silver and crystal for the dining rom, it was no problem, just go and choose it. Well, she did a once-in-a-lifetime splurge, got whatever took her fancy. She was driven round the town, with this great feeling that it was no longer that dirty pool where a girl had to swim or sink, but a place where people like Mrs Chikonki could still be served with special things she'd hardly dreamed of before. She could always use the Mercedes, not a very recent model, but nothing to complain of. The cheeky maids, unpacking, could hardly speak for wonder: pictures, table cloths, copper palm pots, leather writing sets in every room, a whole shelf full of books, sets of romances mostly, lots of love and a happy ending, silver-backed brushes, separate breakfast and tea things, as well as wine and chocolates, and the tins that the big shops kept hidden for their best customers, and she was one of them. But what a price and she must watch her figure. Mr Chikonki bought the spirits, brandy and whisky, and kept them in a special locked cabinet.

And, well, it was all right and she wasn't going to let him be disappointed. It would be letting down the white race if he was, wouldn't it? She did find she had to do a bit of relaxing in the mornings after he'd gone out in his white shirt and smart suit to whatever it was he did do, she never quite found out and most likely, she thought, it might be something to do with politics and she wouldn't understand. Some days, looking round, she wished she could show it all to some of her old set, how they'd have gaped, but she sensed he wouldn't like it and anyway she was above them now. She wished sometimes that he'd let her give some more parties, not just his friends coming in for drinks and never really appreciating the little canapes she'd got the cook to make for them. Just once or twice there were wives and she did hope she'd impressed them, but you can't tell, can you, not with strangers. But she did feel, inside, that she was a lady, the lady of the house, like in some of the Romances she was always reading.

So, most mornings she'd settle back with the radio or the telly and her new manicure set and perhaps a tiny drinkie and a fashion paper. Then in no time it was the afternoon and he'd come back from wherever he'd been and you'd hear him splashing around in the bathroom and then — well, you're his wife, aren't you?

Sometimes important people came to see him. She liked the UNIP man and always agreed with him; sometimes he would even turn from the men's conversation and draw her in. Once there was an official photographer and she was photographed along with her husband and someone from the Government. It came out in the paper but the faces weren't very like. She wondered if any of the old crowd had seen it.

But then something bad began to happen. He started to have belly pains and vomit. She was ever so worried. The German doctor came and spent lots of time and said soothing things and wrote out prescriptions and told him to avoid excitement. Laureen hadn't got pregnant either, not yet, and that annoyed Mr Chikonki, he seemed to think it was an insult to him. He broke some of her table crystal over that. Three of the good wine glasses, but never mind. She cried until he picked her up and began petting her. He looked as distinguished as ever and it wasn't her fault. Maybe next time.

The cheeky girls were whispering. Then Mutinta, whom she'd got rather to like, told her that it was certain that one or both of the other wives were using sorceries against Mr Chikonki, well, wasn't it natural? So it would be best to counter this and what did Madam think? So, if she'd find the money the girls would see to it that the correct things were done and those old sorceries hit in mid-air.

That was expensive. The next day the girls told her that their Doctor had tested and found that it was as they had supposed. He would need certain ingredients which were hard to come by these days. But Laureen emptied her purse and by the next evening Mr Chikonki was certainly better. Of course some people would say it was all nonsense, but she knew better. The stories she'd heard! Not just African superstition like the Mission said, but real nasty: so it's best to be careful.

She began to relax a bit but the worries seemed to go deeper. If — well if anything dreadful happened, what would it be like for her? Had he made a will? That was something she just couldn't ask. But there was the house and the money. She remembered in one of the True Romances how a girl had lost her elderly husband and truly mourned for him, but then a young man had come and seen her in her widow's weeds sitting by a rose bush. At first of course she refused him, but he was ever so understanding and it ended in wedding bells. And what would happen if she fell pregnant herself, and what was stopping that? Surely when you gave up the pill it happened? But she didn't know, not really. Anyway she saw to it that he took the German doctor's prescription regularly, and he seemed more like himself.

From time to time some of the family came to visit, especially that younger brother of his, Mr Chitoshi, who had the garage business. He wasn't as distinguished looking as her hubby. No, he was going bald and he kept making a joke about it, a very old dirty joke, but the brothers both laughed and Laureen kept quiet. This brother had said she should come round to the garage and take a ride in his new Mercedes model; she'd see a difference from her old one. Oh yes, he'd show her himself! And he gave her a look she didn't like. Asked her if she was modern, well of course she knew what he meant and when he kissed her goodbye he took his time and left a nasty smell in her mouth. She wished Mr Chikonki would stop him, but he was always having jokes with his brother and sometimes it looked as if she herself was one of them. She knew Cinyanja more or less, what the common Africans talked, but those two often talked in something she couldn't make out. Mr Chikonki taught her one or two words in it, but they were rather dirty words and she only used them to him in a whisper.

One day she asked Mutinta about her Doctor and had he been doing everything properly to keep off the sorceries. Mutinta said yes and, in case the sorceries were aimed at Madam as well, she had put a little something under the mattress of the big bed. She was sure everything would come right. But she told Laureen to beware of the garden boys. The older one was related to one of the village wives.

In a day or two when Mr Chikonki felt really better they went out in the Mercedes and he bought Laureen another necklace and bracelets to match. She even heard the price and felt quite satisfied that she was being properly valued, by him anyway. Looking at herself in the long mirror she felt, yes, those nasty lines that had been beginning, they've gone, isn't that nice. She'd let her hair grow a bit longer, hubby liked putting his hands through it and that new hairdresser she went to now had some pretty ways of doing it up. There were exercises in one of the fashion magazines, the body beautiful, firming up behind and before. And there were special kinds of smile, some very special only for hubby. She enjoyed doing this. Only for him. She wasn't going even to remember anyone else. Those days were over.

She'd got herself a sling bag in real crocodile with a good inside pocket. Something she'd always wanted in the old days, stared at in shop windows. But the price! That didn't matter now. Hubby wanted her to look the part. Right. She'd do just that. And then one afternoon he complained of the old belly pain, only worse. She gave him a double dose of his medicine and then suddenly he vomited blood like a volcano, all over her silk embroidered cover, all over her hands, all over the telephone as she snatched it up to ring the doctor. But when the doctor came he was dead. Just like that.

Mutinta came in when she called, screamed and ran out. Then the other maid started screaming as well. Then it was one person after another and she got pushed away and poor dead Mr Chikonki was cleaned up and laid out. She had kept on saying about the coffin 'only the best' and it was brought in and the curtains drawn and someone not herself had put his white shirt onto him and there he was on the dining room table, brass handles and everything. More and more people came and she went into the best bathroom and had a good cry. He'd been so sweet to her. Yes, really. And she started taking the bit of colour off the throat and cuffs of her black dress. At least, she said to herself, black suits me. The worst was that younger brother who started ordering everyone about as if he owned the place, telephoned the police, the newspapers, the UNIP office, everyone. Then he took the key of the drinks cabinet off Mr Chikonki's key-ring. He seemed to know what all the keys were for, and in a little he and some others — some she'd seen before, some she didn't know — were looking solemn and drinking out of the best crystal. None of them said a word to her and she didn't know what to do, she didn't want to go into the room with the coffin; she began to feel she was being treated like a — like a black, she said to herself, out of old memories, out of times she'd forgotten. Oh what would her Dad have said! Then two or three of the wives of all these relations came in and told her she must stay sitting in the best room and welcome the mourners as they came. After the funeral people would want to eat, so all must be made ready.

Mutinta, without being told, had finished taking the colour off her black dress. That was nice of her. Laureen put on the dress before going to speak to the cook who seemed to know, better than she did, what ought to be cooked and how much they'd need. Said he'd got money for the meat from Mr Chitoshi. Well, that was a cheek! But a relief in a way. She went into the best room and sat down in the middle of the sofa. Mutinta put a dark scarf over her head, saying, 'Poor Madam. Sad Madam.'

The mourners began coming in and it was dreadful. They touched her hand, she didn't know what to say and they sat all round. More chairs were brought in and she felt she was going to suffocate and if only there'd been just one white face! Not even white, but not black, always black. She began to cry. Several women came with big hankies and mopped her and murmured. But was she crying for him? Yes, she thought, poor hubby, what a surprise it must have been, dying like that. But she was crying for herself as well, all alone in this crowd. Little groups went out and she knew they'd gone to look at him there on the dining-room table with his white frills and brass handles, but she didn't want to go. She didn't want to see him dead.

Tea was brought in. She'd rather have had a stiff drink, but how could she say so. She felt as if she would never be able to move, not even to go to the bathroom. It was only after midnight that one of them, his sister perhaps, but she wasn't really sure, took her arm and said she must rest. The funeral would be in the morning.

She'd been at funerals a couple of times, just looking on when there was nowhere else to go, so she knew what the widow was supposed to do. But could she? Would she have to? She took off her black dress and lay down. In a minute she was asleep.

Mutinta woke her up, shaking her. 'Time,' she said. 'I have pressed the black dress.'

'Oh Mutinta,' she said, 'keep by me, do!'

'But Madam must go front,' said Mutinta, 'just behind poor Master. Here Madam, take clean hanky. Take shoes for walk on.' So it would be like that.

There was a crowd again, but the men this time. She heard them take the coffin off the dining room table. So long as they don't scratch the polish. But they sure will. They put it onto the hearse and then the

women were all round her whispering, telling her she must walk behind.
At last it all started and then she seemed to be walking for ever and it was
petrol stink from the hearse and people crowding behind and her feet
killing her. Now they were at the gate, turning in, thank goodness and
was that the same little priest who'd married them? Anyway, there was
the grave dug and they were all standing round and the prayers went on
and then there was singing and the coffin taken out of the hearse and
brought over. For a minute it was all quiet and they let the thing down
into the ground, oh it couldn't really be happening, but she knew what
she'd got to do because she'd seen it, and she rushed to the very edge,
throwing up her arms. But the women caught her and held her back safe,
thank goodness, and then the grave was filled in and there was a speech
from the UNIP man.

But I didn't really want to jump in there, no I didn't, and perhaps some
of them have known him for a long time, and they must be sadder than I
am. It's not as if I was really one of them, any more than my Dad would
have been, how can I be, I'm different. He was a lovely man in bed, but
we didn't think the same way. But oh, how can I be so cold about it?
How awful I am! And now, very suitably she was crying again and then
someone bundled her into a car and she got the weight off her poor feet.

Back at the house it was all bustle, food being laid out, plates, knives,
steaming meat, hot potatoes, greens, beer, tea, cut bread, cake. That
younger brother of course acting the host. She tried to keep out of his
way, but it was no use. He made an excuse for getting his arms round her
and breathing into her face. She managed to get back among the women,
but she was a little frightened and oh so tired.

At last they began to drift away and she could go to her room. She
took a sleeping pill, then another. When she woke, a bit muzzy, Mutinta
was shaking her, saying 'They have begun to come. Will Madam give me
before they take?'

She sat up, looked at her little clock, saw it was well into the afternoon
of the next day. 'What is it?' she asked, but Mutinta gave her a good pull
up, saying, 'Come, come!' got her onto her feet and then down to the
kitchen.

The first thing she saw was that they'd taken everything out of the
fridge and now they were unplugging it. 'This Madam's fridge!' Mutinta
screamed, but they paid no attention. There was a truck outside the
kitchen door and Laureen saw that they'd taken a whole lot of pots and
pans and someone was at work on the beautiful electric stove with all the
numbers and gadgets. When she pulled the man by the arm he just shook
her off as if she was nobody and went on disconnecting the wires. And
when she turned round there was that brother, Mr Chitoshi, standing
and grinning. 'Oh Mutinta,' she sobbed, catching at her, 'what happens
here?'

'It is the family,' Mutinta answered in a half whisper. And as she said that a large lady, one of the chief mourners, sister perhaps, came through with an armful of sheets from the cupboard and greeted Laureen, who could only stare, then went quickly on and out towards the van. Mutinta pulled at her: 'Now Madam give me—from her room—upstairs—before they take.'

That was it then. The end. The African end. Mr Chikonki hadn't provided for her, hadn't thought. When he married someone different, a white lady, almost white! No, they can't do this, they can't! This black family, they can't be allowed! The telephone in the master bedroom. She got through to the police, but the police were not interested. Someone said to her, 'But Madam, this is not a crime,' and someone else said, 'It is the custom. Wait, you will be seen to.'

'But they are taking everything!' she almost screamed.

The man at the other end seemed amused. He said, 'But of course. It is the family. We are sure they will look after you. The men will see to it. Do not antagonise them.' Antagonise! she thought, these police, these— savages!

Both the maids came up to her room, tittering. 'You give me the little clock,' Mutinta said and grabbed it. Both of them went to the dressing table, looking it over, each taking two or three things, small ones—but hers! Then they opened the wardrobe doors and pulled out half a dozen of her good dresses. 'You give me,' they both said and she just gasped and nodded. 'Goodbye Madam,' said Mutinta. 'You keep chin up, you don't die.' And then they were off.

At least they hadn't taken the jewels and she was sure both the girls knew just where they were. She locked the door. Now she'd have to race to get the jewels safe, put on or shoved into the pockets of the crocodile bag—and I'll fight for that bag, she thought, lucky I have all these big clean bank notes with K.K. smiling so comfortably on them! And that old passport—where had she put it? It seemed to take an age and for a bit she was sure she'd lost it, after all she'd never needed it. But at last it turned up and went into the bag. And now? What a noise, could she face it? She moved the curtain at the back window just a little and looked out. There were two smaller vans now—as she looked she saw four men carrying one of the sofas, in it went. Oh what would Mr Chikonki have said! Or would he just have shrugged his shoulders? No, no. But he was dead. There was a quarrel going on, some of the men fighting with sticks, two of them looked more like farmers. Could they be the other wives' brothers? There went someone with a rolled up carpet over his shoulder. Oh my good rugs! And one of the gold-framed mirrors. I'll have to go down, she thought, and glanced at the dressing table, well, they've left my hair brushes. She tried to smarten herself up a bit.

There was that younger brother. 'Mr Chitoshi,' she said, 'are you responsible for what is going on?' He laughed and so did the other men.

'We are the family,' he said, 'we are in charge of the family possessions.' He added, 'That is our elder brother,' and waved his hand at someone sitting comfortably smoking one of Mr Chikonki's cigars. Yes, she thought, he's the one I've seen in the newspapers.

She pulled herself together. 'But I am his widow,' she said. 'I am still Mrs Chikonki.'

'Not to worry,' he said. 'We shall take care of you. Good care.' And he grinned at her.

She turned to the elder brother—'But they are taking everything! Even the food in the kitchen!'

He nodded and said: 'All belongs to the family. Not to the woman. That is the law.'

'But he married me — your brother!'

'Yes, yes, but you have no family. Now you belong to us. You will go to another house, you will be happy. This house we sell. He—" and he pointed to Mr Chitoshi—'has offered. You will be part of his house.'

So that was the game. 'Could I not go to you?' she asked the elder brother, trying to keep her voice steady. 'Yours is better for a widow.'

'He has offered,' said the elder brother placidly. 'Perhaps he will find you another husband.' Then one of the other men, who was a little drunk, grabbed her. 'We all love you, Mamma,' he said and began to cuddle her up. But both brothers pulled him off her, and the elder one said, 'Now stop. It is not right to say these things when my poor brother is hardly cold in his coffin. Have you no respect?' Several people quieted down and even began to cry a little. So did Laureen, and felt at her arm where the man had grabbed her. Behind them, there was Mr Chitoshi, grinning at her. Now she was really frightened.

The elder brother looked up: 'You may keep dresses,' he said. 'Small things. Now go. We have business.'

'But—' she said, still half crying.

'You will stay here for two days,' Mr Chitoshi said, 'that is proper. You will get yourself ready, then I will come and fetch you. Now go to your room. Stay there.'

'But the house—' she said. Her house.

The elder brother looked up again. 'I have said. The house—we sell.'

And then Mr Chitoshi said: 'After two days the Mercedes takes you to my house. Then we shall see.' And he looked at her as though she had no clothes on.

She went back to her room. There were three women there whom she did not know and when she spoke to them first in English, then in Cinyanja, she saw that they only knew that other language, whatever it was. But no doubt were family. Two of them were looking into the wardrobe; they had pulled everything roughly off the hangers; one had grabbed a silk blouse, the other two had scarves, and one had a pillow under her arm; she switched up one of the big bath towels as she left, but all three went quickly, just glancing sideways at Laureen.

At least nobody had got her bag. If she could stick to that. But then? If she stayed for those two days, at the end of it that man would grab her, that was for sure. And she wasn't having it. These blacks!

Two more women, the sister, smart looking. A sister-in-law, she thought. Then a third, oh ever so old, and it was she who said in slow English: 'The widow must cut her hair. For mourning. We cut it.' And she reached out a skinny hand.

Laureen just gasped. Her hair, her beautiful hair. No!

The sister looked at the old one. 'She has mourned. That is enough.'

But the old one shook her head: 'It is custom.' She came towards Laureen like a—like a witch!

Laureen held her hands over her hair, her mouth open to scream, but the sister said: 'It is village custom. Not town. Let her keep it.' She patted Laureen's shoulder kindly and said something to the old woman in that language of theirs. Then, to Laureen: 'Nice cup of tea?'

But Laureen shook her head, tried to smile and they went out. She turned the key after them. In a bit someone rattled on the door, tried it, went away. She looked in the wardrobe again, couldn't help it. Right at the back there was her wedding dress hanging up, shining white, long sleeves, high at the neck. She remembered it well. But no, no. So what now? That lovely bathroom—she went in, washed hands and face, but of course—no hot water, not any more. The bath salts. The oil. The powder. Cooling down on a hot day. Oh dear. She sat on the bed and counted the money in her crocodile bag. More than enough for an air ticket. But where? And first of all, how to get out of the house, get somewhere safe. If there was anywhere. She turned over in her mind a list of old friends, discovered that there was hardly one of them she could trust, not over something big, not to be really sensible. They'd give her away, not for money, but—well, she'd dropped them all, hadn't she, and it would take too long to explain.

Then another rattle on the door and a voice she knew, Mutinta: 'Quick, open. I come to help Madam.' Could she believe it? Well, she had to. She unlocked and Mutinta slipped in: 'Madam take small suit-case. I carry.'

'But they know me. That Mr Chitoshi—'

'Bad one, him. All bad. That doctor Madam paid. But not able to stop wives hurting. Madam, you pack small, small case.'

Could she trust Mutinta? 'Why you help me, Mutinta?' She couldn't believe it, there must be a trap.

'Sorry for Madam,' Mutinta said briefly, and pulled the small suitcase out from the bottom drawer of the cupboard: 'Madam take shoes.

Walking maybe. Wear two shirts, look like fat!' She giggled.

But it was good advice: two of everything. Hurrying into them, Laureen began to feel excited, hopeful. Mutinta made it all seem fun. Now the necklaces were firmly on, but hidden, the bracelets, the matching brooch. Stick out for a good price, not seem to be in trouble, you know what he paid. Big plans began to shape. 'Night coming,' said Mutinta. 'Then we go.'

'But if—'

'Madam O.K. Not get caught. Something heavy—big shawl—cover face. But we walk quick. Quick.'

They made it. The family was still there, still at it. She didn't dare look at faces, kept her head down. They took the back way, scuttled in and out of the bushes and bamboo clumps, past the parked van. They'd waited, Mutinta pushing her back, when two men came carrying one of the armchairs and got it on the top of a whole lot of other things. Well, you can't cry for an armchair. They'd be up in the bedroom soon, she thought, now the door's not locked from the inside. They'll get everything I left. Had to leave. My nice things. And my poor old hubby not knowing a thing. If he did they'd catch it! And I was ever so fond of him, but that doesn't count with him. And now I'm on my own. Except for the money, and what luck that he'd just given me quite a bit. What was it for? Oh, those malachite ornaments. They'd have looked well on the side table. Lucky I never got round to buying them.

And now they were walking quick, dodging past street lights. Mutinta was cross when the moon came out from behind a cloud. They turned down a side street, then another. But nobody was noticing them and they wouldn't find out in the house till maybe tomorrow. She got a stone in her shoe and Mutinta was impatient till she got it out. How much further?

She was ready to drop when they got to the door, the paint peeling off it, you could see by the moonlight. Mutinta knocked and a child opened. There was a lighted candle, then a small oil lamp. Beside the lamp her little clock from the bedroom. Catching her look, Mutinta giggled and said: 'My clock!' It didn't matter. Funny thing, being here with real blacks in a kind of African hut, though she supposed it was somewhere in the middle of the town, in behind the real houses. Yes, and she felt her own white blood, more than ever. Kind of superior in a way. But it was Mutinta who'd saved her, and she didn't suppose she'd ever know quite why. Sort of accidental, some little thing, a word, a look. No.

There was a mattress on the floor. She kicked her shoes off, lay down, felt it scratchy and lumpy, but never mind. Mutinta pulled a blanket over her, a red blanket smelling of blacks. Funny! She got her hand up over the two necklaces, felt the crocodile bag against her side. She slept briefly, then woke: the lamp was still burning but very low. A child stirred, muttered, went quiet again.

Tomorrow early I'll get the flight to Harare, or maybe Gaborone, see what's going within the next hour or two, so I can take a taxi down to the airport. Maybe Nairobi, some nice people there. Gaborone? There's a casino there, they say, always gives one a chance or so I've heard. You never know who you'll come up with, and I'd be a lone widow with lovely long hair. I'd find someone, a nice white boy, teacher perhaps. And there's South Africa just across from Botswana. If Dad had gone there instead of Zambia or wherever it was in those days, he might have done better. Not married my poor Mum—and then where would I be?

She turned over, but couldn't get back to sleep. Would they have found out by now? Well, they wouldn't have got round to warning the travel agents, not yet. Most likely they didn't even know the name on her old passport. Laureen Thompson. All they knew was Mrs Chikonki. And she wasn't Mrs Chikonki any longer. Though they'd had some good times. Poor dear hubby. All the same, let's face it, I'm back on my own now. And in a way I've brought it on myself, that's what Dad would say. But he's dead too. Well, let's get some sleep.

Nagli's First Princess

THE COUNCIL OF DRAGONS HAD NOT MET FOR SOME time. After all, each of us dragons had so much to do. One has one's hoard, hasn't one, partly inherited but mainly the result of one's own efforts and good taste? Yes, indeed, one's hoard. Earth's veins run with thin gold, but this must be tapped by the smaller creatures, the dwarves and even the men; one then has all the trouble of obtaining the gold by means which may involve considerable personal discomfort, if not actual danger. One may be left for life with a spear head stuck under one's scales. That, in fact, was what happened to Hrax, one of the older and more respected dragons in the northern community. He had even been, in disguise, to consult the Wanderer about it, although no dragon likes to get too near any of the Gods; they have all the nasty attributes of men and considerably more power. Besides, Hrax's disguise, as a fully-manned dragon warship, was uncomfortably tight and made him feel silly.

This spear head accounted for his bouts of bad temper. Hrax was not only liable to go out as far as Skarpdale, biting off the heads of ploughmen and shepherds as he went whanging over, and irritating the Skarpdalers into reprisals which might affect others beside himself, but he was also apt to puff flames into the faces of young dragonlets who, as everyone knows, are not completely fireproofed. Still, the rest of us can consider ourselves lucky not to have any nasty spear stuck just at the back of the left wing where we cannot possibly get at it.

However, an accumulation of dragonish business was building up, and after a while Slaug, the Convener of the Council of Dragons, decided that something must be done. So, with considerable trouble, he set up the whole machinery for calling the full Council together. This involved some complicated business with the clouds which are, anyhow, very forgetful, liable to condense, evaporate and play similar tricks; but how else can one possibly get at the Chinese, Burmese and Polynesian dragons who would be very hurt indeed if they did not get their summons in due form, whether or not they actually attended. Besides, the Chinese dragons in particular, could always be counted on to add tone to a discussion; in fact they were almost always gratifyingly unintelligible. This helped in any debate where final unanimity was desirable.

There would, of course, need to be a banquet and presentations. Slaug rippled round to all his colleagues and broached the matter. The banquet, succulent and flambée, could be arranged, but dragons are not always markedly open-clawed when it comes to presentations, even to respected seniors from abroad. After all, one's treasure is where one's heart is, and who can expect a dragon to rifle his own hoard? Some actions though socially admirable, violate the laws of natural decency. Nor could the less valued pieces be offered to the guests without loss of self-respect all round.

However it was thought on good evidence that the king of Skarpdale and Axe-water had come back from an expedition to the south with considerable booty. No tribute worth having had been forthcoming from this kingdom for several centuries. Men grow revoltingly forgetful. Perhaps one or two of the younger dragons would volunteer? Naturally they could keep the usual percentage and if they got into difficulties they could call on their seniors for advice and even assistance.

Garr and Nagli were two promising young dragons, firm friends from the egg; they had been hatched within a half century of one another. Garr had an unusually long and mobile neck of a shade of green like unripe apples, and with the same polish. Nagli's stretched wings took on all the colours of a stormy sunset. Each had a cave on Blasted Mountain, but so far not as well filled as might be hoped for in time. Garr specialised in golden brooches, Nagli in precious stones. A collection of golden brooches is of course a very usual beginning for any hoard, and looks well from the start when tastefully arranged among ferns and suitable moss. The connoisseur can observe the difference in design and tooling, the older bow brooches and more modern round or horse-shoe shaped designs; a fine specimen is worth a long flight. Precious stones are harder to come by, unless one has luck with a trader. But so many traders, especially those from the east, have unfair anti-dragon devices such as magic mists or rings of invisibility which will even be effective with a loaded camel. Nagli, however, had some fine strings of amber, an Indian ruby, a couple of pearl drop pendants from a lady who had been riding hastily and carelessly from an unwanted suitor — very tasty she had been — and several fine stones set in daggers or sword belts, as well as a good deal of coral. What Nagli longed for was jade. Slaug, who was his uncle, had a beautiful piece of smooth pale jade, a Goddess standing on a flying bat. It was wasted on him, Nagli thought. And old Hrax with that crown set with utterly desirable flat emeralds and moon stones, when, as everyone knew, all Hrax cared for was goblets and golden meat dishes! But the world is like that.

As a preliminary, Garr and Nagli went out ravening and ravaging all down Axe-water and as far as the gates of King Gwydre's city. It was not an unpleasant assignment, for everyone likes a few fat sheep and calves. Garr was not above taking hens, but he was, one must remember, a young and inexperienced dragon.

All this caused a considerable stir and complaint among men both in Axe-water-dale and beyond, who, foolishly enough, had been telling one another that there was no longer any need to take the dragons seriously. A few deft snatchings of children made the parents (who, one would have thought, had plenty of children and would scarcely miss one here or there) rush screaming to the city to insist on their king taking some action. King Gwydre had only recently come back and did not much want to be disturbed. However he felt he must do something. First of all he sent out some relatively lightly armed knights. But two dragons, acting together, can usually manage. And the armour could easily be disposed of, once the head and legs were bitten off. King Gwydre became seriously worried and consulted his Sources of Information. These Sources, with whom the dragons had, naturally, been in touch already, recommended a princess suitably apparelled and decorated, and attached to a tree. Should this little offering be accepted, there would be no more trouble.

King Gwydre had several daughters, so there was no real difficulty, except among the daughters, who should have been delighted with the honour which was being conferred on them. But perhaps they were shy. King Gwydre's sons, also, had ideas of their own and unusually resistant armour and carried particularly long and pointed spears. This resulted in Garr getting a very nasty gash under the chin. Dragons are sensitive creatures, especially when young; Garr found it most painful and alarming. The roar he gave must have sounded almost like a scream, and he allowed his beautiful green neck to go quite brown. Then he disappeared rapidly towards Blasted Mountain, trailing cinders. Nagli came to his rescue with a gallant blast which resulted in putting these particular knights out of action for some time, indeed one of them was partially roasted. But Nagli was left alone to carry on the good work.

Perhaps he worked all the better for being by himself. One never knows with a youngster only a few centuries old; their reactions are often quite unpredictable, unlike yours or mine. So it was with Nagli and the princess, whose name was Ellylo. She was Nagli's first princess, so naturally he felt it was something of an occasion. It must be pointed out that there is no reason to consider the feelings of either dwarves or men, supposing even — which is not proved — that they have feelings. Many dragons are of the opinion that they are mere automata, although the more generally held theory is that they are necessary for the middle process of extracting and working with the gold and jewels whose ultimate and unquestioned destiny is in a dragon's hoard; they must not therefore be entirely destroyed. But that is a very different matter from considering them as individuals. This ought never to be done. Should we ever begin to do so, the whole coherence of society would be in danger.

This princess Ellylo was duly attached to the tree, as prescribed by the Sources of Information. She had a circlet of gold set with pearls, several bracelets and a very handsome necklace with pearls, rubies and sapphires. You would have thought she would be delighted. But no, she did nothing but cry and howl and attempt to make herself unacceptable. Nagli, however, was not to be put off by any nonsense of this kind. He took a long swoop down, circling round the tree with his beautiful wings spread out. The princess went on screaming.

A dragon likes to take his time. Nagli ruffled and rippled through the long grass towards the princess like an enormous coloured wind. And now the princess Ellylo stopped screaming: she stared at Nagli and the human blood went back and back into her heart and her face turned the colour of pale jade.

Now when he saw this, Nagli became quite still and the flames simmered in his nostrils, for it seemed to him that not only was this princess more beautiful than carved jade — jade set cunningly with jewels — but was also much larger and far more desirable. He made up his mind not to dispose of this princess in the usual way, without introductions or conversation. Instead he decided to treat her as a being almost like himself. 'My dear princess,' he said, 'you must not be frightened of me.' And he smiled very pleasantly.

Now it is always most unwise for a dragon to get into conversation with any of the race of dwarves or men or to treat them in any way as one would a fellow dragon. But Nagli had suddenly seen a beautiful picture in his mind. The necklace and perhaps the coronet of princess Ellylo would be given to his uncle Slaug, the convenor of the Council, but the princess was to be his own, moving in form of carved jade with her pale lips and shadowed eyes and translucent skin, for long centuries in his cave. He did not stop to consider the miserable transience of the human body, which withstands time worse than that of the dwarves. But he did realise that the question of transport would be much easier with a willing than with an unwilling and struggling princess. He coughed slightly, and said: 'I have a cave full of treasure.'

Now this was an exaggeration, because his collection was still far from complete, indeed he could not hope to have a really noteworthy hoard for some centuries. But the princess was not to know this; she appeared to be listening. 'All shall be yours,' said Nagli.

The nearer he came the more beautiful the princess appeared to poor Nagli, and the more he longed to install her in his cave, where she would devote herself to him, rubbing his jewels up and cooking him delicious dinners, flaming plum puddings, peppered mustard, and exquisite airy whim-whams of chillies stuffed with ginger. She would, he thought wildly, comb his golden eyelashes, polish his claws, titivate his wings and clean behind his ears. And always she would be gleaming and polished jade.

'Come with me to my cave,' said Nagli proudly, 'and deck yourself with my jewels. I will get you more. I will get you all the jewels in the world.' And as he said this he was making himself a picture of the pale jade princess hung with the spoils of countless other princesses.

The princess was now definitely paying attention. 'Would you really and truly do that, dragon?' she said. And her voice had exciting ripples in it like soft flames.

'Do you doubt me?' said Nagli and tears of hurt indignation stood in his eyes, because after all he had promised considerably more than he was ever likely to be able to fulfil.

'Oh no!' said princess Ellylo, 'but I would have to think it over. And I can't think with my hands tied,' she added.

Foolish Nagli waddled up through the grass and untied the princess. He should have been warned. But he was not. 'Would you,' he said, 'would you stroke my ears?'

'If you're sure you won't bite me,' said the princess.

'Bite you?' said Nagli, 'what can have made you think I might bite you!' And he stretched out his long chin towards the princess, who stroked his ears, and scratched under his jawbone till he gulped with delight. All would be as he had planned. 'And now,' said Nagli, 'are you ready to fly with me? You will be quite safe on my back.'

But what did this crafty and treacherous princess do, but say to poor trusting Nagli that she must go first to the palace and come back with another necklace which her mother would be sure to give her when she heard that her daughter had been invited to a lengthy stay by such a paragon of dragons. She described this necklace in the most appetising terms, great luscious drops of emeralds and a clasp made like a grape cluster of amethyst. Nagli felt quite faint at the thought of it. 'Just shut your eyes,' said the wicked princess — with what diabolical cunning for one so young! — 'Shut your eyes and I will be back before you have had more than two dreams.' And she gave his ears one more tickle.

So Nagli shut his eyes and lay there, smiling and steaming and feeling on his ears the delicate touch of the jade princess. And then — who knows? — perhaps some good fairy whispered to him, though I am well aware that no sensible dragons believe in fairies. At any rate he opened one eye and saw a dozen horrible knights creeping up on him with long, wicked lances, and *no princess*.

One can hardly bear to think of it. Poor, trusting Nagli barely escaped. His nerves were shattered; one leg had a spear wound which dripped blood right across Axe-water and Skarpdale. I am happy to say that this encouraged the growth of dragon root, which, as I am sure you know, is quite fatal to almost all the domestic animals on which men depend, especially the horses which actually help the knights with their cowardly attacks and have been known to kick an over-enthusiastic dragon in the eye.

But beyond that — oh, the shattering of dreams! — Nagli and his jade princess. She was after all only human and can one say worse? No doubt she would have proved a disappointment, but all the same it was as much as his uncle Slaug and indeed others of the senior dragons could do, to put him on his wings again. Indeed, Garr's chin wound healed much more rapidly. That was, after all, merely in the flesh, while Nagli's wound went deeper, as far down in his heart as the shining, flame-lighted hoard in the far depths of the darkest, deepest cavern.

Call Me

I DID AT LAST INHERIT THE DOLLS' HOUSE. I HAD
wanted it all along, but my Grannie passed it on to Aunt Mima and trust
her not to give me a thought, though I daresay she never-ever turned the
key in the lock. Oh, it was locked right enough in her house, though it
had been often enough opened for me in Grannie's day. Poor Grannie,
she lived in one of the top flats in Buccleuch Place and a great view out of
the back windows, but awkward with her getting old and needing to cry
down to the lower flat to bring up her milk and her loaf. I was in
Aberdeen at the time and my eldest not walking yet, or I'd have come
more often. But when I was a wee one myself she was bright and
bustling, the china all washed to a sparkle, and a tea caddy on the middle
table that had pan-drops in it, or else Berwick cockles, and Grannie
wasn't sparing of them.

I'd be sucking away and then she'd turn the brass key in the front of the
dolls' house. But there was always one thing that I couldn't get out of my
mind. That was the difference in sizes of the furniture. The bedroom
furniture was for someone quite wee; there was a small brass bed with a
silk quilt and a chest of drawers that pulled out; one could put things into
it like — I remember — a squashed daisy that I'd laid into my prayer
book from the edge of the kirk path. I was taken to the kirk in those days,
Sabbath by Sabbath, which is maybe why I cannot care for it now.

Then there was a dressing table that opened out, with a scrap of a
blotted mirror inside that one could make stand up and a tiny pair of

scissors, and spaces for other things which had been lost over the years, but I never could make up my mind what they could be. There was what she'd call a chaise percée in ivory with a tiny silver chamber pot in it, a brown and white hip bath with a soap dish, and a hanging cupboard with a coloured picture on the door, but that, she'd tell me, was from her own days. So much of the rest was old, old, and I would suppose now that it could have come from a time when the family was up in the world. Not that we are down now, no such thing, but we would neither afford nor approve the kind of unpractical life that folk led then. Dolls' furnishings in ivory and silver indeed! Yet I liked them.

But I am getting away from the dolls' house bedroom; the other thing it had was a trimmed rocking cot with a baby in it. Well, all that fitted fine with the doll lady who sometimes stood by the dressing table, but was sometimes put to bed with her silk dress off and wearing only a chemise of thin lawn which had been darned in two places, long ago. But the school-room had bigger furniture with bamboo frames, a painted table and a globe that could scarcely have been moved by the bedroom lady. It had pictures on the walls, crochet rugs and some miniature books, though one was a Koran, and as soon as I got round to knowing what it was, I was dead sure nobody would have taught Arabic to the dolls' house children.

But the drawing-room was bigger in scale yet; it had a set of dark wood furniture, intricately carved, from Goa, my Grannie said, and by and by I looked it up in my school atlas. The bedroom lady could barely have peeped over the top of the table or lifted a cup of the flowered tea-set which was laid out on it. There were glass vases too, and cushions the right size for the Goan chairs. There was a swinging glass bird cage with a bright glass bird inside it. Best of all there was a silver teapot and a pair of candle-sticks that Grannie kept polished, and a gilt clock with tiny statuettes, one on each side. Once when I was a child I put in what was clearly meant as a smart electric standard lamp with a pink silk shade which had been given me on a birthday; it seems to me now that it was a great kindness in Grannie not to throw the thing out, so ill did it go with the rest.

Kitchen and dining-room had mixed sizes. There were all the gay-coloured plaster food dishes, turkeys and hams and sausages, gigots of meat, cakes and oranges, goblets of purple wine that couldn't come out. Here there was a dining table from Goa, the legs and sides darkly carved. The centre-piece was a three-tiered china stand, very pretty, my favourite thing when I was a wee girl, and on the dining-room mantleshelf a carved chamois under branching trees. Swiss, it would have been. Kitchen and tableware were the right size for the bedroom lady and, what was more, the cook with her cap and apron was the right size too. But then there were wooden pails and jugs and a churn, from Germany I think, and meant for someone bigger. And there was a pussycat in a basket which was almost tiger size but luckily sound asleep. Once, said Grannie, there had been a gentleman, her husband, and a little girl in pantalettes. But they were gone.

Whenever I got the lady out of bed she had to go right down to the kitchen to consult with the cook among the pans and the kettles and the girdle that were the right size for them both. The lady had a mauve and green dress and tiny black boots painted on to her china feet. I remembered the pattern all my days. Grannie said she was called Lady Mousiekin, but the cook was just plain Bella. The lady's husband was called Sir Ranald Mousiekin. 'Did he wear a kilt?' I asked.

'No, my dear,' said Grannie, 'a kilt looks badly on a doll, just the same as a lassie looks badly dancing the fling. Sir Ranald wore the dress uniform of an officer, tartan trews, a well-fitting jacket and a small sword. There was a gillie too, with big whiskers. But some way, while I was growing up, those two disappeared, and the young daughter as well. Someone must have taken them.'

'But who could it have been?' I asked. It was such a sad thing!

'Nobody could say and they told me I was too old to play with a dolls' house.'

'I'll never be too old, Grannie!' I said. I kept on asking questions. Grannie didn't know the baby's name, but I called him Wee Dougal; he hadn't much of a face and was all wrapped up. I didn't care to unwrap him because he mightn't have had a body.

And there they stayed, shut in, all the time Aunt Mima had the dolls' house, up in that top attic in Morningside. She'd had a sad life and wasn't tired speaking of it. It seems she had been engaged to be married in 1914 when she was a young girl, but he had been killed. He was in the Black Watch and Aunt Mima still had cuttings about the battle of Richebourg L'Avoué, yellowed pieces from the *The Scotsman* and then, the casualty lists and his name ringed in black. I hated seeing that and if she showed it me once she showed it a dozen times. After she died I found all those bits of paper and his photo, and some old letters stamped 'Passed by the Censor', from him no doubt, all tied up with ribbon; I burnt them at once. Why couldn't she have let me have the dolls' house, me with a young family, though it's a fact they were boys and mightn't have appreciated it? But no. If I'd had a wee girl, she said. But it was I myself wanting the dolls' house. I dreamed of it sometimes.

Of course Grannie was almost bound to have left it, with the rest of her good furniture, to Aunt Mima who was her daughter. It would have looked queer leaving it to my father and I doubt Grannie would never have skipped a generation with anything big, though she did leave me her garnet necklace and ear-rings, not that I ever wear them. But some way it seemed hardly fair, Aunt Mima keeping it shut all those years; she didn't even want me to see it when I came over, as I did a couple of times in the year, oftener even, as she grew older — and worse tempered. And then she died and there was nobody else to leave it to. Or so I felt.

Well now, the first thing I did was to open all the drawers and take the lids off everything and give it all a good dusting. I couldn't find the big ashet with the two chickens and when I opened the dressing table the scissors were gone. Oh, I was that cross! There was a chip off the china centre-piece in the dining-room and of course she'd never bothered to polish the wee teapot and the candle-sticks, as I did, the very first thing. But then, in the drawer of the kitchen dresser under the soup ladle, there was this paper and all it said was Call Me. It was written small in brownish ink and in a hand I didn't know. But what could it mean? I was fairly puzzled by this for I knew well enough it had not been there when I played with the dolls' house last. Yes, I puzzled my head. Who wouldn't?

Call me. You'd think I could have laid it by, just an old scrap of paper out of a dolls' house, but some way I couldn't. I felt a need to call — someone. I have never in my life been scared of ghosts and bogles and such; that was something which had passed me by altogether, even when I was a wee child. But I thought, well, whoever it is, I'll not call *her*. Aunt Mima was bad enough in real life. But I called softly Grannie, Grannie. I'd never-ever have been scared of her, even if she'd come back in a shroud. She'd still pet me up and give me pan-drops and laugh with me. But there was no answer, not even a shiver.

I began to shift the furniture in the dolls' house. You know, I had never asked which of the family had been to Goa; I just took it for granted. Once, later on, I had asked my father, but he had no idea and was not interested. It came to my mind suddenly that I ought to call whoever it was in Goa that had made the furniture too big and get him to alter it — such fancies one has! But a person cannot be called without a name to call him by.

So there I was, making up stories to myself, and the boys coming in for their supper. Alastair was at the University by now, but he'd a habit of having one solid meal a day in his home! They'd all been teasing me about the dolls' house and how I'd got it at last. So I wasn't going to speak to those lads about the paper with the writing on it, whoever else I spoke to. I'd the queerest feeling that if I'd had a daughter — but three boys are enough for anyone surely! — I could have told her about it. I'd tears at the back of my eyes over this very thing. I tried to put it out of my mind and when it would not leave me, when it kept jagging at me, I had a wee talk with my husband late in the evening, trying to make light of the paper and how there must be a sensible explanation. He was quite concerned but said to me that I should throw the piece of paper into the back of the fire. 'I'll do just that,' I said, and indeed I meant it, but the sitting-room fire was out and we were in our beds and tomorrow would be time enough. He said, too, that he himself with such a problem, would find help in reading the Book. But he knew well enough that I was not that way given. Yet, out of fondness, I promised that I would do that as well the next morning.

But tomorrow came and it seemed to me stupid to go to the lengths of burning the paper; that was like something in a cheap film. In real life one just laughs at oneself and forgets all about it. Only that was not how it was working out. I felt a great curiosity growing in me, I just had to know who was to be called — and why. So when the house was empty I went back up to the dolls' house and I got myself a cushion and sat down on the floor and called by name every one of the dolls: the two who were there and the lost husband and child and gillie. I even called the baby in the cot. But what I'd have done if there had been an answer is beyond me. There was none of course, but if there had been would I have kept my head or would I have been scared and bolted back downstairs and rung up my husband's office, though he never likes me to do that? Or what?

And I kept on puzzling: why in the kitchen dresser? When was it put there? Was it some kind of revenge by Aunt Mima because I had a husband and children and she had none? But I knew her handwriting and it did not match up with this. The paper looked as if it had been cut along the edges; could she have found it in an old letter and cut it out and laid it there? A crazy idea and I knew it, but I could get nothing to fit and the afternoon was wearing on and it darted across my mind that it could have been in a letter from that laddie who was killed in 1915. But was it his handwriting, and, if so, had Aunt Mima, once upon a time, called him and he had not come? For if he had she would have been different. Somehow I knew that. And besides this was nonsense. I knew I had burned his letters, all, all, so I could not compare the writing, and I began to feel a grey sadness pressing me down, a kind of guilt, and with it a strong determination that I would never, never, call Aunt Mima.

Did I read a chapter in the Book? I did not. That too seemed to me not just genuine, in spite of my husband truly thinking it could help me. My Grannie could have got comfort from the Book; I remembered how she'd had bookmarks with flowers painted on them to mark the pages she liked best. But today's world is different. I wondered if Aunt Mima had been helped at all by that kind of reading, but I thought not. I thought her pain had to be borne without this sort of poultice. Nor could it affect my own trouble, which was not pain or loss but an anxiety which I could not quite pin down.

How did it end? Ah, there, I'm afraid you have me. For it has not ended. I put back the piece of paper and shut the drawer and made myself a good strong cup of tea to bring me back to my right senses. And now there grew up in me a determination to put back the piece of paper and shut the drawer for all the rest of my life, but I would put more than the soup ladle on the top of it. I went out and bought a piece of good white material and I hemmed it round into threee table cloths to fit the dining-room table, each with an initial M for Mousiekin embroidered in the corner. I put the iron over them and now they are folded up neatly in the drawer on the top of the paper, with the soup ladle above them, and there they will stay.

I like to show my old dolls' house to visitors and I can tell you, I was just delighted when Alastair's girl-friend came in one evening and asked to see it. In no time she was looking at everything, picking out the prettiest, asking could she make some small re-arrangements and promising me that she'd somehow find a doll the right size for Lady Mousiekin and with the same kind of china face. She'd look in one or two of the old shops along the High Street, she said, and when Alastair started to laugh it was she who shut him up. She'd another notion which I find myself taken with: that she should try for a doll the right size for the big furniture.

'We could even,' she said — and I liked the way she'd said 'we', yes, I thought it boded well — 'have an Indian doll, to go with those chairs from Goa, a lady in a lovely sari. How would you like that?'

'I think it would be right,' I said, 'but they could never meet, could they now?'

'No, no,' she said, 'we'll keep them apart. It will just mean a trifle of re-organization.'

Of course she and Alastair are not exactly engaged; that would be too old-fashioned for them. But I wouldn't wonder if the next thing might be a wedding, even if it is not the kind of good-going wedding that we had in our day with a fine cake and a sit-down tea and photographers and plenty of drink but not too much. No, they'd do it their own way and doubtless for a while they'd both be working. But later on, they might have a wee girl. Yes, like I was once myself.

And then I could leave the dolls' house to her, and she would be certain sure to open all the drawers and she would find the paper and read it. And who would she call? Never Aunt Mima; for she is deader than the dolls. Her name will have been forgotten, only something on the flyleaf of a few old books. No, my grand-daughter will never call that one. But who will she call? Maybe me.

Endangered Species

K.G., AS HE WAS MOSTLY CALLED, WAS BACK IN THE city. His tour had been rather a success, the villages friendly. A fresh tiger skin for sale had been spotted; this had been traced back to the sportsman-poacher who had shot it and all the existing Indian law had been brought to bear, without compromise. It was made abundantly clear that it does not pay to shoot tigers. There had also been words overheard and brought to his ears. A back lane had been pin-pointed with a finger flip and a young tiger had been found shut into a narrow barred cage in a court-yard.

It had not been totally easy to get the cage moved, even when the tiger was duly tranquillised, but between cash and threats it had been carried to the edge of cultivation. K.G. had stood by with his rifle, just in case, but, when the young tiger stretched and found the bars gone, it had disappeared into the jungle in two splendid bounds. He wished now he had taken his camera instead of the gun, but if he had could he have induced the locals to lift the cage? Now he must find out which Zoo — or possibly, in India, a private owner — had offered how much. Stupid when tigers breed so easily in captivity. But people are stupid. Breeding like tigers. No thought.

K.G. enjoyed walking, even in the city. He took his usual short cut to the office: a lane jammed with sellers of grain, meal, pulses, spices, weighed out for bargainers into screws of newspaper, next them cloth folded or hanging, nails, tinselled marigold garlands, tin mugs and brown cooking pots, bicycle tyres, cigarettes, kettles, sweets, cheap Japanese enamel ware, bangles, bamboo ladders, anything and everything one might but didn't want spilling out of the dark little shops, to be peered at, handled, tasted, praised and complained over, the din of voices and radios momentarily scattered by a honking bike, the exhaust stink mixing with the spice smell. He stood back from it among the bargainers, avoided stepping on a pile of fruit skins, and took the shouting, scurrying main road, the jam of buses and trucks and cycle taxis, back to his office. Always a rush hour in India.

He unlocked the door, switched on the fan, picked up a letter which blew gently off the top of the pile. He smiled at his wife's photo and carefully dusted a little smudge off the glass; soon he would be at home with her. The whirr of the fan replaced the violent street noises, became too backgrounded to hear. The letter was a reassuring one about his special clause in the Nature Bill, soon to come up. He took up his report, re-read part, looked up across his desk; was it strong enough?

There was a photograph of a tiger on the wall across from his desk, a good enlargement from one he had taken from the hide with his new lens. Full face. He stared at it for a moment. It stared back. Yes, it was one of his very best photos. You don't always get the eyes like that. Advancing out of the frame, flickering with tiger colour. The genuine thing. He blinked and it was still there. He could hear the heavy, snarling purr. The tiger. It was communicating.

'Sir,' said the tiger, 'they killed my wife, but it was you who saved my son. I am the Tiger Rajah. I wish to thank you.'

'Please,' said K.G. courteously, half rising from his desk. 'It was the least I could do. Delighted, dear sir, that I could be of assistance.'

The Tiger Rajah came nearer, the enormously powerful paw stretching out of the frame. But the claws retracted. It appeared also that there was a collar of thick, polished gold, whose jewel drops reflected tiger colours round his neck above the immense thrust of shoulder muscle. 'I will give you a wish,' said the Tiger Rajah. 'Do you wish for success in your work?'

'Well, I do not want to appear boastful,' said K.G., 'but I believe I am already successful in my work.' No, he didn't want outside help!

'That is good,' said the great tiger, 'but would you care for a rich and supremely beautiful wife?'

'No, please!' said K.G. 'I am married and although my wife was not rich or much interested in riches, and although she is not perhaps supremely beautiful to others, she is to me.'

'Enough, enough,' purred the Tiger Rajah, 'some wish will come to you. I will wait.' And he withdrew himself into the photograph and perhaps, thought K.G., perhaps the tiger had never stirred from it. Perhaps a wisp of sleep had come on him and he had remembered his

granamother's stories. Tiger Rajah and Cobra Rajah. Well, cobras were
not yet an endangered species.

He flicked through the correspondence, drafted two letters to be
typed, checked a report, making notes against some doubtful figures.
If only people thought less about pleasing him and more about
accuracy! Then he switched off, locked up, walked out. And now home;
Vaneeta would be waiting. The light was beginning to tilt up towards the
tree tops and balconies, but night was a little way off. He walked
strongly, but constantly halted by little crowds, shopping, standing,
talking, looking on. Better take a cycle taxi. He hated doing this, hated
the kind of poverty that drove men to this ignominy. But home
was waiting for him. He chose a terribly battered looking one, the man
on the cycle thin and drawn, the hood tattered. Even the pride of
decorating it no longer there. In some cities they were at least painted
up. Not here. Pressure on people all the time. Poor bloody India. Too
many people.

A cycle taxi pushed past them, two women with shopping baskets and
billowing saris. His own taxi was slowing down a little, the man's leg
muscles bulging and contracting as he half stood on the pedals. Another
came level with them, a thin boy pedalling two men sitting back with
their slick attaché cases, each of them twice his weight. K.G. hated
having it all again, the noise, the horns, the thump and clatter, the harsh,
always irritated voices. They seemed to be stuck now at the back of a
loaded lorry. If only he were on a jungle path with nothing but the faint
scrape of leaves, the gentle converse of birds. There or home, only not in
this sea of trucks, cars, taxis and cycle taxis, people, people. The street
compressed between advertisement covered buildings all densely
crowded; at the back of the shops, room after room with couples
copulating, with women cooking, talking, eating, giving birth. I wish,
he said, half aloud, there were fewer people.

It seemed to be a total traffic jam. Well, they were near the big
crossing, the concrete fountain that never worked, the policemen in their
raised box. Another corner and they would be there. After the crossing
the crowds thinned out. Oh, better to walk! He paid off the man, got out
and wriggled his way across to the pavement. There was a string of
trucks, there were bullock carts, and only the bullocks not shouting,
resting unmoved. But the people. Suddenly there were people running
back from the corner, pushing, screaming. He had better see. They were
terrified. He might be able to help, at least quiet them.

He had seen terrified faces before. He thought momentarily of a jungle
fire, five years ago. But that terror was nothing to this. It was spreading,
drivers and pedallers had jumped off, were running, women had dropped
their baskets, were screeching inhumanly. In the small shops they were
putting up their shutters. Twice he caught at someone running from the

corner, asked but got no answer but a shudder. He pushed his way through them to the corner.

The Tiger Rajah leapt out of the sky into the street, the so empty street. No people. It was, yes, astonishing but not really alarming. Only take care, be calm, be wise. No people, only smashed trucks, taxis run off the road, no drivers. The Tiger Rajah said: 'I have started on your wish. It was a wise one.'

'But what have you done?' K.G. said, trying to keep his voice steady. 'My Lord Tiger, where are all the people?'

'You wished for fewer people,' said the tiger. 'I agree. Now there are fewer people. But perhaps not more than a quarter lakh fewer. I shall continue.'

K.G. looked down at the crossing where the policemen had stood, directing so much traffic. Nothing. 'Where are all these people, Lord Tiger?'

Tiger Rajah gave a purring laugh and stretched out a paw. 'I caught them,' he said and K.G. noted with a certain interest the unsheathing and sheathing of the talons.

'And then?'

'They are no more. None of them.'

'But — ' There was no blood. Nothing. 'Where?'

'That I do not know. Not in India. Not on this earth. Where? That answer is not given to me. Come, my friend, I shall go elsewhere in the city. It is easy for me. Your wish shall be fulfilled.'

'No!' said K.G. 'This is not the way. I un-wish it. If you do this once more I shall begin not to love tigers.'

'As you will, my friend. But see, it was their karma. Had it not been, how could I have fulfilled it?'

'I am not sure that I believe in karma,' said K.G. He pulled up an over-turned stool and sat down, his head in his hands.

The Tiger Rajah lay down beside him and looked up with eyes as green as still waters shadowing thick growth of paddy fields. Without thinking K.G. had reached out a hand, brown and smooth against white and orange fur, to pet the great tiger between his ears. 'What, then, do you believe, my friend?' the tiger asked.

'I suppose I believe in progress,' said K.G. Some small birds had come down and were pecking at the grain bubbling out of a sack in front of an empty shop. It was so quiet. The Tiger Rajah must even have silenced the loud-speakers. How soon would it be before the emptiness was filled up again?

'Progress is competition, I have heard,' said Tiger Rajah, 'and that is a snatching of rupees from weak to strong. Does that make happiness?'

'Well, no, not always, but much happiness for those that ride on the back of progress.'

'That is to be like tigers.'

'Perhaps. But remember, my Lord, even tigers, even strong tigers in thick jungles, must be wary of traps and guns.'

'But also they have friends,' said the tiger and licked his hand; his tongue was startlingly rough. 'If there is progress you must run, run, and you will never catch it. It is many years, I think, that you have had progress in this city. Progress and competition, running after rupees. How few of those who were here before your wish were happy! Perhaps if I had found one truly happy I would have left him, who knows.'

'My Lord Tiger,' said K.G., 'you may be partly right, but I am now very unhappy because I made a foolish wish, not understanding.'

'Do not be sad, my friend,' said the tiger, 'it was your karma to have this wish, as it was theirs to be here. Karma is happiness because there is no more competition. No progress, you would say. The soul rests. And now, if my friend does not wish me to fulfil his wish, I will go.'

'But wait,' said K.G., 'ask all your tigers to know my wardens and never to hurt them, and perhaps also you will turn the hearts of the State Legislature so that my clause in the Nature Bill will go through!'

'All shall be done, my friend,' said the Tiger Rajah and, raising a paw, he flipped at his golden collar and then in one bound was far, far away, with K.G. staring after him into the eye of the sun.

K.G. stooped and picked up the jewel from the collar. In his mind he was picturing it lying between Vaneeta's breasts. He walked slowly away towards the real world. Beyond the crashed and empty buses, beyond silent streets. To people. In a while he found himself back in a street, a normal street of people and traffic and noise. Had it happened? No, it could not have happened. And then he saw a knot of men, more and more coming, discussing, gesticulating, shouting, already someone making a banner: Demand Government Protection! So, yes, it had happened and suddenly it came to him that just possibly Vaneeta had been in that street. She did not usually do her shopping there, but if she had wanted something special for his homecoming and this thing had happened and there would be no more Vaneeta — . He signalled wildly for a taxi, told him to hurry, hurry. They lived in a small modern flat with a balcony, you could see it from the street, her flowers but not herself. He paid, he ran, raced up the stairs, knocked, yes, it was all right, she was there in the kitchen, her voice, her smile, perhaps nothing had happened, it was all a dream. No, he had the jewel in his hand. 'See,' he said, 'I have a small thing for you.' She exclaimed over it, for it was very beautiful and she had so few jewels. Her father, a good man, had not been rich and as for herself and K.G., they were modern, no worrying too much about dowries and such. Ah look, it must surely be a ruby!

'But where did you get it?' she asked. He answered that a friend had given it to him. She frowned just a little, a sweet, dear frown: 'but what had you done for him?'

'Oh, nothing wrong,' said K.G., 'I had helped his son over a small trouble. That was all.'

They sat together in the scent of the balcony flowers, looking up from the food into one another's eyes, happy. She had found a ribbon and twisted it through one of the gold loops in the ruby's surround, a master goldsmith's work surely! Now it lay on her throat, moving with her breath, just as he had imagined it would. Setting off the delicate, so much loved, creamy brown of that kiss-soft skin. The tiger's ruby tamed. Yes, all was well. She took the dishes through and switched on the radio.

He began to listen. Yes, and his skin tightened, yes there had been a terrible disaster in the city. Scientific opinion definitely states a new type of offensive weapon, creating a vacuum. Two or three voices of announcers now, crossing one another. Army chiefs deny — the Americans — many thousands totally disappeared. Prominent banker's empty car. Buses and trucks careered into one another, smashed but always empty, no corpses — the police say — the army — an industrial accident — the professor of Physics says, could have been a black hole loose in the planetary system — jumble, jumble — some who escaped babble about tigers — a disaster fund has been set up — widows and orphans — unheard of catastrophe —

So, it was true. It had happened. In reality. He had made it happen. Or had he? Surely not? Their karma as the tiger had said, that was it. If he could accept it. But could she? He glanced at the ruby, the Tiger Rajah's parting gift. And in what world had it been before homing to Vaneeta's silk-smooth throat?

She had been listening too, standing beside him, staring down at the little black radio, horrified. At last she said: 'I think we should give this very beautiful jewel to the disaster fund before I begin to love it too much.' She put her hand to her throat, to break the small thread that held the gold loop. There, it snapped.

'Vaneeta,' he said, 'you are always right.'

Out of the West

HE THOUGHT SHE WAS A SUMMER VISITOR, HE DID
indeed. And when he found she fancied him, he went full steam ahead.
He would maybe have been a bittie more careful if it had been a local
lassie, more especially if it had been one of his cousins, and he had plenty
of them. Aye, he'd have gone into reverse right enough there! But a
summer visitor, ach, she would go back at the end of the month and
everything forgotten and no kind of difficulties.

But the thing was, she was no kind of a summer visitor, that one.
Indeed, I can hardly like to say what she was. Well, I will try to tell the
story.

But first I must say that Colin was a handsome one, well grown, his
hair black and a wave in it and his eyes blue with a ring of darker colour
round them. There had been a fair few lassies that had fancied him, but
mostly they had been all for the marrying when it came to the bit, and he
had been not just that keen to tie himself up with a nice cosy wee house
and the evenings sitting by the fire and his own wages going into the
housekeeping. No, no, Colin was not for that.

But this one had said nothing about a house and settling down. No,
that would never have been in her mind. It was herself had spoken to him
first, on the flowery machair at the back of the sand, at the tail of a long
summer evening, the sun sinking small and away in the far north-west
over the wide empty Atlantic. But he was not slow to answer and soon
enough he got his arm around her waist, and that was only the

beginning. No, I do not know just what she said, maybe nothing much, but at first he was boasting away to the rest about this lassie and the good clothes she wore and the nice smell you felt on her, and then about the long clever fingers she had and the soft hair. But in a while he began to shut up about her, aye, tight as a clam, but he went around with a smile on him and a way of walking, so it was clear to the rest of us that he had got beyond the hair and the fingers.

We were all keen to hear, for indeed there isn't much ploy here, not like the big cities, and often enough we'd not see a film with a good bit of love in it from one month's end to the next. So we got a bit of drink into him and sure enough he talked. For it is at those times that the words come to you right. I mind of him saying that when you had your face into her neck, in under the hair, you felt you were at the bottom of the sea and the great waves swinging over you, and again he said that running his hands over her and she breathing kind of quick and moving herself, it was like being in a boat on a day of fresh wind, and the lift and dip of the jabble. We were at him to say how far he'd gone and what like it was, because, though it is a thing nobody will put into words, yet one always has the hope that some day this will be done. So we led him on to speak of the lifting of skirts and the unbuttoning of this or that, all that you guess at coming true. 'You had her at your mercy,' we'd say, 'but little mercy did you give her, not you, *a bhalaich!*'

But he only fell into laughing. 'I wouldn't say,' he said, 'who was at the mercy of which!'

We liked fine to think of one of ourselves having his way with a summer visitor and leaving, maybe, his bruises on her.

'Did she cry?' we said.

'Not her,' he said, 'she laughed like the waves on the shore.' But what is the satisfaction to be got from words the like of yon, that you might find in a book of wee poems that you'd get for a school prize?

Now, Colin was working in the Forestry, a steady job but no great pay unless you got overtime, and mostly all the young folk were keen for that. But after a while he began to say he had a notion for the fishing. His father had been a fisherman right enough in the old days, and Colin had been out with the boats plenty when he was a boy. But the fishing had dropped off and gey few of the young fellows following their fathers' trade. So when Colin said sudden one day that he had a notion to go back to the fishing, we all said he was daft and how in all the world was he thinking of it. But he smiled in a kind of stuck-up way and said we should see.

Colin had a young brother Alicky, who thought the world of him. He was in the Forestry too, but when Colin said he was going to the fishing, Alicky said he would go with him. Colin was thinking to go to the lobsters and there was an old boat that had been lying up for a while so he could get her cheap. There were plenty hazels up the glen, for it was a good while since anyone about the place had been making creels, and the two of them went at it over the week-end.

Alicky had been going with a neighbour lassie, and this Jeannie was put about, the way Alicky was not taking her to the pictures on the Saturday night as he had half promised, so she kept on at him, how was he thinking to throw up a steady job and go stravaiging off to the fishing, and where did he think he would get the money he had been putting by every week towards them getting married. For she was after that, was the Jean lassie. So by and by Alicky says that it is this lass of his brother's speaking about the fishing and persuading Colin into it. 'She'll just want to see him in a blue jersey,' says Jean, 'fine I know — the summer visitors are daft on the fishermen! Why, there was that one that kept on painting old Bashie in his sea-boots! Me, I'd sooner a man in a decent suit, but them from the towns, ach, they'd think you'd get a better squeeze — '

'He says right enough she knows the sea,' says Alicky, kind of troubled.

'Women dinna know the sea,' says Jean. And then a kind of unchancy thought comes at them both, but neither of them speak it. 'Anyway,' says Alicky, 'we'll give it a try.'

So off they went with their old boat and their new creels, and, true enough, they had the Devil's own luck. Or maybe that is not what one should say. But never a blank creel, and often enough two or even three lobsters, and hardly a crab among them. And there was another thing. It is a law these days that you cannot sell a berried lobster, that is, a lobster with eggs on her, and they say it is because of lobsters getting scarcer and the need to preserve them. But what's about what they say! The money is scarce too and mostly everybody takes a hard brush and scrubs the eggs off the berried lobsters, so they'll not be breaking the law. And it was noticed that Colin and Alicky had no brush with them. One of us asked, daffing, where was the brush. 'No need,' says Colin, kind of sharp. We thought maybe he was keen to keep the law, and indeed you can see it is sense if you can spare the money. But it was not that with Colin. It was just the way they got no berried lobsters, and Alicky wondering at it. Aye, that was a queer thing, right enough.

When we saw how well Colin and Alicky were doing and the money they had coming in, we were all saying to ourselves that there might be something in the fishing after all, and old Bashie that had sold his boat to Colin was biting himself, the way he'd let her go so cheap. There were a few old creels about and others were made and the wee harbour busier than it had been this long whilie back. But it was the queerest thing, none of the rest of us had more than fairish luck at the best, not a right wage to be got out of it, and plenty berried lobsters forby, and that though they had watched kind of carefully and were fishing the same grounds as Colin's boat.

Well, there was speaking! We'd a notion at first that Colin might be using rabbit bait, but no, it was the same as the rest. But it does not do in a wee place, no it does not do at all, if one man is luckier than another. Not that much luckier. All kinds of folk begin to be against him that were his friends before. And this was just how it was.

And still Colin was meeting this lassie out on the machair and none of us able to find out where she stayed. For it was clear she was not one of the visitors at the hotel, nor yet the boarding houses, and there was none even at the bed and breakfasts that matched up with her. She could have been camping right enough, or coming in a car, but surely one of us would have known!

And there was this other puzzlement about it. Some way we never could come on them close, least of all the way it would have been the best laugh to find them. We would see him with his arm round her and the two of them close, but by the time we might be up to them they would be away. She looked to us kind of quiet; she wore her hair long and old fashioned like in the old Sunday school pictures of the martyrs, and it was a dress or a skirt she had on, and none of these wee handy kind of shorts that the lassies wear these days.

But if we were ettling to see closer, wasn't it Alicky's Jean that was keenest of all. This was partly with Alicky saying to her that his brother was having fine times with his lass and she not saying no nor pushing his hand away, aye, or anything else! For Jean was one of the sort that are all for waiting till they have the man tied up well in church and maybe they have sense, for it's terrible the tricks a man will play and him wanting it bad. Or so they say. But most of us some way have always half behaved ourselves. One is feared to do the very thing one wants most. And besides, one can get that fond of a lassie that it is more pleasure to do the leastest thing she wants than to have one's own way. It is queer, that.

Anyway, Jeannie there got herself all worked up against Colin's one. At first Alicky would not listen, for he was terrible fond of his brother, but in a while Jeannie got working on him, and at last the two of them decided to make a right hunt of it and see could they catch Colin and his one, so that at least Jeannie could take a good look at her and say if this was a decent ordinary lassie or, as she suspicioned, nothing but a shameless hizzie. So it got to be dusk, or almost. They went about it cannily, trust Jeannie — dodging and crawling along the edge of the broken ground where the machair turned to dune and the rabbits had been at work. There wasn't the length of a house between when they got a good sight of Colin and the one he was with, close in each other's arm and her long hair streaming. Some way Alicky felt a shame on him to speak, he had a mind to turn and go back, but Jean nudged him till he gave a shout. 'Hullo there, Colin!' he said, and saw his brother spring away. But Jean had her eyes on the lassie, who twisted herself over quick, facing her. Yet she did none of the things Jean herself might have done, the like of smoothing down her green silky dress or rolling her loose hair up into a decent bun. She just cast her eyes on Jean, saying nothing, and it was a scunnering look.

And then came something above all terrible, for she walked away and she walked to the edge of the machair in the dusk across the flowers and she stepped down onto the sand, and Colin ran after her and took her by the arm, but she snatched her hand away and went faster, went sliding down the pale strand as a wave slips back into the sea, and she was into the water and in a moment she was gone. Colin turned on his brother and his face was twisted with unhappiness, and he said 'You see, you see —' and then he gave Jean a hard smack across her face. But Jean was in such a fearful scare from that scorching look she'd had, that she scarcely felt it. It was not till the bruises showed the next day and she minded that Alicky had said nothing, had not cared at all, that it came back to her what Colin had done.

For she turned and ran, leaving the footmarks that went to the sea's edge and the two men together on the strand, and what they said to one another I do not know at all. But maybe they spoke of the time when they were boys together and believing the old stories, before ever they were men grown and only believing the newspapers and the wireless.

Not one of us knew that anything out of the ordinary had happened, for they said nothing to any of us, and Jeannie was holding her tongue. They went out in their boat the next morning with the creels ready to shoot, and there was nothing at all different in either of the two of them. They were not speaking much, but when a man is going off early to the fishing his mind will be on it and he will not be talking anyway, so there was nothing in that.

And the next thing was that another boat, on towards midday heard shouting a long way off, the way one will do across water, so they got their outboard going and went across and there was the brothers' boat but only Alicky in it and he in a terrible state. 'She came for Colin,' he said and he pointed down into the sea and he shook and shivered. So they took him into their boat and made for shore and sent for his mother, and then after a while they thought to go back to the empty boat and lift her creels. But there was nothing in any of them.

The Son's Story

YOU SEE THAT TREE? YES, THAT BIG FELLOW, THE ASH tree. There's a fine view if you stand under it and look away, right out to the downs, great walking country. But my Dad, he always sat facing the tree. You'd speak of the view and he'd smile but he didn't bother to look round. Not at least if he was sitting the way I remember him, very straight in the back with his legs crossed and his feet sticking up. I never could do that, though he tried to show me how, but he did, easy, and then he'd go off into whatever it was, and once he was there it was no use trying to talk.

Me, I don't reckon to understand what it's all about. Religion and that, it doesn't touch me, I haven't felt the need of it, not yet anyway, and if I ever did it would be too late wouldn't it! But my Dad, it was lucky that he'd got religion before he needed it, before it was any real use to him as you might say. How? Well, it seems he began to take to it when he was growing up, a first year medical student. That was why he'd gone to stay with some cousins in Singapore, feeling they knew more about it in those parts. All this was long ago, when the Japs had started winning their war against all expectations. It all happened before the people in Singapore had time to think, so to speak, and then the Japs set up those foul camps of theirs for the prisoners who had just never believed it could happen.

By that time my Dad was already kind of deep into some kind of Buddhism; it had been quite the thing for the University kids. My notion was that Dad had fallen for one of his girl cousins, but he wouldn't speak of that, wouldn't want to remember it, even. She had a foul time with those Japs in another camp and died in the end. I think he told Mam about it later, but not me.

Well, he found himself helping the doctor in this big prison camp, kind of medical orderly, getting to know the ropes and a bit about treatment. Now the only way to get anything was to boot-lick the Jap commandant, go through the motions and do anything else strictly behind his back. The doctor was mad to get more medical supplies, he knew the Japs had them, oh yes, the stuff was there all right, but not for the prisoners who were thought to be the lowest of the low, just because they'd surrendered, or someone had surrendered for them. There were some badly damaged prisoners, burns and that; he told me but I don't recollect the details. But it all sounded real nasty and a lot of pain, most of all in that climate.

Any time there was a minute to spare Dad said he used it for meditation, it made him better able to do the work. But how did you manage it, I asked him. Well, he said, it was better than just being angry as otherwise you were if you started thinking about what was happening and likely to happen. Or you'd get to making plans that weren't possibly going to come to anything, or else crying over what you'd lost. Some of the prisoners thought he was nuts or that he was sucking up to the Japs, for it seemed they let him be, sort of looked at him and passed by instead of yelling and barking at him, the way they did with the other prisoners. It helped a bit when rations were low, he said, you could find yourself able to give away a handful of rice.

It wasn't only rations of course; it was drugs of all sorts. They'd had things to start with, morphia or something of the kind. Pain-killers anyway, for the real bad cases. He used to give the injections and he was in charge of boiling the water. Getting it sterile, see. The camp was full of infections. The latrines, he said — well, you can imagine. Or really, I suppose, you can't. I couldn't myself when he told me, it didn't seem real, didn't seem possible that human beings could make other humans suffer like that. But they did. And it seems they still can. There are all those things you read about in other parts of the world boiled down into a few sentences. So you can forget them quick. That is, if you're somewhere else. But my Dad he was there. He'd to clean the latrines and burn dressings — that is if they let him light a fire and burn away the stink. But sometimes there'd be days, he said, when he couldn't get out of it for one minute, to go back to this meditation which gave him strength to go on. If you got too tired, he said, you'd go off past the doors that have to be opened, into total illusion. I'm not sure I follow that, but it seems that was the way he thought of it. But it did strike me that total illusion must be like some kind of a real nasty movie, dirty and frightening and you knew it couldn't have a nice ending. Poor old Dad.

And then the doctor found out that his drugs were being tampered with, half a bottle taken and then filled up with dirty water, the lock on the medicine box pulled off. Yes, and some of his instruments stolen. He had a flaming row with the camp commandant and was shot out of hand. There was my Dad kneeling over him and the doctor just muttered look after my patients and then he was dead and the Japs standing round laughing and the commandant looking black murder. My Dad wondered a little if he would be next. But then, he said, the look split and went past him and he left the dead doctor and went back to the patients who had been got into a kind of thatched shelter. Kept the sun off, see. But not much good for the rain, he said.

Well, there was one or two in real bad pain, waiting for the doctor to come back and begging for their injections, asking, crying, for morphia. And the morphia was finished or spoiled. Nothing else in the medicine box. In a while one of the Japs brought a bottle and said it was morphine, but my Dad thought that was a trick, could see it somehow on the man's face. You know the way the German Nazi doctors in that same war but the other side of the world, experimented on men and women, yes and small kids, the concentration camps, saying it was scientific research; I don't know that the Japs ever went to that length, not their style quite. But my Dad didn't trust that bottle, not with the Jap guard grinning the way he did. For a bit, he said, he didn't know how long he was in total despair and could only hear the patients' moaning and crying. One of them was a woman, they'd punished her for something. He didn't know what to do. And then suddenly he did, my old Dad. He filled a syringe with the boiled water and it seemed that as he did it those doors opened — that was the way he put it to me — and he told the patient that now the pain would go and put his hands onto the poor chap. Well, it seemed to work extra well, the chap said thanks for the morphine and went off as quiet as a goner. Same with the others and the woman smiled as she slept. And the Japs were watching.

He did it again, three or four times, to the worst patients, and every time it worked. But he was flat out at the end. For a while, he said, he was in darkness, whatever he meant by that. But he managed just one go of this meditation of his and the Japs went on watching and then he was going to give another of the patients some kind of medicine — I think the poor guy had diabetes or something of the kind — and one of the Japs came to him and took it away, frowning and shaking his head and then put his hand in his jacket pocket and said, 'Those bad. These true. Promise.' And it seems they looked at one another and the Jap said something else, kind of religious the way I account for it, so my Dad believed him.

Well, it seemed that from that time things looked up a bit. The Commandant ordered a proper funeral for the doctor, not just a hole in the ground. And they took away the bottles that had been tampered with and even found him a few things that he needed for the patients. The surgical scissors came back, he said. And then one day there were flowers on the top of the medicine box, put together in the correct way, he told me, but when I asked what he meant he couldn't exactly explain, I suppose because it had sounded a bit silly to me: some kind of pattern, like in a church.

It went on for a long time, days and days, months and months. Two of the patients died. Others recovered. That woman did; she used to write him a long letter every Christmas — oh for years. New ones got ill and came to him. He lost count. And maybe he didn't want to talk about it. But it seemed that he made quite a success out of most of the patients. It seems, too, that he was able to get more time for his meditation, because instead of laughing and poking him, some of the guards began to help and to take a bit of trouble. They'd speak quiet and nice to the sick ones instead of shouting and hissing, and it seems that one or two began to sit in meditation with him, but a bit behind, and go with him wherever it was he thought he was going.

Soon enough they were right out of medicines, and then some of the Japs began to tell him about local medicines, things that grew in the forest or even on the edge of the paddy fields. And somehow they fixed with the Commandant that he could go and get them. A lot of them worked quite well and what was more, he was able to gather leaves and berries to stew up for camp food; they were short on everything. But he kept on with whatever it was he had done for those first patients who got what wasn't real morphia. Well, he tried to explain it but it never made sense to me. Because pain and what is causing it is real, see? And what he did couldn't have been real. Or not in the same way. He and the Japs might have thought it was, but it couldn't be, could it? You see, he tried to use words to explain it to me twenty years later when I began to ask questions the way kids do. And Mam didn't really understand, only she said it was all true.

Dad never finished his medical course. A pity in a way, but maybe he'd have found it hard to stop believing some of the things he did believe, and he'd have had to do that, wouldn't he? Learning real scientific things, they wouldn't have mixed. Instead he became a botanist; he even had a plant called after him, though not what I'd call a pretty one. Mam had a bit of money so it was all right.

But he went on with this meditation lark and sometimes we'd have all sorts of holybolies coming to the house and once it was some Japs and he told me that one of them had been a guard at this prison camp — fancy, him coming and touching Dad's feet — I saw that myself. So there must have been something in it, though what, beats me. But I grew up keen on engineering and I had a bit of luck with jobs, so here I am. In the real world, though Dad wouldn't have looked at it that way.

I suppose I feel a bit the same about the University physicists that I meet sometimes and we get on a treat till they try and take me into their way of thinking, for they're dealing with the same set of objects and movements that I'm dealing with, but in ways that don't seem to me real in my sense. Any more than Dad's realities that I was always outside of. There we were under the same tree, me looking out at the fine view and my Dad with his back turned to it and looking in at something that can't be real. And yet it seems to have worked in that ghastly old prison camp where nothing else could have. And when he died he seemed so sure that everything was all right.

So where are we?

Telling to the Master

AT EACH SIDE THE HEAVY, THICK MARTEN AND beaver furs brushed softly, intimately, against his arms. He moved closely along them, knowing that the opening would come and he would pass through it. He was used to the almost dark, the deep forest feeling. It was part of his training, as were the whispered repetitions, fur muffled, the continuous hammering of knowledge, the murmur of the great rush-thatched beehive. Happy he was to be back. The fur curtains revealed an entrance; he pushed gently. There was the roof post, the shelterer, the strong one. He knelt and broke the small clay pot he had been carrying in his hand against its foot, which stamped so deep and strong into the earth below, a trivial offering but acceptable from a homecoming student.

He passed on into the warm, totally fur-enclosed hollow in which the Master lived, thinking and making his calculations and sometimes teaching. Some light sifted in from the raised centre of the roof, but the overhang of thatch, necessary for keeping out the weather, somewhat dimmed it. There was also a floating wick in an oil pool, but the Master saw what he needed inside his head and had little need of light. He did not even bother to decorate himself; he was too well known, both to the Goddess and to men, for this to be wanted.

The young man, whose name was something near to Patric, took the Master in his arms and kissed him. They touched and smelled one another. For a little time the Master stopped thinking, became ordinary; it was restful and happy for him. His face creased into pleasure. By now it was almost a year since Patric his student had left, fully decorated and clothed honourably, carrying a cord of shells, a flat of barley bread, some dried meat and his bow and arrows against his next meal. Not that he was likely to starve. He would go by way of places where people lived; the sequence of these places was kept in his head, the distances and sun directions. The people there would know that he was a student and would soon be a prince of learning. They would give him shelter, food, perhaps a night's wife and pass him on, beyond the even and cultivated country, the small dykes, the planted fruit and nut trees, through forest and marsh and hills.

And so it was. The mid-day sun threw his shadow always in front of him, the rising sun on his string hand, the setting sun on his bow. When he came to places of learning he would greet the Master. He would also honour the house posts and the hearth. If there was a Goddess place that too would be honoured. In some that would be the first thing, if it was She who spoke into dreams. In such places he would sleep as instructed and then he too would dream and find answers. But there was no place so large as his own great house of learning and no stones so staggeringly large, so overwhelming as those he knew. Nor were these people as skilled in measuring and the foreseeing of events that came out of the measurements. Yet most of them at least would know and honour the time of sun-death and sun-birth. In many there were stones that told, at least in a simple way, the times of the moon. Once a stone had fallen and they had not liked to touch it, but he, telling them what must be done and himself setting the first hand on it, had got it in place for them.

There had been some difficult days and nights when the space of walking between the places of people became very long. He was among hills and lakes that had never known eyes or hands on them; he slept sometimes in trees, hearing wild beasts at night, snuffling of bears or grunting of wild pigs. A flint must be well aimed to pierce an eye; he could do it if need be, but it was better to keep away, to leave the beasts in their own world. Once, lying along the branch of an oak, he watched the rising of the delicate new moon, out of the notch between two black hills, the Lady reborn. If there had been people there instead of wild beasts, they would have used that notch to tie down time.

When he came down out of these violent hills into people's places they spoke with different voices, so that sometimes he had to laugh, or they laughed at him. But many words were the same and he was recognised for what he was. In one a woman of wisdom remade his decorations, using the same colours. Even if he had not been a student, ordinary people would have welcomed him, given him food and warmth, for are we not all one kind, one family? A stranger coming to a place with news and perhaps skills, lights a little lamp. Strangers, coming alone, are good. Sometimes, too, he would meet some man or woman in his own discipline and then there would be little problems of understanding, since the big words were the same, just as the proverbs or riddles are the same among hunters or farmers or flint miners or fishers or root gatherers, even if the ways of speaking, or the small words, are different. He told all this, sometimes in bursts, sometimes silent for a time while he gathered up his memories, seeing himself in strange places, and the Master nodded, approving him.

He counted in his head the places of people which he came to and left and also the places of learning. There were tens of them and again tens. He had come late to a place on a small rise and when he woke in the morning and drank milk which had been given to him the day before, there were wide waters stretching. He had seen the sea before, two days journey from the place of learning and the great Circles; he had eaten fresh fish there, not like their customary salt fish. He had not liked the taste at first, but took to it later; they were the Lady's fish. But that early one was the sea of the high sun and this was the sea of the sunsetting, a different colour and smell. Already it was colder, though the wind had a good, new taste at the back of it. Later he knew it was the taste of the brown and gold waving plants that grew in the sea's edge. He went on, the picture and pattern of where he was to go still clear in his mind. There came a river to be forded as he had known there would be, a ford with stones, knee-deep, and after that rough going and in the end a crossing of the cold sea in a skin boat, expertly handled. And then he saw the marked rocks and he blessed the cups and mazes of the Goddess, and after that, as had been made clear, he came to the place intended from the beginning, the place of measurement.

'And then?' the Master asked. He had listened carefully, nodding and from time to time chewing a piece of some strong-smelling plant. But it was the august smell of the Master himself that filled the room, that came in gentle waves from the fur of walls and floor, welcoming Patric back. It was so good to know himself again in the great house of learning, not having to make decisions, only to tell and be taken into the memories of others. But if only he had more words!

If only he could show the Master the great thing that caught him after he came to the intended place, or indeed before that, after he had seen the guiding, reassuring cup-marks. He had strangely not been afraid, not even in the skin boat crossing over deeps between hills and other hills. 'They spoke to me, those kneeling with the paddles; it was hard to understand, only that I was one of the expected.'

The Master nodded. 'What did you give them?'

'A shell,' he said. 'A shell of our own sea. It was borne in on me that this was the right pay. And so it was. Yes, so it was. From then on I did the things which my hands and heart told me; it was as though I was a leaf in the flow of a river. Most of all having seen the rock marks that showed me we were now all Hers.'

'Ah,' sighed the Master, 'as I also on my young man's journey. And were there others? Yes, yes, that would be so. How did they place you?'

'All of us were on the long ledge at the side and back of the stone, separated by counts of days and part days, ready to tie down time. I was closest to the stone, being from the furthest place. That ledge has been made smooth and hard by many footsteps. You will remember?'

Again the Master nodded. Such things brand themselves on the mind.

Patric went on: 'Each of us had a checking wand, peeled white. As each saw the last moment of light he placed his wand. There is the shivering time. The moving of the sun seems to stop, a night and another day, a night and another day, the wands touching and then, as time is accomplished, the spread backward among the wand holders. This way was the stone checked and she who was also the stone could be set free having taken the light into herself to keep for nine months. Was it so in your time, my Father?'

'Yes, it was so. At first light he to whom had been given the checking wand and had been admonished to lay the year's light into her, must, having done so, take her at first light and tie her to the stone, pegging her feet into the ground as time must be pegged. You also, my son, it seems to me, did that thing.'

'Her body was smoothed thin over her bones, thin and smooth, but it leapt like a fish when I speared it, gently as you had taught me, not like the spearing of hunters or farmers. She smelled of the leaves of knowledge which she had eaten and which I tasted from her open, hot mouth.'

'What did she tell you after you speared her?'

'She told me about the lines which are not seen by hunters' sight but only by the sight of knowledge, the lines between us on our green earth and the earths of light. She told how our shadows crossed, speaking as a teacher although she was young, thin and white as a young unsuckled lamb, so that at first I wept for her. When afterwards I took the pegs and cords from her feet I wept over her bruises, but she herself did not weep. She laughed from her open mouth because of what I did to her and because of the sea tides and the growth and fall of leaves, because of the stars walking round us, looking through chinks of darkness, of all that is entering and leaving, spinning and crossing, making darknesses by day fearful to those without knowledge. But we who understand, as I did then understand and shall understand again when my mind has been cleared, we are not afraid, knowing that the lines separate, that light will return. She and I held it in our joint minds and because of that we are cherished by the Goddess and our knowledge will run like a hidden river for all time, growing as a river grows. All that knowledge picture was

given to me by her through a long unsleeping new day and the night that
followed. The first night of the new time. After that she left me, but both
of us were filled, she by what I had done for her, and myself by what she
had passed to me.'

'And the wand-holders — all of you?'

'They too had become truly men. There were others from the
Goddess. That way we worked on what had been told — the sand was
good for long sight lines. — And my own one watched us from far, and
she, I believe, having passed on this knowledge, closed on it and waited.
Is waiting now.'

'Is waiting now. And the children? You saw them?'

'So beautiful. Without fear yet utterly courteous to strangers. Strangers
such as I was. Had been. Until she did this thing out of her body, making
me a whole man.'

Stirred by deep and beautiful memories, the Master understood,
smiled, but must question further. 'The teachers?'

'They too were beautiful.' Patric shut his eyes to see them better and to
get words for them. 'Being below the Goddess, yet women, ageing into
further wisdom. The marks of the Goddess showed blue on the white of
their arms, live spirals. As my own white lamb will be marked. Their
faces were netted with lines as it might be the lines joining and crossing
the great circles. Their eyes . . .' He could not describe what it was to be
looked at by those eyes which had once been the eyes of just such a
maiden as he had speared. The remembrance of those eyes came back
stunningly into the fur-lined familiar chamber of the Master, as though
these teachers were also there, with them. The Master, sensing the depth
of Patric's remembrance, did not speak but laughed low a little, he also
remembering the un-sleeping night. They stayed so.

Silently a man slid in through the thickness of the fur curtains, carrying
a bowl of beer still faintly bubbling, still warm with its own life; he knelt
in front of the Master, who took the bowl, relishing the feel of the even,
stone-polished grooves, the stone-polished lip against his own. He drank
deeply and his stomach gave thanks in a comforting belch. Patric took the
bowl next for his own comfort; there had been no beer so carefully
brewed anywhere on his travels. At the farthest end they made an
altogether different drink, out of some kind of flowers that grew there, or
so it was said. But the fish had been very good.

A woman followed, again silently, offering flat rounds of barley bread,
hot and crisp from the baking stone, and on each meat and honey. They
ate quietly. For a few breaths the Master slept, Patric watching him,
wondering what dreams were coming into him. There was a roll of soft,
pale inner skin beside him; he had been marking it with a stick of charcoal
and a measure, the strides and arm-breadths of measuring made as small
as the tiny nicks in the smooth bone. Patric longed to know how soon

where and what was to be thought out and made, what honour was coming to which fortunately chosen diggers with antler picks, miners in the flint pits, makers of levers and rollers, twisters of rope, chewers of the skin strips. All, all would become people of the Goddess, as he himself was, as all who by understanding had pinned down and tied one after another of the natural and fearful mysteries. As also the white, thin body of the maiden who would in turn become a teacher, since all goes in spirals towards the centre. And those in the outer parts of the centre, miners, diggers, preparers, they too were within the network of protection, unafraid, brothers and sisters with the one mother.

The Master woke and nodded to Patric. They went through the fur tunnels and, blinking into daylight, out to the great mound of the ditch. From here a man could look far out over the barley fields and the sheep fields and the forest lands where the pigs rooted and fattened and the children herding them climbed and swung and played and sometimes found cast antlers and carried them back running for praise and pleasure. Here too went hunters and protectors and every man and woman from time to time would cast a glance up towards the place of learning where all finally would be made plain. So, standing there and in full sunlight the Master and Patric tossed out the beer they had been drinking in glittering golden drops, in arcs of great circles, in symbols of understanding.

It was good to be home once more, and yet Patric knew in his heart that the time would come round when he must move again. There were far places, beyond yet further seas, places which could be seen, sometimes veiled, sometimes shining with mid-day sun, and here the Goddess must show herself to the people, show herself equipped with power and knowledge, able, through her teachers of whom he was already one, to demonstrate the mysteries of measurement and prediction, the external spirals. There were many things yet to be understood; that was the ultimate joy of learning, the opening up of further questions. Where he had been, the day was longer, and when it came to the other turn, the nights were longer. So they had told him. If, later, he was to go where he felt he surely must go, this would be still clearer, or so it was said by those women with the blue-netted arms, the teachers who were to be believed. It could be also that the movements of animals and fishes, the flight of birds, would be on the other circles. Why does a circle always meet itself? The tight inclosing. Why? How to begin the understanding? What to cast out? All must be worked on, thought about, measured, given its place in the great network of the Goddess, giver of all life, all measurement. Would the Goddess, in her own good time, allow her people to know all, to follow her totally, perhaps, yes, perhaps to become, even for a short moment, totally as she herself was? Had this indeed been so for the speared one who had made him a man? So much to know. He sat there on the edge of the great mound which was in its turn the edge of all light, all growth, and his life appeared to him in its totality. Year upon year of work and worship and the happiness of nearing, nearing to whatever it might be. Work, life, death.

He knew this would happen to him. It was accepted and therefore good. But for now he was home in the place of learning. They had told him that there was a new great house to be built for yet more teaching. Trees had been felled and dragged. Boys had been sent off, honourably hair cut and straw crowned, to find the antlers in the further forests for the picks. Girls, with coloured straws woven into their shining plaits, had gone with songs to cut rushes, knee deep in water and mud, each with her curved flint knife, something her mother treasured, not to be dropped. There they must bind the rushes into bundles and load them onto sledges, changing to the sledge songs. And all the time fathers and mothers were preparing the fur curtains for the new great house, carefully working on the small, soft skins, as he remembered his own mother working while he leant against her knees. Or else those with some knowledge might be thinking and measuring. All this was continuous, all in order. This was the centre of greater and greater circles, the focus of the ellipse, the mother of the right angles. There was no place for idleness or ignorance or fear.

Nobody likes a Refugee

NOBODY LIKES A REFUGEE. THEY ARE A NUISANCE.
They cause trouble. They are frightened and unwashed. They do not
speak our language, at least not the way it should be spoken. They smell
of over there.

All the same I think we have to help them, though it is good when they
can be passed on. I remember very well that time in Lobatsi. Yes. I was
much younger then and more afraid of what might happen to my future.
It was not so long after Independence and I was still excited about that, as
many of us were. I had passed my Cambridge and I had qualified for
work in the Ministry of Education. Yes, I was a real Government Service
man and it was at last truly our own government, even if there were still
many whites in it, one of them my boss. But I had won my interview.

Well, I went over to see my aunt. We are from the Baralong and my
aunt was a proud woman. Once she and my uncle, who had died a few
years before, had land, a good farm across the border in the Republic.
Yes, it had water and they had built a brick house with three bedrooms,
as well as sheds and places for the plow oxen and the hens. She had a
garden. How often she spoke of it! But it became a black spot in a white
land, so the Boers took it, paying very little for the fields my uncle had
cleared and fenced and nothing for the house, since they said that no
white would live in it. Yet my aunt had kept it so clean you could lay a
blanket down anywhere, and it was well thatched.

People spoke for my uncle, mostly other farmers, even Boers, for my uncle was well known and liked by all. But it was no use except that they let him stay until after the harvest. Then he must harness the oxen to the great waggon with all their things from the house and my aunt threw dust on the last fire she had lit and perhaps she cried and she and her children got themselves onto the waggon and they turned their backs on what was no more their home.

They crossed into Botswana which was then Bechuanaland and they made a farm, although much of it needed to be de-bushed before the next ploughing. The Baralong are good farmers and there were cousins who helped, among them my father. So it was not too bad. But my aunt was always grieving for the old house and the fruit trees she had planted, which had to be left and would be bearing fruit for others. There was less water in the new place, though the grazing was good enough. I used to visit them and meet my cousins. Then my uncle died and my elder cousin who should have done Junior Certificate failed, perhaps because he had been too sorry about his father. Moswetsi, that was his name, and his mother managed the farm well enough, but when I went to visit he sometimes became angry and sad because I had stayed on with education, and he had missed.

My aunt cooked nice food although she always complained that her kitchen was not like the old one. This time I brought her gummy sweets and half a bottle of whisky which I had shared with a friend. Myself, I do not like the taste of whisky, but it is the most expensive, so I liked to put down my own earned money and ask for it, more especially if there were white men at the bar who could see me pay proudly. This whisky I had bought out of only my third pay check. My aunt liked the whisky; it made her able to laugh a little and tell stories. I remember she told me about Plaatje; he had been some kind of a relation, I think. In all her stories the bad people had been the Boer men. This I could believe and I was very glad that new Botswana had shaken them off. Or almost.

Well, the next day was Sunday and we went to the church. I like to sing a few strong hymns, but I do not think they mean much, not to ourselves. My cousin Moswetsi, who was with us, slipped out after the second verse and I could see through the window that he was speaking with someone. His mother also seemed to see this and I could tell that it made her not happy. But that was all, for the time. Later in the day Moswetsi and I took a lift into Lobatsi. In those days it was not so grand as it is now, the abbatoir did not look the fine way it looks today and the shops were smaller. But it was more than that. We in Gaborone were lighthearted because of Independence and all our plans and the big Government buildings and the Mall and this feeling we had that everything must go well now and we had all voted, so that now we were a democracy and as good as the big countries. But in Lobatsi people went dodgingly, not looking at one another, nor greeting loudly and with laughter. Not everyone, but enough to make me uneasy. I found myself thinking that this was because it was so near the border with the Republic. I tried to speak of this with Moswetsi, but he shook his head. It seemed to me that, although he barely greeted one or two persons, yet he exchanged looks with a few. I waited for him to speak.

He said no, no. Yet I knew inside myself that he was not yet speaking from the heart and perhaps I had made him anxious, so I said we should have a drink and we should go to the Cumberland Hotel. As you know, that is the big place and indeed I thought to myself that perhaps I had been too bold and after all and in spite of Independence we could be treated coldly or even thrown out. But then I thought no. I am a citizen of the new Botswana and I myself am part of the Government, though as yet only a small part.

So we went in to the bar and several white men gave us hard looks and two of them whispered and laughed and I hated them. So I wondered if I should ask for whisky so that I could show that we Batswana could ask for anything and were as good as them. But then I thought that was a show-off and they could laugh at me secretly, so I asked for beers and when we got them another white man looked in a nice way and raised his glass to us. So for a while we sat in a corner and watched.

Then Moswetsi began to seem uneasy and said, 'Let us go,' and we walked along the road a little way out from Lobatsi and we spoke about the whites and so long as they were not the Boers it was all right.

In a while we saw a white man with a camera and he seemed to be taking photographs, as the tourists from everywhere are always doing, even of the most common things, so this was nothing new. The man walked slowly under the trees with the camera slung over his shoulder. He was wearing a jacket buttoned tight and suddenly it seemed to me that there was no shirt under it. Moswetsi said: 'Come, we will see,' and he walked following the white man.

I said, 'He is taking many photographs,' and Moswetsi said, 'Yes, but is there film in his camera?' And I was surprised, but I said to myself that white people sometimes do mad things.

And now we had come a little way out from Lobatsi and I thought we should begin to look for a lift. But Moswetsi was walking quickly and soon he was beside the white man and seemed to speak with him. They moved off the road to where there were some bushes and I asked myself what could my cousin be doing and whether we should stand and sign for a lift, since it had begun to be late and nobody could take photographs even if what Moswetsi had said was just a joke against the whites.

My cousin came and stood beside me. He said: 'The Boers took my mother's farm. The same Boers would take this man's life.'

'Why?' I said and then I began to understand, so now I whispered, 'They are chasing him? The police?'

'We must get him to Francistown,' Moswetsi said. 'That will take two days. You must keep him in your room in Gaborone.'

This made me angry. 'No!' I said, 'A big no. I am a Government servant. I am not interested in politics.'

'You will do this for my mother who is your aunt,' said Moswetsi, and I did not answer. I wanted to go back to where we were before. I said: 'It is time we got our lift.'

'Yes, yes,' said Moswetsi, 'but it is a certain safe lift, not any one. And I shall leave you when we get to my place and you will take him on to Gaborone.'

So we waited and I very much did not want this thing to have happened. Before, I had seen myself on a straight road that might lead to great advantages. And now I would perhaps be breaking some law, for I did not know why the Boers hated this man and he might have murdered one of them and he might have a gun as well as an empty camera. But my cousin said: 'It is good that our Botswana is now an independent country, and we can choose what way to go.'

So I began to think that after all this was so and we could decide who were our true friends. But still I would be going into trouble. Yet my cousin was so certain that I would do what he asked that I began to accept that the thing must be done. And soon there came a certain truck and Moswetsi stepped into the road and made a sign and it stopped. Then came the man out from the bushes and when the truck started he was sitting between the driver and me. We dropped Moswetsi off and he and the white man shook hands and passed certain words together and then we took the long road to Gaborone. Most of it was a dust road in those days, though it is a fine highway now.

I did not like the man's smell; perhaps he had not washed for too long; and sometimes he made swallowing noises. I talked across him with the driver, who was not from the Baralong but from Mahalapye, up north. He was an educated man but we did not speak in English since we were speaking about the one who sat between us and stared at the road rushing backwards under our lights and now and then there was a small animal or a bird that flashed across.

This driver told me that the South African police were after this man to be a witness in a big trial, saying what they wanted. A white man could be police-hurt just as well as a black and he had been much threatened. We all know well what is done in South African prisons. Now it is the same for the whites, the driver said. Yes, said the driver, all that unless he agrees to witness. And he will not do that.

'Yet he seems not to be a strong man,' I said, for he had sagged back, and I saw he had not been able to shave.

'No,' said the driver, 'he is not strong. But God might give him strength.'

'He will need that,' I said, and I began to pity the man and wondered what was to be done.

The driver said he was taking the man as far as Gaborone. Later, he said, there will be a safe lift to Francistown.

I asked could not the man go by train, but the answer was that many of the train people were still from the Republic and not to be trusted even if now they were our citizens. That is not so today, but in those days the railway was not properly ours. So it seemed I must keep him safe until the next lift came. 'Do not let him go out of your house,' he said. 'I will come back perhaps tomorrow. He must not be seen.'

'Must I feed him?' I asked, and the driver said yes.

So it came that I took this man into my room, which was in one of the old houses, and I gave him a blanket and he slept and was still sleeping when I left for the office. It was a difficult day for me. I had many figures to copy and add up or perhaps subtract. In those days we must do all that by hand; now the small computers make it easy. But not then. I went over and over my figures and my boss became impatient. I made a small mistake. Oh, I cursed this refugee man who had made me so anxious.

He slept most of the day and after work I brought sandwiches and made tea. In the dark I took him out to shit. Late that night came a knock on the door. The man was most frightened. But I went and it was my cousin Moswetsi and someone with him whom I did not know, but he had a truck. So this white man whose name I never knew was put onto the truck and we all wished him well, but I was most glad not to see him again. No, he never told me his name and I did not ask.

'That,' said my cousin, 'is your share of payment for the farm.' And I knew how he and his mother and even his younger sister had talked for many evenings about their farm and wept for the beautiful days there.

But my boss had found that small mistake in one of my sums and he was very angry and said hard things about my education. And I washed the blanket because it smelled of this man. All he had with him was the empty camera which he could use in pretending to be a tourist, and a little soap and a pair of socks. Even, he had no cigarettes. I never asked him his name. I did not ask, had he a wife, a home, what he did. Better not to know. But he had ink stains on his hands.

Later my cousin told me that this man had got safely to Francistown and the plane that took the refugees away. There was a powerful white man there who saw to it and protected them. But it was many days before my mistake over the adding was forgotten. I am not happy to remember it, even if it is now long ago.

Today I am a married man with an office that is wholly mine and my aunt is no more. Also the refugees who came from South Africa at the time of the terrible trials come no more. We have other kinds of refugees today, from further north, not white. Some are good people, but have lost their homes. They are at Dukwe now. But some among them are not good and are sent from the Boer Republic to make harm.

That is most difficult, for how can we tell which are the true refugees whom we should help, although we hope very much that they can be passed back to their old homes near Bulawayo. Yes, it is hard to know what to do. But it is a most sad thing to be a true refugee with no home, and always, always we must help them since we ourselves now have our own home and our own country. Which is Botswana.

The Money They Must Have Spent

ARE YOU LISTENING CAREFULLY? I MUST EXPLAIN. You're telling me, aren't you, that everyone thought I'd been murdered. And the body buried or thrown out to sea. It was in the papers. How silly! You thought so yourself? No! But you say you did. Me, murdered. Oh dear, isn't that dreadful. Yes, I see it must have upset you. But now here I am again and quite alive and — and happy, like I never was. You remember, don't you? Even though I was always trying to hide it. As one ought to, so as not to worry other people.

And now you say I ought to tell them that I wasn't murdered after all? But how can I? It sounds — well, downright silly, doesn't it? How can I possibly go along and tell them, here I am! And after all the trouble and expense they've had. As you were explaining to me. The Special Branch and all. Looking all round for what-you-call-it clues. Digging holes. Frightening people. Oh dear.

You see, we haven't been reading the papers, Bertram and I. We were so happy, we couldn't be bothered. Didn't listen to the news, even. And he — my husband — you say he's gone off to America. Having a good time. Well, I just hope it hasn't been like his old good times — with some other poor girl. Look — if I was to say I hadn't been murdered, he might ask for me back! They couldn't make me do that, could they? Oh dear, perhaps they could. No, no, I won't! You must help me. I wouldn't say anything, only I'm worried about the money they must have spent, looking for — well, my body I suppose.

You see, when I had decided that I just couldn't stay any longer, when it all got just too bad — I knew that even you wouldn't believe me if I told you about him, half the things he'd done — I thought it all out. I left that stupid old car — much too big and fast and I never could make out all that nonsense on the dashboard. I just drove it up onto the moor and got out and walked. I felt sure someone would find it and take it back. I'd left the key in on purpose to make it easy for anyone who could drive. Most people in the district would know it was his and they might have thought he'd say thank you and give them a reward. And I didn't take my smart jewellery, only just a few useful things, my watch, well that's almost a part of one isn't it? But not, well, not those expensive presents he sometimes gave me . . . afterwards. Presents I hadn't wanted anyway. Not from him! I couldn't do fairer than that, could I?

Oh it was such a relief! — you've no idea. I just started walking. And then — then I got to where Bertram was, and everything was suddenly all right and I wasn't frightened any longer.

Well, you know about my husband, what he was like, what he did, what it was like being near him. I only told you a little, just the edge. And he'd been getting worse. Of course, if I'd understood ten years earlier, instead of trying to help him, being a good wife, at least that was how it looked from my side, things might have been different. I was so young at the beginning, much too young to understand and I hadn't had a real education, so he could always look down on me. Treat me like dirt. And he, well he was beyond helping, beyond even talking to, at least by a wife. And the things he did — oh you wouldn't believe! What he did to me and said to me, I just curled up, I can't even try to remember them. How he even thought them up — ! Horrible. And nobody else knew. I managed to keep it from the servants. They might have been on his side — at least, that awful butler. I don't know. Anyway they wouldn't have understood half of it, not how frightened I was, not knowing what he'd do next. When I think of it now I'm sure that what happened to my dog — you remember little Sparky, don't you? — was his doing. I couldn't believe it at the time, not how anyone, not even him, could bring themselves to do that to a poor little dog. But later I knew it was him. The way he laughed after I found my Sparky, all squashed and his eyes — oh I can't bear to think of it!

You know, I did tell Jim about it — well, not all, I couldn't, I was ashamed. I felt awful. You remember Jim, don't you, the tall one with the ginger hair and those ties? Well, it came over me suddenly, at that big party for the Americans and I'd had two glasses of champagne. And Jim was ever so nice at first. I cried a bit and he mopped me up. And then he got me to go to bed with him, sort of sympathising and patting me all the time, kissing me ever so gently and that was nice at first. It was so different from my husband, even if it wasn't true. My husband had never been gentle, not from the start. He liked making me cry.

Jim was different. He whispered nice things to me. When we were in bed together, just the two of us like in the old movies. Not like real life. But you see, it turned out that Jim was married; I didn't know that till later, but it meant he couldn't, so to speak, rescue me. He didn't even want to, I saw that. You know, I hoped so much he would want to. But it didn't happen. He was in the same world as my husband, went to the same parties, played the same games, he wouldn't have given up any of it. Not for me. And people began to talk, so of course Jim backed out; I don't blame him, he had other people to consider, most of all his wife. At least I hope that was the reason. I hope it was because he really loved her. But it meant I was back where I'd been, only it seemed worse.

And then Bertram came, to look at some of the furniture. You know, don't you, that was his job, the thing he was so good at, clocks, chairs, bureaux, cabinets, the lot; we had some very valuable things, though I can't say I miss them at all. There were half a dozen clocks scattered about that big house, a grandfather in a very fancy case, a buhl clock with a little chime, and two others which had come from some Austrian collection, I can't remember the name. They all showed different times and my husband got annoyed with them — well, that's one thing I can't blame him for — and then someone told him they knew of an expert. And that was Bertram.

I didn't even notice Bertram at first, I was so wrapped up in being unhappy and trying not to let it show and wondering whether it would ever stop. Then one day Bertram was looking at a little chair from the bedroom, that was broken, and he asked me how it had happened. He was looking at that chair in a sad and kindly way, running his hands over it — yes, it was his gentle, clever hands that I noticed first — and saying he was sorry that this had to happen to something which had been made more than two hundred years ago. Made by men who had prided themselves on knowing everything about how a chair should look for both strength and comfort, and the beauty that goes with that, and it had been used ever since, all these years, without being hurt, but now — and he shook his head. Of course I knew just exactly how it had happened and why. I knew the nasty way that poor little chair had got itself worked into a kind of relationship between me and my husband. He knew I was specially fond of that chair, and so he'd picked it up and — oh dear, I hate to think of it, even! It was like my little Sparky. Meant to be wicked. Meant to hurt.

So Bertram looked from the chair to me, looked full in my face and back again to the poor little chair, and suddenly I was crying and he put his hand onto mine. And I caught myself thinking, Oh this is just Jim all over again. He doesn't mean it. He'll just go away. But it wasn't, no, my dear, it wasn't like Jim. Or anyone else. It didn't take me long to understand how different it was. So after a bit we made up our minds, Bertram and me. It was as simple as that. I'd only got to disappear, not to be there. There was so little I wanted to take, nothing that would remind me, and he'd got this other job lined up. You see, Bertram is so good at all sorts of things, anything to do with wood or lacquer or inlay or ivory or touching up, anything with tiny screws and brushes — oh I do so love to see him at it when he brings something home to work on! And I'm learning, I'm learning to do it myself. I think I could be good with bindings; I like books if I don't have to read them. And why should the police have got it into their heads that I'd been murdered?

It's so stupid! And they even had to drag in poor Jim — and what can his wife be thinking of him now! And these newspapers you brought, saying they've been hunting through the woods and digging up where they think I might have been buried! Such a waste of time when those policemen might have been catching burglars. You know, when I got round to reading about it and thinking of all the money it must have cost, and the trouble it had given to so many people, I was quite ashamed. All those clever Special Branch gentlemen who could have been looking for swindlers and comparing handwriting and telephoning to the Bank of England, all put on to question everyone about poor little me! Those people at the hotel, not that they knew anything, but it must have been dreadfully uncomfortable for them. And the police don't seem able to stop. So what ought I to do?

I'd like just to say no, no, you can leave off, I'm quite all right, all I want is to be left alone, I wasn't murdered; but if they knew that they'd be bound to be angry, wouldn't any of us be! Wasting their time. And then, well, you see, don't you, they might try and take me away, take me back. To him. To my husband. Away from Bertram. And I couldn't go with them. I couldn't do that, no, not possibly, I'd kill myself first. Truly. Then they'd have a real crime. And I'm so happy, surely they could just leave us alone.

So what am I to do, dear? Please help us. Me and Bertram. Oh, you think I should write a letter, explaining, only giving a wrong address? Or no address at all. And you'd post it yourself, perhaps in the middle of London or somewhere? Oh that's ever so nice of you! It wouldn't be wrong, I'm sure. But who ought it to go to? Not my husband. Not Jim, oh I couldn't do that. But who? Oh no, I couldn't send it to the Chief Constable of the County! I don't even know him. I saw him once at the races, and he looked as if he might be cross. He might try to find me — and I'm sure he's ever so efficient. But even if he didn't manage to find me I'd be frightened all the time in case he did. Not frightened like I used to be, but still —. No, I have an idea. I might write a letter to that nice young policeman who lives near the bridge, he has one of the old chestnut trees growing right in front of his police station, a real picture in

May. He was ever so nice when my poor Sparky was run over. If he was run over. If. I'm sure that nice policeman would understand and want to help me.

But then, he'd have to tell the others, wouldn't he? And I do feel so awful about the money they must have spent hunting for me and digging holes, when here I've been all the time, and being happy and learning how to bind books. I feel guilty about all that, I mean properly guilty, as if I'd done something wrong. But I haven't, have I? No, I'm certain I did the right thing. But I couldn't write that letter and get my nice policeman into trouble and wondering what he ought to do. Let's think again.

I know! That is, if you don't mind. I'll write a letter to you from Australia, some place called Wallaboloola or something, saying I ran away because it was all more than I could stand, and I won't say a word about Bertram or anything else. Just something about kangaroos perhaps. To make it sound right. And you'll have to say you threw the envelope into the fire before you read the letter, so there won't be a postmark. But they can look at my handwriting so that they'll know it's really me. I expect the Bank will recognise it, they were always complaining about my cheques not being legible, oh, half in fun of course, because they were really quite nice; they knew a bit about what was happening to me. The girl who cashed my cheque could see I'd been crying. Yes, the Bank would know my writing and I'm sure the Special Branch would enjoy having something to show I hadn't been murdered. What do you think?

Not yet? Why not? Do explain. Oh, because of the time it might take me to get settled in Wallaboloola and the letter to get back. I see. But think of them going on worrying about me being murdered and spending all that money! Bertram is worred about that too. He feels we ought to try and pay it back, but I don't see how we can without being found out. So the sooner I can write the letter, the better. I could put in koala bears; I suppose there are still some in Australia? You see I do feel uncomfortable. All that money they must have spent — all, all for nothing! And I'm so happy now.

Death of a Peculiar Boar

'THE WITCHES,' SAID GWILYM PETIT NOIR, WHO WAS also called the Little Black King, 'are getting very troublesome. I wish someone would do something.' A witch had just carried off one of his younger daughters. He was not much perturbed himself. He had enough daughters; all of them would need dowries unless they were exceptionally beautiful, in which case they might be bargained for, but none of them were that beautiful so far. However the rest of the family were fussing. His eldest son, Elifri, said he would lie in wait and fight the witches when they next came, but Gwilym, who found this son very useful for keeping the kingdom in order, said he was to do nothing of the kind. The witches were no joke. They used unfair weapons. It would be better to have a tournament and attract some of the ambitious young men. 'If only we could get one of Arthur's lads,' he said, 'we'd fix the witches.'

Elifri ap Gwilym was annoyed. He was sure he could fix the witches himself. But his father was putting more and more of the dull parts of ruling the kingdom on to him. The Little Black King was more grey than black now, except for streaks in his beard and his rather bristly eyebrows. And he got tired and cross riding round in his armour, and not sleeping in his own bed. So Elifri ap Gwilym the heir had to go the rounds of the kingdom with the men at arms and collect the rents. Then he had to drive back the rents, maaing and bleating or else bellowing and tossing their horns and occasionally bolting.

Also he had to do justice. He would not have minded that so much, except for the annoying fact that, if people were not satisfied they appealed from him to the Little Black King, and his father was so delighted at being appealed to that he almost always reversed his son's decisions. Very occasionally Elifri had to take action against a giant or some ravening creature out of the wild woods. But he never quite had the equipment, and when he asked his father for a really good sword instead of the old family bone-hacker, his father said that what had been good enough for his ancestors ought to be good enough for him.

The second son Tegid was not a warrior. If he could get a good hunt three days a week, that was enough for him. Tegid had been fostered by a man who was a great hunter himself and indeed was apt to turn himself into a beast of the chase from time to time, usually round about full moon, so as to refresh his memory of how such beings acted, and he had bred up his foster-son in the same useful ways. Tegid was not so good at the doubtful arts as his foster father had been. He was able with great trouble and fuss to turn himself occasionally into a stag, but as often as not he could not quite manage the horns, and had to go about with a hand or a lilly or some such nonsense sticking out of his forehead. So usually he just hunted.

Naf and Cadwry were much the same. It took a lot to worry them. But the witches interfered with their pleasures too. One day those nasty women took off a couple of hounds, leashes and all, and they were forever flustering the hunt by flapping across just when things were going well. It takes a good horse and an unimaginative rider not to be put off by a witch's toot-toot and the black whizz of bat or broomstick under one's nose.

So Tegid, Naf and Cadwry were all in favour of a tournament, and the girls naturally were sky-high. The witches were always bothering them, causing minor ailments, turning the cream, breaking the warp threads on the loom, or addling the setting eggs. Not to speak of carrying off poor little Gwaeddan, who in any case had a very bad cough, which was probably the witches' doing to begin with. The two eldest, Gwenllian and Tangwen, decided they must speak to their father about it; for it might be just one of his ideas and only going to be dropped when things went well. On the other hand if it was done properly — and if any of King Arthur's court *did* come — well, that would be dreams come true!

They waited till they got him in a good mood, with the drink taken but not to say drunk. They had been through all the chests in the bower, they told him, dropping their deepest curtseys, but there was really nothing — no, not a thing! — fit to wear at the tournament. Besides, their little sisters Enrhydeg and Teleri, were getting big now and would need to be properly dressed like princesses instead of running round in rags. This was all, naturally, for the greater honour of the Kingdom.

The Little Black King had been talking about his tournament for at least an hour already: in his mind it was already a vastly gay and successful affair with himself as the host. And here were these two girls coming in like sluts and spoiling it all. But — yes, if they were dressed, well, they could make their contribution. Gwilym Petit smiled at them. 'And you two,' he said, 'you, my dears, will of course be the prizes.'

Gwenllian looked at Tangwen and giggled. 'For the best knight!' she said, and a delicious warm feeling flowed all through her.

'Properly dressed,' said the Little King, frowning, 'and with jewels. Perhaps.'

The two girls curtseyed again. Jewels! 'Oh my lord,' said Gwenllian, 'I must have a cloth of gold dress.'

'And I must have cloth of silver,' said Tangwen, and added, 'Pearls go with cloth of silver.'

'Rubies go with cloth of gold,' said Gwenllian. 'Big ones.'

Gwilym Petit sighed and wriggled resentfully, thinking of it in terms of oxen. But he admitted that something of the sort was a necessity, and that, when Naf and Cadwry were going round the country, as they would now have to do, announcing the tournament, they could see what was to be picked up in the way of suitable wearing apparel.

'If we are to be prizes, my lord,' said Tangwen, 'we shall have to stand in the tourney ground.'

'Under a may tree,' said Gwenllian drowsily; the whole idea was getting deliciously almost too much for her.

'And we shall need mantles of vair,' said Tangwen. 'Then we shall look truly worthy of our noble father.'

Naf and Cadwry spent a really delightful time riding round, sometimes separately and sometimes together, announcing the tournament. Most people had heard of the Little Black King and the boys were heartily welcomed by several old friends of their father's. One or two spare princesses were offered to them, and Cadwry, whose tastes lay in those directions, actually married a snug little blonde in Wessex. She came away from her father's court riding pillion behind her husband, and it was most unfortunate that he should, while taking a short cut through the Red Knight's country, although he had been warned against it, have been unhorsed and lost her (as well as a good horse).

The Red Knight, following his usual custom, added the lady to his unrivalled collection of blondes. When, some hours later, Cadwry came to with an atrocious headache, some minor abrasions but otherwise no great damage, he was at any rate relieved to think that he had put his wife's jewels for safe keeping in under his mail shirt. One bracelet bought him a new horse; the necklace would do for one of his sisters. When he and Naf met next he said nothing about being a married man. Indeed he had thought so well of his few days' experience that he almost got married again, this time in the Cotswolds, but found out in time that the proffered princess had been the victim of rather an awkward enchantment.

Both the young princes took part in several small wars, to oblige their hosts. Naf killed a very unpleasant-looking dwarf, who, it was generally thought, must have been at the bottom of last year's harvest failure in that particular kingdom. He also came under the influence of a hermit who told him a number of surprising things which he felt he would have to think over. About God, for instance. The brothers arrived together at the court of Arthur the King or, as he liked to call himself, Roman fashion, Emperor. They were both somewhat abashed, but were well received at the Round Table, and, after they had bathed and had their hair cut, given such a feast as they had never come across before, both for variety and solidity. Nor were the dishes and drinking horns ever less than silver, blown glass and walrus ivory. Yet the hermit had said to Naf that none of this signified.

When they came back it was high summer and all preparations for the tournament well forward. Elifri and Tegid had been busy accumulating the necessary funds, for a tournament needs a full Treasury. Not every one of the Little King's subjects was sufficiently loyal to appreciate this. Elifri had to apply considerable pressure, and he really did not care for thrashing the heads of households, setting the women off into screaming and even attempting to attack him. He was able to get fairly satisfactory contributions from a few of the merchants and moneylenders, but it was all very boring and unpleasant, not to say un-knightly.

Naf was of course aware that his brother's activities had all been in a good cause, but still he was uncomfortable about the hard looks and sometimes almost treasonous anger among the Little King's subjects, as well as the occasional burnt steading and crying children. That hermit had said something about oppressors too. Yet surely it was in a good cause? The tournament had been set up to get rid of the witches, and surely that should appeal to everyone? But not all of them seemed to understand this. Naf had never done any worrying before and he disliked it acutely as an occupation. But once you start it is not easy to stop.

The two brothers had, by the end of their trip, a mule laden with wearing apparel for their sisters, as well as some jewellery. The load included a couple of kerchiefs, real Roman silk, which were a present from the Empress Guinevere; she had been most kind and condescending. Gwenllian and Tangwen were in raptures and there was a whirl of cutting out and basting up and sewing on of ribbons and tassels, and screaming and laughing and snatching and slapping from the ladies' bower. The two little ones were washed and the nits combed out of their hair; then they were allowed to dress up. And in the middle of it all a witch sailed in and made off with a nightgown of pale pink samite.

And now the guests were arriving. Several of King Arthur's knights came, including Gwynn, Goreu, Howel of Brittany and Teirnion; Gwalchmai himself, the May Hawk, had said he might look in later if his own quest was over in time. There were one or two kings and princes, Peredur of the Forêt Sauvage, Morffran from the Castle of Hollies, the local man Cradawg, descended from a notable line of giants, and a number of others, some with ladies, but most in a bachelor state. It was altogether very lively, and the travelling merchants got wind of it, followed and brought their delightful foreign wares. Gwilym Petit Noir was in his glory. He ate and he drank and he gave gifts and received them, and he fixed up marriages for Enchydeg and Teleri, the younger girls, who were now looking presentable, but not, of course, for the two prizes, Gwenllian for the best knight and Tangwen for the next best. Both of them walked about, rustling their skirts and displaying their jewels, in a dignified and yet alluring way which they had been practising for weeks.

Cadwry was extremely uneasy in case the prince, his brother-in-law, were to turn up, in which event it would be difficult indeed to explain away the affair of the Red Knight and his poor dear lady wife. The whole thing might end in a very nasty war. And impossible to take anyone into his confidence! Naf kept on about what the hermit had said, which unfortunately made nonsense of only too many important things, such as princesses and tournaments. Most fortunately, however, the Wessex prince did not turn up then, nor indeed did he ever do so. But it held up Cadwry's other possible matrimonial plans.

Elifri and Tegid found that most of the hard work had fallen on them. Elifri had been shot at twice in the course of his collecting of voluntary contributions from his father's subjects, and once the head of an arrow had gone in under the edge of his hauberk and made a nasty graze. He had not taken much trouble to find the culprits, either. He had a nasty feeling that they had a cause. Elifri was interested in justice. And he could not bear seeing his sisters going about showing themselves off. It made him think even iller of women than he thought already.

Tegid had to arrange the hunts and, as there were so many guests, he always ended with a rather bad place himself and no sport. However, you got an idea from that of how the tournament would work out, and how the more practical aspect of the campaign against the witches was likely to turn out. One or two of Arthur's crowd were impressive, Morffran was an accurate shot, but Peredur of the Forêt Sauvage was as strong as a bear and cared nothing about what danger he might be walking into.

There were only two raids by the witches, probably for reconnaissance. In one of them all the lights went out and they swept through Gwilym Petit's great hall, whistling and howling and croaking like a mixed pack of evil animals. When the candles and torches were lit again it was found that a visiting knight lay dying in the rushes with a barb in his throat, a hound bitch near to littering was split down the middle and several ladies had gone mad. The other attack was in the open and some kind of revolting black cloud was dropped, which clung stickily and stinking to the heads and hands of those present, and only wore off after several days. The only casualty was due to a bolting horse.

However it looked very much as though the witches would manage to spoil the tournament if they were given half a chance, so one evening it was decided to issue a challenge to the Principal of the College of Witches and have an all-out battle before the tournament. They must put the witches utterly in their place once and for all. There was discussion as to who should lead the assault, but no mad enthusiasm for this coming from most of those who gave their opinions; the witches had an unpleasant habit of turning their opponents into low forms of life. After a time Sir Gwyron the Boneless remarked that no doubt they were all aware that the witches would have no power of enchantment over a chaste life. Virginity was not absolutely necessary, so long as one had confessed and obtained absolution, but — several kings and knights backed out rather self-consciously, but at the same time preening themselves and glancing at the ladies who were listening from the back without of course taking part in the debate. But Elifri said explosively: 'I knew I could do it myself!'

'Is that so?' said Morffran politely, and looking away from the ladies, 'You have the qualification?'

'Never had time for women!' snapped Elifri, 'Can't see what it's all about, can't see what my father — Sooner a good horse myself, any day.'

'Is that so?' said Morffran again, with even greater interest.

The challenge was duly sent and accepted. Peredur of the Forêt Sauvage and Elifri were in the front line, but many of the others, including Morffran, were close behind them. There had been a rush to confession and a certain smugness among some of those who had spent the next few hours on the chilly chapel flag-stones working out their absolution. In spite of this, however, the witches managed to work on Sir Gwyron so far that he grew a thick furry hide, striped in parts, and ever afterwards talked with a peculiar snuffle. But there were those who said that this was merely his giant blood coming out.

Naturally the witches did not rely too much on enchantment, and there was some fine fighting and quite a number killed on both sides. Elifri did well with the old family sword, better than some much more expensively armed; he was sure some of the Round Table Knights had been watching him, and a report would be sent in. Perhaps — yes, perhaps he would be able to get away from the kingdom and his father's subjects and his own sisters. Finally there was a parley. Peredur and Elifri ap Gwilym had a long and lively talk with the Principal of the College of Witches; it did not appear to the others that they had reported the whole of it. But at any rate the witches agreed to withdraw entirely from the Kingdom of Gwilym Petit Noir, which was the desired result. Plans for the tournament could go ahead.

Although Peredur, who was utterly fearless and madly strong, had killed most witches, several others had done remarkably well. By common consent Morffran of the Castle of Hollies was the second best knight. After him came one or two of Arthur's court, though Howel of Brittany had been severely wounded by a witch's barb. Tegid and Naf had done reasonably well, but Cadwry had contrived not to be present; he had not felt himself qualified to avoid enchantment.

The day of the tournament was fixed, and just as well, for stocks were beginning to run short and Elifri ap Gwilym thought gloomily that it would be up to him, once again. Gwenllian and Tangwen were getting very excited; it would be a good thing when it was all over and they could relax. Indeed it would be fortunate if there were no incidents before that; Tangwen had already thrown a sharp-cornered box full of preserved toads at her elder sister. She found Morffran much to her liking; so did Gwenllian. Even after confession and absolution he had been polite: more than polite, even. He had magnificent dark eyes and long lashes. Whereas Peredur had looked at them, when he did look, in a rough and careless way and as though they were rather distasteful; he laughed like a dog barking, and he had large hands with ribbed nails that were never clean or trimmed. Morffran, on the contrary, washed his hands and face every two days at least. And he was definitely unmarried; everyone said so. The Castle of Hollies was by all accounts warm and comfortable, with ample stable and guest room and a good water supply.

The great Gwalchmai, Arthur's sister's son, whom the south English called Gawain, did turn up, for he was always one to keep his promises, on the evening before the opening day, having duly punished a king in the North East who had spoken disparagingly of Arthur and the Round Table. Gwalchmai was somewhat tired and the great golden Spring hawk on his helm had a dinted wing. The Little King's daughters all hastened to prepare his bath; Gwenllian soaped his back, and Tangwen, head modestly averted, held a warm towel. The two younger ones were able to have a good stare. Yes, he said, he would certainly break one lance, but no more. He was too old to compete for such fresh young prizes, would leave that to some lucky lad with hot blood to match their own that coursed so sweetly and showed under the clear skin. Oh, thought Tangwen, peeping round the towel, if only he had felt like competing! She wouldn't have cared about the Castle of Hollies. But Gwalchmai must have had his pick of all the noble ladies of Britain.

The Little King was of course all over himself at the great honour. Gwalchmai was set at his right hand and if, late on in the evening, after the wine had circulated, he did yawn slightly during one of Gwilym Petit's stories, well, he had made a hard journey to get there in time, and he must be ready for bed.

It was a fine day for the tournament with great clouds blowing. Everyone was there. Even those who had been most annoyed at having to give voluntary contributions thought they had better make the best of it and at least see all that was to be seen. Largesse was scattered at intervals and some of them got something back.

The two girls were arranged on a dais among flowers and cushions. They would know by the evening. Everything had been arranged for a quick wedding. But of course the victor's wishes must be respected. His damsel, princess or no princess, would be given to him in her gown and jewels and remain his property in her bare skin. The sisters might have very different destinies, according to the mood of the two winners. Yet an insult might provoke retaliation, not from the Little King, who was bound to accept the consequences of his own tournament, but from the other relatives of the two girls, not to speak of the bards, who had all come flocking for whatever they could make out of the story.

Crash bang went the tournament, with hog-maned, hairy-heeled stallions going a-wallop and spears breaking and knights thrown and battles on foot, where the combatants tended to lose their tempers, iron hitting iron and wood splintering and leather or strong cloth tearing. Gwalchmai, after his round, in which he was duly victorious over two kings and an Irish knight with green hair, sat back and rested, not always even observing with professional attention the combats which were going on all over the tournament field, but considering the problems of his uncle, the Emperor, and the jealousies of the Round Table.

People were shouting for Peredur of the Forêt Sauvage. He had knocked over one opponent after another, had seized one round the body and crushed his armour in, had thrown another to the ground during the sword play and jumped on him till he yielded. But Morffran was doing well too; he had an agile hand and a quick eye, had leaped from under a falling horse which might have pinned him and was particularly expert with the small axe.

By the end it was clear to all the observers, including the two most directly involved that Peredur was the victor and Morffran the runner up. One of them was going to get Morffran. Under their breath the sisters whispered insults at one another. The next was a knight called Alun the Broad, but he was recently married and had brought his lady with him. She was a gay and gentle one, and they seemed to be devoted. The three knights rode up to the Little King and saluted with their swords. He, all in a flurry, presented the golden garlands. Alun the Broad turned and rode along the front of the main pavilion until he came to where his lady was sitting. He knelt to her with his garland and she answered, to the high pleasure of the crowd, with flushing cheeks, a wet mouth, and a frank and fair embrace.

The Little King was then seen to be pointing at his two daughters. But it was more than clear that Peredur was shaking his head vigorously. There was a consultation into which Elifri came, speaking with considerable warmth. It was all too exciting for some of the ladies present, who burst into tears or hysterics. Tangwen slapped Gwenllian, who pulled out a handful of her hair; both screamed and pretended to faint. Morffran was looking in their direction. Their father got to his feet and approached them, waving back the rest of his court.

'My dears,' he said, and coughed, 'Sir Peredur tells me that he has made an arrangement to stay with the Principal of the College of Witches to take a final course in — what did he say? — yes, to be sure, the Arts. He feels that marriage would, in the circumstances, be inappropriate. And your brother Elifri tells me that he has come to the same arrangement. Most inconsiderate of him. I shall need to have the taxes collected early this year.' He paused and coughed again.

'And Sir Morffran, my Lord?' asked Gwenllian, breathing jerkily through her nose.

'Ah yes, Sir Morffran,' said the Little King. 'He has offered to take Elifri's place as heir to the Kingdom.'

'But —' said Tangwen, 'but — the important part —'

'That is the most important part,' said the Little King with rebuke in his voice. 'However. And he is proposing to marry both of you. One wife at the Castle of Hollies. One here. Considering himself as two separate persons: for certain purposes. A new idea. A very clever idea. Very clever indeed. Sir Gwalchmai thought so too.'

Gwenllian looked at Tangwen. And Tangwen signed to her to go on. 'But can he —' Gwenllian began.

'He tells me so, he tells me so!' said the Little King, rather loud and fast. 'Says he sees no difficulty. And with Peredur not wanting to marry and Alun married already, there is a great deal to be said for this plan. Morffran appears to be an unusually able young man. And it will mean that everything stays in the family. What those dresses of yours cost me in sheep I wouldn't like to say. I really wouldn't. And each of you will be able to tell him from time to time, of some agreeable little surprise that would be acceptable to your sister. From her husband. You see, my dears?'

'But can a man have two wives, father?'

'Exceptional men can do so, I understand. In exceptional cases. Which is just what this is,' ended the Little King cheerfully. 'So come along, my dear girls, and be given to him. Everything has been very nice indeed, I am sure. A most successful tournament and these wretched witches professionally dealt with just as I intended, and after that we must all have supper.'

The girls looked at one another again. They were, after all, dutiful girls, as their father was always saying at the times when he was not shaking his head over the selfishness and frivolity of the younger generation. And besides, neither of them wanted to be the one to back out. So the little ceremony was satisfactory to all concerned, as also the banquet which followed. It was certainly a great relief to know that there would be no interruptions by the witches. It was also a relief, in a way, to know that many of the guests were proposing to set off home the next morning, although of course there were a few who were in bed recovering from their wounds. Those ones did not, however, make such inroads on the meat and drink.

Morffran of the Castle of Hollies sat with a wife on each hand. Gwalchmai sat on the further side of Gwenllian and was bored. The Little King had the wife of Sir Alun Le Broad on his right hand; he found her charming. Sir Alun was frowning. Peredur and Elifri and Gwilym himself were talking eagerly about the possibilities of the Arts course at the College of Witches in Gloucester. It seemed that the Principal had quite taken to Elifri and had promised him an enchanted sword at his graduation. And after that there would be more than a chance of the Round Table if he went to the Emperor Arthur. Naf and Cadwry were discussing tournament form with some of their guests, leaning across the table and illustrating points with fingers dipped in red wine. But Tegid sat by himself, scowling. Here was this Morffran taking the place of the heir to the Kingdom and all so as to get the girls pushed off onto someone! Why was he not the heir, now that Elifri was going off on this course? He knew all about the Kingdom. And he himself had organised all the sport and seen that this one and that one got the best place, and then they never even thanked him but put it all down to their own cleverness. Clever — them! They would see next time; and then there was to be a hunt for the remaining guests the next day. Morffran had been easily persuaded to stay on. And then Tegid had his big idea.

Everything was ready for the final hunt. The ladies rode out on their jennets, both Gwenllian and Tangwen looking somewhat sleepy, but much less nervous. The men had their bows and arrows and hunting spears. The cries of the beaters were coming nearer as the half-circle closed. Tegid was not about, but perhaps he was organising the beaters: a splendid host, Tegid, always thinking of the comfort of his guests. 'Takes after me,' said the Little King.

But Tegid was in the middle of a bush, working furiously at his idea, trying to remember everything his foster-father had told him. There must be no mistake. Especially about the tusks. You had to get a real purchase and then rip. Using the neck muscles. Tegid concentrated.

Stags and hinds dashed in, wild pig, a magnificent white forest bull with enormous horns which fell to Sir Gwalchmai, hares and foxes, innumerable birds at which the ladies behind flew their hawks. Some of the hunters were now on foot, including the bridegroom, Sir Morffran, who might have been showing off his undoubted agility to his wives. Suddenly, and from an entirely unsuspected angle he was charged by a monstrous boar with huge and dangerous tusks. All would have been over with him, possibly as man, certainly as husband, to judge by the way the boar was about to attack, when Naf, from quite a distance and with great luck, threw a spear which went stright into the boar's eye and brain. The boar fell over, dead, within a yard of Morffran.

Tegid was never seen again. There was a lot of talk at the time, naturally. It was put down to direct action by rebellious subjects, several of whom were suspected, caught and tortured without any satisfactory results. Most of this was done by Morffran, who took his duties as heir presumptive very seriously and duly gratified the Little King with two grandchildren a year for some time.

But it was as well for Naf that he never got to know that he had killed his brother, because what the hermit had said was working in his mind. If in addition to the comparatively minor crimes of assault, arson, rape, robbery with violence and so forth, he had added the crime of fratricide, he would have had to take the whole matter very seriously indeed, especially as he had eaten several large slices of roast boar. As it was he made a pilgrimage to Rome which turned out to be very enjoyable, once he got used to all the foreigners.

If a Thing can be done Once

GOODWILL MOGESI AND AGREEMENT KWEYO WERE
students. They had come from different homelands, as these were so
studiously called, although for the moment that had been dodged. Both
spoke school and town English. But student is a dirty word in South
Africa, especially if the student happens also to be black. And, yes, they
had been demonstrating. So the police picked them up and the usual
things happened to them. They were finally returned to their families in a
rather bashed condition. Agreement Kweyo was able to walk. He was
swearing under his breath and sometimes changed over to crying with
mixed pain and anger. But Goodwill Mogesi was dumped limp, his head
hanging down, out of a police car. His mother and his young brother
carried him in, saying nothing. His eyes were shut and there were many
bruises on his face and the little smudges of blood and the red marks of
cigarette burns on his hands and other parts. They laid him down on a
blanket and his mother began to wash him. Her face was hard and angry,
but her hands were gentle. Her thoughts went back. As a young girl a
long way from the city she had lived not too badly; her father had goats
and even a few cattle; she and her mother worked in the fields with the
other women, but at least they could talk and sing and get on with the
hoeing at their own pace. It was only later that the anger began to grow,
after her marriage and living in a place without land.

Goodwill opened his eyes and looked into hers. 'They hurt you, my
son,' she said. 'Those devils in the police place.'

'No, no,' he said, 'when they started the interrogation it seemed to be time to leave. They had only this lump of flesh and bone which has just now —' and he gasped a little '— started to hurt, and you will put cool cloths on me and I will soon be well.'

'You took yourself out of it then?' she said, and sat back on her heels. 'I did not know that could be done in these days.'

'If a thing can be done once, it can be done again,' said Goodwill.

'Where did you go?'

'I sat in a tree but I held tight in case I should fly.'

'There is no tree near the police place.'

'That I know, my mother. But when your own father's grandfather was in the great battle he quickly made a tree into which, although he was wounded, he climbed and was not speared by the enemy.'

'That has been said, yes, but it was a long time ago. Are you sure, my son? Is not your mind wandering?'

'No, my mother, it is all clear. When I was in the tree I looked round; I saw your roof, my mother. Far and small, like a toy. Indeed I saw you.'

'What was I doing?'

'You were hanging the washing. My blue shirt was in it, the one which is almost new.'

'Well, I might have been doing that. But I still cannot truly believe. It is certain that my great-grandfather was treated with medicines before the battle and that is not something that happens today. It is another kind of battle. Not called war. And as for the medicines, no-one believes. Or do they? Have you — perhaps — found *tshitlo* that worked?' She wrung out another cloth. There was still blood here and there.

Goodwill did not answer for a time; his hurt body in which he now found himself was indeed sore and he was finding it difficult to escape from: indeed, it was occupying too much of his thoughts. At last he said, 'No, my mother. Not entirely. But I am in a straight line from him, the old one, the man-who-was-not-speared. Also I am a student of science at the University and I have had to think about time and about what is real and what is not. Perhaps I have learnt a little. But now I think I must sleep.' He shut his eyes, pulled up the blanket, then suddenly lifted his head again and said to his mother, 'Find out more about what the old man did.'

She shook her head and her teeth showed, but her son did not see this. And she knew at the back of her mind that she would have to do the painful thing which was asked of her. There would still be those who could speak if they were asked.

After this for a while both Goodwill and Agreement were quiet and diligent students. They did much reading outside their courses; some of this was science and philosophy. But there was also as much African history as they or the other students could come by. Such books were not always encouraged, but yet it was possible for a diligent student to remake the censored, blanked-out chapter of the History of South Africa. They talked much about ways of outwitting the various authorities which kept freedom and happiness so far from them. Suddenly also Goodwill found himself taking a great interest in botany. He would go out with a small tin case to hold plants, and large spectacles on his nose so that he looked totally harmless. The policemen stopped him and asked what was in the case. He showed only flowers and they laughed at him. However, that was not all of the things which he was trying to find. At last on a day he pounded up roots and stalks and other things which had been come by here or there and made a *tshitlo* with which he anointed his friend Agreement Kweyo, having made certain formal supplications.

He left his friend for a while until the strengthening began. He tried to think but could not because he was already on a course. Then, when Agreement's eyes had changed and darkened, when he was no more Agreement but Anger, when he began to rock on his toes, looking for an enemy, Goodwill killed the white cock and held up the bowl of *tshitlo* and was himself anointed by his furious friend. Before this his mother told him of certain doings that were attested for her father's grandfather, though she had been uneasy and afraid of speaking of them. She also told him the words of a praise which had been made. They were proud and angry words and were in his head now. Goodwill became Illwill and he too looked for an enemy. Both of them knew which enemy it must be. Both of them had by now trodden upon and forgotten any of the Christian teachings which they had believed in and without which they would not have got either their names or their education.

Now it must be said that a certain police captain, an Afrikaner, became suddenly aware that out of the sky had come two birds volleying and screeching murderously down on him, but whenever he thought he had either bird in the sights of his gun, it was not there. Totally not there. Whichever of his white policemen he shouted at also became aware and in terror of the attacking birds, and in a short while all were running and swearing and screaming, and bolting the doors of the police station behind them, and some were vomiting and others were getting under tables and wetting their trousers, or holding their hands in front of their eyes and sobbing. So when the telephone rang, ordering them to go immediately to a riot area they could only say they were under attack themselves. By then two or three of the police had drawn their pistols and were firing them at wherever they thought the birds were and it ended with more than a few wounded and one man dead and bleeding on the floor of the police station.

Other police came in armoured cars with the sirens howling, but fear and anger and confusion spread and there was great abuse and fury and yet no enemy to be seen. In a while some small children came and looked at them and laughed and ran away and told the whole township, so that the police were altogether made shameful. The grown men and women spoke carefully in front of them, but the police knew very well that they had been made a mock of and weakened in the eyes both of the people and of their superiors, and yet they could not understand how.

Now this had been a pleasure to the birds, but it did little good. When they could use human thought and speech again, Goodwill and Agreement both understood that this was so. The power of the *tshitlo* was out of them and they were themselves again. It was clear that what had been done was useless, although it had given them so much furious delight, as war and the disgrace of enemies would have given to their plumed and tasselled great-grandfathers.

'No,' said Goodwill frowning, 'we have been behaving like savages. As they tell us we are.' And he laughed mirthlessly.

'There is one policeman less,' said Agreement.

'And that one may not have been the worst,' Goodwill answered him. 'And now I know that we have made ourselves less like the men whom we hoped our children would be.'

They spoke to one another, half looking away, very quietly, of how it had seemed to be, although the feeling was dying out of them. 'The beak at the eyes,' Agreement said, fingering his own face.

'The power in the feet,' said Goodwill, and looked down at his, now safely trapped in his old sandals. 'The tightening of the talon muscles for the moment of strike, oh tear and hook out that soft flesh on the face!' They looked at one another and their breathing was hard and disturbed.

'But it was not real,' Agreement spoke anxiously. 'Only a seeming. To ourselves. And them.'

'All the same — '

'No. We were wrong. This will not do what is needed.'

'Yet it was given to us. The power. By our ancestors.'

'Perhaps in their time — '

'Yes. It is true. Things have changed. Even my mother knew that and did not wish to tell me.'

'Yet she did. And I also spoke to my grandfather who is still with us. He as well did not wish to speak of it. But I bought him brandy to loosen his tongue. Certainly these things have happened.'

'Or have not happened.'

'Came to us from our ancestors. But now?'

Goodwill got to his feet. They were some way from the College. There had been blood. He remembered buying the white cock. Money his mother had given him for a new coat. Or half new. He remembered the prickle and heat of the *tshitlo*. They must have missed a lecture. Two lectures. Or no lecture. The sun was almost the same place in the sky. But had a yesterday come into today? However it was, they had been away from college. Excuse. Excuse. Death in the family? Best if they hurried back. Both were known as diligent students. Excuses would be accepted.

'Meanwhile,' said Goodwill, 'we will only sometimes come out of the body. When necessary. However this may well be soon. If we students become more involved, and that is most likely. Wanting perhaps better education, who knows? Or the kind of equipment those — others — have. Or in sympathy with — many things.'

Agreement nodded. This trick could indeed be useful. The next time there was a demonstration they would not need to be afraid of simple police pain. Even a term of imprisonment, a 90 days and another 90 days, that could pass. It was this play with time and form. The power of the ancestors shifted into a shape for today.

'I will show you,' said Goodwill, looking ahead of him at the buildings they knew so well and which ought to have been so much better: if money had been available. But not for their kind of University. No. That was something they often spoke about, digging away at shortcomings and grievances until they were sore and angry and not able to work properly. They slipped in at the gate of the College compound.

And if the examinations went as they should, Goodwill would become a technician. He would work with white men who might be jealous but equally might be helpful. They might even be friends. Yes, that was possible, might have to be faced, happily enjoyed, with one part of oneself. Only one part.

Agreement would become a teacher and he too would move in a double world, partly between time and space as now. Or it could be between a homeland which was entirely unacceptable today, but which yet held the ancestors of yesterday, who could be called upon. Or else it would be between his small life and a total Africa, an Azania idea which was as hard to seize, as slippery and full of false reflections as a concept in physics or a great soap bubble, too difficult to think of. Not yet. Not yet.

So the two students were back in their college with these notions slipping in and out. They would be hearing what had happened in the township with much piling on of detail and comment and they must be duly surprised, incredulous, but joining the others in a suppressed pleasure. How long had it taken in this world's time? Was it days or hours or no time at all? This was waiting to be discovered. Only after that could there be any preparations for another step.

A Little Old Lady

NO DEAR, MY LOVE POTIONS NEVER GO WRONG. NOT, that is, if properly used. It's a rare pleasure to think how many happy marriages have started here in my little old cauldron. What do I put into it? Ah, that would be telling wouldn't it? You'd be surprised. Quite simple some of them, obvious you might say. But others, no. And I can't pass on my little secrets. Why not? Well it's against the rules. Whose rules? That's something we don't talk about, dear, not even to nice girls like you. Ah yes, I don't see you coming to me for a little drop of something! Not till you're older. You've come for something, haven't you? Or you'll tell me I'm sure, after our little chat. Some people you know, they never have need of a love potion, not if they're lucky. And if their luck holds.

But you can't tell, not always, if someone's going to be lucky. Or sensible. Or able to read the instructions: which are quite plainly written in ordinary doctor's Latin. Now and then people are in such a hurry, I can't think why. Virgins tumbling off their unicorns as often as not forgetting their handbags and pomanders and such. And the unicorns always go galloping away; one whiff is poison to them, poor things.

I can't be held responsible for accidents. And they will happen. Not that it's likely with you, dear. Careful, that's you. Yes, I can see. But there was this king, a bit on the middle-aged side, but what's that compared with a crown and sceptre and all that. What happened there — yes, it was a lesson to all of us, anyone who's not careful about the instructions. This king of Cornwall, he was a cousin of King Arthur, so I've heard. Yes, he sent one of his knights to see if I'd got what he needed, and so I had, just the very thing. Freshly made, smelling as sweet and powerful as a young man's sweat. I put it into the prettiest little flask I had, for I do believe in packaging, sometimes a mere glance starts it all up. It had the directions written in my own handwriting, you couldn't mistake them. It seemed there was an Irish princess whose father had agreed but the child was young enough, quite inexperienced, the tiniest bit frightened, poor little thing, so it was a case of just those few drops of something before she met her new husband.

So there they were on the boat coming over, the Princess with her maid, the young Knight who'd been sent over specially to look after them, very trustworthy he'd always been, and of course the skipper and crew. There was a fresh wind, so they told me afterwards, and the poor little girl was dreadfully seasick, hadn't been on a long sea trip before. What was to be done? Well, she had this maid with her, an Irish girl, and you know what these Irish girls are like, never thinking twice, didn't bother to read the directions, and thought it was a cure for seasickness. And that poor little Princess Iseult, leaning over the side, sicking up all the nice things they'd had at the palace the evening before they left. Too much mead probably, it can be quite upsetting. And what with that and the wedding day coming so close, something had to be done, and this Irish maid of hers brought her my potion, thinking it would stop her vomiting. And so it did, so it did.

For she fell in love quick as a blink with the young Knight who was in charge of taking her safely over to King Mark, and the change of ideas acted on the stomach like — well, like the sort of cure this maid thought it was. As for the young man, Tristan his name was, he didn't really need a potion; men can mostly do without if there's a pretty face and come-hither look on it. But at the same time he didn't think it was right, considering that the King had given him the responsibility. Oh very awkward it was and nobody came out well in the end. For it went on and on, long-lasting that potion was. And all because of that silly Irish maid not reading the directions.

And what might your trouble be, my dear? Just tell me. I'm never surprised, not at anything. Oh, he turns into a frog as soon as dawn comes and hops out, then hops in after supper and when he's in bed with you — ah, so you don't want a love potion exactly, that side's all right. A bit chilly when he's still half froggified, yes I can quite see that. But one must put up with little inconveniences. Well, he must be under a spell and I'm sure we can do something about that. It's not uncommon, but you must remember, dear, that there are always some frogs that can do it their way, turning themselves into men, or even into pretty girls like yourself, just for the night. So you see it's a kind of a two-way thing.

You quite see, don't you? Now I must ask you a serious question. Are you quite sure you want him to be a man all the time, for I could manage it the other way, in fact it might well be easier, so that he'd stay permanently froggified? In fact it would come cheaper. Then you could always shut the door on him if he got tiresome, or get one of your brothers to stamp on him, and it wouldn't be murder because it would only be a frog. No? You're fond of him. Turns you on. I see dear. In fact you want him about all the time. Who is he, do you happen to know? Haven't asked his name! Now that's careless, it really is careless. I wouldn't have believed it of a sensible girl like you.

You think he might be a prince? Very likely, very likely, it's the kind of thing that happens to princes. It's usually a jealous stepmother wanting her own son to be the heir. But ask him, dear, ask him. He might think you were forward? And then if he does happen to be a prince and if he's offended — ah dear, now I see why you are asking about a love potion. But then supposing he isn't a prince? And supposing he's only a frog in disguise? I don't like that bit about his not wanting the light on. You see, dear, one must think of everything.

So you'd like me to lift the spell, if of course it is a spell? Yes, well I shall certainly give it thorough consideration. It will need some special ingredients. And above all I shall want something belonging to him, any little thing, a glove, a button, a penny out of his purse. Oh he's not wearing anything at these times, very inconsiderate my dear, you might catch cold. I suppose a snip of his hair would do. Nice curly hair, you say? Well then I would have to match it up, quite a lengthy undertaking. I couldn't consider it without a down payment. No dear, I must be honest with you, and of course if he did turn out to be a prince a pot full of gold would be nothing to him. But as we agreed, didn't we, he might be something altogether different and not so nice. But that would be nothing to do with me.

Well, I shall leave you to think it over. We've had quite a nice little talk, haven't we. Come back if you feel like taking the risk, but bring me something which definitely belongs to your — ah, your frog prince. And of course the down payment.

A Matter of Behaviour

I AM NOT ONE FOR MAKING DISTINCTIONS BETWEEN
one sort of person and another. And besides, there are matters of
behaviour which I myself, as a teacher, have tried to establish. You see,
Elsie was a tinker — that made her different. It was no use talking about
regulations. The fact was that mostly all the tinker children came to my
school in winter, maybe two terms, but then they would be on the road
again, all summer, everything they had learned from me forgotten. Then
in August, when it came to a new start, away behind all their own age. It
was hard for the tinker children, right enough, though they were healthy
apart from scratches and rashes that their mothers were not bothering
themselves about, and maybe they were learning another set of things on
the roads the travellers took, deer and birds, a fox or maybe a pair of
weasels running the road, what's called wild-life these days. But could
they put it in writing? Not they, so they'd be laughed at. Not by me, but
by the other children, for no child is kind by nature.

But as for wee Elsie, her mother was dead and her Dadda only wanted
the boys off on the roads with him when it came to the end of April and
the good weather calling at them. So Elsie stayed with an old auntie that
had the use of a shed and a row of kale and two cats. She barely missed a
day off school. When I saw she could read to herself I gave her a few old
picture books that I was throwing out and soon enough there was a tink
reading the best in the class.

More than that, she was trying to keep herself clean, which was more than the old tinker wifie did. The way it was, my children would never sit next the tinks. It was the smell off them, you understand, wood smoke and little washing, with no soap. But if you lived the way the travelling folk used to, you'd not have much chance of looking a bath in the face. Mind you, it is different today; many of them with the smart caravans, the same size and make as the tourists' or better. You'll not see a woman lugging away between two barrow handles the way I'd seen them when I first took on a single teacher school with a roll of twenty dropping to fifteen, away in the west. No, it was different altogether in those days.

But Elsie managed to wash herself and her school clothes, though they were nothing great. But I found her bits of decent cloth she could work with in the sewing class. She learned to knit and I unravelled an old jersey of my own, a New Year's present, but too bright altogether for me. But for all that Elsie was slow at her writing. She persevered, yes, that she did, and she picked up arithmetic, so long as it was about real things, and indeed that's how I feel about it myself. Once she was in Standard Two she made friends with a few her own age, two from the Forestry houses and one, Linda that was, from the Post Office. Respectable families and they'd ask her for tea, or rather their mothers did, maybe three or four times in the year, and pleasing themselves to feel they'd been good. But all the same they never let it drift out of their minds that wee Elsie was just a tinker.

She grew up to be a handsome figure of a girl, so she did, with that bright hair that most of the travellers have, and bright blue eyes to match it. I'd seen less of her once she went on to the Grammar School at Oban, and left on the stroke of fifteen, for the old woman was getting less able to do even the bit of cleaning she used to do and when her father and the boys were around it was Elsie who had to wash and mend their clothes and see to their dirty heads and all that. So it was hard on her. She would come over to me an odd evening and I could see she'd been crying.

Well, the years went by and, as you know, I married and we moved around, first to Dumbarton, then to Glasgow itself. But I'd enough friends around the village that would be pleased to see us both, and my own wee Ian when he came. So I kept up with the old families I'd known and I saw Elsie turn into a fine young woman, even if she had no time for anything beyond what she had to do, and then suddenly she was married.

This would have been in the early sixties, with things brightening up and all of us sure the bad times were past. There were only a few at the wedding and the old wifie was safe in the kirk-yard, but Elsie's father had smartened himself up with a red rose in his coat and so had the one brother who was still about. I liked the look of the bridegroom. His mother and sister were there and doubtless wondering what like of lass was coming into the family. Truly, I was afraid the two tinks might make a scene and that would be hard on Elsie, but they were scared to say much. They were foul drunk by the evening, but the others were well away by then.

I went to the wedding myself. I thought it would have been kind of nice if one of her school mates, Linda or Jessie perhaps, had been there to see how bonny she looked, poor Elsie, but none of them came. (Linda was courting at that same time and married the next year. I was at her wedding too, but it was a bigger affair, with a two-tier cake.) It was only strangers or part strangers in the church, come just for the taste of a wedding. Elsie was wearing high-necked white and I wondered was it a bought dress. Her hair showed flaming under her veil and I didn't wonder a man would fall for her.

He seemed a very decent man, a welder from a steel works, and his folk pleased that I had come and at my present of a set of tea cups, the same I'd give to any one of my old pupils if I'd been to the wedding. They went back to one of those small towns that were springing up, Edinburgh way, but not for long. The year after they moved to Corby in England. She wrote to me from there. I think she was a wee bit scared to be out of Scotland and not always understanding what people said to her. I was kind of surprised to hear from her, but all the same I wrote back and the next year she wrote again, asking me if ever I was in the south could I not come over and see her.

I thought this hardly likely, but as things turned out my husband was sent south to a branch his firm was setting up in Kettering and that was only a bus ride from Corby. I remember it well, a beautiful, rich countryside, parts of it Buccleuch land, so what were the Buccleuchs doing this far south was beyond me. There were well-doing villages, pretty old cottages and gardens packed to the gate with rose bushes. But Corby itself was given over to steel, rows and crescents and long streets of workers' houses and all that was left of the old village not knowing itself in the middle of them. There was a great chimney, alight with flames from the furnaces below; you could see it for miles. They called it the Corby Candle.

There was a Scots club and pleasant enough to be among ken'd folk, even if they were from the far ends of Scotland. They would have concerts and that; time and again there'd be a hundred folk standing to sing Auld Lang Syne. But some were terrible home-sick, worst the ones who had come from towns along the coasts, whether it was Peterhead or Campbeltown. They missed the sea sorely, here in the very middle of England. But the fishing had gone down and the money was away better down here. There were others from Wales or Cornwall or anywhere at all, but it was the Scots there were most of, and who made up the best part of the clubs, the Labour club as well.

So Elsie met me and took me back to her house, talking all the way. It was a modern house, in one of the crescents, two bedrooms and a smart bathroom. And almost all the furnishing bought: a lounge suite, the kind you'd see advertised, a table with a pot plant, new kitchen stuff, only she'd brought her old kettle and her griddle, for you'd not get one in England. But she had an electric iron and there were my tea cups, not a chip out of them. Everything was kept shining and a biscuit jar, I mind that, which they'd won in a Labour Party lottery. She showed it all to me, piece by piece, and told me not one bit of furnishing, not even the suite, was on the never-never, but all paid for. 'And nobody knows I'm a tinker!' she said and when I laughed and said she shouldn't be ashamed of that, she clutched my hand and said, 'You'll not tell!'

So I said no, no, and laughed a bittie and then she took me out to her wee garden in front of the house, all newly planted with small rose bushes that still had their labels on. They'd a drill of potatoes and a few cabbages at the back. Her wee girl was at play-school — yes, they had that and all — but there was a baby boy in a pram out among the rose bushes, asleep, with a soft fuzz of orange. I said to her, laughing, 'I see he has your colour of hair' and I can still hear her saying back, 'I could wish it was black!' And her husband, just coming back from work, had dark hair. They were that friendly, both of them, and I went over there from time to time, with my Ian who was about the age of her wee girl. She talked sometimes of the days she'd been at school — she'd still got the books I'd given her — but not much about the other girls, only a mention of Miss McSporran who had been the infant teacher and well liked by all my pupils.

But then, as you know, my husband was moved back to Scotland and we settled down in Hillhead. I remember the last time I saw her she had a big stomach, but full of content and looking forward. So the years went by and I sometimes thought of Kettering and Corby and wondered how the friends we'd made were doing and sometimes we'd send cards. But mostly I was glad to be back in Scotland with my husband and my own two, both shooting up taller than myself, and Ian talking of what he'd be doing after University. For my own part I was doing supply teaching, but I had begun to lose touch with my profession. And indeed, teaching in Glasgow is away different from teaching in a village.

And then, in the late seventies and eighties, the bad times came on us, with the yards closing down all along Clydeside and where were the orders going and the men on the streets not knowing where to turn, and all the anger breaking. And not us alone, but industry everywhere, what our forebears worked for and built up, coal, steel, shipping, the great companies that had seemed to be there forever. It seemed strange to me, since we had won the bitter war with Japan and tried and executed their Generals, that now they could be the ones who had all the factories, or else it was the Germans who had them, while our men who had fought, the older ones, in that war, were now thrown out with nothing but their old medals and the dole. What had gone wrong?

At first it did not hit us and our friends just so hard, though salary rises that my husband had expected just didn't come through. What we felt most was the terrible price that everything was, the way you had to pay a whole pound for something that was only worth what used to be half a crown in the old days. And then, well, everything got worse. But you'll know that. At least I had my two educated.

The works at Corby went. The steel industry was cut down so that it was hardly there; we didn't know what worse would follow. How had it happened? It seemed we couldn't make steel as cheaply as other countries, or it was not the kind that was wanted. We couldn't understand. Only we knew it was a matter of money, not of men working. And when money talks there's no place for people, for ordinary men and women, the like of Elsie and her man.

Well, it seemed that there could be small industries starting up here or there, maybe taking over premises in a small town and not doing too badly, at least for a few years. You've heard of T.T. and McV? Yes, well they started up somewhere west of Bathgate, on some waste ground there was, and it seemed there were jobs going. A few of the Corby men heard of it. It was nothing like what they were used to and you wouldn't see the furnace men going, but those who'd been on the lighter side and willing to take training, they might have a chance. At least they'd be nearer home. The wages were nothing near Corby, but better than the dole. Yes, it had come to that. They cursed the Tory Government and this man MacGregor — but no Scot! — who'd been put in charge of the steel industry, but they went up to the new place for interview, remembered to say Sir, and were taken on. Elsie waited to hear. They sold most of the furniture, the best bits, the ones they'd been proud of, the lounge suite, the Hoover, the washing machine.

Well, I know the rest of the story by hearsay. He started work. For a while they were in one room, not easy to keep decent. And then they got half an old house, a bike ride away. The two older children, the girl and the boy, started at the new school; the girl was well up in Secondary by now and promising well. But the third child, another wee boy, was still at home. There was no kind of pre-school in those parts. The nearest was a bus-drive away and most likely full up, let alone she couldn't afford the bus fare. She tried to feed the children well and her man best; that's the way it is for most of us women.

Well, she went to a jumble sale. The children kept growing and had to be clothed. Some of the jumbles were away better than you'd get at the shops, anyway the shops where Elsie could go. The wee one was with her of course, he was a red-head the same as his brother, though it's not a true red but more of an orange. You'll know it, I'm sure. There's always a bit of snatching at the jumbles, and so it was this time. It was just bad luck that she met with an old school mate and they knew one another. Yes, they met across a boy's jacket and Linda — for it was her — said 'Ah, it's you — you dirty tink!' and a man behind said 'What, playing tinkers' tricks on us!' And poor Elsie ran out of the sale with nothing, just hauling the wee one, pulling him along crying, and maybe the good folk walking past would have stopped and scolded her, and when she got back in she saw that her purse was gone out of her pocket.

So she put the wee boy into the bedroom with what toys they had and half an orange, and herself went into the kitchen, turned on the gas and put her head in the oven.

That was how the two children back from school found her and had the sense for the boy to run to the corner and ring the police — and lucky the 'phone was working. The ambulance men found the two children practising the artificial respiration they'd learned at school — and they'd turned the gas off. And it all came in the evening paper and I happened to read it. It was only a small piece and I only read as far as the name because I was waiting for my Peggy to come home before I'd put the kettle on and I wondered could it be Elsie. But the next morning there was a photo in the paper of the two children and I could see that the girl looked like her mother. I knew they'd been in trouble, that the man had lost his job in Corby, but she hadn't written to say where she was. No, she'd have been ashamed. But now the shame was worse. And now I was ashamed too, that I hadn't got round to writing and finding out how my old pupil was doing.

I rang the paper and got her address, saying I was a friend, and the very next day I made my way over. I remember once when I'd visited at Corby, my own Peggy asking me 'Is she really a tink?' and I said 'Yes, and I'm telling you who the tinkers were. It was they who made the weapons for the High Kings of Ireland that came over to the west of Scotland: all those beautiful swords and shields!' For that's one of the Tinker stories, though who's to know what's true and what's not? But I felt I had to get another picture told and believed, even if it wasn't the right one. Maybe it is and would account for a lot; in the old days, before my time, the tinkers really made and mended all kinds of metal things and were more welcome then than they've ever been since.

So off I went and found poor Elsie lying on a lumpy old sofa they had, wrapped in blankets and the big girl, allowed off from school, making tea and keeping an eye on the wee boy. I'd brought some cakes and we all took our tea together. I could tell from what the girl said that her father had been in a terrible taking, coming back from work to find his wife carried off to hospital and the two children, though they'd done well and the paper said so afterwards, all to bits and no tea made.

The next time I went over she was getting on fine and ashamed of what she had done, but she told me how that name that Linda had thrown at her had been that sore on her, she had just felt that nothing else she could ever do would be any good. Nothing would ever get the bad name off her back and it came out that the boy had been called a tink at school. Nobody at Corby had ever said anything against them, but now when they came back to Scotland — and she burst into tears, the poor thing. I could have sorted that Linda who had thrown it at her, and both of them my pupils. Sure as I'm a living soul, Linda would have seen that story in the papers, but not a cheep from her. Most like she'll have forgotten Elsie's married name, so there she'll be sitting at her ease. And me forgetting Linda's married name, I'm not able to get at her! But I'm hoping that someone calls her something worse than a tink, this side of Judgment Day.

Thirty Pieces

WHEN THE TRIP WIRE AND THE SHOOTING CAME ON them suddenly out of the black night, Jimmy had only one idea, not to get killed. He had been with Tagariro and there'd been a light riem between his wrist and Tagariro's hand. All at once it went slack, dangled, let him go. He turned and ran, doubled up, and the nasty zing like a hornet striking close at his ear and, once, a stone in the path split suddenly, throwing up chips at him. He went on running, stumbling in the dark, keeping on. The riem caught in a bush; he crouched and managed to unknot it from his wrist. And Tagariro, had he been killed? Probably, or he wouldn't have let go. Killed. Somehow they'd got half friendly, talking a little, exchanging grins. Better if Tagariro was dead now, not caught to be hanged.

He changed direction a bit, still running. In one bit of his head he wondered what had happened to Livingston and Lucky, his vanmen, prisoners too. But there wasn't a thing he could do about it. Go on running, almost out of shot, right out of shot. Unless the shooting came nearer. So keep on running, stumbling in the dark, hurting yourself but what of it. He was running uphill now, his breath coming in gasps, catching his feet on stones and roots: keep on! — lucky they'd left him his boots. But which side of the frontier was he? Couldn't be sure. Had never known this part and they'd been more and more cautious the last two days, dodging, moving at night. If he got to the top of the *kopje* and lay there till it was light, maybe he would be able to see some kind of mark.

He was thirsty but that was now something he was used to. He said a prayer. Funny, he and Tagariro used to say a prayer together sometimes, made him feel they weren't quite enemies. Funny. He slept fitfully, woke at full day, the sun beginning to filter through the bushes.

Where was he? He thought and thought. He could have taken a better compass direction if they had left him his watch. But of course that had been the first thing to go. Still, God had taken him out of the valley, no the Border, the Frontier of the shadow of death; it could have been for some good purpose. But he must eat. And had nothing to give in exchange. There had been that shilling in the lining of his coat, but he had given it to Chengetai, the only thing he had, and he didn't regret it. Couldn't. Not ever. The good Samaritan, the woman of Samaria, they must have been the same, surely.

There looked to be some kind of small village down below. He had to chance his luck. If he was ever to get back. Mum must be worried stiff. A beer, a cool beer. No, think of something else. He started downhill cautiously, a right place for snakes. But saw none. The village was further off than it had seemed. Oh, if only it could have been *that* village. Impossible, they'd left it three marches back. At last he was greeting a couple of elderly women, and asking for water; after a long stare one of them tipped her jar for him; it was so good. And what else? Suddenly he knew he wasn't looking at this village as he had done all his working life until the last two weeks — if two weeks had been what it was. These weren't a bunch of *munts,* but people, yes, people, living in homes — not mud huts they way he used to think. Where there were different kinds of welcome. Or not welcome. Cautiously he went with the two women. He did not ask for food, but when he saw a full pot of porridge he said admiring words, and when it was offered pretended to refuse out of modesty, then accepted and ate with lip-smacking pleasure and praise. They laughed and in a while the headman came; there was some roundabout speaking. Jimmy asked the way to the big road, was told, thanked his hosts, set out. Now, he felt, he might make it.

The road, when he came to it, was very empty, but he thought, from the look of the wheel tracks, that it was used, at least daily. He sat under a bush and waited. First there was an ox-cart going the wrong way; the man did not return his greeting, only cracked his whip and hurried on his yoke of oxen. In the old days, he thought, people were friendlier. What have we done, Jesus, what have we done? For this must be us, not poor bloody them. Communists? Phooey. He'd seen them close to by now, hadn't he? In the old days he'd always chatted away when he was round the villages with his van, no bother picking up words. But during — when? — this last week maybe, there'd been real talk. Mandiwana spoke good Queen's English when he liked, been to school. Argued, got the better of him even. And now? Zing, you're dead. Best like that.

At last there was a truck going his way; he stood up and hailed it. The driver halted, looked at him: 'What the hell you doing here, man?'

'I was kidnapped, escaped, have to get to some town. Must let my old Ma know.'

'You aren't by any chance Jimmy Kitson?' He nodded. 'Man, you've been given up for dead. The papers'll have fits. Get in. How was it — real bad?'

He didn't answer for a moment, thought about it. Yes, it had been real bad at first when they took him and the two vanmen, Livingston and poor old Lucky, off the van, waving pistols about, threatening, taking everything off them all, and then giving away all the meat and vegetables in the van, yes giving it, not to customers, no. To skinny, battered men and women, half naked, the poor. Yes, the poor. Like it says in the Book. That first night. They'd tied his ankles and there'd been this guard with a gun, glaring if he moved. They'd been hating him. Yes, he was scared stiff. But after a few days that hating stopped. He could tell them apart, began to be able to talk, most of all to Tagariro and Mandiwana. They'd given him back the snap of his old Mum. Yes, he was guarded, sure, and they kept that riem on his wrist. And there was the day he bashed his hand with the rock slipping and it went septic. That had scared him, been bad. But it had led to Chengetai. He answered at last: 'Bad at first.'

'I'll bet.' And then there was this pouring out of abuse. The so and so *munts*! All that he'd heard a hundred times and it didn't mean anything, he couldn't go with it. The driver looked round, lighted a cigarette for him, shook his head: 'You've had a proper doing. But you'll be looked after now, don't worry, man. I'm taking you straight in to the police. They'll compensate you. And what's more, they'll get those black bastards. By God we'll all get them.'

Jimmy leant back, shut his eyes, forgot where he was, only woke fully at the police station. Yes, there was that cold beer. They let him phone his Mum, that was all he wanted; then the questions started, not nasty, mind you, but they had to know, above all what route the terrorists had taken before they got to the frontier. Which villages had helped or hidden them. What headman they'd spoken to. 'We'll need to take you over the ground,' said the officer, 'sorry, old chap, but it has to be done. We got to show those bastards it doesn't pay to help the terrorists.'

'I'd like a shave,' Jimmy said.

After he'd seen a reporter and answered a dozen stupid questions which somehow didn't connect with what had happened, they went off in the police trucks. He couldn't concentrate on anything they said, not even when they told him they'd found his van, empty. It didn't seem to interest him the way it should. He did ask about Livingston and Lucky. But it seemed likely that they'd been killed in the shoot-out. The army couldn't be expected to know one black from another.

Ten terrorists, the reporter had told him. Then who had got away? If it had been his vanmen they'd come back. Or maybe it was Mandiwana. Or Namozwang. Or Tagariro. He'd told the police that must be all of them; better to please the police. And that reporter. Now he was with six whites, pale hair, reddish skin, well fed, one in his teens, why did a young chap go into the police? Well, he got to understand that later on. And there was this big black corporal, hell of a big chap but not from these parts, from down beyond Gwelo.

It was making Jimmy afraid, himself, being with them. But the officer said to call him George, that was better, that opened things. But not too wide. Mostly, Jimmy was tired, he kept dropping off, riding in the police truck. Dropped off like a child. When he should have had his wits about him.

They went right back to where the van had been taken. Most of that lot there had been interrogated already. That was why they looked — well, when men and women have been scared stiff, beaten, kicked, seen it done to their kids, it gives them a look. They were due to be taken away to one of these protected villages the Government had set up. 'For their own safety,' the officer said, 'and ours.'

But these were his customers. He just had to say something. 'Look man, that means they got to leave their crops, their beasts, their little homes, what's more the graves of their old Mums and Dads, like a churchyard, kind of. Is that right?'

'Oh they'll squeal. But there's a war on, Jimmy. Remember that.'

'Yes,' said Jimmy, 'that's right.' No use arguing. It would be done. His poor bloody customers. And they had that feed from my van: the ones that had no money to buy. A war on. He pointed the way they'd gone. Here was the first village. Naturally when they saw the police, everybody denied they'd seen any terrorists or a white man prisoner. But when they'd been beaten enough they howled and said yes, it was true. Then the handcuffs came out and matches were put to the thatch. But Jimmy didn't want to hear or look.

The second village was the same, the headman getting the worst beating. It was one of them, trying to save his own skin, pointed out the next stop. Well, he'd save some of his skin and the thing was, it saved Jimmy from having to tell, himself. He didn't want, dear Jesus, he didn't want! The police had a bit of fun, chasing old men or girls. Oh, they behaved correctly, but these *munts* had to be shown it didn't pay. In a village further along they shot a couple of dogs and chucked them into the well. Always, always, leaving pain and destruction. And Jimmy didn't want.

So, in the evening, to the village where they'd taken him with his red, swollen hand, hurting all up his arm, scaring him. And they had found for him Chengetai who was, he supposed, a doctor of some kind. Oh gentle, gentle. And that was her house, that cone of thatch beside the tree. 'No,' he said, and suddenly his voice had come awake, had hardened, 'This isn't the place. No.'

'That *munt* in the last place told us —'

'You don't have to believe him, man! He got it wrong, it wasn't here. I'd have remembered, sure I would.' She came to the door of her house under the fringe of thatch, but he must not see her, must not let her see him, in case some look passed — . 'Get this, George,' he said to the officer, 'we were going faster then, had got food that last place, took off into the *kopjes*, making for the frontier, see? Going fast, didn't touch another place.'

'You sure of that, Jimmy?' Oh, how to make it sound right!

'Look, I should have stopped you two, yes, three miles back, we must have turned off there, hell of a scramble, big stone fell on my hand, crushed it.' But it did not hurt, not after she — and if only I could show her I am healed — . 'You know, George, I must have dropped off when we passed the place. Yes, it was that *kopje*, they called it Spider Hill. I can show you.' After that it was short marches to the frontier. Dodging around. Not a road — . He'd got to fill it in, make it sound true, got to! 'But this village — definitely no!'

'Could burn just one house, show we been here?' That was the young chap, just liked burning, the way a kid would. But luckily the officer called him off. One of the trucks turned. And then the black corporal, who had been ferreting round, making out he was better at the job than the whites — and these people up here were no friends of his — he came back with a small boy gripped round the ear: 'Says he saw you.'

Jimmy made a great effort, said to the officer: 'You know as well as I do, George, they'll say anything. Thinks he'll get out of a hiding if he says yes to what's put in his mouth.' And then, as the officer hesitated: 'Come on, George, who d'you believe, him or me?'

Well, that was that. The boy was let go with a good kick in the arse. They turned back. And if only I could have spoken to her. Told her it wasn't my fault. But I saved her, didn't I? But she didn't know. And she would have put her fingers onto the scar of the cut, onto my cheek, my lips. Gently, gently. And now never.

They went back and tried again to find out about Livingston and Lucky. Ten terrorists dead. But they wouldn't have known which bodies were which. Poor old Lucky, one more black man. So how many could have got across? Did Mandiwana? Did Tagariro? That was something he'd never know. Another never. He shouldn't be thinking this about terrorists. Stop it, Jimmy. His van was all right, a bit of paint would make it like new and he got some compensation out of the fund. They bought him a new watch, it went better than the old one, but he didn't care for it too much. And he saw his Mum and the neighbours — they'd made a kind of banner saying 'Welcome Home Jimmy'. That was nice.

He and Mum went to church and again there was something about him, a bit of thanksgiving, that was nice too. Maybe God had been looking after him. Maybe it was God's doing that they'd taken him to that village and Chengetai was there and healed him. A woman of God. If he could see her once again. And maybe God had strengthened him to lie to the police officer.

It was a few days later, and Jimmy was tinkering with his van, thinking every now and then if only old Lucky would turn up with that hat of his and his way of grinning at you. And then the police officer called, and another man, sweet-talking him: 'Very useful to us you've been. Very co-operative, the kind of man we need. And you know this country. Would you like to help again?'

He got the drift. He shook his head.

'No? Why not? You know it would pay you better than that old van! Pay you quite handsomely, we'd see to that. No danger, all you'd need to do would be to go round a bit — with the van if you like — talk and listen. You're first class at this lingo of theirs. Then you'd report back.' He shook his head again, refused a tot of brandy — he'd been brought up not to touch spirits. The senior officer went on, probing, cajoling: 'Look, man, we'd leave it to you. All we want is information. Might be good, everything quiet, everyone happy. You see? Or might be able to warn us, help us to save lives. Don't say no, there's a war on, Jimmy.'

But Jimmy didn't want to hear any more. 'Look George,' he said to the police officer, 'there was this chap almost two thousand years ago, got paid for this kind of job, and his name now means something bad. No, folks, I'm going back to my old van round. Not going to have to hang myself later. No.'

Poems

The Child Jason
is brought to Chiron

And the Kentaur, dewily laughing,
Caught him up to his breast half-way,
Said: 'Look, see, I am the craftsman!

'With a sight I shall make keener
Than the eagle's, on the wind leaning,
You shall see the plane leaves greenly

'Dancing against the sun; the brook below there
With its long snake's body every moment flowing,
The brook Anauros, hasting, slipping from the snow fields:

'Miles off the young heroes, your friends, coming from the hunting:
The winter shapes of the oaks by chill winds stunted:
The shape of clouds before thunder.

'Your ears shall be certain of hearing
As, through her cropping, the deer's are,
That her ways in the dim wood may be fearless.

'You shall hear the dawn wind in the grass heads:
The lifting, slim feet of the marsh birds:
And the stones slipping in the mountain passes.

'*You shall smell as the fox does, questing:*
Every fresh breeze winnowed and tested
For faint scents that may nest there:

'*Earth scents and flower scents better*
For heart's joy than feel of bright birds netted:
And your own body in the sun sweating.

'*I will make you taste as the bear does,*
With long tongue and paws sleek and hairy
And the honey sweetness through his heart tearing:

'*All pleasant things, hill sheep's haunches roasting,*
Apples and cakes, spices that kings' ships boast of,
Clear wine, warm in the mouth and the guts it flows to.

'*I will teach you touch as a snake, harmless*
And warm on its stone, stretched out with scarlet
Slit tiny tongue over the still dust flicking and darting,

'*With all its length feels the rocks' ridges and hollows;*
Or like a bare nymph with spread fingers lolling
Between cool, wing-filled air, and earth grassy and solid.'

And the Kentaur, quiet and wary,
Smiled at the child staring:
'*This too, if man can bear it: —*

'*You shall see some day, my dreamer,*
A sight real not seeming,
Phoibos Apollo and the lyre at his breast that gleams there.

'*You shall hear one morning in spring time,*
As your head whirls and tingles,
The glade suddenly full of the Muses singing.

'*As your heart checks and falters*
You shall smell, and after, always,
The dark March violets through their bright hair falling.

'*You shall touch, not in pride nor folly,*
But with bowed head, heart unsolaced,
The hair of the Muses and the still hands of Apollo.'

So the Kentaur, secretly smiling,
Took the boy Jason, amazed and silent,
For all the days of his childhood.

Valley of the Kings

Slipping down, down past the place of the serpents,
Through the tunnel not of love but of horror:
Horror for the uninstructed, the damned, those who disobey the Gods
As Akhnaton did (but his name is obliterated),
You come to the half world.
This is the world before sleep, more dreadful than sleep, for in sleep there is
*   nothing,*
But here — and you cannot wake — here are the creatures of nightmare,
Snake-heads, jackal-heads, ibis-heads, and hawk-heads,
Crocodile-heads, tube-heads, girl-headed birds, walking snakes,
Cobras with vultures' wings, staring owls, and here the striding
Slack-breasted hippo, funny and not-funny.
They see you uncoffined, uncorrupted, though the Canopic jars
Heave with corruption. They see you taking the way of the scarab.
They whisper: what does he eat? Thinned wine and eggs boiled hard,
Pomegranate seeds, meat: but he will taste nothing.
What does he listen for? The tinkling harp. But he will hear nothing.

Remember, oh remember, you in the two-headed boat,
Remember the correct words and the correct offering.
You think the army of days will help you, but Osiris is judge.
Do not trust the Gods. That is the God of writing,
But he writes only of the mazes of death, not for life nor knowledge.
This one is Truth not-Truth. They may decide to call
Out of Nile mud the crawling twilight crocodile.
The Goddess is not Love, she is dreadfully elongated,
Racked between dawn and dusk. And observe below you
The chained and headless bodies of wicked commoners
To whom the priests gave no pass-words, such as they reserve
For the Royal who is also their whip and their sword against enemies.
(Yet Akhnaton once himself welcomed, himself preached to
Syrians, Hittites, laughing and rejoicing Nubians.
How can his name be certainly obliterated?)

How long, how long in the Under-world? You do not know.
Stars, stars and a pale sun pass through the body of the Goddess
Who has become hardened, become one with the coffin.
Lift up your hand to the great beetle, to the scratching legs,
To the dry, cold wing-cases: will he lead you out?
Up through the suffocating rock, the limestone,
Up to the dust? Oh, I have forgotten my learning,
I am lost among death and half-death, among the snakes and the beetles
And the Gods who are about death, death and drying up.

What is this? Is it a clue? I can read it; it is a Greek alpha,
Alpha for Alexander and, in time, for omega,
Alpha for life, for the release of the Gods,
For the smiling lip, the lifted foot, the wavy
Hair, yes it is hair, not merely a head-dress!
Alpha for the Greeks who woke at last from the nightmare
(Not remembering Akhnaton, whose name had been almost obliterated).

What if the Romans come, defacing and looting,
First of the imperialists, who make their own,
Very own nightmare, and different, for the defeated?
Best to destroy everything Egyptian or that might make the Gippos
Believe in something other than Rome. And the gold, also, useful
If melted down into respectable ingots.
What if the Romans come, when Alexander has been?

The nightmares outlast defacement, outlast Empires,
Outlast the Mysteries, when Isis at last became Love,
Outlast the cross and crescent. Outlast Freud and Jung
Who were on terms with them no doubt. What must we do?
Is there no way to escape from the death stories,
Unless Akhnaton comes back, to tell the world a secret,
Something to do with waking and brotherhood?
(We think, we are afraid, he has been obliterated,
Only, it is just possible — .)

Siren Night

Whoohoo go the goblins, coming back at nightfall,
Whoohoo go the witches, reaching out their hands for us,
Whoohoo goes the big bad wolf and bang go his teeth.
Are we sure we shall be the lucky ones, the princess, the youngest son,
The third pig evading the jaws? Can we afford to laugh?
They have come back, we always knew they would, after the story ended,
After the grown-ups shut the book and said goodnight.

When the windows went, Margaret was under the piano,
Bernice was behind the sofa. IT didn't see them.
At the third explosion Tony was under the bed clothes,
Hugging the hot water bottle. IT didn't see her either.
Next time IT might get any of us.
We had better be careful, better make the right gestures,
Better not laugh too much.

Whoohoo go the goblins, coming back to look for us.
The pale children are asleep in the Underground,
In the rabbit burrows, in the roots of goblin wood.

Whoohoo go the witches, stirring up the cauldron.
I can hear them now over our roof, can't you?
Wasp-wuzzing of the fly-king, the devil's own, high over London,
Round and round over the cauldron, sticks of noise stirring it.
Let us talk about something else. They may think we don't believe in them,
As the grown-ups didn't believe.

Let us shut the book on them. Let us switch on the gramophone.
Let us be rational, let us disbelieve in magic.
Countrymen of Handel and Haydn, countrymen of Beethoven,
You are not playing goblins, you are only wanting to kill us:
Wanting to frighten us. If you frighten us enough, you win.
We are a little frightened, we who have been happy,
We are not frightened enough to become what you want.
We set our will against yours, the will of London,
If you kill us, we only die.

Whoohoo go the goblins and cold, cold their fingers.
Some day the story will end, the book be shut for ever,
Sleep will be sweet again and sweet the waking,
There will be no more goblins.

We are only a little frightened.

London Burning

London again, London burning again,
Again death and civilian pain.
Blitz talk on the side walk,
Foot steps on glass crunch,
Again phone calls in the morning:
Are you all right darling?
Again meeting at lunch
Roof spotters and rumour swappers.
Again importance of wardens
And again in train-jarred tunnels
The crammed pale shelterers
In from the snow's light flurry,
Warmer down below,
But the stuffed hours go slow
Living against the grain,
And we guess but cannot know
What breakfast time will show —
London again, was it London again?

Not like the old blitz, we say,
And up to noon, confident, almost gay,
Stick up our broken windows, plan, write, chatter,
Hope for news of friends, queue up for rations,
But by tea-time, even, night begins to matter.
Blankets in shelters, thermos filled, perhaps
Tonight might be quiet, perhaps only shrapnel,
Perhaps in a year's time it will be all a dream, perhaps.

Better get it over early. There it is. Those bloody sirens.
Get the babies out. Don't run, it'll be all right.
That's only barrage, only our own flares, go slowly.
Ruth, daughter-in-law, Ruth, where thou goest —
On the floor, in the small light of the torch, close over your baby:
If my body could shield you both from blast, take it,
Let the glass fangs bite me — But no, but no,
The thing I feel at my throat, that I will not show,
Is only my heart pattering, not London shaken
As the giants' hideous ball-game bangs overhead,
Banging no doubt over Berlin, does that comfort
Ourselves, or their bombs them, or is it something
From the implacable heavens, not to be avoided? —
If your number's there, it comes.
Shelterers of Europe, after the storm is over
We shall have this in common for our re-building,
Mortar of fear and endurance and a special laughter
And nightmare knowledge of the whistle that brings death.

Is it lightening? Yes, surely. Can we stand up?
Over for tonight. Pick up the babies. Did Anne get home?
Let's make tea. Gas pressure's low. And there's nothing like
A nice hot water bottle after a blitz.

London again, London burning again.
We were lucky that time the incendiaries dropped in the river;
But you can't expect such luck to last for ever.
London again.
Going to work tired, blitz talk in bus and office,
Re-filling buckets, blitz talk in shop and kitchen.
Going with a history book to a library,
Hoping to look up a reference,
Returning books to the library, there is no:
There is no library.

London again, London burning again,
Men and women, dog tired, asleep along the train,
Under familiar cosy slogans, Knightsbridge for Harrods, Green Park,
Piccadilly for Doughboys in the screamful dark:
Giggle and slap but half an eye on the time,
Get home, get in, get down, Big Ben's nine chime
And the news broken and the radio darting and stopping
And again the barrage and again the whistling dropping.
London again, London burning again.
Oh my city, my soul, city of the plain,
I, like Lot's wife, like Whittington, turn again.

Comfort

A woman comforts a man, staring
Beyond his pillowed head, thinking
Of other things, of needful cooking and sewing,
Bright flowers in a vase or the idea of God.
She is giving only her body.
But the man is comforted, he does not know,
Blinded by customary eyes, lips, breasts, tender hands,
That the woman's mind is faithless;
It is not with him.
Nor with any man, for to her all men are children.
She has been sucked by baby men, giving them freely her body
As now she gives it.
Suckling, she thought of other things,
Staring out gently over small, breast-pillowed heads, thinking
Of necessary things.
Faithless.
The woman alone.

A man comforts a woman, partly
For her sake of course as he tells himself, but also
For delightful dominance, for a slight but pleasurable erection,
For the sense of ownership. And the woman is comforted:
Strong shoulder to weep on, clean hanky to mop tears.
She clings, could love and obey. Almost.
But no!
My tears are dry. Goodbye,
Thanks ever so!
My goodness, what an escape.

The Talking Oats

The Talking Oats.

There are too many trees in Scotland. You cannot listen
Because of the noise of the trees. The wind gets in them
And then they shout, make their own noises: boom,
Rustle and rattle, gossip of leaves all day.
I cannot listen to the voices of Scotland
Because of the talking trees. They will not be quiet.
I must go where there are no trees.

Harris where the smiling women carried turf in creels,
North Uist famous for barley.

Whispering oats in the Western Islands,
You let me listen. What do you say?
The wind passes. I hear voices.
Things that have been. Things that are forgotten.
Whisper, whisper.
Voices in the wind ripple of oats, voices
At the back of the blood, at the back of the brain,
Below the deepest roots of the trees, the blown shouting trees,
Below the oats, below the rocks, below the islands,
Behind the ploughing and sowing, the harvesting and threshing,
At the back of life.

Voices.
> They are under the stones with the others. They have gone back.
> They are un-born again.
> He keeps the stone knife.
> She the black necklace.
> They are not sick any longer, they do not call us,
> They are inside.

> There are new people other than our own people.
> We did not know.
> They have long knives, other than our own knives.
> We do not know if the strange knives could kill us.
> We do not know how other are these people:
> Whether they speak words:
> Whether their stones are our stones:
> Whether their dead are born again.
> We have only seen them on the hills,
> Watching through the thick heather, crawling.
> Shall we be able to stand and speak to the strange people with the knives?

> He came in a coracle, from somewhere, with a cross made of olive wood.
> He baptised six families; they made a church out of turfs.
> Thorkettle Hammer killed him on his own altar
> But forgot to break the cross.

> This woman made a new milking song and got honour, of the kind
> She wanted, at the milking. She went with her head high.
> Later, she died in childbirth.
> The pipes were going, crying and shouting at me
> Of honour and killing, driving my hand to the knife.
> In the din of the pipes I stabbed him. The drones went on in my head
> Through the blood and the screaming and the urging to flight and the
> > stumble over the threshold.
> My clan were between me and his brothers, held them for a time.
> I was into the heather, between the rocks; the small birds started sideways
> > from my feet running;
> The wind was in my face and the noise dying out of my heart.
> I looked behind and they were after me, at the green edge of the crops.
> I was up on the ridge, and down, I saw the place I needed.
> They were very near behind me and I running hard in silence,
> The plaid's weight thrown off me and left red in the heather.
> And I came to the church wall.
> I touched the door; I was in; I laid my hand on the altar; I faced them.
> One by one the swords' blades went back into their sheaths.
> I had sanctuary against them and they hated me for it.

The dinning of the pipes had gone out of me and I was empty,
And I wished my enemy were alive then, and by my side.

My brothers and I
Are the best bowmen between here and Eaval
Often we are shooting our arrows
Through the holes of the pierced cross, or at the wild geese in winter.
I shot a seal once
That was chasing the sea-trout up into Torogay pool.
Easy I shot, and laughing;
He sank in the brown water, his red blood thickened it.
Because of that shot, my father got his lease
Of Malaclett where the mill is. He is a bad farmer,
And we too, we are better with our bows
Than at the plow-tail.

The seal-men come ashore on certain winds.
It was a seal-man took MacRuari's daughter,
Mairi, who was a good one at the spinning.
You have to shoot them
With a silver bullet; they dive at the flash; yet a time comes
When you can kill the seal-men.

This man saw the Prince land. He shouted with the others,
Pressing close round the Chief, shouldering to get nearer.
He would have gone with him and died, as his brothers went,
But the next day he broke his leg, slipping on a rock; he lived
To be very old; he was always telling tales of the fighting;
And the young boys believed him.

Her uncle was carried off as a child by the ones we know of;
They kept him seven years; he forgot everything.
Then he came back one evening, mazed and full-grown; all he remembered
Was the name of the collie, Shulach; and the collie had died
Three winters before, at the lambing. But after that
He took to the music; there was no piper in the islands.
That had his gift, though he made queer tunes sometimes,
Oh, queer enough. And now the girl has a queer look on her,
We think she might go the same road as her uncle.

> *The wind passes. The oats whisper again,*
> *And the voices are of things remembered and half-remembered.*
> *For what is a century or a century and its half*
> *To distinguish it from yesterday and the day before?*
> *Voices of Scotland, whisper out of the oats.*

Voices:

It is said they had the right to do it, by law.
Maybe so.
We know where our homes stood and upon what land.
There are some things we are certain of: not legal things,
No. But another kind of rights. The land was ours by right of
Seeing and touching and smelling: working upon:
Having security with: it was ours by these rights.
And then it was sold and we were not part of it.
They came from the south with their sheep and little lowland phrases

And words of a pinching lowland usage: they burnt our homes.
It is customary after that to think of such people as enemies:
Customary in the Islands.
We were permitted shelter below high tide mark; it was then past summer

And the autumn storms falling due.
There were babies to be born, begotten in spring, before this;
There were old folk, looking on death.
The tides came and went.
Their sheep gathered our harvests.
Some of us were shipped to Nova Scotia, to the hard coasts and the cold.

Some went to prison; the more fortunate died
And so remained with the land. These things are certainties,
Although not to be taken note of legally.
There is one more thing certain.
That is the end of the clans, of the trust that kept us
Together, clansmen and chief. Our chiefs sold and betrayed us.
We will think nothing now of betraying any chief.
The customs officers made me row them out.
They were less than welcome.
It had been a grand year for the barley
And the stills on Pabbay were all working.
I thought what to do, rowing the short, hard stroke; I watched them

Sitting grim in the stern. I thought about prisons
And evil coming to Pabbay.
As the swell rose under me, I brought her bows across:
And the rock clawed and caught.
They were wet landing, and late. Late enough for Pabbay;
There was nothing there for them to find.
Only men without courage need go to prison.

Some years we would work on the sea tangle
Gathering and burning, getting our rents out of it.
And all at once nobody wanted it.
We needed to look elsewhere for the rents,
Elsewhere, Mother of God!
And maybe the money not to be come by anyhow.

The ship is sailing for Canada; we have food in the ship;
There was little food at home.
Past the noise of the ship I remember the quietness of Scolpaig.
I remember the dun calf and the red calf
And the pet lamb that was my own lamb,
The soft smoke and the curlews crying at dawn.
Ah, better for me to be leading sheep at Scolpaig
Than cutting the great trees away in Canada.
Aye, better even to be digging potatoes
That were little and scarce, but rooting in my father's croft.

Knowing the great good to be got by education
I sent my lassie to the school.
They were needing to do their sums and all in the English;
It was hard for them, though they were cheery enough.
But they spoke to one another, whiles, in the Gaelic.
And the schoolmaster strapped my lassie
For speaking in her father's tongue.

A man was drowned at the North Ford with his horse and cart.
The sands shift. The tide is sudden. He could not swim.
He had been afraid after Mass. His mouth was dry with fear
Till the sea wetted it.

We went out to the fishing.
There were no fish in it.
The trawlers had come and taken them.
That was our living.
How would a man be brave, how be skilful
With nothing to be got from it, nothing?
The Lord's wrath is upon us, he has chastised us with trawlers
For sins we did not know of.

They wanted to leave the island, although there was fair grazing
And one could grow some crops. But there were no peats there:
You had to row them over and in winter
Nobody wanted to do that. So they kept on complaining
And writing to the Board. One autumn they were moved from the island.
But the new houses were damp; the old people all died that winter.
Some of the young ones are moving back to the island.

In my father's time they would be shooting the seals,
And clubbing the creatures, it might be.
The skins would sell for sixteen shillings, or make coats.
The worst of the seal-oil would be burnt in the cruisies;
But the best of it would be for drinking. The children
Could stand the winter well with that inside them.
It was good against colds and chest pains.
Now they protect the seals against us shooting them,
And likely it was cruel enough in the old days;
But our children are getting ill in the black months of winter,
And there is no seal-oil.

I had seven sons by my man: a bonny brood and troublesome,
And for years I would never set foot outside the house
For the work there was to do. Yet I was half happy,
And there was always porridge enough to go round.
They got what education there was, at the schoolhouse,
And reading the Book, at home.
Donald and Dugald went to Canada, got farms there, married.
Then came nineteen fourteen.
Both the two enlisted in the first fortnight. Donald was killed.
Dugald came home once, writes at New Year, is doing well.
Sandy was working at home on the croft, when the war came;
He left the drill of potatoes half dug, went off with the Camerons
And died of measles in an English camp.
After that Ewan, who had liked Sandy best of anyone,
Could not settle, went south, spat at a sergeant-major;
He went to prison and took to the politics,
And married a Glasgow lassie of his own kind;
They live in a single-end, had two bairns there;
Wee Sandy died, Jess has a scholarship;
Ewan has been out of work these three years.
Neil was too young for the war; he was a douce kind of lad,
Feckless with beasts; but one year he got a paint box
And the next he was off too; he was in Spain when we heard last,
Him and his paints.
Seamus writes oftener; he has only been gone two years;
He is in London at one of the big stores there,
And doing well. London is further than Glasgow.
It was over-strange for me. But there is one more son,
Kenneth, who stays at home on the croft, doing the things
His father did, not reading, not asking questions.
I am lucky indeed to have one staying. And yet, and yet
If he had been as good as the rest, he too
Would be gone.

Is it dull in the winter with the short days and the storms?
No indeed it is not. The boys who have been gillies,
The girls who have been housemaids in the big houses
Or in the summer hotels, come back. They are full of talk
By the end of October. And then we have the ceilidhs,
Sitting around the peats, singing and story-telling. You would not believe
What marvellous queer stories get told in winter!

It is an unlucky house.
So many have died in it,
Bonny lasses with a high delicate colour,
Dropping like roses in an over-great heat,
Their young brothers taken with loss of flesh, with coughing.
It is an unlucky house, surely,
But where else can we live?

All winter the lads would be playing each other at shinty:
There was a cup they played for.
I do not know where that would be, now.
But they went off, to America, Canada, and the south,
Every year more would be gone.
And the war took the last of them.
The lads that are growing up now think nothing of shinty;
They are playing at football; they can go on with that
When they too go south.

In the old days we lived on porridge and mutton,
Now we can shop with the best; Argentine beef,
Canadian flour, good quality, white and dry,
New Zealand butter and Californian peaches,
South African apples. And the picture papers.
It all has to be paid for. Yes. But the tourists
Are as thick as wasps this season.

I gather little shells below on the shore,
Between half tide and low tide gathering:
In the cold months when money is scarce in Sollas,
I market the shells in London, where they eat them.
When times are good I get twenty shillings a bag.
But is it work for a man?

My husband's auntie is still one for the weaving;
She makes her dyes: crottal and soot and iris root:
Hours and days she takes for them.
Her tweeds are nice enough and would last you half a life-time.
But they are ill to cut out and who would be tailoring them here?
Myself I get my dresses by mail order from England;
It is the grand catalogues they send you with coloured pictures:
I pin them up in the room.
By next year the stuff is worn through, but I am getting a new dress,
And no work at all for anyone!

They had the wireless
Put in at the store last year. And now we go there
To get the morning weather forecast.
They tell us when gales are coming; we take the creels in;
They have saved us gear and boats.
There is the news too, and talks, which do not concern us.
But the music, och well, times it is nice enough,
But it is not what we are used to.

That year we had the scarlet fever
The postman took it. But he stuck to the mail car,
Handing out the letters and all.
He said it would take more than that to get him down!

If the land is sold, what security have we?
Will we be sure of staying here, in the houses we know,
Or will we be scattered, not knowing what to do,
Seeking for new tenancies, packing up the bits of things,
And maybe one of us getting ill or another leaving us
And the whole thing broken?

They say there were giants in the old days, giants and fairies,
If I were a giant I would walk out of the island
And the wet and the wind and the loneliness. I would put my curse on it,
If I had a wish I know the girl I would wish for:
Chrissie from the big house. If I were one of these old giants
I would be picking her out between my thumb and forefinger
And walking away with her. But I am no giant
And even if I get to Glasgow, what then, what then?

The wind passes and the long ripple on the oats.
Is there any new thing under the sun, under the wind,
New voices for Scotland?

Voices:

    Above the line of the sand,
    Pale-shining, oat-coloured machair,
    The twelfth rainbow of the day stands up, stands up,
    With a double green and a double violet.
    Soft is the rain on my left cheek and my left temple,
    Washing away the salt of many sprays.
    My hair is wet to the tips
    But the sun will dry me,
    And dry the drenching grasses.
    Soft is the sky above Harris.

    Lobsters have done better this year. It was cold in the south,
    So the English lobsters never took the price off ours.
    We sell them in Billingsgate, which is London, in England.
    Myself, I have never tasted the lobsters.

    The red tin church is the Established;
    The Free Church is stone and slate;
    And there are two-three F.P.'s along by the school-house.
    And that with the cross?
    Oh, that is the ruins of Old St. Ultan's.
    There was a spring there once, just past the tide mark,
    But now the pebbles have been washed up by the storms and filled it.
    The Ministers are always telling the young folk
    Not to be dancing and holding ceilidhs and that;
    But there are not many young folks church members now.
    Nor many old folks either.

    This man walked all day on the moor, saw no coveys, but observed
    The insects trapped by the sundews both long and round leaved.
    He made some notes and will be coming again.

    If I allow my neighbours
    To commit wickedness,
    To break the Lord's Day,
    Even for the Harvest itself,
    That is the beginning of the road
    To hell-fire, to the punishment.
    Better punishment on earth
    Than for all eternity!
    The Lord do so unto me and more also,
    If I do not punish my neighbour,
    Even though in so doing
    I punish myself.

I was myself the wee red-head you minded on,
Playing with lobster pots and old tins at the tide edge.
But the thing came on me, to learn. I left home in delight and terror,
Saw my first trees at the Hostel, sat for my scholarship,
Went over to Aberdeen, holding my limbs still in the train,
With everything a wonder, the stations, the shut-in book-stalls,
The new noises and smells and the perpetual English
In which I must learn to think. So I took my degree
And walked the wards. And in the end I came back.
Everything was as it had been, everything,
Preventable disasters accepted like day and night!
I cannot speak because of the great anger that is on me.

Lewis can outvote us
Whatever the rest of the islands think:
And there's democracy for you!

They have been going together for long enough;
It is time there was a woman to mind the house
And care for his father and his auntie,
The two poor old souls,
And they in a house with no conveniences.
And indeed there will be little pleasure in it for Maggie,
But they have been going together for long enough,
And what will folk be saying?
It is time they were serious.

The aeroplane crossing the gap in the hills tells us
That it is near dinner time. We stand and stretch
And watch it away. When Angus' boy was sick
Suddenly, they fetched him away in the aeroplane.
He would likely have died in the old days.
But now he lives; that is he, digging potatoes; he can do a full day's work;
He would have been a big loss to the family.

A boat of our own.
Do they say we could get a boat of our own, a crew of us,
And do we dare?
They would give us a loan on it and all, the Head Ones,
But —
We have no money, none of us.
We come home with a little
But in a few nights it is away.
The whisky takes care of that,
And how would a man not be hospitable?
So this loan would be on us.
And if the fishing was bad,
As it has been in times past, so often,
In twenty years there would be no boat, no money, nothing.
I think we cannot dare.

They come here for the elections,
The Labour ones and the Conservative ones,
Shooting their necks out,
Speaking plenty of this and that,
In one part of the world or another.
They go back to the London Parliament
With all these grand noble thoughts in their heads
Which put out the thought of us and our wee difficulties.
It is a far cry to the Islands
And MacBrayne's making it no easier.
When the election is over
We will be forgotten, the way we always were.
If we had our own Parliament
And it sitting in Scotland
The head ones would not be so far,
They might be folk like ourselves.
But that is not the way of it,
So when they come here,
We will applaud the speakers,
Since that is a matter of courtesy,
The Labour ones and the Conservative ones,
And the good old Liberals forby.
Our applause will be pleasuring them surely.
It might be best to vote for the one with the most money,
But me, I am not troubling myself to vote.

There is no hurry, my soul, dear yes, no hurry at all.
Has not the gate been lying so since my father's time?
Was not the doctor taking ten years to marry the district nurse?
Are we not the lucky ones to be living at all, and eternity on the two sides of
    us?
So why bother your head?

I am come back.
In England they thought me a foreigner.
Yet they were friendly to me, kind folk,
Asking me to their homes.
There was nobody there but had a bath-room;
There was a great choice of work;
They were bold lassies, but friendly.
Later, I was at Arnheim.
Yet I am come back.
How will it be now,
Oh my island, my soul,
Will everything be the same?
Or will I too get a bath-room,
After Arnheim?
Will we have work and security and the time to think,
Which things alone give folk the right chance to be friendly?

For all of two hundred years
Someone has pushed us around,
Landlords and trusts and agents,
Rooting us up:
We want your land,
Go off to a worse place,
Make your living there if you can!
Later, in the days of security,
It was the priests pushed us around,
The priests or the ministers,
And the lay preachers the worst of the lot.
Now, when the rocket range crowd
Push us around again,
We will go the old way about it,
Letting ourselves be pushed,
In spite of all the speeches in Edinburgh,
Going where they want,
Getting what we can out of them,
Learning, learning,
For a day maybe to come
When we will say no to the pushers.
I wonder now, is it too late for that day?

Along the highest tide mark
A scatter of tiny shells;
Oh light and delicate
From very far away
Down the long Gulf Stream,
Surviving only by fragility.
How, ah, how to survive?
Thirty years back
There was speaking about lobster ponds for the fishermen,
The way we could get central marketing and all that.
Year after year there was this speaking
And nothing done, nor yet ourselves expecting it:
Speaking seemed plenty.
But now, look there are two lobster ponds and the marketing,
A Lewis man at the head of it,
And the fishermen in great trim with it all.
Who would have thought that speaking could come to this?

The van was taking my eggs.
I was tied, so, to the van.
Ach, biscuits!
Now I am free of the van,
Our own lorry takes them
To our own packing-station.
I will tell you the way it was:
There was a man called Roddie MacFarquhar.
Some way he woke us up
To see our own live strength and work with it.
Now I laugh at the van
And eat no more biscuits!

On the machair at Gerinish
The concrete slides softly in,
Slides softly deep and hardens.
The rockets will go, the strangers will go with them.
But we shall be left.
We and the concrete
On the spoilt machair of Gerinish.

To get the grant, we would need to write down the acres,
But how at all to measure the common land?
It had always been so. Not like the inbye fields
That we know foot by foot. And the wee hills and corners!
Terrible altogether.
But the boys from the school, they came and measured it up:
Wonderful, that. No bother with their sums.
In my day the school was a place you sat and sat
And longed to be out. But today, it seems, is different.
And maybe better.

No, no, the man is not gentry, he is one of ourselves.
We in the grazing committee, at first we thought
He comes from the College, he must be different.
But no.
He stands a head shorter than the most of us, also
He came as an adviser, almost Government.
Yet see what he advised us.
See the green fields that were once black peat: from our own shell sand:
Guess the weight of the lambs: see the good money coming!
They call him an Islay man, he may have been.
Now he is one of us.

There is a thing I am needing to keep clean.
I have not the right words for it.
It could be between a man and a woman,
Or between a man and his work.
It is as hard as the granite and as clean as the air,
But I have not the words for it.
It could be between a man and other men,
Or between a man and his country,
I have not the words for it right.
Maybe they will come to me yet.

Buganda History

Remember with the cords, with cowries,
Remember through the line of the widow, the favourite sister,
In the bark-cloth mazes of the pillars, the dark, the narrow forest
Whose canopy is not flowers, not leaves, but a high hollow
Where the bats hang with the memories, almost obscured,
Remember before the future, the great snake, swallows us all.

Behind the bark-cloth arras, in the black eaves, the Sybil
Possessed by the Kabaka who once possessed her, centuries back,
What does she say?
Heirs of the Katikiro, starved princes,
Thin man whose beautiful grandmother became a drum,
Speak to us kneeling out of your dark. Unravel
Hard knots of old palm fibres. Make speak to us
Dry voices of the jaw-bones of the great fighters
Wedded to drums. When the beat speaks to the new moon
Let us hear the tale of our forebears:
Who comes, who goes, how strikes the leopard, whose thin spears sunder
The thick leaves of the past, the orchid growth of myth.
Unravel the dry palm knots, remember, tell us,
Lest we feel fatherless, lost in the terrible present.
Give back our past.

Absence of Indians

Who knew rocks, heights, thin waterways, nuts, berries,
Who knew caves in the cliffs, pine cones, small rodents,
Whose arrows sang and stung jack rabbits or deer leaping,
Who danced and painted, made music, had homes here,
Who would have known the use now lost of leaves and sea shells,
Who could have kept their land but for the shotguns,
Who could almost have trusted the sheltering friars,
Who were killed, killed, killed by the ranging colonists
Spreading ownership, defacement, dirty scorn, our revered ancestors
For whose sins we are now paying, dreadfully paying
In the absence of Indians.

Stories

Mary and Joe

HER HUSBAND LOOKED UP FROM HIS NEWSPAPER. 'Jaycie seems to be getting into trouble again,' he said.

She nodded. 'Yes. I had a short letter from her. I wish — oh, Joe, I do wish she could take things a bit more lightly!'

'Get herself married,' said Joe.

Mary didn't exactly answer that, but went on: 'I know so well what she feels about politics. After all, we both had Liberal sympathies in our time — hadn't we Joe? But — it's more than politics to her. Much more. And when she's feeling like that she seems to forget all about human relationships.'

Her husband grinned a bit. 'Not like Simon. Nor yet my little Martha! What time did that kid get back from her date? Oh, well . . .' He finished his coffee. 'I must be off, Mary. I'll take the car — right? How's your own stuff going?'

'Not bad,' she said. 'We've got all the routine tests for the new skin grafts to check before we can get on. These internal ones are a bit tricky.'

'Poor old rabbits!' said Joe lightly and shrugged himself into his coat. He respected Mary's work, knew about it, but somehow didn't care much for it.

Mary, however, was thinking about the next series of experiments and checks while she cleared up the breakfast dishes. Dear Joe, couldn't he ever learn to put his stubs into the ash-tray! She left a tidy place for Martha, who was running the bath upstairs and singing to herself, saw that there was plenty of cereal left in the packet, and all the time the shape of the work was clear in her mind.

The basic genetics couldn't be simpler. Blood from two different blood groups cannot, as everyone knows now, live together in the same body. Equally, cells of one genetic constitution will not accept cells of another — and we are all, except for identical twins and 'pure line strains', if we happen to be mice, genetically different. What happens is that the grafted cells produce antigens, and the host cells in reply produce antibodies which destroy the grafted cells; without very special treatment nothing stops this so long as the cells come from a genetically different individual, although recent transplants have managed to get round the antibody reaction, if the donor is sufficiently near, genetically speaking. Yet grafts from another individual do take in certain favoured positions, such as the cornea of the eye and in bone structure, where probably they turn into inert scaffolding but as such are accepted. Out of all this a whole series of experiments opens up, some having to do with tissue cells which behave abnormally, as in cancer, others with exchanges between individuals at such an early stage, for example, in the egg, that antibodies are not yet being produced and the exchange will take. This, then, was the field in which Mary had worked for a couple of decades, exchanging views with other workers in the same field and occasionally going to conferences when the family could spare her. It was an absorbing and in many ways a happy life.

On her way to the big teaching hospital where she worked she bought another newspaper. It looked as if these strikes were going to develop the way Jaycie had said they would in her letter. It is odd, she thought to herself, how often things do work out the way Jaycie says. But if they bring in the troops. . . . She couldn't really think about it sensibly. She hadn't got the data. Jaycie hadn't been home for six months; it wasn't that she didn't get on with the others, and dear Joe always going out of his way to be nice and welcoming, but — well, sometimes it seemed as if nothing they did at home was worth her attention. She would try, especially with Martha, yes, she would try, but it was like a clumsy grown-up talking to kids! Jaycie could be annoying. Yes. And yet — people followed her. A great many people really. And whatever happened her mother loved her.

The newspapers were beginning to get on to Jaycie now. They had ignored her at first. Put things down to anyone and everything else. After all, it was a bit awkward for them having to do with a woman who was beautiful but apparently had no sex life; they didn't know what to try and smear her with. But now — Mary wished she knew, wished she could read between the lines. Were they frightened? She had been too busy these last ten years or so to think much about politics. When Jaycie turned up: yes. But when she left Mary went back to her work thankfully as though to something simple and relatively clean — though some people wouldn't think so! Back to thinking about problems of genetics and immunology. And an undertow in her mind always busy on the other children and dear Joe and something especially nice for supper and perhaps a show at the weekend and the new hyacinth bulbs to plant. But now it looked as if all Jaycie had said last time was going to develop into something she would need to think about, something real. And dangerous.

But this was the hospital stop. She had come by bus, for it was an easy journey and she didn't care for driving herself. She was apt to get abstracted and slow down, so that people hooted at her, but here in the bus she could work. She knew the conductor would call her, amused if she was deep in calculations when it came to her stop: 'This is you, doctor!'

She got out, nodded to a colleague, and walked a bit abstractedly along the corridor with the marble bust of the Founder, on which young Bowles had, as usual, hung his hat. There was a lot of routine work and checking. She could do it with half her mind. But instead of concentrating on the next phase she kept on thinking about Jaycie. Had she done the right thing to tell her? Had she? Had she? Or would it have been better to let her believe the same thing dear Joe believed, the story about a sudden overwhelming fascination — women's magazine stuff really. But easy to make up and equally easy to believe. Much easier than — whatever the truth was. You couldn't expect anyone to believe that and still remain normal. And she had so wanted that: the lovely solid, warm, normalness of dear Joe. If she hadn't told Joe the lie to which he never afterwards referred they mightn't have had their life together, they mightn't have had Simon and darling naughty Martha. No. No. Any other way didn't bear thinking about.

Yet perhaps she should have told Jaycie the same — lie. If she had done that, Jaycie too might have grown up to be a normal girl. She might have fallen in love and married, and then there would have been grandchildren, lovely normal babies and the happiness that goes with them. Or if Jaycie hadn't felt like that she could have done some absorbing, professional job. She could have been a scientist like her mother perhaps or an architect like Simon, one of the thousand satisfying things which are open to modern men and women alike.

Why had she told Jaycie? Mary thought back, frowning. It was that time when Jaycie was so depressed about being a woman, about the undoubted fact that there were rather fewer females than males of undoubted genius. That it is so much harder for a woman to take the clear, unswerving line towards — whatever it might be — because women are ordinarily more pliable, more likely to be interrupted, more aware of other people's feelings and apt to be deflected by them:

especially if they are loved people. She remembered Jaycie sitting curled up on the sofa, her chin dropped on her hand; and she herself had been standing beside the fire, so much wanting to help, but knowing that Jaycie needed more than the comfort of a mother's arms around her.

Jaycie had said: 'I suppose, Mother, that's what it means to be a Son of God, as they used to say. You go straight to the light. You know.' And Mary had said yes and had felt something gripping at her, a rush of adrenalin no doubt! Jaycie had said: 'No daughters of God, of course!' and had laughed a little. And then she had stood up and looked straight towards her mother and said: 'But I too, I know. Directly.'

And then Mary had to speak, had to tell her. It was, after all, true. And since then Jaycie had never curled up again on the sofa. Never seemed to want the comforting arms. And Mary had hardly liked to touch her. Only on the rare nights when Jaycie slept at home Mary used to go up to her room when she was asleep, so deeply and peacefully it seemed, and stand there and want to take the one who had been her baby into her arms and share and share and comfort. But luckily she had managed the self-control never to do anything of the kind. Because if she had tried it Jaycie wouldn't ever have come home again. She was fairly sure of that.

Mary had forgotten to make her own sandwiches, so she went down to the canteen for lunch. There were rather more newspapers than usual being read. Young Bowles was having an argument with another of the lecturers; they frowned at her, but perhaps not deliberately. The Professor made some sympathetic remark to her about Jaycie. Nice old bird, the Prof. But who did he think Jaycie's father was? Simple enough; that wasn't the kind of thing he thought about.

Things looked worse in the headlines of the evening editions. Mary seldom bought an evening paper, but this time she felt she had to. 'Look, old girl, don't worry,' said Joe. 'They — they always write this sort of bilge. Makes people buy their rotten old papers. Nobody takes it seriously.'

'It's so childish of them — calling names!' she said, and stupidly found herself crying.

'Jaycie wouldn't give a damn for that, would she now?' said Joe cheerfully. But all the same, he thought, if only she and her crowd know when to stop!

'I bet Jaycie likes it!' Martha chipped in and, of course, in a way that hit the nail on the head.

Three days. And suddenly the headlines got bigger, blotting out any other news. Now she was stuffing things into a small bag and Joe beside her was talking. 'I won't try and stop you, Mary, if you feel you must.' And she wasn't listening to him, wasn't thinking about him. She was only thinking about Jaycie.

They hadn't done anything really out of the ordinary to Jaycie. And the police as a matter of fact hadn't been the worst. But nobody who wants things to go on as they are — and that goes for most of us — cares for someone who is intent on changing them and looks likely to succeed. An agitator is bad enough; a successful agitator is not to be borne. There was something about Jaycie that made her audiences believe her; she never lied to them, not even at a big meeting with the lights on and the voices clamouring, the time when lies come easy to most people. But Jaycie stayed steady and unmoved by that temptation. You couldn't catch her out.

But it was not during the actual arrest that most of the damage had been done, nor even when she was questioned. At first the police had been rather inhibited at doing their worst on a woman. But — she got them annoyed. Not reacting the way they wanted. Then they let go a bit. But the really nasty thing was the accident — at least they said afterwards that it was an accident — with the petrol. Apart from everything else, Jaycie had lost considerable areas of superficial tissue and skin, including some on the face. Too much for safety. Very much too much.

It had perhaps not been intended that she should get to an ordinary hospital. But Jaycie had more friends than was usually supposed, and in some curious places. Someone took fright and reversed an order. The body of Jaycie was bundled into an ambulance; she might well die before getting to hospital. That was to be hoped, but she didn't.

At the hospital they knew Mary by reputation; most of them had read one or two of her papers at least. But someone who has been a printed name at the end of a scientific paper looks different when she is the mother of a young woman who is probably dying of shock and what have you and who has been considerably disfigured. Who will be up for trial if she recovers. But she won't. Even in the hospital some of them felt that this would be just as well. Doctors and surgeons no less than other citizens have a considerable interest in the preservation of the existing order of things. They were, of course, extremely busy in Casualties. That was to be expected after the last few days. But it did account for the fact that the House Surgeon paid little attention to what was happening at this particular screened bed. Mary got the Ward Sister to agree. Then she took the skin grafts off her own thighs under a local anaesthetic. It was not really at all difficult. She had often worked with this type of scalpel like an old-fashioned cut-throat razor. It took the strips off neatly, though it is always rather a peculiar feeling to do such things to oneself. The slight reluctance of the skin to the blade and then the curious ease of the shaving off of the strips can be felt by the operating hand but not by the anaesthetized tissue. The sister brings the necessary dressings. The new, still living skin is in place over the cleaned burns on the young woman's thin, partly broken body.

The Ward Sister couldn't help noticing the extreme care with which the mother was laying on the skin grafts over burned cheek and neck and forehead, above all the corner of the mouth.

'I couldn't have done it,' she said afterwards over a nice cup of tea. 'Not on my own child. My own daughter. Nice looking she must have been, you could tell that. And there was the mother going straight ahead, not batting an eye. And bound to be in pain herself. And all for nothing! There were no preparations, not what's needed before a transplant, so it's as clear as day, those grafts'll never take, and that poor thing will look a proper mess if she lives. And that's not likely.'

'Bound to stop her speaking at these meetings, that's one thing,' said another nurse who had been reading the papers.

'That scar tissue's sure going to twist her face,' said the Ward Sister. 'Remember that woman we had after the big Palladium fire? Shocking wasn't it? This'll be worse. But mind, agitator or no agitator, she gets proper nursing!'

The morphia was wearing off. Jaycie was whispering in half-sleep, arguing and refusing. Even like this her voice kept much of its strange persuasive beauty. The Ward Sister was whispering to the House Surgeon: 'I know these skin grafts can't take; you don't have to tell me! They'll slough off. If she doesn't die first. Do more harm than good. But the mother — well she's kind of distinguished; I couldn't very well say no, could I now? Besides she had some theory — oh, I can't remember now – yes, yes, it'll be worse for her when she sees her daughter's face the way it's bound to be. I know. But don't you fuss now! Haven't we all got our hands full these days!'

After that there was rather less scope for fussing about any individual patient. The wards were jammed with temporary beds. Mary waited beside Jaycie as she gradually awoke into pain and mastered it. They were getting short of analgesics by now, and besides Jaycie had said quite firmly that she needed none. Mary did not ask for much herself; the pain, though at times severe, was bearable. On her own thighs the skinned strips were healing by first intention; all had been aseptic from the start, competently done. She helped the Ward Sister when she could. It kept her mind off what might be happening at home. For the usual channels of communication were no longer functioning. The military had taken over successfully, or had they . . . .? Perhaps not.

Days and nights went by. In the third week the Ward Sister, still surprised that Jaycie went on living when so many had died, said to herself that now those skin grafts were lifting, would slough off like a dead scab, leaving everything worse. 'They can't do anything else,' she said. Then you'd begin to see the mess the scarring was bound to make of her face. And that wouldn't be nice for the mother.

But the new skin didn't lift off, didn't die. The edge of it visibly and redly lived and grew on to the damaged flesh in healthy granulations.

The thin scar lines would be there, but not the hideous twisting and lumping of raw flesh. You took off the dressings and there was the undeniable fact: the skin grafts had taken. The area of damage, the revolting wounds were covered in. No wonder Jaycie lived.

The Ward Sister shook her head. It shouldn't have happened, but it had. In a way, however, Sister was rather pleased; the doctors were wrong again. Them and their theories that they were always having to change! And it just showed how, in spite of all the troubles and difficulties of overcrowding and medical shortages, good nursing — her pride, the thing she insisted on in her ward — had somehow done the trick.

The House Surgeon looked too. He wouldn't commit himself and he hadn't time just then to look it all up in the text-books. Later on he'd mention the matter to his chief. But after a while, with Jaycie getting stronger every day, he and Sister decided on a few tactful questions. The odd thing was that Mary found it comparatively easy telling them. She didn't mind what the effect on them might be of what she was telling. Indeed, she hardly noticed. She had plenty of other things to worry about. It was much less easy telling Joe.

For he came at last, bless him, bringing all sorts of delicious things to eat. Yes, they were all rather hungry at the hospital; supplies had been cut off, there hadn't been much news either. 'Oh Joe,' she said, 'dear, dear Joe, is everything all right?'

'Yes,' he said, 'and my little Martha turned up trumps. We never guessed what a head that kid had! And I got Simon on long distance. Naturally he couldn't say much, but he's okay. Now, Mary, what's all this story about skin grafts?'

Mary said: 'Jaycie had a very large area of skin torn and burned off, on purpose. Joe, they — they were so horrible to her. Some of her friends told me, they didn't mean her to live. I didn't realise people could be like that about politics in this country. Though I suppose they really are everywhere when it gets serious. You know, she was very nearly dead when I got here.'

She stopped for a moment and dabbed her eyes. It came fleetingly through Joe's mind that this might have been the best thing. For the world, for things as they are. For himself and Simon and Martha. Maybe for Mary herself in the long run. But he wasn't going to let himself think that just now, not with his wife sobbing on to the edge of his waistcoat. He stroked her hair, a bit sticky and unwashed and the white collar of her dress all mucked up, poor sweet.

She looked up a little and said: 'So it seemed to me that the best chance was a skin graft.'

'But Mary,' he said, 'a skin graft's no good from someone else. Even I know that!'

'It's all right from someone identical: genetically the same.'

'But Mary you aren't, you can't be . . . .' Joe had an uncomfortable feeling, though he didn't quite know why.

'Because of the father. His genes make the child different from the mother. I know, Joe, I told you a long time ago that Jaycie had a father. Joe, dear, dear Joe, I only told you that because I thought it would upset you more to think she hadn't a father. There now, you are upset —'

'Mary darling, don't worry about me. I just don't understand.'

'She didn't have a father, Joe. I — I never had a lover. I was — well I suppose there is nothing else for it, I was a virgin, Joe.'

'But you had a baby. Sweet, you can't have been.'

'I was. You see, something started one of my ova developing. That's all. Oh, that's all! It doesn't sound too odd that way, does it?'

'But what could start it? What's the stimulus?'

'It might be anything I expect. Some — metabolic change.'

'What was it with you?'

She did not answer. Even now she could not think quite calmly. It might have been imagination. It must have been. Lower than far thunder, higher than the bat's squeak, the whispering of a million leaves. Sometimes the murmur of wind-shifted leaves in summer reminded her. It couldn't possibly have been what she was certain it was. She took a breath: 'Whatever the stimulus was, the ovum developed normally. The child had to be a female, an identical female. Without the Y chromosome that comes from the male and goes to a male. I don't know what happened in the process of chromosome division. Of course, there was the possibility — perhaps the probability — of a haploid. Of the chromosomes splitting unevenly. You see what I mean, Joe? But they didn't.'

'That — that was odd,' said Joe, looking away from his wife's face. 'There must have been — some kind of pattern making machinery behind it —'

'You could call it that,' said Mary; 'yes, of course, Joe, you could call it that. But the way things worked out, Jaycie and I are genetically identical.'

Joe swallowed: 'Did you — did you know this from the start, Mary?'

'Not for sure,' she said. 'But — when she was a baby I started by taking the tiniest pinch-graft from her to me. That took. But it wasn't certain. I mean, it was almost sure that my antibodies wouldn't affect her graft. But it wasn't sure the other way round. So, when she was a little older, I tried it that way too.'

'But if you were genetically identical, Mary, you — you'd have been as alike as — identical twins.'

'We are, physically. But there's a big difference in nurture, Joe, as well as age. I'm going grey and wrinkled.'

Gallantly he said 'No!' but she only smiled a little.

'You see, my dearest, there's a different best treatment for babies every generation. And then — we started thinking about different kinds of things. Using the same brain perhaps, but —'

'I'd have thought I'd have noticed,' Joe muttered, 'seeing you both all the time.'

'You were used to me, Joe. And besides, by the time she was adult, you thought of her as herself. Though you've always thought she was like me. You were pleased she was like me and not — like someone else. Weren't you? And I always had a different hair-do from hers. On purpose, Joe.'

'And all that time, you never told me, Mary.'

'I — I couldn't. Not by then. The other thing — we'd got used to it, you and I — as a story. Oh Joe, you wouldn't have liked it!'

'No,' said Joe, 'no, I suppose I wouldn't.' He looked across the crowded ward at the bed; one of Jaycie's friends was sitting there with a notebook, questioning and taking down the answers. Jaycie's friends were going about openly now. Beginning to take over here and there, to put Jaycie's ideas into practice. Bad, bad. At least, that was what one had to suppose. The alternative — the military alternative — had not succeeded. There would be no trial for Jaycie. Instead, there were going to be changes. Changes he knew he was going to hate. Even if they were supposed to be going to be good in the end. A lot of people were sold on that, but not Joe. Changes — everything changed before it was done! His own whole life: set another way, not the way he wanted! But all the same, he thought, this was the baby he had accepted when he got Mary to say she would marry him all that long while back. She was a sweet baby right enough. Pretty. Those great eyes. There was always something about babies that got you. Maybe, he thought, I shall have to accept Jaycie's changes and not say a word. Because of Mary.

Mary went on: 'Perhaps that's why she's always been a bit different. Why she's been — single hearted.' She wasn't going to let Joe know — not ever — that she had told Jaycie before she told him. That would hurt him, and she couldn't bear to hurt him any more. She was Joe's Mary as much as she was Jaycie's. Almost as much.

'So you don't know what the stimulus was,' Joe said half aloud. 'You don't know. It's — Yes, it's a bit scaring, Mary.'

'I know. That's why I told you the other thing. The easy thing. And you were so sweet. Forgive me, Joe.'

'That's all right, Mary. Funny, I sometimes wondered what the other chap was like. Whether Jaycie took after him. Whether you ever thought about him. And now there isn't another chap.'

'No,' said Mary, 'No.'

'And you got the doctor here to take this skin graft —'

'I took it myself,' said Mary. 'There's nothing to it if it's done in good conditions.'

'Didn't it hurt?'

'Just a bit afterwards. But not nearly as much as thinking she was going to die. Goodness, Joe, any mother would do it for her child; jump at the chance of doing it if it was to be any use. But of course it wouldn't be any use — normally.'

'Yes,' said Joe. 'Yes. But you've always liked normal things, haven't you, Mary?'

'For everything but this, Joe,' she said, and held on tight to his hand. Deliberately and with a slow effort he made the hand respond, warmly, gently, normally. For the hand left to itself had wanted to pull away, not to touch her. Not to touch.

Take-over

AS A EUROPEAN I COULD NOT, OF COURSE, TAKE PART
in the revolutionary movement of the late twentieth century in South
East Asia, but it was well known how my sympathies lay. In fact the
revolutionary council did me the honour of asking my opinion from time
to time, even occasionally taking my advice. Certainly I was able to help
a little over their external image and to counter some of the straight lies
that were being spread. They sent me back twice to put their case in
Europe and America; I believe I had some success, though what can one
man do?

It was impossible for anyone other than the medical team to go into the
city itself until the epidemic had worn itself out. The team had the most
modern type of protection against the terrible infection risks, but even so
there were a couple of deaths in the early months. Plague must have been
like this in the old days. Gradually it became less virulent. At last, after
rather more than two years, we were allowed back. The first clearing of
the ruins and what had been left in them had been done by para-military
units, again in protective clothing, but there were no casualties, so now it
was thought safe for civilians such as myself, though outsiders and in
particular the Press and television representatives were not yet allowed
in. One photographer had disguised himself and sneaked in, but had been
caught and would probably have been shot but for the intervention of a
few of us who talked the Committee out of it, explaining how badly this
would be thought of in other parts of the world.

When we actually went in some of us felt some anxiety, though we were assured that it was quite safe. My own anxiety was not for something as trivial as my own health, but for what I would find in a certain place. I had managed to make certain that this was where I would be sent. We started from the camp and then had to make our way through the smaller streets which had not yet been cleared; although we were armed, we had been instructed not to shoot rats or small animals. They could be dealt with later. But it was possible that larger predators might have been attracted, probably jackals or wild dogs of some kind. Someone had said there had been a tiger viewed, but that was probably an invention. All I noticed myself were the squirrels and once a harmless snake. We separated at what had been the monument and I looked up at the hotel; for a moment the upper part seemed unchanged, the rows of windows softly dazzling. Well, we would see. It was quite simple to walk up the steps and through the swing doors.

My companion had been a kitchen worker. It was quite usual for young Arts graduates like Salim to take such jobs, which usually meant becoming politicised. He had some hair-raising stories about kitchen bribery and what often happened about the stores. I think he had also helped in the elimination of some senior but much disliked bosses. But that, after all, was two years ago. Since then he had been working as a literacy teacher. A nice chap and knew his way round the hotel, especially the lower ground floor complexes. I gathered he'd had a girl-friend in the cosmetics and hairdressing section; but she seemed to have disappeared. He only mentioned her with a kind of sideways casualness.

The last time I had been to the hotel myself was just before Christmas two and a half years ago. There had been great bowls of white orchids with genuine imported holly through them, as well as a decorated Christmas tree, a real imported Douglas spruce. In Australia we always made do with a young casuarina. There had been other bowls of orchids everywhere, and real gold orchid brooches and bangles in the show cases. Yes, it had been like that. And a fountain with lilies in bud and blossom and yet more orchids. Easy enough to see where that fountain had been; there was dried scum in the basin. And there were the long counters and the notices still up.

Behind the counters it had all been elegance, warm, welcoming, by trained staff and for that matter, efficiency. The girls all spoke English as prettily as they dressed. You changed your money, you picked up your letters or your key; it had all been so smooth. I went to the back of the counter with my torch and took a bunch of keys. There were papers lying, files snapped in place, a desk computer no doubt untouched all this time, even money: worthless stuff. I had to grope for the keys; even with a torch it was darkish behind the counter and somehow I felt awkward. I came away with as many as I could carry as well as the one I specially wanted. I looked about. Something unpleasant had happened to the carpet and of course with no lights one was liable to trip. The ground floor windows had never been important and now they were blocked with greenery, mostly the bougainvilleas and alamandas which had ramped away instead of staying neat little bushes in tubs.

Salim had been downstairs. He came up with an armful of tins. They would be all right, he thought. Naturally everything in the freezers had gone; if you opened one the smell would knock you down. As for the cellars, there had been special orders, which we obeyed. They were no temptation for Salim, but would have been for me if things had been different. They used to have some really marvellous hocks. I remembered them. And there was no reason why they should not survive perfectly. 'But you must see the vegetable kitchen,' Salim said. 'Cucumbers, beans, pumpkins, peppers, many, many seeds and those little plants, how they got back on us when the wet got in! Everywhere! I could make us a meal straight away: you know there are fruits burst, there are mango and pawpaw seedlings, little oranges and a grenadilla climbed out of the grating. Even the rice sprouted! Ah, but that needed sun, it shrivelled away. But oh, you must see — wherever light came in.' He was laughing a lot; it was nice having something to laugh about.

It surprised me a little to see how quickly the plants had taken over the ground floor of the hotel. After all it had been in the middle of town. But there had been a piece of formal garden at the back, well looked after, and beyond it on another piece of land, a few big trees which had made a pleasant background for the big swimming pool and the terrace. And in front there had been a row of tubs, begonias, lilies and so on. And there had been two monsoons between then and now.

When the front windows were broken, whether by storms or wild animals or, well, whatever else there might have been, leaves and seeds had blown in and then came the monsoon rains. So now there was a spreading of mixed weeds and a few creepers had started adventuring about, climbing up the chairs and tables. Birds had come after honey or berries and mice or rats had been at the upholstery. Very comfortable those chairs had been when I was waiting around, hoping that someone could be induced to see sense. But they never did see it; they were so deep in the security of making money, just as Lily had been so deep in music; so that nothing else seemed to get through. And I had my Christmas present for Lily on my knee. So beautifully packaged; I remember that.

We looked into that very delightful informal restaurant — you didn't even have to wear a tie — facing onto the garden that had been so delicately landscaped by a Chinese expert. He would have been furious at the big weeds swarming over his dwarf trees. Here the plants and their animal followers had just walked in over the sills. There were even some wild orchids among them, the little white ones. That was the table where

Lily and I used to eat salads and fruit and talk about — yes, probably, ourselves. But the ceramics, the bright silver and brass work, the linens, the sharp light on the wine glass, the flimsy pretty curtains and lamp shades, where were they? Nowhere for Lily and me, not a chair whole or clean. I caught Salim watching me. But perhaps it was not out of unkindness or suspicion.

We found our way up the stairs. They were not very grand, for of course everyone used the lifts, half a dozen of them there had been, always bright and polished when you stepped in, and a smiling lift-boy to be tipped later — if one remembered. I thought of forcing open one of the shut, dark doors, just to see, but then decided not to. The first landing was astonishingly overgrown and one corner heaped with a huge fungus that appeared to be housing quite a population of little nasties. Once the windows were gone it was easy for all sorts of spores to drift in and settle cosily. The floor covering had rotted away as quickly as if it had been pieces of dead wood on a rain-forest floor.

Perhaps it was as well that things did rot. I found my first casualty on that floor with a knife still in his ribs. Or perhaps hers. Salim looked at it coldly. The flesh had been very tidily eaten away, probably by rats, though something larger had been at the long bones. There were a few tatters of cloth. Probably a man, but his wallet had been gnawed, except for the metal clip — gold, was it? — so that I wasn't able to make a guess at who it had been. I couldn't help hoping that the flesh-eaters had made as good a job of other corpses.

We unlocked two or three doors and went into another room where the door had been left open and had swung so violently that it was half off its hinges, the pre-monsoon winds I expect. These had been air-conditioned rooms and on the whole the windows were still shut. But patches of fungus had spread; some of the bathrooms were thick with it. The room with the open door had been cleared out, but the others had plenty of evidence; one, even, had the beginning of a letter on a neat little typewriter. I stopped long enough to make notes, but the atmosphere was unpleasant. The rooms had of course heated up during the hot weather of two years, with no air conditioning. I felt choked. In several I noticed bottles intact, a discreet breaking of the laws which were enforced against the poor. I found it had mixed associations for me: some rather powerful. Salim always tells me to cut that out. It is easy for him, engrossed in his present and possible future.

Our assignment had been just to get an idea of what had happened in the city during the two years. The events of the first three months were sufficiently well-known and documented. In fact there were far too many photographs; almost everyone either had a camera or quickly looted one. But after that, with the specific weapons of the counter-attacking forces causing complete withdrawal from the city which, however, was by now lethal to its new conquerors, nobody quite knew what was what, only that the counter-attack had petered out. World developments elsewhere had seen to that.

So now it was important to make an assessment of the city. If buildings were in reasonably good condition they might be re-used. Possible uses had not yet been considered in detail, but that would certainly be on the immediate agenda.

We next took a look at the swimming pool, which was on the first floor level, partly over the garden-view restaurant. I had not much wanted to do this in case there were remains. At one point several men and women, deservedly in a way, had been taken, condemned, tied and thrown into the pool. I had known some of them and though the relationship had been one of irritation and anger, I still did not relish this kind of confrontation. But that had been cleared up; the bodies, Salim said, had been fished out and taken to the mass grave in the Botanical Garden. After that the water had partially evaporated in the hot weather, since the circulating and purifying mechanism had of course stopped; but the pool had filled again in the rain. Yet it was totally changed; leaves had drifted in and rotted; there was an abundance of larval life in the brownish shallows where the shining blue tiles were almost obliterated. 'We should get some fish to clean this up,' I said to Salim, 'otherwise malaria will spread.'

Salim said doubtfully that he would try. I believe he is doing this now. One interesting thing was that seeds had blown in from the slight overhang of the next-door trees and there were healthy saplings already prising up the mosaic where the chaise-longues and little tables had been, with young men like Salim scurrying about with drinks and sandwiches and ice-creams, accepting tips but thinking — what? Well, one knew now. The umbrellas had all blown away, but some of their stands were still there. Wicker chairs, too, had blown into a corner, become overgrown and now had birds nesting in them; the wicker had blended in better than rusting metal and plastics. There were ingenious spiders' webs too and bright metallic-looking beetles picking up a living. Quite a take-over.

We had to go on to the upper floors. It was much the same, except that twice we came on corpses inside locked rooms and they were totally unpleasant, not having been cleaned up by predators. The smell was terrible until we had smashed some windows. Salim was making a list of useful consumer goods from pencils and torches and gift packages of soap to spectacles and watches and on to radios, tellys, typewriters and computers. There was clothing still hanging in some of the wardrobes but we agreed that the smell of mildew, and worse, made them unacceptable except as waste for processing. In the upper floors the windows could be opened. Sometimes an adventurous creeper had got this far. One couldn't help a slight feeling of applause. Good luck to them!

And so we came to the room I was afraid of. I had the key, but it was not locked and it did not have what had been burning into me since I volunteered for this particular mission. In fact the room was tidy; the violin was in its case. Salim made a note of it; he had never seen one close. I explained that the damp and heat would have affected the strings and probably warped the body, but this could perhaps be restored. The body looked all right; it had survived almost three centuries, though in a cooler climate. Salim touched this thing from Europe gently. I was trying not to think of her hand, her cheek and shoulder. The piles of music seemed to be only slightly mildewed and frayed at the edges; the same with the books, and all the little things she couldn't travel without. There was a scent bottle there, half full. It would have been terrible to open it. And know. And know. Beside it was a letter from her agent about an American contract. I looked at the date. Yes, it was the week before when I had been trying hard to warn her. Apparently she had answered it. If only she had left then. If only. But she hated being hurried, wouldn't take me seriously.

The letter to me. I had half expected it. Yet, when I saw it propped against the mirror which by now was blotched, but still unbroken, I found it difficult to keep my hand steady. I am not sure how much Salim knew. Probably something, but his and my definitions of love would be strangely different, more so than our definitions of justice. She wrote that yes, I had been right and she had been silly, hadn't she, but now it was too late and if I ever found this letter I was not to be sad or angry. She was going down to sit somewhere outside among the flowers and when she heard the shooting coming close she would take enough of her sleeping pills. This of course had been written after the fatal 11 a.m., though she had not dated it. The television set in the room had been left on, though now it was blank. I wondered what had been the last thing shown on it. I folded the letter and stood looking out of the window. Which flowers? Perhaps in front among the alamandas and tall fuchsias, the ipomeas and jasmines which were going to be set free. She had always enjoyed sitting there watching the traffic, so varied and bright coloured, from the front row of the dress circle, so to speak. Laughing about it. A few days must have gone by while her body still sat there, her scarf still blown in the broken sunlight. Then all corpses had been cleared from the streets, thrown into trucks and taken to the Botanical Gardens.

When I turned round Salim had opened the sliding doors of the cupboard. What I found it hard to take was not so much the dresses and the furs, but the row of shoes. They seemed to be waiting. I went out very quickly. I had not even looked to see if she had left any of her jewellery. If so Salim would have taken it out, carefully noted down everything and as carefully handed it all over to the correct official body in the Department, for ultimate sale. That is something I do not want to know about. The letter ended with love and a little laughing and remembering. She must have gone to sleep among those flowers, those plants which were going to win, to take over from us humans.

We spent the whole day going over the hotel, making notes, not speaking to one another too loud, and then suddenly it was night. I think somehow we had both irrationally expected that the lights would go on and though we knew perfectly well that nothing of the kind could happen, yet we were surprised and rather upset. We decided not to go back but to bed down on the comfortable banquettes in the main reception area. Neither of us felt like going into a bedroom. We opened a couple of tins and a bottle of soda water, gone rather stale. It was perhaps simpler for Salim than for me: we had won, that was good. I kept a question mark over both; it was only that we'd had the same enemy. Was that enough? I didn't know, only I was sure I did not feel like a winner. But over exactly who or what — now? When we lay down there were constant small rustlings and a strong smell of jasmine, perhaps also something sharper and earthier, but certainly a plant. Whoever else had won, they had. Later the moon rose and its light came filtering down onto us through thousands of eager and growing leaves. Forcing and teasing and tearing their way into what had been human territory, but would soon be theirs.

Far from Millicentral Station

AS THE EXPEDITION WORKED FURTHER NORTH IT became increasingly troubled by what are vulgarly called flying saucers. These, normal enough, as we all know, at high altitudes, were now skimming at under twelve metres. The patent ventilating shaft of the larger of the two Veriwarm moveable huts was quite severely dented, and this in spite of its monoprion content. And yet, most unfortunately, not one had come within the reach of Dr. Spong, the leader of the expedition, noted in three hemispheres both as geologist and as astro-selenologist. It was probable, he thought, that some type of interference might be devised which would bring him in contact with these fascinating objects of controversy. The patent ventilating shaft, clearly, had not been enough. Not nearly enough. A complete interruption of the normal parabolic flight would be necessary.

Now this should have been simplicity itself, but that there was something about the velocity of these so-called flying saucers that escaped Dr. Spong as it had escaped his predecessors. Nothing worked out and yet, he thought, if once some quite elementary difficulty were overcome all would go smoothly. If once this elementary difficulty could be identified it would be overcome! As leader of the expedition he had much organisation and routine work on his hands, besides the nightly writing up of the reports which sometimes took him well into the small hours. It was at these times that his mind would stray away from the matter in hand and he would suddenly — oh but almost! — reach a blissful comprehension of what would be necessary and achievable, even within his budget. And yet always some link was missing.

He did not like to involve the other members of the expedition, specialists all, in his peculiar difficulties and worries. Not one of them quite shared his astro-selenologist angle. And yet if that involvement had been possible! But the leader of the expedition was, somehow, aloof. Even from the more senior members such as Dr. Millicent Butter. This lady, a D. Phil. of Milan University — for she was widely travelled, having found it necessary to escape so frequently — was the official botanist of the expedition and was indeed one of their most distinguished members. Her papers on the mycellia of the phycomycetes and the geotropism of Hypholoma Fasciculare had excited considerable interest in mycological circles; and it was not for nothing that one of the rarer and, to a trained observer, lovelier of the green algae bore her name.

She was also a not incompetent archaeologist; but she had early found something a trifle distasteful about much which was discovered, so different from the sex life of our dear algae. Dr. Millicent Butter had a long-standing aversion from certain forms of non-academic human activity. This, unhappily, had somewhat marred her happy philosophical and botanical months in Milan. Even the Professor himself, a married man she had understood — but then the Italians are notorious for such activities! Dr. Butter was never afterwards able to hear the word professor, and it was unfortunately one of the words which tended to crop up in many specialist conversations, without feeling a slight *malaise*. Beautiful, embarrassing, treacherous Italy! But in what surroundings could a woman be sure, yes sure, that no activities could obtrude themselves? Even among the most apparently arid pre-graphic potsherds one was only too likely to be brought into archaeological contact with them.

It was thus with considerable interest, but also with a certain distinct anxiety, that Dr. Butter discovered that this northern expedition, in general so congenial, so adequately clad, had begun to come across the traces of an early settlement in which both Norse and Eskimo influence was apparent. Almost too apparent, perhaps. 'Oh dear, oh dear,' said Dr. Millicent Butter to herself, nevertheless carefully placing the fragment of engraved walrus tusk between layers of cottonwool and laying it on the lid of her vasculum. The fragment would have to be shown to Dr. Spong, so embarrassing. Yet who, if not dear Dr. Spong, could be trusted to regard the fragment with the cool, the non-engaged, eye, which was so essential? She must, yes indeed, she must, find a moment when he was alone with no possibility of interruption by any of their younger colleagues. And yet, would not that — ? So unfortunate, this insistence on animal fertility, so recognisable! Whereas the reproductive cycle of the phycomycetes had a delicacy that, indeed, made them what they were. Conscientiously Dr. Butter searched for the other part of the engraving although with a strong feeling that it was more than fortunate that this was nowhere to be seen: that the design had broken, so to speak, where it did. Although on the other hand, and archaeologically speaking, the complete design would be of great significance. But here, on a protruding rock, Dr. Butter observed a most interesting lichen. She stooped over it with her pocket lens in her right hand; and at that moment a flying saucer unfortunately bisected her completely.

Dr. Spong, meanwhile, had been noting geological formations. And yet, all the while his dream had been with him: oh to have the possibility of examining a flying saucer! Oh to solve the problem of interference, to discover the normal parabolic flight, which so teasingly offered him no opportunity, somehow meeting with some finally restrictive power! Imagine, then, his delight when he saw one actually descend without rising again! He rushed to the spot, closely followed by the zoologist of the expedition, Mr. Cyril Leakin. To their joint horror they found the projectile, still warm, between Dr. Butter, who was, however, as far as her right half was concerned, continuing her examination of the interesting lichen.

'Dr. Butter, Dr. Butter!' said Mr. Leakin in great agitation and with a curious gobbling effect which, indeed, he noted at the time. But 'Millicent!' groaned Dr. Spong, for the first time allowing the name actually to pass his lips. The right half of Dr. Butter thereupon expressed herself normally, though with a certain *gêne*.

'Please do not distress yourselves,' she said. 'I am not in the least incommoded.'

'Delighted to hear it, delighted!' said Dr. Spong. 'But — are you sure?' He had the most curious impression that the left half of Dr. Butter had produced something which in another, and of course intellectually inferior person, might have been an unseemly cachinnation. The left half of Dr. Butter was not botanising. On the contrary, she had found the other fragments of walrus ivory which completed the design.

'Now there, old boy,' said the left half of Dr. Butter, 'is something to write home about.' Without any help from her other half, which was now delicately removing a morsel of lichen, she laid the fragments deftly, if left-handedly, together. They portrayed a most interesting scene of early life: of fraternisation — in a sense — between the two cultures. Mr. Cyril Leakin blinked. It went somewhat beyond his subject, zoologist as he was. But Dr. Spong was now eagerly regarding the missile.

'No,' said Dr. Butter, and both the geologist and the zoologist had the remarkable impression that the two halves of Dr. Butter were now speaking together. 'I have nothing to complain of, and perhaps you would like to examine the missile. I feel it most fortunate, dear Dr. Spong, to have been the means of gratifying your interest.'

Dr. Spong took a step nearer. But it seemed to him in a way —
impious — to come between Dr. Butter. At the same time, he could not
help observing the faintly crystalline structure of the missile, which was
more nearly triangular than had appeared from any observations of the
same type in flight. It was his great opportunity, both as a geologist, as an
astro-selenologist, and, yes, as a man. Why had it never occurred to him
that the simple, the utterly efficacious solution to his problems lay in the
hands of Dr. Butter? Of Millicent. But — in the hands — ? No, no, why
allow himself to be bemused by such purely verbal complications! His
way was clear. His intention gleamed before him, at long last clearly.

'May I — are you sure — ,' he said, 'Millicent?' It was the left half of
Dr. Butter which answered in a slightly flippant way.

'Come right in, Spongey dear.'

Mr. Leakin winced. It was so unlike Dr. Butter even to have taken
cognisance of the nickname which some of the junior members of the
expedition had conferred on the distinguished geologist who was leading
them. The right half of Dr. Butter gave a slight start and appeared to be
immersed in closer study of her lichen. But Dr. Spong seemed unaware
of any peculiar or undue familiarity. On the contrary, his face lit up as it
rarely did, even in the midst of the most exciting controversy in the
Senior Commonroom. His hand went out towards the missile. The left
half of Dr. Butter, still delicately fingering her archaeological trove,
smiled with unmistakeable purpose; and Mr. Cyril Leakin tiptoed away.

Miss Omega Raven

THE OTHERS WERE ALWAYS QUICK, ALWAYS FIRST.
Was it because of what they did to us when we were young, when they
took us out of our nests before our feathers were more than quills and fed
us this other food and made us sleep and put the little wires on to our
heads so that we could look back and forward? We became different. And
yet it seems I became the most different of all. We knew what was ahead
and how to get it. We knew, not deep inside where there is no choice like
knowing in our necks and wings the moves of the mating flight when all
is Now. No, not that. We knew with the parts of ourselves that choose.
Thinking, they called it, remembering, looking ahead. I was the latest
hatched, damp and flabby, my beak making squeals, the pieces of shell
still stuck to me. I had not seen my mother. I opened eyes and saw him,
the God-man with the special food. He became her. I had to follow him
to do what he did, to become him. How else? Yet because of that I was
more changed. But they took us a long way in the dark in a box and made
us fly. By then our wings were grown. We felt a need but did not know
what it was.

When we flew we were in a different place with open stretches of rocks
and trees, but no built walls. But inside we knew it. We knew the ways in
which we were going to live. The food. And there were the mates. Oh
beautiful, with the deep part which has no choice, I knew this was my
need. I must get one. I must get the most beautiful, the best, shining dark

of feathers, bright of eye. We must dance together in the air. That was what wings were for. We forgot the humans who had reared us; we forgot to look forward and back. But perhaps I did not quite forget. Perhaps that was what went wrong.

I did not at once leap into the air, crooning and bubbling, to chase the top bird, the raven of ravens, Alpha Corax. My feathered tufts were slow to come to the erect and welcoming sign which should draw him, yes, to lay his neck over mine. Others did it, my hated sisters, jumping with touched beaks, ruffling, courting, crooning. And the mates responded, answering with the same love notes, the same stiffening and relaxing, so that feathers ruffled and beaks snapped. It was clear already who was top, who could peck whom, though it had scarcely yet become clear to us female fledglings. Even during the courting dance when air became buoyant and welcoming, inviting to enormous heights of glory from which one could dive flashingly, the wind booming one's feathers or even when the mate, turning on his back, invited with his beating spread wings but warned with beak and claws. One after another the couples began to take flight. But I — I? Surely I could not be the one left out! But I was. For me and for one other, no mate. There had been two more of us than of them. Or perhaps two of them had died in the rearing. She, the other unmated, was even more hateful than the wives. Each of them had taken the rank of her husband and would keep it for life. We ravens settle each with her own mate for always.

This way each took orders and gave orders, each pecked in punishment and was herself pecked; it was the same with the husbands. Only the most beautiful, the bravest, the top raven Alpha Corax, gave orders. Nobody pecked him. He led the flock to roost or to hunt. He watched and warned for enemies and sometimes attacked. His beak was sharpest.

But I was lowest of the low. She — the other unmated — pecked me and I had to accept this, jumping away from food, not pecking back. All that was in the deep part of me. I could not escape being how I was. There was no choice. But also I was angry and that anger was in the other part of me driving me to plan. That part of me thought of a future in which I would not be pecked. I knew I was becoming ugly. My feathers were draggled. I was thin, for I always got the worst share, either of flesh or eggs or the rarer grain and nuts. No wonder I was a pecked-on with nobody to peck. Had God-man made me this? If he had not made me something other I could not have questioned what I was.

So things went on. The beautiful one watched and led us to food; so did his wife. She saw with his eyes, she too led the flight in which I was last. And I knew two opposite things: in the deep part of me — that this was how it was. But, in the outside, the changed and choosing part — that this was not for always and one day there would be a choice and a plan. But the choice did not come. The mates made their nests, beautiful, enviable, with heathers and grasses and earth and small sticks, lined deliciously with worked, soft grasses and feathers, ready for eggs. Once I tried to sit in a nest but how I was driven out, with what pain and anger! I tried to join in flights, I tried to croon and preen to each of the males but I aroused nothing in any of them, since they had only one image in their constant minds. They also had been in the hands of the God-men but now they had forgotten. I being alone, could not forget.

Then came the chipping of the eggs, the young, the tremendous drive and bustle of feeding. I looked on, knowing what it was I missed; it was I who was driven from the dead lamb that was feasting us. It was I who saw the God-men circling us, with what intent I did not know, yet believed it was not evil. It was not they who had left me hungry. They spoke to one another or so I supposed. I also saw that they took some of the nestlings while they fed others with their own kind of food. The mothers were disturbed briefly but none of us could feel that the God-men were enemies. They were only high beyond us, beyond the top of the Alphas; they could give orders. They could peck us to the bone and any of us must submit, but because they had also fed us they did not do that; they did not need to. The one on whom my nestling eyes had first opened was there. He looked at my thin and draggled body; he had brought pieces of food, not their own kind, but good raw meat. Our best food. He gave me some and I tried to gulp it quickly before the other unmated could see me and drive me off. Yet she came, and her black beak drove at me; feathers flew. The deep, inside part of me was making me cower and accept. But the one I had not forgotten, the God-man, had shown himself; it was meat he had given. He sent the knowledge of choice back into me. In a moment she was the pecked on. I made her feathers fly! It was impossible and it had happened.

Once pecked, she accepted. That was the first lesson. For both of us. I hated her. I could not stop pecking. Even when the God-man picked me up so that she could run and then flap away. Through the wriggle of my held wings and the straining of my body I felt his hands thinking about me. My beak wanted to peck, my claws to scratch; the one I had opened eyes on. He held me but it came to me that I also held him.

Then there was a feast again. A cow had given birth. She moved away with the calf, leaving what else had come out of her red and wet in the grass. That was for us. But now I had one to peck and drive off if she came near me and the one who before had pecked her could not at once change to pecking me. The old pattern had been made. Yet because she too had been with the God-men and had been partly changed by them, so that she had choice, she began to know that I had taken the place of the other and also she was afraid in case I did not accept it. Sometimes her pecking was not hard. But I did not attack at once, not when she was with her nest and her mate.

The leaves of the great nest trees had spread and become green to live the leaves' life. Then they browned and drooped and loosened and the leaf flocks swirled briefly in air and then drooped and were still and useless. The young birds began to fly. But from every nest the God-men climbing quietly had taken one. I was watching, the mothers not always. They and their mates swirled and clattered and called uselessly, and yet they all knew, in the part of their minds that looked forward and back, that the God-men had the right and this way was best for all.

And now cold days began and we all scattered again, though the pairs kept partly together. There was less food in winter and less light time to find it. And I began to peck back at the next above me. I did not want any mate; it was the wrong season. I wanted only to be top. By the next season I could take this one's place, but it was not enough. What then?

The God-man came. My own. Was he top God-man or was it possible that all were top? They did not seem to hurt one another. But perhaps they did in some way hidden from ravens; who could tell? No use asking even if one knew what or how to ask. What is asking? So it went. But one day the God-man was gone and with him in a box went the wife of Alpha Corax, the top raven. Where had she gone? We did not know what to think, only that all were perturbed. She, with him, had led the foraging parties of the ravens. He was used to her being with him. He called; she was not there. He made the croonings and the mating cries; she did not answer. But all of us felt something in the deep part that wanted to answer, even before the season of mating. There was movement and small noises. Feathers rose and a posturing walk began. And then my own God-man looked at me and he too made a mating cry and he lifted his arms flapping. He was me. He had taken me from the egg and changed me so that I could hatch out of the old patterns. And then suddenly it was I who was answering Alpha Corax; it was I who was with him, who had taken top place. I was the same as my God-man, my top God.

Now it was I who would have Alpha Corax, the top bird, the most beautiful, the raven of ravens. At mating time we would dance together in the air and then we would build our nest. But today, now, he knew and acknowledged me. I was alpha today. I could peck the one below me and not one of them could peck me. I would become beautiful and glossy; my feathers would always lie smooth; I would bite and swallow all the bloodiest of the food. I would have the best nest, safe, not out in the edges.

All this happened. It happened to me. Now I am mated forever with Alpha Corax. Yes, at first there were those that rebelled, that had it in the bottom of their minds that I was still the pecked one, Omega Raven. Yes, some of them tried to peck me. But how I pecked them back, scattering feathers and blood! For I remembered the other food and the little wires that made me more than myself. I remembered God-man who made me into top pecker, breaker of custom. My God-man, top God. God-man and I.

The Factory

THE FACTORY PEOPLE HAVE BEEN EVER SO NICE,
really they have. They needn't of; they'd kept all the regulations, strictly
kept them. We couldn't have had the law on them in spite of what Ted
and the newspaper man said. But it's been a bit of a shock, I won't deny
that. Above forty years I've been on the farm and my husband he'd been
born there. You get to belong with a place and know every brick you do.
Not that I wouldn't sometimes say, 'Wouldn't you like a nice job in town
and not the cows every blessed morning and evening of the year?' But
that was what he wanted. You know he wants it yet. He misses it.

It was a calf died first and the vet, well he didn't know what to make of
it; ever such a nice man, Mr. Thompson the vet, but I haven't seen him
now not for a year and he used to drop in most every week and eat a slice
of my cake. Kind of fits they had, the poor little dears, heifer calves they
was. And then the cows began to take sick but they didn't die, not at first,
only the milk went off. You know, I wonder sometimes if anything ever
ailed any of the folk that drank the milk. The next to go were my ducks. I
found them dead in the long grass. Thought it was a stoat, I did, but there
wasn't a mark on them.

It was then the gentleman that used to have the trout fishing began to
notice there was sick fish floating belly up. That got round to Mr.
Thompson and he took samples of the water and sent 'em up to London.
Clear water it was, all along the river; many a nice bunch of watercress I
picked off the edges in the old days.

We'd all been ever so pleased when the factory came on the old mill site. It was giving a bit of extra work and men stayed at home that would have needed to go and get work in the town in the old days. I remember me saying to my husband why wasn't that there when our boys went off? Once they go, you see, there's nothing to tell of them, they wander off. One of them's in Australia now, a terrible long way, and then there's our Ted. He had a job up in Yorkshire. Yes, I used to think if the factory had only come sooner. And they could have given their Dad a hand with the Sunday milking so he could have lain in bed once in a while. Well, he can do that now.

It was before the samplings came back that poor Rover took his first fit. Oh, he was ever such a good dog, he could bring the cows in on his own. We put him on the rug in front of the fire and gave him milk. But he died. Mr. Thompson, the vet, was there and he couldn't understand it. There was my poor husband with Rover in his arms and Mr. Thompson standing there ever so upset. Mopped his eyes, he did. We were that worried about the cows too.

I found one of the kittens dead the next day, the black and white one. That settled me. I sent off a wire to our Ted saying as how there was trouble. I didn't tell my poor husband but I got Ted's room in the attic all ready. He came the same day and we heard about the sample. Well, they found there was a trace of something, a long name it had and must have come from the factory. Mr. Thompson was ever so puzzled. He couldn't see how so little could have done so much harm. But he rung up the factory and there was a Government man, who come down to see about it. That was the day my hens began to go but they went quick, one big flutter and then dead.

And there was our Ted in a proper rage. Talked about suing the factory. There was nowhere else could be blamed. Two of the cows had died by then, the rest were poorly. Mr. Thompson said we must stop selling the milk. Not that there was much to sell. I gave it to the kittens that were left and wondered if I should have. You know, I kept on catching myself putting out scraps for Rover.

Ted went off up the road to the factory; his Dad tried to stop him, said it wouldn't do any good. But Ted went steaming off and his poor Dad went back to the cows. There was another one going. One of the neighbours was giving a hand to bury them.

Ted was a long time gone. I put the kettle on to boil and then took it off. There was a dead rat outside the door. I never thought I'd grieve to see a dead rat. It was late when Ted got back and he seemed terrible downhearted. 'They showed me the regulations,' he said, 'it appears they kept to them. Took me all over they did. Safeguards. Checks. Warnings. The Government man, he saw them too. Nothing wrong with any of the chaps working there; special gloves and all they wore.' There wasn't anything I could say. He went on, 'You don't know, Mum. Regulations. Stacks of them. So then this is an act of God. Where's Dad?'

But I didn't hardly like to tell him that his Dad was down at the cowshed, cleaning, cleaning, cleaning where the dead cows had been. Taking down the boards with their names — Daisy, Cowslip, Elsie. Burning them.

Mr. Thompson came in. He had been up at the far end of the wood. There was a young fellow there with a pair of golden retrievers, pedigree dogs. The bitch was due to pup in a few days time. It was the same story. Mr. Thompson was worried because old Mr. Hugget at Rose Cottage always had a pig at the back and it seemed the pig began to sicken, so Mr. Hugget took it off to the slaughter house; they didn't see anything wrong with it. Then he started smoking the sides and ham the way he had always done. But what was going to come of it when he started eating the bacon? Mr. Thompson was ever so upset over this. But I couldn't somehow seem to care.

It was after that the newspaper men began to come and we had our photo in the papers. It made a break like for we were feeling that low all of us. The cows were all going or gone. The rest of the kittens were dead. Every blessed one of my ducks and hens. Ted and the newspaper men they began totting it all up in money what we'd lost. But we couldn't think of it that way not at first. It was just that we'd always had these living things round us all our lives. A quiet farm is not a farm at all somehow.

A gentleman came down from the factory. He explained how it wasn't their fault; they had kept strict regulations, and what they were making was ever so useful, a poison spray to deal with some kind of insect that had come from abroad. He kept using long words we couldn't make out. He offered us a cheque for £800 and a paper for us to sign. It seemed a lot of money to me. Most years we didn't make the half of £800. But there was the milk and eggs that we kept for ourselves. I didn't know.

Dad was for taking it, saying as it wasn't their fault and nothing in law that they was bound to do. But Ted came in and he had one of the newspaper men with him. Ted took the cheque out of his dad's hands and tore it right across. All that money! It was vexing.

And the newspaper man he said to Dad, 'Are you aware, sir, that you will have to leave your farm? It will be unsafe for stock for many years.'

'Who says?' Dad asked, dazed like.

'That's the verdict,' said the newspaper man. 'Ask your vet.'

'Of course if that were to turn out to be the case,' said the gentleman from the factory, and he looked kind of annoyed, 'we would see that compensation was on a generous basis.' All these long words, and Dad and me struck of a heap. We hadn't thought. Not of that one. Not of having to leave the place.

But it was true. Mr. Thompson said so too. I have been to the farm since. We try and keep the glass in the windows and the tiles on the roof. But the weeds! You've no idea the way a decent field grows up all anyhow. And coming through in the yard everywhere. Why couldn't this stuff kill the weeds instead of killing our beasts? And you hardly see even a sparrow.

But they gave Dad this job cleaning and caretaking. Maybe you would say it wasn't a man's job. And his heart's not in it right enough. And they put us in a little house with roses and all in the garden, oh ever so nice they've been. I don't know what we would have done but for the factory.

Like It Was

THEY ALWAYS TOLD ME, DON'T GO BEYOND THE TREE.
And pinched so I'd get it in my head. The tree with the rocks round it.
Up top. See? And then Gran would give me a bit of a punch like. So I
never did. It wasn't that near and I'd get stuck looking the other way if
ever I caught myself looking where I'd been told was wrong. I knew well
enough that if I did look I'd want to go there straight off and if I got
there, if I touched the stones or swung on the branches, I'd find myself
going beyond. And then.

But one way and another I never had much time to battle with myself
over it, what with Gran always at me. After a bit I got to know she
wasn't my real Gran, it was all because of some big mistake. Not my
mistake. Something far back. And I wasn't to ask about it. Nor about a
lot I'd like to know. They'd lay into me if they caught me asking.

As well as that, there was so much I had to do and if I shirked it I'd get
told off, not just by Gran but any of them, so I never had that much time
to look at the tree, let alone going to it. Then, when I was older I started
off myself on the young ones, telling them they weren't on their lives to
go near the tree and how I'd wallop them if they did. I had to take it out
of someone, see. But, just because of that, I did begin to look at it myself.
The funny thing was, the tree was always the same size, same shape. I
didn't take notice of that at first, it had just always been there, like a
locked gate, like morning always coming and breaking up our dreams,
and the work bell clanging: things that just repeated themselves. And

then one day I noticed that I was taller than Gran, so next time she tried to punch me, I just gave her a push and over she went. I could have given her a kick, but I didn't. I was afraid of what she'd say to the others. I didn't want to get punished. Said it was an accident, ever so sorry. She didn't believe me, I could see that, but she kept her spite in, for the time.

So that was when I made up my mind to go, anyway far enough to see just a bit beyond the tree, to see why they'd said I mustn't, to see if there was really anything. So there I was, starting off and for a time that tree didn't seem any nearer and I began to wonder, first, was it real and then was it worth it. It looked as if there must be some reason, even if none of them got round to saying it. But why hadn't they?

It wasn't difficult going, no, just a bit uphill. The tree came nearer and I was thinking to myself, shall I touch those rocks? See if they're hard, like, or mossy. Or what. And then it began to look as if the rocks were moving. It looked now like they were animals asleep. Then one of them got up, and it was a cow right enough. A cow. And we'd always been kept short of milk, had to be first down to get more than a drop. So, if there was cows about, who got the milk?

Now I was scared of animals, all kinds, downright frightened of them, didn't know what they mightn't be up to. And all the time those things lying under the tree seemed not to be sure if they were stones or animals. Creepy, that was. And some way, I couldn't see past the kind of ridge that the tree was growing out of, to get a sight of what they'd warned me against. So I just went on, kind of cautious but feeling I'd got to find out about what it was I could see lying around that tree and sometimes it was rocks and sometimes it was cows lying down. Or what else?

Once I got nearer there was this cow smell, strong. I didn't know if I liked it. Maybe not. I went on, quite near, wondering if they saw me. They were spotty kind of cows. One of them stretched out her neck with that floppy bit dangling and her great fat tongue licking up into her nose. 'Stroke me,' she said. Somehow I wasn't surprised, not really. Felt it was just right, nothing difficult. The cow shut her eyes and swallowed a bit while I stroked her and hoped I was making myself pleasant. I even half hoped she would stand me a drink, us being so short of milk, but she didn't. It mightn't have crossed her mind, and I didn't begin to know how one got it out of a cow, or where to start.

I got kind of sleepy, standing there stroking that cow while she heaved and rumbled and sometimes gave me a great floppy lick and in a bit asked me would I like to be a cow? Well, I was a bit scared to say no straight out, so I said well, not yet. Then from behind the cows came another animal, it was a sheep like in the holy pictures they sometimes showed us, and this sheep wanted its nose stroked and sure enough after a bit it asked would I like to be a sheep? And that wasn't the worst of it, oh no, it was other animals, you've no idea. Somehow with the way we were always kept so busy, I didn't used to have time to look at animals, let alone think about them or talk to them. And there's some I can't like, but they all seemed to be there. They'd somehow been behind the tree. All those animals. Not farm animals, no. I didn't know the names for half of them. So that was why I wasn't to go beyond the tree, I could see that now. I got to half expecting the tree itself to speak. But that wouldn't make sense, would it?

Well, I went on saying no, no, to the animals, as was only sensible. Who'd want that kind of life, tearing at one another or getting knifed at the end? Not me. But then, when I wasn't thinking, it was the tree taking its turn, and a lovely smooth reddish bark and kind of scales that lifted off to lighter smoothness underneath. Before I knew there was me stroking and getting the green smell of the tree and when it put the question I just looked up into the leaves, all quivery and live and new and in no time there I was. That tree. And now it came in my head quite clear that everything alive, animals and plants, they'd all wanted to change with me. You see, I'd felt it funny a bit, the way even the grass and the weeds kept clinging and brushing, like they wanted something. And the tree wanted it most. But why?

Now, what I don't know and never will know is how long I stayed inside that tree, being that tree. Silly, doesn't matter, maybe it isn't true. But the seasons went by. The buds all along my branches, hard and sticky, waiting, paining, to burst. And then the leaves coming, staying, falling, and the small flowers, scenting and scattering and leaving little lumps that reddened into berries, slow and certain. Then the pull of the wind, my roots, holding me straight, their delicate ends catching tight onto the crumble of earth. The tree knew loam and sand and peat, it knew the sky's look and the suck of rain. Inside the tree I had forgotten that what I'd come for was to see beyond. Maybe there wasn't any beyond. If there was it didn't matter to the tree. Nor, really, did the animals matter. I saw or maybe I didn't see but I felt some way, how the cows were driven off for milking, rolling over from under my branches, the swing and itch of the heavy bags and the pleasure of eating while the milk was taken out of them, the long chewing and the smell of all warm together.

Other beasts were driven and there was a short terrible moment and then they were dead. It was like that with the old cows too. And some beasts tore and killed each other. It was all right, you know. I understood all that. If I'd once said yes to them I'd have felt the terrible moment too, smelling blood. Instead I smelled green and pale, taste of thin honey. There was no clear end to anything.

Yes, I got sort of dreamy in there, just couldn't bother to be anything but me. And the tree was me. And then that terrible wind came, late in the season when I was heavy with leaf. If it had been winter I'd have got by, no problem. But that wind, shifting, catching on the laden branches, it seemed to put a twist on me. I began to feel my roots pulled and stretching and the earth not holding them. More and more of the delicate fibres that fed me with all the earth goods, were breaking off. Then one of the big roots snapped and the bruised stump came up through the turf. Nasty that looked and felt, sickening. Yes, then I began to feel a bit queasy, not quite there. There was the crunch of the root coming up and through and then my trunk, my beautiful smooth trunk, beginning to lean over and the leaves shivering, the twigs tensing for the crash that was coming. That, at last, came.

But me, myself, the way I'd looked at myself, well, somehow I'd sucked up all the strength of the tree, all those slow seasons back. So I just walked out among the broken bits. I stroked along the trunk, picked off a few scales, but I knew it wasn't me any more. That tree was finished; I knew that. I wasn't going to do anything about it. There was a bit I'd learnt, by now. If I'd listened to one of the animals, I'd have changed its way, that was sure. Instead of getting tree strength I might have got beast strength, fighting and hiding or eating all day and being part of a herd, not ever getting beyond.

Now I stood up and looked with my own eyes over the edge of the world at shapes which maybe I wasn't meant to understand, but all the same I might come to terms with them. Yes, it seemed somehow I'd be able to make them part of my own strength. This was what it was all about, what they didn't want me to do, no way. But why? I picked up some of my own leaves and looked at them: pretty things. Before, when I was the tree, I hadn't thought of them as separate. They'd been part of my breathing and growing, kept busy on taking in and sending out. Like, I thought, I'd been before all this. Now those leaves could go back into the soil where other trees could use them again. I knew that. It was all right, what I wanted.

I started to walk back and I knew I was strong, much more than when I'd started out. I knew my own bones and guts. Right, then. I saw Gran coming at me, angry. I thought, she's trying to scare me like she used, stupid old cow, like as if I was a kid still. Just for a breath I felt the old fear twisting in me. And then I thought of the other old cows, the ones that got driven away at last and made into shoe leather. She just had time to shout, 'You went beyond the tree, you saw the rocks, the animals, you naughty girl, you!' Just like before.

I had to stop that, see, for the others as well. The first time hadn't stopped her, only made her worse. This time I'd got to make sure. I took a swing at her. It didn't seem anything much, but I was tree hard and down she went, screeching and screeching. I was pleased to see her on the ground and I let out one good kick to her face and that was it. I got it right this time. No more Gran. I just thought once, if it had been my real Gran. But it wasn't. Just something I was told to believe.

So I just went on. Past those bad places I'd known. There were some kids around. Good if they'd the guts to follow me. But will they? I don't know. Up to them. Two of the others came up, tried to stop me, but, me being solid like, it didn't do them any good: tore their hands on the bark, or so it looked. Stupid to try it. Yes, that was the end of them. So why'd they try to stop me? Why'd I let them all that time ago? And me working for them all the years I was growing. It seemed nothing but silly now, something I'd grown out of. Maybe some of the kids might have another think now, seeing it was so easy. Might pick themselves up and go out to the tree. For there's bound to be a new one out there: stands to reason.

Can't say it matters to me, how I look. Never did. How you see me, that's all, and your choice. Nice for me to be moving free, hands, leaves, that's all the same . . . Don't look up if it makes you dizzy, it doesn't matter to me. Just you go the way you want.

If you're looking for me, here I am. See, if I get kind looks, I'll shelter you, feed you, help you. You'll be all right with me. Just take care not to touch where my root broke.

After the Accident

NATURALLY I KNEW THE CHANCES. IT HAD ALL BEEN
plotted with a standard margin of error and for those who, like myself,
knew which ancestors had been in fallout areas, the probabilities were
reasonably clear. Of course many of the mutations were lethal, though
not always at an early stage but when they were late-stage, one might be
involved in considerable unpleasantness. So it was better to avoid the
whole thing. As a young girl I had been somewhat obsessed with this:
inevitably it took me into history and biology. Once one was aware of
the connections, the tension eased off.

But I was affected by the Better Humanity writings and tele-
propaganda. I saw this return to genetic normalcy and advance to super-
normalcy as something desirable, deeply clean, to be reached for. And I
was well aware of the flaws in my own make-up. Most of my friends had
the same problem; most of us had been constrained, reluctantly on the
whole, to turn down date-mates whose heredity would have increased
the problems. If a man appeared to be lying, as some of them did, lies
being so much a male weapon, it was easy enough to check up on the
probabilities. The records were open, at least in our sector. Occasionally
one of us would take a chance, but there was always an element of guilt.
Those who were genuine Better Humanity converts had of course to
agree to instant destruction if the result was not perfect. And how seldom
it could be!

Naturally we dated and all that, but did not mate, and, as time went on, found a certain lack. In this comparatively empty world which the Great Accident has given us, we wished to give and not merely in the matter of data, observations, and synthesis. We wanted to people some of the new spaces, as they became tenable once more, to sample some of the new growths, the genera of plants for which names had perhaps still to be found, to see how rapidly adaptation and selection could take place. Above all we wanted to meet some of the cut-off communities who were also in the Better Humanity network, not merely over telecommunication but face to face. Yes, how we wanted to give! To be fertile. But — Better Humanity? There were moments when we shivered away, back to other dreams.

My own sector had barely been space-interested. Before the Accident space travel had made sense; the beginnings were there; now it had become academic. And yet, once the techniques were there, even on brain level, it was not possible to disregard them. At least not for some.

That was how Hari arrived, gliding into my life like a virus into a cell. But — a virus of happiness, delightful, but as impossible as other viruses to control. He had managed an inter-community capsule, of a kind none of us had envisaged. Both it and he were new. I took him off and he did not seem unwilling. Nor would I have expected him to be.

He had been working on one of the main space-travel projects; his own capsule was a by-product of this. The work was slow of course. So much had to be improvised: not the ideas but the methods of carrying them out, especially now that large-scale power methods were no longer possible. Many of the necessary raw materials had quite simply been destroyed during the Accident. Others were in no condition to be touched. And the space projects needed considerable groundwork. It was only gradually that I realised that under Hari's lightheartedness there was a feeling of hatred against the makers of the Accident which was even greater than our own.

We all have hang-overs from earlier cultures. There came a time when Hari showed me a small ivory carving of one of his goddesses — Kali, I suppose — with a recognisable head of a late twentieth-century statesman in each of her eight hands. Three were Asians, four were European or American, one was African. I wondered whether there would have been exactly the same choice had it been made elsewhere. But I was more interested in the ivory, whose grain I recognised. 'Have you seen one of them?' I asked. 'Dead,' he said and added, 'One of the central vertebrae usually snapped. The main leg bones were adapted to the weight, but if they got into wet ground which they usually did, looking for fruit trees or high crops to eat, the strain on the middle of the spine, which took most of the weight when getting out of the mud, usually did the trick.' He looked away from me and went on, 'The one I saw had fallen on two or three houses; it took us a day to get it off. I was still a student in those days. There were some children squashed into mud. Yes.'

'Are they all gone?'

He nodded. But I would have liked to see an elephant fifteen metres high.

Most of the worst giant mutants had been destroyed or more usually had died out because of their own inability to come to terms with their environment. But there were occasional lurkers in the less populated zones. Such really nasty ones as were left were almost wholly aquatic, since water is more accommodating than land to large displacements and easier to hide in. We used to read sometimes about swimming in seas or rivers in the old days, surf riding and above all underwater exploration. How wonderful it must have been! I ask myself whether pre-fallout people ever realised how fortunate they were. Such activities are hopelessly dangerous now.

There was still work to be done on many other mutants, especially of course the bacteria, which had developed with predictable rapidity. Some had to be eliminated, but there was always the danger of fresh invasion. And there were the happy-making viruses which, however, had to be strictly controlled, as we learned through some very alarming periods of trial and error. But at least we biologists were never bored.

Some of the work we were doing was quite new to Hari, and of course there are few things more enjoyable than explaining one's work to an intelligent listener. Quite apart from little things like the sudden, excited movement of a hand catching at one's own, the bright widening of deep brown eyes, there is the mental effect on oneself: new aspects are suddenly uncovered; something which has puzzled one for weeks shows itself in a curious flash, which, if one could catch it — and this was largely a function of the listener — short-cut hours of plodding and worry and fake analogies. But such exchanges of intellectual sympathy must be mutual. I listened to Hari talking about space travel, and listened just as carefully when my fingers were also tracing his eyebrows or pushing back his black wavy hair.

It started from his explanation of the simple, but to us new, technique of his inter-community travel capsule, which traversed the danger areas where fallout reactions were still predictable. After his account of the type of travel mechanics and propulsion, he began to talk about the plans for landing on heavy and light gravity planets, of which the former seemed most likely to have possible atmospheres and some kind of life. Much of this was based on work done before the Accident, but now perhaps we could get a calmer and longer term perspective. There had even been some survivals of plants which had been specially designed for human food during space travel and on arrival. And here came the next step: the colonists.

It would be at the earliest fifteen years, at latest twenty-five, before any possible start; we could not get together the enormous and costly pre-accident space-travel gadgetries. In fact our methods were based on a different philosophy of techniques. But training for colonisation would take a long period, in fact it could not be started too young. I did not see where this was leading until Hari explained that he had looked up my records. He seemed to be rather ashamed of this, though I could see nothing wrong with it. Such records are, and must be, public. Apparently this was not entirely so in his culture, at least for women. He had equated with his own. There was a very high probability that the gene pattern would be such as to produce the perfect high-gravity colonist, almost legless and with certain other modifications from the normal human evolved for an earth environment: the ideal of Better Humanity.

Would I?

I went through a difficult time. At first I was deeply shocked, I could not bear to see Hari again. Then I did see him one day, standing very still, looking desperately sad and carrying a long piece of silk. I had of course heard of silk, but had never seen it, or rather only in one of the collections where it had partly crumbled and did not appear at all desirable. We had, after all, plenty of textiles. But it was interesting and attractive, and so was his sadness. He did not speak a word of what had upset me, but when at last I spoke to him, he told me that this was the kind of dress which his sister sometimes wore. As a matter of fact it was quite true that he had a sister; I saw a picture of her, a tough girl in lab jeans carrying a spanner. But quite possibly she did wear this kind of dress sometimes.

I did not put it on at once. He held it up and played with the silk, which certainly produced beautiful reflections. I touched it with one finger. He threw an end over my shoulder, and his fingers brushed my neck, accidentally on purpose. No doubt if I had genuinely not wanted him I would have reacted badly.

But I did not. I let him dress me in this silk: this fancy dress so different from standard lab wear or play wear. I became confused, the length of silk wrapped me and tripped me. He began to talk about his sector of humanity. Much of India had escaped, or had not escaped but was now habitable, and being cleared of mutants. I began to think I wanted to become somehow involved in it. And then he was showing me gods and goddesses in deep colour stereo: pictures one could wander into. Not that Hari believed in them as such, any more than I believed in my own religious hang-overs, some of which are pretty enough. Yet, as I fixed my attention his gods began to affect me. And I wanted them to.

By the way I have not yet made my work clear. I am, of course, a biologist, but I was also developing a technique of intellectually aware appreciation of historical objects and artefacts, which could lead to a reaching out into past lives and consciousness, which could in turn clarify historical problems, especially those where one was quite out of touch with contemporary motives. It was particularly useful in dealing with pre-fallout situations where our ancestors had allowed themselves to be pulled into the most extraordinary and evil activities through religious or political convictions.

Some people said all this was pointless: better to ignore the incomprehensible past when we had so many of our own immediate and directly fascinating problems. I remember an argument I had about this with Motaba, a friend of mine. I had been concentrating on something directly concerned with some of her ancestors: the impact of the Christian missions in southern Africa. I had come across some old letters — so curious, which archives did and which didn't escape the Accident! — and I was concentrating on them, especially the slight change in hand-writing when certain highly charged words occurred. I was now looking for typed material of a slightly later date to see if this change would still occur.

'I wish you wouldn't!' said Motaba, one fine-boned hand on mine, but oddly a different shade from Hari's, who was, however, not a cross.

'You're getting angry,' I said, 'why?'

She said: 'It was all such a waste! Five generations back — only that — my grandmother's people had to become Africans again. It was good that they did — No!' She caught my eye. 'Not good, Chloe. But it had to be done. Because of what you are reading about. But it made my people do horrible things. Horrible!' Her face went into a twist. She was thinking of a story about a mission which had not withdrawn in time and of her great-great-grandfather, who had started as a mission-Christian but ended — well, it was all over. Or was it? The story hurt still.

I said: 'What I'm trying to do, Motaba, is to reconstruct the reason for the missions first going in and then staying on.'

'To open a door to trade,' said Motaba bitterly.

'Yes, yes, dear Motaba, we know all that and it's a bore. I'm getting down behind it. You'd be interested if you could bear to think about it.'

'But it doesn't matter any longer. Everything's changed. We're different. My people were converted by the mission. My people tortured and murdered the mission. That's past. Nobody could behave like that any longer: like my people or like the mission. We've moved on.'

'Sure?' I said.

'Yes! We've moved on to molecular bounce. Oh, Chloe, it's so marvellous, isolating the states; when it all clicks together. It's not in the same world as murder and conversion — is it? So why bother? Aren't you thrilled about bounce, much, much more than those old letters?' She was excited, she pulled my hair gently. Yes, bounce was all right, but conversion was still real.

I said: 'We have to know everything about belief and conversion reactions because they still go on. You're keen on Better Humanity, aren't you, Motaba?'

'Yes, Chloe,' she said, clearly trying to be truthful but to keep all emphasis out of her voice.

'And I am considering becoming pregnant with a mutant,' I said.

'No,' she said, 'No! Even if you are so much in love —'

'But I'm not,' I said. 'Only I'm thinking of leading an experiment.' She covered her face with her hands, muttering something to herself. I rubbed it in: 'A mutant, quite a long way off standard. Now, Motaba, remember your great-great-grandfather.'

And I felt that she had, that the shock which was greying her lips came from deep in. And it was something which I shared; we had all accepted part of the ideology. It was fascinating, for I could feel the same thing, but attenuated. The converted soul coming up against a nasty fact. Yet we were in a civilised environment. But how civilised was it? Where was the breaking point? My research on the letters might give me some of the data for that.

And, using the same techniques, I began hard concentration on Hari's gods and goddesses. There was the eight-armed Kali again brandishing the weapons of technology. There were beast-headed avatars, many-faced Siva. The four-armed dancing god Hataraja was more beautiful than a normal, indeed a perfect, human. There was the inelegantly bodied but attractive elephant Ganesa, there was the half-human monkey, and the lion with the head of an angry, overeager man. There were protruding eyes and tongues, semi-serpents. There was also a very strange trio of gods from Puri in Orissa, and they, above all, were like some mutants, stump-legged and stump-armed. At first I was alarmed and half angry, clutching out of their reach toward Better Humanity. Then I began to accept them, as I had accepted Hari's silk.

I knew it was all on purpose. I knew that Hari and his whole space-travel setup had planned this, talking it over carefully; they had made the pictures of the gods, and I was not the only object. I knew that Hari's mind was not on me, but far ahead on his high gravity planet. Not that he would be there, only his children. But that was as it should be, between scientists. Yet I could not have accepted it without a certain degree of thought-changing, of alienating myself from earlier resolves. I ask myself, could I have accepted if Hari had moved with less beauty, if his sadness and quivering joy had not affected me so deeply, if his hands adjusting the silk, had avoided the delicious nerve touch? Is a true answer possible?

During my pregnancy I asked him many questions. He wanted more colonists and I helped him to find mates among my friends with suitable genetic make-up. Another genotype was of course necessary for those who would act as mechanics during the space voyage, probably doing repairs, internal or external, while in a state of weightlessness. But Hari was not a suitable parent for these; he had to concentrate on colonists. Apparently it had not worked out with any of the mates in his own sector: all had produced lethals. However, this was partly due to sloppy methods of recording and partly to the fact that they had apparently no drug like our neo-thalidomide, which would allow potential lethals to develop. The only thing they used was a local extract with a somewhat uncertain action; it had not yet been at all thoroughly analysed. In fact, it may turn out to be better than neo-thalidomide. One does not know yet.

At an early stage I had an amniotic fluid analysis; a lot could be discovered from the chromosome arrangement — or misarrangement. It appeared that the predicted result of the meeting of zygotes was happening. Looking at the chromosome pattern, it seemed to me probably male, but certain elements were jumbled about and unclear. I could not be sure. And if the colonists were to breed successfully, sexes must be separate.

I began to take neo-thalidomide. And yet, every now and again I was shaken. Perhaps all women, in some curious way, suppose that their first pregnancy will produce a divine creature, something of consummate beauty and worth. The experience of many centuries has not altered that. This time I knew that, whatever I gave birth to, it would not, by human standards, be divinely beautiful. Yet it must be given love if it was to survive and have the confidence necessary for its task. Could I manage that?

I was concentrating meanwhile on Hari's gods and on the state of mind of those who had made them, who did not insist that divinity could only manifest itself in the perfectly human. And I was not neglecting my work on the African missions. I was watching Motaba and her reactions to my pregnancy, my deviation from the genetic norm to which she had given the enthusiasm of conversion. But now I thought that I had better be more certain and asked for an X-ray. While I waited I explained that this was an experiment, designed to solve some of the problems of space travel.

Those who had seen the earlier chromosome analysis had assumed that I would discontinue the pregnancy, if it did not discontinue itself, as it would probably have done without the drug. The research physician in charge at the centre was herself a very keen Better Humanity convert. The walls of the clinic were covered with stereos and even imaginary pictures of the recognised ideals, in the several branches of mankind and their crosses. I noticed that India figured less than Africa as a basis of mixture and was obscurely annoyed.

There was some surprise that the pregnancy had continued. The X-ray picture of the foetus showed a colonist. What I had intended. But I was suddenly afraid. 'Don't you think, my dear,' said the physician in charge, looking very gravely at the shadow picture of the still curled foetus, 'that this experiment has gone far enough?' And for a moment I almost said yes. 'Stop taking the neo-thalidomide and the thing will probably abort on its own. We'll look after you. Give me the tablets, Chloe.'

I can remember how near I was to putting them into her hand. But I remembered not to. The interest of the experiment succeeded in containing my fear; I reacted as a biologist. I said, 'I don't think you quite realise the nature of the space-travel difficulties.' And as I said this I suddenly knew that the foetus with which I had doomed myself, if that was to be part of my reaction, was not forever: its destiny was not of this world.

There were weeks and months more to go. Motaba was still not reconciled. 'It is the example,' she used to say. 'You may have good reason, Chloe, but others might be encouraged to — to mate thoughtlessly.' And then she added, 'As I almost did once.'

She told me about that, how she had longed for a child, tried to persuade herself that it might be normal; but her gene pattern was too bad. She had given up what she so deeply wanted. And I saw in her the recapitulation of African conversion, as it might have been her great-great-grandmother. They, as it happened, were almost unaffected by the Accident; the damage came on her European side. She looked so deeply sad that I could do nothing but say, with formal hate: 'The Accident Makers.'

'The Accident Makers,' she answered. It was these occasional moments of ritual anger and intention of violence that were sometimes all that kept us steady and orientated towards life.

At my next checkup I had confirmation of something that I was beginning to suspect. The foetus was developing into something very broad. The shoulders would make a normal delivery impossible, especially for a primipara. A Caesarean was simple, but if I was anaesthetised it was possible that the malformed — or rather, experimentally formed — baby would be destroyed, and I could not risk that. If only I could get hold of Hari! But he was now occupied with the fourth of the possible mothers and, as I knew, something beyond logical persuasion was necessary with each. I thought of getting one of them to stand in, but felt it might be too much of a shock and could induce them to terminate the experiment. One of them was an old friend, but less stable than I am. I knew that Hari had encouraged them all by telling them that I was the first experimenter, the leader of the team, and I have a good reputation as a biologist. He and I, discussing it, felt that six possible colonists might do for a start. It could be seen after a few years how they were developing and whether the same or a different type of genetic pattern should be used for the next batch.

However, I spoke to all those who were likely to be present, emphasising that this was the first stage of an experiment in applied genetics. And then Motaba said that she would like to be present. She did not express it, but clearly she had the same fear as I had; and her loyalty to her friend was stronger than her loyalty to her moral feelings, if one could call the Better Humanity drive that. And I recalled a passage in one of those old letters about a lapsed convert who also, guiltily, was loved and helped. But would any of them, tangled as they were in the Better Humanity principles — most doctors had become involved — be entirely trustworthy with — and now I said it to myself clearly — my child?

I went under the anaesthetic with considerable latent fear. I dreamed of rushing along cliff roads, and in and out of caves, under a treble moon. I knew this was the landscape of another planet. I knew that the air was unbreathable before I was plunging into prickly darkness, clutching for something — something. I woke and saw Hari's face upside down. 'She sent for me,' he whispered, sloping his head at Motaba, who was also there. 'She could not trust herself. But how could you keep me from this stage of the experiment?'

'Where?' I said, 'where?' For I could tell by the pain which was beginning to be apparent that the operation had been concluded.

Motaba picked up something with tight shut eyes. Hari said, 'The first colonist.'

'Is it,' I asked, 'male or female?' Obviously it would be incorrect to say boy or girl.

'Definitely male,' said Hari. So I had been correct in my view of the chromosomes.

'And otherwise?' It dizzied me to move. Motaba pulled the wrapping back and her fingers were trembling; tears crawled down her cheeks. The head appeared thickened and slightly flattened; this was to be expected and need have no effect on brain volume or content; the outer ears were an odd shape, which might be the external sign of a useful modification of the eustachian tube and inner ear.

'Leg stumps,' said Hari succinctly, 'arms shortened, some digits absent, but can grip. Spine as decided. Shoulder and pelvic bones modified. Congratulations.'

For a minute I swirled back into sleep. It had been a success. And disconcertingly I dreamed that I had borne a normal human baby and knew that this was what I wanted on one level, but could never have. Yet, thinking that I had achieved it, I woke. And saw Motaba's face of grief and accepted the truth. 'Give it to me,' I said. I touched its pale brown, very delicate skin. 'What do we call it?' I said to Hari. His eyes too filled with tears, in spite of our mutual success. I wanted to cheer him. 'I know your sector calls their children for their favourite gods,' I said, 'but we can't call this one for Krishna. Clearly.'

'Clearly,' said Hari, with a shake in his voice. 'Not Jaggernaut,' he said, and I knew that we had both thought of the black, stump-legged god of Puri, 'That was never — living. Make it Siva. Of the many avatars.'

'Yes,' I said, as the first colonist opened blank bright eyes from under its heavy brow ridge. And then it opened its mouth and yelled: for me. And my heart turned over. It was my achievement. My child.

Out of the Deeps

IT WAS OF COURSE THEIR OWN DOING. NOT THEIR fault; that would be meaningless. But when they crawled out of water, when they started to copulate on land, developing arms and legs and at last brains and hands, the thing was there. Communicating through air by voices they lost communication through mutually touching water; they lost the great echo belts far down round our liquid-enveloped mother; that made what followed almost inevitable. Almost, for they had a glimpse of what they had become before the end came to them. We tried to show them and teach them. At first, as with children, we played games with them, even allowed them to shut us into enclosing spaces to learn communication. Yes, we even tried to communicate through air by voices like themselves, though a few of them were learning our way. Strangely, they thought they were doing us a favour, they felt they were superior. A large deep sea octopus will sometimes do this, waving forty feet of suckers, and the same is true of some of the sharks, but it is not a very pleasant thing to communicate.

It had taken hundreds of years and terrible pains to get so far with them. They had come on our bigger cousins whom they called whales and murdered them with every possible cruelty. But our cousins too tried to show them better ways, the sacrifice of self, refusal to leave the gashed and bleeding, the screaming body of the harpooned child. They clustered round the ship, heavy with plunder of what had been living flesh; they attempted to communicate, to show forgiveness, to be willing to be friends. It was useless. For a time the slaughter was so terrible that we were compelled to hate them although it already seemed possible that there was a chance of fellow-feeling developing. But as the slaughter dwindled our hatred rationally dwindled with it. It is productive of nothing to continue hatred: a pity for them that they could never learn that lesson. Instead, they always had to have enemies. That had become a necessity to them.

Our forefathers and foremothers, whom we of today were then, thought about their land-living, handed fellows with brains as big as our own but with this terrible inheritance of enmity and violence. It was most extraordinary. These human men and women knowingly lived in intense discomfort, crowding all together in what they called cities, making cell structures out of cement, like corals without beauty. This they did although it had been put into them by their genes and from very far back, that each must have a piece of territory, a space that he or she owned exclusively. A strange thought but coming on to land had made it inevitable. Now the crowding and the wish fought with one another in their minds. The land which they supposed they owned gave them food of many kinds in great plenty, as well as beautiful and ingenious toys with which they could do many kinds of things that they took with great seriousness. But here too this pattern of ownership overcame sense in their use. The more they had the more afraid they became of some others of their own species taking it. Even when they became able to communicate with our fathers and mothers they could not drop out of these far back patterns, which might have been of use in the days when they were a struggling species, but had now become as stupid as sharp fangs on a grazer.

Remembering back into the body of my far back mother I know that she was determined in some way to save the land dwellers, all the more because it had become apparent to us that their toys had developed into objects of terrible danger, certainly for them, perhaps even for ourselves. She allowed herself to be caught in a net. The meshes were painful; they trapped and twisted her beautiful fins. But she succeeded in relaxing and in time was loosed into the water so that at least she could move; she was at that time expecting to give birth to a child.

It was not unpleasant in the space and there were others of the ones they called dolphins, many from other seas, who let her know what had been happening and how ill or well they had succeeded in their task of communication. There were several humans swimming with them whom they found pleasant, playful and eager to learn. These humans had set up useful toys to help with the problem; there was already some interchange of ideas, though both sides found the sounds made by the other somewhat ludicrous. The humans also saw to it that our food was plentiful and to our taste, so that one or two of us who were not genuinely set on perfecting communication became lazy and would only play. But none of the humans were attempting to hurt us. Thus my mother was assured by all her friends that she had no cause for anxiety; insofar as she might need help at the birth of her child all was prepared.

All went well with this and the humans were particularly delighted with the child, which was a lively male; my back mother allowed them to touch and measure him and in this way became in closer sympathy with one of the male humans who was called something like Djon. After that she and he spent much time learning to converse, for their advanced communication might be called that. She liked to feel him when he swam beside her. His skin was thin and changed colour and he needed to come up often to breathe; he was a good playmate. But he appeared to be anxious and often split-minded, as though part of his large brain was elsewhere on some other problem.

By now ourselves, the dolphins, were no longer kept in the enclosure but were out in the open sea. But naturally as our object was the furtherance of communication with humans with a view ultimately to getting them into an easier and more sensible social and moral position, with regard both to ourselves and to other humans, we stayed with them. My back mother and Djon communicated for hours every day. Often he would ride on her back, which was a pleasure for both; apart from words each could sense if the other was tired or depressed or for that matter happy. She became more and more convinced that something was wrong, was making unhappiness, not only with him but with the rest of the humans. So did the rest of us.

And then gradually the whole picture became clear and horrifying. These humans supposed that they had an enemy; they feared and hated this enemy with something akin to madness. They thought that this enemy would attack them by water in huge and dangerous toys that went below the surface and which the humans could not see and therefore feared the more. The fear had sent our friends into wickedness, which they knew, themselves, was abhorrent. But others, who had power over them had planned it. This plan was that we, the dolphins, should be made to feel friendly toward these enemy toys and should approach them. But each of us was to carry unknown to him or herself a deadly container that would burst, destroying not only the underwater thing of the enemy and all the humans inside it, but also the dolphin carrier of the deadly material and indeed any other inhabitant of the nearby water. No wonder Djon was unhappy. Because in his odd human way he had grown to love my back mother and indeed the other dophins, and yet he thought he had to destroy her because of this insane hatred which fought with this love.

The child was still suckling but was beginning to eat fish and other normal food. She felt he could be left. The essential was to stop this madness. We too planned, while pretending to the humans that we were reacting as they wished. Several of us offered our services and our backs to be ridden, for it was clear to us that the only way to intervene was to show these humans that the others whom they thought of as enemies were truly the same as themselves. Yet it was a long way to the land where the supposed enemy lived and we were doubtful of our powers. Then suddenly a new chance appeared. A large toy belonging to the enemy, as large as an island, had, they said, been sighted. It had done nothing dangerous as yet but they were afraid, oh, they were deathly afraid of these other humans so like themselves.

Quickly we got together, my back mother and those of the rest who were most anxious to help; all began to play with their special humans, got them to mount on their backs. Then they set off toward the enemy, eager to help toward human sanity, thinking they could explain to both sides. On they went, on, and became aware of mounting terror and anger and then that their riders thought that somehow they, the dolphins, had become part of the enemy, were owned by the enemy. This was so strange that at first they could make nothing of it. My back mother and her friends tried their hardest to communicate, to explain their purpose, but were met by intense anger and fear. One of them riding had a belt with a toy in it that spat fire and death; he took it out but Djon cried out to him that he was sure my back mother on whom he rode, whose sea-smooth body he felt between his gripping legs was no spy, no enemy. They shouted at one another and the rest of us tried to make them hear us and we came nearer and nearer to the dark island of the enemy humans whom we wanted our friends to meet and understand. We thought that was possible. It was not.

Suddenly from the large toy of the enemy there came a noise crack, there came death. For the enemy, equally afraid, had thought that we and our riders were attacking them like a school of South Sea sharks. The foremost dolphin and his rider were both killed at once. One or two of us dived, slipping our riders off, but my mother knew that she could not take Djon to the depths since he was constantly having to breath air, and she would not leave him. In this way they died together, their blood in one stain. In this way my back mother again became one with the great ocean, with the deep echo-layers, with past and future and most, with the future that was still immature in her male child, who was in time my grandfather's grandfather.

In the next few years other attempts were made to bring sense into an increasingly mad human situation. With more difficulty and less success, although there were always a few humans, who in their dim way, understood the danger they were all in. Ten years. Twenty years; the long running of waves between one shore and its opposite, the land dwellers hoping to destroy one another. Our cousins the whales did what they could and the seals, who are not large brained and could not understand the urgency, helped a little, so that something came through to the few humans who lived in the very far, very cold north, and to a few who for some odd human reason were engaged in digging out earth and making their elaborate, peculiar toys in the equally far south. But not to the many millions who crowded and feared in the cell cities and were not happy with the toys that they had made.

Thus the end came and we, forewarned, were in the deeps. Here and there was breathable unpoisoned air, though some of us died with the humans whom we had tried to protect from themselves. The land died. Nothing could live there. And slowly the seas cleared and emptied of any human thing. There are no more of the dark, death-dealing floating islands today. The waters are ours with their past and their future. We do not mean to leave them. A few humans are left in the two cold ends of our mother but we do not think they can meet. Not yet. Perhaps in a thousand years when the middle barrier of destruction eases a little. We hope so and we are trying to teach the few humans so that by that time they will become more dolphin-minded. Ourselves, going far below, can pass the barrier. We have had to start again to show these humans that they can trust us. If they can be brought to help themselves by understanding, we will tell each group that far away there are other humans, not enemies but infinitely to be loved and cherished. One day perhaps humans will start again knowing that out of the waters, from which they should never have come, helping will always be theirs.

The Valley of Bushes

THREE TIMES DURING THE LATE SUMMER THE OLD
women made the hearths for the fires, carefully smoothing the special
clay over them. The girls brought in the bushes, pulling them with great
attention root and all. Then on a calm day came the burning and at last
the sifting of the ash. This was hand work and special songs went with it,
always curiously muffled by the fine, beautifully coloured material of the
masks which all wore on these occasions. The light ash was tossed and
scattered and then came the sieving of the darker, heavier part and on the
sieves, made and used for this alone, appeared the nodules of metal which
had run together in the heat of the fire.

The girls and younger women learned the songs, some praising the
cleverness of the plant which had gathered the precious and dangerous
stuff out of the soil, some telling of their great-great-grandmother — but
how very far back was she? — who, taking the shape of an enormous
butterfly, first whispered to the plant and learned what it was doing.
Sometimes these huge blue and bronze butterflies still came and all
gathered round and watched and praised and were glad, speaking with
low laughter to one another over what secrets might be being passed.
There were many other butterflies that came and it was always possible
that one of them might also one day pass on some simple and enormously
important fact. A special butterfly: something or someone else disguised
as a butterfly.

Yet for the moment all went well. The sifted nodules, praised and handled and washed like small infants, were taken downstream to the men, weighed and beaten together into such shapes as were considered luckiest. All the handlers, men and women, wore gloves, beautifully made of tenderest kid skin; these were stripped and left in running water, down-stream of the village. Nor did anyone eat or drink during the hours of burning, sifting and packing. These rare metals which occur here and there through Earth's surface layers, are often poisonous when their natural scatter is gathered into visible form. So it was in the Valley. Fortunately, the effect on the lungs was minimal, though the masks were always worn.

After their shaping, the heavy pieces were packed into leaves and then into kid-skin cases; after that into baskets ready for their journey over the mountains. The traders at the far side were equally careful. What happened at a further stage of the trade was not their affair. On the journey back came presents for everyone. There were guns and silk and medicines, including spectacles for the elderly, tools of many kinds, down pillows and brandy and finer woollens and furs than any from their own valley; instamatic cameras and small expensive bottles of scent and torches with spare batteries and hand mirrors, watches, salt and sets of chessmen, for there was much chess played in the evenings; cases of such fruit as they did not grow and beautiful sparkling drinking glasses and fine Chinese washing bowls, jars of honey and ginger and new kinds of musical instruments, though they did not care for transistor radios since the sounds that came from them were uncouth and in jarring rhythms. Not seldom the men brought back plants which might prove useful: as the coffee plantation, the better bananas and nuts, the opium poppy to be used in moderation during the winter months and many roses. But never never to encroach on the preferred ground of their own bushes.

Often they heard stories of wars and religions in the outer world and felt happy and cosy not to be part of it. They also heard about aeroplanes and helicopters and had seen many pictures of these both in war and peace. It was clear to them all that such things were not welcome. It was clear also that they might all the same come to the valley and that plans must be made accordingly. There was no surprise then when the speck in the sky was sighted and watched as it grew and came lower.

'This it? You're sure?'

'Yes, we're going to find out what we can. Then back. While the weather holds. These mountains —'

'Yes, next time. With the money raised. In force. But we have to have samples. There's a man coming!'

'Yes. Apparently unarmed. And several women. Looks all right.'

They tried several languages — both were good at this. The third man followed but said nothing — languages were not his thing. In fact he was a botanist or had been, but there had been an unfortunate incident involving a misclassification. So now he was doing a bit of trading, a bit of painting, making notes for a book that never got written, reading old copies of learned journals and trying to make up his mind whether or not to stay on. He kept wondering what truth there was in the story about the bushes and if so which they were. Certainly some plants, especially perhaps marine ones, but also a few in singularly unpleasing parts of Australia, have unsuspected powers of collecting minerals. But this particular one! The chelating agent must be most peculiar. Well, they must see. There were in any case some interesting botanical specimens around in the Valley, quite apart from their particular interest.

The two crew men stayed by the 'copter, occupying themselves with the engine. All that had been arranged and paid for. The others went ahead. Quite soon communication was established. After all, those who came down to trade were bound to have a large vocabulary so the trading language served insofar as it could be stretched. It was not known what kind of government there was in the valley, but probably a chief and council in some form. Naturally gifts had been brought.

The man took them down to the main village; it was attractively built with well smoothed timber and nicely trimmed thatch. There were even glass windows — trade no doubt. More people, both men and women, the latter mostly elderly but handsome and well dressed with silk showing at neck and wrists of their heavy coats. They were brought into a large house where food and drink were offered and accepted, the gifts laid out and inspected with interest but not so far taken up by anyone. There did not appear to be a ruler of any kind.

The third man had hoped for a tour of inspection and yet it might be unwise to raise the question of the bushes so soon. As evening came on more food was brought and now the possibility of the visit to places of interest was raised. And what did they want to see? Ah, now, this was it. Although samples had not specifically been mentioned there seemed to be some embarrassment. All three were aware that the elderly women were listening — had they in fact understood? Did they know the trading language? Had they ever left the village? The men appeared to be quite pleased. 'What have they said?' the botanist asked. Suddenly he was thinking that if this expedition turned out as they all hoped, if above all he could get a specimen of the fabled bush, if he could isolate the chelating agents, he would make up his mind, he would go back, he would have a place again in the scientific world.

'Tomorrow, they say.'

'To see – everything? They admit that it is true?'

'Oh, they were quite open. Seems we shall have a conducted tour.'

'These old women —'

'Might be some younger ones tomorrow!'

The evening meal was delicious. Local herbs must have been

extensively used in preparation of the game stew; the botanist tried to identify them by the smell, sniffing at the excellent gravy in his carved horn spoon. Beside him one of the elderly women patted his shoulder and smiled. There were comfortable rugs to sleep on and indeed it had been a somewhat anxious and tiring day. Now one could relax. They slept. The next morning they did not wake.

The men of the valley went back to the 'copter, this time with guns which they trained suddenly on the crew men. 'Go!' they said.

'Where are the others?' one of the crew asked in the trading language but backing away towards the 'copter.

'They are staying here,' said one of the men. 'You go!'

The crew men had wisely insisted on payment in advance so they got off as quickly as they could. It was a near thing getting over the mountains but they made it and in time reported to the police, not that anything was likely to be done.

The expedition was suitably and quietly interred. Several of the elderly women appropriately veiled went through the wailing as was only proper for guests. As the earth was being shovelled on it was noticed by one of the old ladies that a very large blue and bronze butterfly, that rare beautiful visitor, flitted out from the trees and dipped for a moment towards the moist loam before taking its way on.

'She has come once more to greet and say goodbye,' said the old lady, deeply satisfied.

Somewhere Else

THAT WATER HAD SOMEHOW CHANGED A LONG TIME ago. If it had ever been just ordinary. But yes, they said once upon a time it had been drinking water. Good water. Clear, nothing in it. Or had it been? Nobody really knew: not when, not why. Better not to ask, not to talk about it. You had to live and that wasn't always so easy, though certainly it could always be done if you followed the Rules. But the Rules made it boring and straight-lined. That was what it looked like to some of the kids. But there was something you might get to know which explained things: there are a lot of selves in just one body and a good idea not to let them all out. That was established grown-up conduct. Established politics you might say.

So: the lake was there, the water. It was called the pond because that made it look smaller, more containable. A pond was something people could some day handle. Perhaps you could even drain it off if you were prepared to get wet. But that was something nobody was prepared for. Not after what had happened or seemed to have happened. But that too was a long time ago.

'How long?' young Fred asked his grandfather, old Fred.

'Before my time,' said old Fred, scratching in his beard. 'They said the skin came off their feet. Kind of eaten. Other things too. But all that could have been something, well, not how it was. But could have been. Nasty though. Right nasty. Don't you go near now. That's a Rule: see?'

But of course young Fred wanted to. And if he did, it was the same with Madg. Or Mad as her brothers called her when they pulled her hair. Young Fred didn't pull her hair, or not often. He told her things instead. He had somehow been learning things, but not the proper exam things which were all in words with meanings nobody would ever want to know about. The exam was all ancient history, boundaries and politicians with funny names, Queens and Prime Ministers, conferences and treaties and shouting and money figures so big they floated out of sight, so you couldn't believe any of it had ever mattered. Exams were what you had to see but couldn't use, not ever. No, not like you use crops and shelter and play inside the Rules, welcome to incomers if there was enough over, and ways of easy dying at the end. Exam history was a kind of huge decorated set of ladders and platforms with silly names, not real at all though you weren't allowed to laugh at it, oh no, not till after the exam and then you mightn't want to, not, at least, if you had got to the top and out.

But Fred had been getting at old piles of books that it was nobody's business to throw away. What was in them was mostly something called biology, but not in its proper place which was safely inside ancient history and only to be carefully used by those who could be trusted and who had been through the exam and out at the other side. That is to say it might be all right for people like old Fred himself, who knew more than you ever credited him with about the living earth and also about the living atmosphere, but that wasn't something anybody wanted to discuss, yet you had to know that long unhappy word, though you didn't say it. It might be all right for some of the communicators: but not for you. Well yes, part of it was about cows and sheep and that was good. But never go beyond. That was a Rule, wasn't it?

There had been that time when the communicators had got everything wrong about what to expect and a lot of people had just died. Now it was better; you knew what to expect and also just what sort of biomass to produce for your own survival, as well as how to keep the makings for a different type for next time there was a roll-over and a kind of earth and atmosphere environment which meant a different kind of crop and stock handling. Yes, the communicators had got some bits right. They knew when a roll-over was due. Old Fred gave them credit for that. Funny all the same, to think there had been times when people in one part went on living the same, growing the same, more or less, for nobody had counted how many generations, keeping the same kind of biomass to fit themselves into. But that was in another time and somewhere else. Every time there was a change and a roll-over it was God's will, or so the communicators said when it happened. But the new ones knew quite a bit more. Why? Well, did you have the right to ask? Old Fred just laughed.

It was easiest to go on the same way. But old Fred had a suspicion that young Fred had been having ideas. He had spoken once to his grandfather of those books he had found jammed behind the history books and biographies and maps of places that didn't even exist any longer and all those stuffy old dictionaries in the school library. Full of ideas, those books were, talking to one of the lad's other selves, waking it up. Maybe a good thing. Maybe not. Better for him to wait till after the exam; he could surely keep himself quiet for that long. You see, old Fred had been nudging young Fred into being a communicator. Himself, he hadn't quite made it when he was a lad, a bit too clumsy with figures, but he knew plenty about it by now. More, he had friends, was always the one to welcome communicators when they blew in, talking their own kind of language, knowing what the extra words meant.

Schools were supposed to teach words, not meanings. But sometimes they taught meanings by mistake, and as often as not that made for wrong answers in the exam. Once meanings get loose, kids pick them up. Those books ought to have been put right away where nobody could get at them. Some fool teacher ought to have done that. But all the same. So long as young Fred got through the exam and then got noticed by the communicators. But old Fred could fix that. That skinny kid Madg picked up from young Fred but had the sense to keep her trap shut at home. Just as well really. They hadn't wanted another girl in the family. Old Fred had got her out of a walloping once or twice.

Exam time was coming near and the school had got edgy, at least the ones that wanted to get on. So why did young Fred make up his mind that now was the time if he wanted an answer about the pond, instead of always being shut up, even by his grandfather? Well, it was partly because he'd seen that if the exam went well, you'd be squeezed, only one self allowed out. Of course, it was a good squeeze in some ways. You'd get more things, if it was getting things that you wanted; a bigger share of the cake, the biomass and all that, and to be respected, that is if you like respect, and if you can keep your other selves from getting out. And then, you might end up as a communicator and that was all right or supposed to be. You'd know when the next roll-over was coming, wouldn't you? But it meant being chosen. How? Well, young Fred hadn't bothered and of course the way it looked, it was right out for Madg. She couldn't even have spoken about it, not to anyone. You only get laughed at, get smacked.

In fact she only talked about that sort of thing to young Fred and a bit carefully even to him, and of course to her cat. In the time between long ago before the Pond, and now, cats had somehow got brainy. Able to communicate. Or so some people thought, at any rate some children. It was very early morning before anyone was about, that the two of them started out to see whether the whole thing was a nonsense. Or not. Four of them if you counted the cats.

They had nicked enough for eating until it was over: whatever it turned out to be. That had been young Fred's job; there was never enough to spare in Madg's family. But old Fred always kept a bit by him, in case something turned up. For you never knew, did you? They didn't say much but walked along the road until it took a bend, and they knew quite well why it had been made to do that. They just looked at one another and went on. Then they followed a path which might once have been a hard road, but now all sorts of spikes and prickles had crept over the edge and narrowed it so that they had to carry their cats. It was full day by now but not very bright. They even had a little whisper and look round, but there didn't seem to be anything wrong, not yet.

But then they began stumbling over nasty great lumps of bricks mortared together and bits of metal among them, you couldn't tell what for. Young Fred was just going to pick one up, a kind of pipe it looked like, when his cat jumped and bit his hand. 'We could be getting near,' he said, and kicked the pipe carefully with his boot.

'What do you think it will be?' Madg asked.

'Don't know,' said young Fred, 'but we got to see, haven't we?'

'That's why we came,' said Madg, 'but my cat, she's worried.'

Fred nodded. Both of them knew that the cats would somehow know of things that they themselves wouldn't know, because people didn't have certain kinds of pick-up. That was why cats were important as well as to be loved, why almost everyone had a cat. Old Fred had three.

Then they were over a kind of lump in the road and a bit of brick wall still standing but being pushed over by tree roots and thick brambles. There were big trees here, but it looked like most of the lower branches had been broken or maybe nibbled. You couldn't see far through them. Then suddenly you could; there was a tree down and they climbed on to it. 'There's the Pond. Nothing much to it,' said Madg in a voice that she made flat, not pointing one way or the other. Young Fred grunted. The cats were wriggling against their necks and digging claws into their jerseys.

It looked kind of all right, a nice bit of water you might play in. There were ripples, sure enough, but that was the wind, wasn't it? 'Could be deep,' said young Fred.

'Could be,' said Madg, and then, 'We've seen it. Doesn't look much.' It was a kind of question.

'We got to get near,' Fred answered. But as he said it his cat stuck a claw deeper and gave the miaow than means "no". They looked at one another and crept a little nearer, one hand stroking a cat. The ground under the trees looked a bit funny, holes here and there, earth pushed around, almost as though someone had been at it with a spade. Now they could see a mud bank, greeny-brown strands wet along the water's edge. And beyond? A ring of water moving. Something seemed to be coming out and as they kept on looking it seemed like a nasty shape. Too many legs. Or pincers. Or eyes. Sort of scaly. Could they be real?

Madg's cat jumped straight out of her arms and up a tree and almost spoke. Madg almost understood. She jumped for the branch, caught it, slipped, saw another of the same coming out, got a toehold on the main trunk, was half up and there was young Fred there already giving her a good pull and the cats snuggling and it seemed to be all right.

So long as there was nothing that climbed. But there were more coming out, wet. Out of the Pond, here and there. And when they came close some of them looked — if you could bear to look — like the small things that live in ordinary muddy water, like you could fish them out and tread on them if you wanted. Because of you being bigger. Being people. But now they'd got big and you'd stayed the same. For a minute or two you didn't see them and then one came pushing through the leaves and seemed to be smelling round the tree trunk, tried it with one of those legs. Both cats jumped to a lower branch and spat furiously, then made a big effort and did a pee and shit down onto the crawlies. That seemed to clear them off quick. 'We could do that,' said Madg, 'if we had to.'

The cats came back up, shivering, then found a higher branch. It was better, you could put your feet on the branch below and lean back against the main trunk. All right unless — well unless those things could climb. If they climbed up behind where you couldn't see. But the cats were moving round, taking care. And it seemed that the beasties were finding enough of what they wanted, digging into the ground mostly. Young Fred was whispering: 'Those walls and things we saw — my notion, long time ago they made something — it got into the Pond.'

'But what? What did they make?' she said.

He was thinking of something he had read in those books he oughtn't to have read: an odd word. 'A mutagen,' he said, 'some kind of chemical that acts on the cells: what we're all made of. What we pass on, you and me or — that lot. Altered their eggs. Looks like these ones could be the sort to have had eggs. Changed the pattern a little. So little you couldn't have seen, not at first, but in all that time between long ago and now it got to be a big change.'

'I see,' said Madg, trying to imagine all that great loop of time, and then pointed. There were other things coming out of the pond, one quite close. It was lizardish with great golden eyes and a ridge along the back. The cats mewed fear and anger, but Fred and Madg watched carefully. By and by one of the lizardies reached up a long pink tongue and pulled down some leaves, then settled on them and ate messily. Just leaves. But it reminded the two kids that they were hungry; they shared a piece of bread and a thin slice of cheese. Fred said: 'We ought to be getting back. The exam —'

'I shan't pass anyway,' said Madg, 'I know it. But they'll hammer me at home. Just because I asked to try. Anyway I'm not going down. Not till those first things are back where they belong.'

'Let's try the cats' way. We can pee from here. You can, too?' She nodded. 'And I want to take the stupid old exam. And you must too, see, Madg. Let's work on it. What we'll be asked. Let's go over the Queens. They always ask something silly about them.'

'They just put them in to make us think we girls had a good time once,' said Madg. But all the same they started on them: Assolutina — blonde. Bellefronta — mid-blonde. Condrophile — auburn. Despolasine — brunette. Everingia — ash-blonde. Fragolifolia — deep auburn — And Good Queen Goo. But they stumbled a bit and stuck on L. Still, it took their minds off whatever else might be coming out of the Pond.

The day turned hotter and there was a kind of film on the surface of the water. You couldn't see properly to the other side. But it did seem as if some of the things which had come out were going back in. The cats seemed more settled. 'Shall we go?' asked Fred. Madg nodded, she was getting stiff, bits of bark sticking into her. They decided to pee on the ground before climbing down; it would be safe after that to wait a few minutes to look out for the best way back, uphill a bit, keeping clear of everything that didn't look just right. Fred had a good strong stick, Madg had stones to throw, there were plenty lying about. The cats jumped onto their shoulders. They started off and even laughed a bit. Maybe they wouldn't see a thing.

Then Madg's cat gave a sharp warning cry; out came her claws and her teeth showed. In front of them was a dreadful yelping, a pain cry. Both ran towards it, then stopped short. A fox cub, newly coming out from its dark nest, is forever nosing at new things, poking and smelling at them, and this had just happened. Now one of the pincers shot out and gripped him, then there were two, from two of them, one tight on his foot, the other at his nose. What did the cats think? The cats thought come away, come away, danger, leave it! The two humans felt this, felt it strongly, but they couldn't just go, no they couldn't — the fox cub was like them, ordinary, red-blood, furry, crying. They had to help! But how?

Fred hit out with his stick, but hadn't got near enough and there didn't seem to be a soft place, he couldn't make the pincer shift. His stick broke on hard kind of scales. The eyes on their stalks waggled at him. Madg got closer, though her cat was clawing to stay up on her shoulders, was spitting and screeching. She shut her own eyes and hit down with her sharp stones, first one, then the other. That was better than the stick because whatever it was let go of the fox cub's nose, but turned at Madg herself, waving pincers. She yelled and jumped, but it scrambled at her, got her by the foot, but luckily over her shoe. They were old clumpy shoes, too big for her, but she'd stuffed them with socks and she kicked hard with the other foot. Then young Fred was kicking too and suddenly the pincer-thing was knocked right over and the under-side with all the little waving legs was soft and heaving, trying to right itself, and the two cats leapt on it with all eight clawed feet and in a moment its insides were scattered and torn, pink and yellow, and it was dead and the pincer let go of Madg's shoe.

'We got to get that on its back!' gasped Fred, and knocked with a stone at the other; so did Madg but it didn't work until Fred got hold of the struggling, snarling, twisting fox cub and pulled both it and the pincer beast right over, where the cats could jump in and do their thing. For a moment the cub lay on its side, released but bleeding, exhausted.

'We ought to splint the leg, it's broken' — Madg pulled at Fred. But the little fox had twisted and leapt clear away, back to its earth, dragging one leg but fully alive. It had given Fred a nasty nip, but the teeth hadn't got far in. 'I'll do you up!' Madg cried at him, but wondering what with.

'No!' he said, 'no time — come on!' and caught her hand while the cats jumped onto their shoulders again. But were they going the right way? It was uphill, that was all right, but where were the remains of whatever it had been, the bricks, the pipes? Both stopped long enough to find two good sticks that wouldn't break easily and more stones. Which way now? Fred's cat pushed her face hard against his cheek, made him turn. The trees thinned out enough for them to see. In one place there were three of the pincer-creatures digging, throwing up earth. They kept well away, hurrying, Fred's arm feeling sore, but what of it. And then Madg stumbled over a lump of brick edgy under a moss heap and they knew they'd got safe. In a few minutes they could run and the cats running beside them instead of weighing them down. Oh they were tired.

But they didn't stop till they got to the real road, then Madg pulled off the leg of her knickers, which were a bit torn anyway, and did up Fred's arm which had almost stopped bleeding. They found a pool, ordinary water, they were sure of that, and washed as well as they could and petted the cats and washed their claws because of what might be on them still. 'Will the little fox be all right?' Madg half whispered.

'I think so,' said Fred, 'only a bit lame.' And he thought now, it was funny, if it had been up near the sheep they'd have shot it. But down here it was like one of themselves, like a person. Not changed. So one of your selves would have killed it, another self would have saved it. And which self was thinking now of the pincer beasts? He went on: 'I wonder if there are others. Down in the mud. Or if —' But he didn't go on. It was clear enough what he was thinking. After a bit he said: 'You know, Madg, here we are, just outside whatever happened —'

'Whatever goes on happening,' Madg muttered, half to herself.

'And back home they're getting by, having just enough of everything. The right biomass. And the exam. And doing the same things everyone else does. And, you know, the Rules. And not asking questions. And all the time —'

Madg nodded: 'Yes, all the time. And they wouldn't believe. I couldn't tell them. Could you?'

'There's one or two I could tell. Or half tell. I just might. And all the cats will get to know. They're pleased with us, right enough, aren't you, cats?' The cats purred unmistakably. 'Maybe they won't be so bad to you at home when they see the way the cats think. You might even pass the exam.'

'Me? No way.' She was wishing now she hadn't asked so hard to be let try it.

'That old grandfather of mine, him I'm named for, he might think different. Even about you. He might think you'd pass. It's him I'm going to talk to. Made up my mind.'

'About — all this?'

'Yes, about this. He kind of knew I'd be bound to do what we did, the two of us. And he might have some way —'

'Don't tell me he can fix the exam! No, not even your grandfather.'

'But there's beyond the exam. There's the communicators.'

'Oh Fred! Would you want that? To be a communicator? Like — like being caught with pincers. Or catching other people. Almost.'

'Don't Madg!'

'The communicators, they make the Rules, don't they? That's kind of pincers.'

'Madg you can't go saying that!'

'Yes I can. Now! You want to be caught, Fred? Or catch other people?'

Fred looked round, caught her hand, whispered: 'I wouldn't be caught. Not me! Maybe I'll drop one of my selves, that's all, only not my real one. I've got ever so many! So've you, Madg, if you once get to see them. You don't believe me, Madg. But we bashed them, didn't we? It's all part of the same!'

'Fred, you are a one for talk! Would you still speak to me if you got to be a communicator? I tell you, I'll get proper lammed for this. Before they notice what the cats think. My Dad and my brothers, they mayn't even let me try the exam. Oh well, we'd best get along. Anyway, I've seen something they haven't. Couldn't have.'

'If only what we'd seen had been something — well, something nice. It could have been.' Fred was suddenly feeling very sad, very soft about Madg, very fond of her.

'Maybe if we'd waited long enough?'

'Thousands of years, that would be. I know that now. Don't you go home, Madg, till I've seen my grandfather. Then he'll come with us. It's going to be all right. I just know it is. All my selves know it. And — and now we've seen the worst about the Pond. Once you know that you needn't be frightened. And one of your other selves can see how to use it. When I'm a communicator I'll do just that. Madg, I'm feeling wonderful!'

'Are you?' she said. 'I wish I was.'

'You're going to be. I'm seeing to that.'

The funny thing was, old Fred seemed to have smelled they were coming. Stood at the door and pulled them in quick, both of them, not just young Fred. 'Well then,' he said, 'what was it?' He sucked at his teeth while young Fred told him. 'Damn lucky,' said old Fred. 'You go breaking the Rules. Asking. Looking. You got to wait till after the exam. Wait, I told you, didn't I? Like seed. Not your spring-time yet.'

'The cats know,' said young Fred.

'Them cats,' said old Fred, and fidgetted about a bit. Then he looked at them straight. Both of them. 'Well, if you're that kind — both of you —' He glared a bit at Madg, chumping with his teeth, and she tightened herself for whatever was to come. '— You just have to pass the exam and then — You, girl, you don't go home. You stay here. I'll fix it.' And suddenly Madg's cat began to purr ever so loud and its paws kneaded softly into her shoulders.

'But — but —,' she said, thinking about her brothers.

'Scared, are you?' said Fred. 'After you killing one of — them things. All for a fox! Stupid, aren't you? Never you fret. I'm fixing your Dad. And those brothers.' He nodded at the cat and saw the girl take a deep breath and get her colour back. Odd that it was a girl. But that's how the penny drops. Shoes, she'll need. Maybe a skirt and jersey. Can do. As to the exam, that wasn't difficult, not with what he knew. About certain things. And people.

'You don't speak, not to anyone,' he said, frowning at young Fred. 'Not till after. Not anyone. See?' And then, speaking to both of them: 'After. And if you think that pond is the only one, I'd have you think again. I'd have you think about the biomass. Not just here. Somewhere else.'

He went over to the cupboard. There was a cold pudding. Good though, nice bits in it. They were hungry, so were the cats. They finished it up in no time. Things were kind of almost all right. Best of all for Madg.

That's as near as I can come. Yet.

Conversation with
an Improbable Future

YOU WANT TO KNOW ABOUT TIME BLACKOUT? HOW
we managed those space journeys which take so long even in our own
little planetary system, and intolerably longer further out in our galaxy?
Those were the years of the first space age when it became clear that there
must be some way of bridging the time gap between earth — dear old
Gaia — and — there. That problem was, in the end, solved. But it was
only the beginning. You know that?

Yes, you want to know how we deal with the time factor in deep space
beyond our own thinking and imagining? Still more, beyond yours.
Well, I will try to make it clear and not use words which had not been
invented in your time. In fact I will try to make it, what you might call,
human or domestic.

This business of time black-out was not always as simple or as
reasonably safe as it is now. It had been clear for a very long time that for
real space exploration, not just dawdling round our own solar system,
and after that our own rather disappointing galaxy where so few systems
had taken the necessary steps towards producing life, something else had
to be found. So, human beings having spent so many millennia in
problem solving, this one was tackled.

Valuable lives were lost or badly damaged before anything
approaching total control of the ageing process, which is the human
measure of time, could be achieved, and ageing held up during the period
of unconscious, unmoving existence. At first when it ended, there had

always been severe damage on parts of the total being which would, for one thing, make it totally impossible for those so treated ever to act responsibly, in a human way. Damage extended from the still unexplored complexities of the brain to other centres. The willing experimentees might well have regretted ever recovering consciousness.

Remember, it all started on a small scale, trying out and discarding methods, some of which had given appalling results. That went on until it was safe and sure. Hundreds of years. Not all scientists are interested in space exploration. I am not, myself. There is so much else. But hundreds of lives went into time research. Thousands, almost as many, as brave and more farseeing than those who died in the old useless disasters of war in your time.

I believe that the best way to clarify all this is to tell you something about myself and how I and my closest relatives were affected by the actualities of space blackout. But remember, although you ask to know, I am not an expert in this subject. I only know what everyone knows. That is, everyone in my time. My own special interest and knowledge is of something else. Otherwise we could not now be communicating.

The experiments of space research had to go on. So much of the human impetus which in early days went into destructive activities such as the exploitation, both of the remaining riches of our own Gaia and of the human mind and imagination, and of course the final obscenity of war, now strained up to the furthest unknown. Risks had to be taken. New kinds of pain had to be produced and if possible assuaged. There were always enough volunteers to take the appalling risks. We are proud of them.

Gradually some of it came to be understood. First, the lapse of a few months, then a year, ending with a complete waking to full energy and remembrance. Experiments in Terran laboratories were about to be replayed in shorter flights in our own galaxy, which might mean, say, a five year black-out. But in every space-ship (as they were then called) there were others who would remain normally conscious and ageing in what must have seemed almost a prison, who were responsible for the voyage. The complete black-out of a whole expedition with the navigation totally under automatic control was still to come.

But come it did. This was the beginning of space travel as we know it now and shall go on knowing it. Had it not been developed by our honoured and infinitely courageous forebears, we would never have had the possibilities which we now have of making communication with other intelligences and sensitivities.

It became increasingly obvious that the apparent impossibilities of inter-world or inter-universe communication had to be solved at the same time as those of the total black-out of the crew. The actual problems of unmanned flight were solved rather quicker as nonsentient working parts usually stick to their jobs even in unusual conditions. It became assumed that unmanned flight was the only rational option. Everything was set for early and totally dependable warning of any object, however tenuous, within measurable distance. It was of course nothing like visibility, but would react to any possible sign of otherness.

Then came the great jump. At last we need no longer think in the old terms of light years. The new terms were of total destruction and total reconstruction. There were centuries of controversy about whether it was a true continuity of life. Some very odd ideas much like those of some early religious systems were being re-considered, since some of these seemed to be making the same kind of picture of what was involved, which was as far as we could get at that stage. But of course we had to reckon to get out of our galaxy and into the chosen one, on the exactly chosen satellite of the exactly chosen sun or even major planet, which meant that all the humans must be awake during the critical times. For this was when unforeseen things might happen. So it was normally the leader of the expedition who set his or her self to be the first to end the black-out. If all was going well the next thing was whoever was to make the coffee, a pleasant little ritual that almost all groups stuck to, so that it would seem to be a normal waking. There would be jokes about breakfast television, dating back almost a millennium, and for some a kind of reconstruction of a last breakfast which must have been so many years ago. Sometimes there were tears.

But here a little of the training that the expedition had gone through came in to help, switching all minds from past to immediate future, into possible, even probable, danger, but assured excitement and in-volvement. Well, I am only setting down this bit of history for those who take it for granted that everything has come easily, that in fact things were always like they are now. We forget that people in even a slightly earlier day may have had other feelings.

Today the usual pattern is for the old-fashioned time black-out procedure until the expedition arrives at the limit of our own galaxy, or rather at one of the insetts between it and deep space. Then the new technology takes over. This means that some Terran time has elapsed. After that, time, as we think of it, has no meaning in the otherness between galaxies. Does that seem impossible to you?

I want, here, to shift to something else which was recognised in your time, but became much more important in mine. This is an introduction to my own story which I shall tell so that you will understand some of our space age problems. We now know considerably more about animal, and specifically human, bonding. I mean that between adults and more importantly that between mothers and children too young to have any but maternal bonding. In our time, most women who decide to have children give one or two years of their life to the first bonding, which means the assurance of love for the life-time when the child, having this base, can and does reach out for others. As you know, our life expectancy is rather longer than yours. When it comes to space explorers, these Terran interludes do in fact keep many women in splendid shape for certain essential kinds of work, research, artistic achievement of various kinds, sex and motherhood, above all for inter-species or inter-world communication. Continuous space exploration is apt to alienate people not only from Terran affairs, which may be a good thing, but also from easy Terran contacts. Women especially come back for a reasonable length of time, at least a single passage of the seasons, the beautiful Terran seasons, thus keeping the necessary Terran feelings in a normal state. It takes at least a month to absorb the inevitable, sometimes painful, changes, including those in one's own family.

I remember well how it was with my own mother. After her first, very successful expedition, when she had managed some communication with a new life-form, she had stayed on old Gaia for almost four years, partly, of course, in preparation for her next voyage, but also to give birth and bonding to two children of whom I myself was the first. She had as usual opted for a girl. But it was both of them; my father was, I believe, almost too excited about the whole thing. Indeed I think he still is, when I see him. But I have very vague childhood memories of him, though my psych-tests show him up quite well. But his expedition left soon after my brother was born and there was a long gap. It can of course be awkward for a really bonded pair if their home base times fail to synchronise at all. This happens rather too often for galactic well-being, or so some of us think. Now, for instance, our father has been out of touch for some twenty Terran years and we cannot expect him back, they say, for another five. That is if all goes well. We all know we have to avoid anxieties about which we can do absolutely nothing.

Still, there I was, a developing three year old and my little brother almost two and well aware of dear Gaia, the lovely world about him. We have both been to a memory clinic, so as to have our baby profiles filled in. That was exciting; it always is because people often find something, usually very small, but all the same important, which has to be put right. In fact I had an odd little thing to be dealt with: alarm at heavy rain drops coming down a window and out of sight. It had never been spotted.

Anyway I got a clear feeling of my three year old self. It seems that the birth bonding of mother and child, which leads to the expectation of loving relationships between all humans, was a success and by three years old I was totally capable of making and keeping friends. My brother was almost as well bonded as I had been, but it might have been better for him if our mother could have waited another year. However her next expedition was due to start and she had to have the final pre-flight month of intense preparation. Anyway, by now I was out-going, making all kinds of bondings with people and with the many lovely animals of Gaia.

So the severance was harder for her than for me. She took a whole case of mini-holograms of both of us, using up the usual space for personal music; this she could normally share with someone who had the same tastes. Indeed I think she had holograms of most of the family and friends; there is always an enlarger on any space voyage. But those old holos, which I am keeping, are not up to modern standards.

Apparently neither of us baby children noticed her going in any damaging way. We still felt the warmth of the bonding and transferred it to others. My brother — that is, Peachy, the architect who is responsible for the third Mars station, which some people don't like but others rave about — came out with a small element of suspicion. But I must remember: you don't know about him in your time. This suspicion of other humans sometimes flares up, but less now that his new bonding is working out so well. I wish you could meet Peachy's bonding; she is really gorgeous.

So we grew up and began to be watched and to acquire appropriate skills. I was into the Arts. I loved dancing and by now found it more fun to dance with boys. So what would our mother be like after eleven years away from us? And after the process of destruction and re-construction which we dimly knew about but somehow felt was impossible? Killed and come back to life (for in a sense that is what it is), could she be a real person? Anyhow it was going to be very, very exciting and what dress should I wear? Peachy said not to be so silly and pretended not to care, but worked himself up in spite of what our very sensible advisers were saying and doing to help us. Eleven years — so now we were almost grown up. We stared at the holograms, wondering. Would she now be like her half sister, my aunt whom I loved, who had a few wrinkles about the eyes and mouth and was beginning to get tired more easily? It was the same with the mothers or bond guardians of most of our school friends; Terran life length was pulling them down. I knew our dear aunt was bound to be much older than her sister, who had already been on two expeditions, but surely even our mother must be showing some signs of middle age?

And then she came and she didn't seem to be old at all. She was just like the old holograms except for the scar up her leg and we didn't see that until a few days later when we were all swimming. I managed to ask her. It is clear that no healing process takes place during time black-out. Sometimes of course a body may be in very bad state, so that the waking is inevitably into great pain and danger. That's just one of the things we have to take into account. Mother's hurt leg was still itchy, I know, and so probably was the remembrance of what had caused it. That unwelcoming little planet!

When she first hugged him, Peachy bit her. Of course he got over it very quickly, in fact he still refuses to believe he did it. But she and I were friends from the start. After all, she was physically in her twenties; there wasn't much of a gap between us. In no time we were talking and laughing together like old friends and I was so proud of her, showing her off to my school mates.

She had some information which was of deep interest to the top planners, filling out or explaining the many records she and the rest of the expedition had made five years back, on that planet, though it seemed like last week to her. Once she woke up crying out after a dream of the thing which had curled on her leg and left the scar, even through her space uniform which should have kept anything out. One of the others on the expedition had it across his wrist.

She settled down with us for a year to start with, enjoying the wonderful colour changes of the Terran seasons, back now to what they must have been before that terrible bit of history that we call money-and-bombs. I am not sure yet whether you yourself have actually passed through it, or if it is still waiting for you. I hope the former.

Yes, those years when our mother came back were a marvellous time for us, a new playmate, someone to be totally loved and trusted, who didn't get tired the way older people seemed to do, who could dance all night, swim all day, and whom we could surprise and delight with new songs, games, art objects, ambitions. After a while she began to tell us about the expedition; it was so different coming actually from her own live self, not just a programme. Questions, questions! We were enchanted, wanted to go on for ever. We loved our aunt, her half sister and our bond-guardian, and were aware, somewhere underneath, that she would mother us again, once this new mother left us for her next, already half-planned expedition, which we could feel was always there at the back of her love and our trust.

What does all this do for people? I think it helps in the necessary process of freeing ourselves from wanting things, above all wanting to love and be loved in an exclusive and permanent relationship. This is growing up, becoming wise in the classical sense. We mustn't hold on, but, living and loving, we must take all possible risks. Few of the known space explorers died in bed or in Terran surroundings, the bosom of old Gaia. But many of them are still active in work or play long after their great-great-grandchildren are no more living — unless they too are space dwellers. Luckily perhaps, the explorers, those who can face the reality of disintegration and re-integration, are rare. Often the strange longing, not to be contradicted, skips a generation. Peachy, for instance, has a daughter who is steadily going that way. She is basically a geologist and I wonder if those genes come from her grandparents or through her architect father always hankering for new materials, dreaming about them and what could be achieved if — . But by the time his daughter might have found them, he would be too old, his architectural imagination dried up. It seems that we may still have misapprehensions and muddles and miseries, in spite of all our good intentions, because at some point in our lives we seem to ask for them. But perhaps they are needed or we wouldn't know how lucky and happy we are most of the time.

Our mother only stayed with us for two years; we knew it couldn't last and towards the end of the second, among the blaze of autumn colours, she was sometimes, it seemed to us, deeply elsewhere in the nearing shadow of the black-out and what lay beyond. They were going back to the same galaxy and the same hot little sun, but to a new planet which they had sighted, watched and measured, in various ways. The general assessment seemed promising; it might well be less inimical than the last one and it might even be possible to establish some kind of communication, the essential aim and prize for any space explorer. That scar had started to bleed and afterwards had taken its time to heal completely. But she never let either of us worry about her. That only started after she left and then not until the time when there was a nasty space disaster — but not to her expedition. Our aunt was very good about it.

It had taken mother some months to get back to physiological normalcy, but after that she returned to ordinary Terran monthly rhythms, usually timing with my own. We used to laugh about it. This, of course, always stopped during voyages. The one she was looking forward to was her third expedition and I was well aware that she was caught, she could never want to give it up now. Her work and reward was the increase of knowledge and understanding between Terran and non-Terran life-forms.

Of course it was not necessarily the humans who managed to break the communication bar, but some of the various animals at the main communications centre. There are some delightful families of dogs and jackals which are particularly keen about this and well accustomed to space surroundings. There are otters and a few bears. It is thought that the whale population may be equally good at communicating, but it has its practical difficulties. Perhaps you don't know about this. Your relations with the rest of the mammals are not I am afraid always happy. We do better. Yes, and there is one elephant who seems extremely competent. He did a wonderful job on one planet where the inhabitants had developed in a curiously parallel way. He wants to go back there.

Mother's first expedition had been very rewarding on communications but not this second one. She had tried various techniques, but never managed to break through. She had also used various risky methods. Very risky, but useless. It was in trying out one of them that she had acquired that wound on her leg. Yet in a sister planet all might go well.

That first expedition had been so marvellous; she had been going over all the results and videoing what she could during her first pregnancy with me. My father had been on the same expedition, but as a geophysicist. He and she had argued endlessly and happily and had ended by deciding on a baby. When she told me about it, I began to understand how she had hoped in some way to influence me, her unborn, to be a space explorer. But that hadn't worked. The genes said no. Yet when she talked to me about this first expedition, I kept on thinking how old is she, really? But what is really? I found myself, in spite of our warm bonding, just a little frightened.

So I became certain of one thing. I was not going into outer space. I didn't want to. It was too big, worse, it changed people. I wanted to do smaller, more compact things. At that time I did not know what, but I did know I was good with my fingers, and that some space patterns and some colours seemed to go together and make me gasp with pleasure and interest. It was my dear aunt who showed me ways of manipulating, not only these colours and patterns, but their caught shape as well. It was then that she told me that she and my mother were almost the same age. I could hardly believe it. She was still a good walker and rider; she had one of the new hybrids, a lovely, intelligent creature who could for instance do simple arithmetic, and really enjoyed being ridden, the faster the better. But my aunt's skin had aged and wrinkled and her hair had lost some of its brightness. And there seemed to be interesting things that she wouldn't bother herself to understand.

When I was old enough to ask her those kinds of questions, she told me she had never wanted children of her own, but had love to spare for others, the love which Peachy and I took for granted. In spite of that love, we couldn't play with her as we did with our so young mother, nor expect the same kind of reaction. At the same time we felt that our aunt was someone who was well able, if and as we needed it, to give us a hand on the steep road of growing up. Of course we had other advisers and teachers, but while our mother was back with us we didn't see so much of them.

And then she was off again, on her third expedition, and all the games we had been playing stopped being fun. We knew she was still loving us, but she wasn't there. There were things which we knew, suddenly, we would never do again, not without her. We had gone into another stage and had shut the door.

It was a longer gap that time. We were into our late twenties, knowing what we were going to do with our lives, working fairly hard and very enjoyably. Peachy was having his first taste of success; he was mad about materials, discarding some on aesthetic or historical grounds, adapting others; he was on the edge of a girl problem too. And I — I was trying out what I could do and being encouraged — I think that doesn't always happen in your time. It wasn't only my aunt; there were plenty of people with time to listen and advise or explain and they didn't hurry me. First I started as a jeweller and then as a potter. I was entranced with the shapes I could make and that others could make or had already made; my aunt insisted on keeping far too many of mine. I loved playing about with some of the new crystals and metals and minerals brought back from space expeditions, so many light years, backward or forward of our own Terran ones.

And then I became deeply interested in some of the time problems, but I didn't know quite how to tackle them. Only this was leading me into museums and into absorbing art history. I wondered, rather uneasily, if we were really doing any better than, say, the early Chinese. Obviously our lives, our social behaviour, all that, were infinitely better, but what about our art? How did those Chinese men and women, so far back, do what they did? What was motivating them? How did they think? So this put me right back into communications, my mother's thing, but through time, not space. It could be communication, first, through objects, holograms, books, the vast stores of videos and poly-videos and then — well, we are communicating, you and I. Perhaps not very well, but I feel that I am translating fairly well into your idiom. Yes?

So, by the time our mother came back, we were both settled into our own lives, fascinated by our own problems, taking risks and sometimes succeeding, discussing with colleagues or being quite alone, thinking.

So here was mother with these curiously old-fashioned ideas and actions and of course wanting to tell us about what she had found out and seen and achieved, but somehow not quite realising that we were in some ways ahead of her. She looked, well, embarrassingly too young; her movements seemed wrong. We got impatient sometimes, but our dear aunt somehow kept in close touch with her sister, although she herself was settling into gentle ageing, her hair whiter than grey; yet her mind was still acute, though with odd little gaps. She was still working on her interests; she had been a botanist and sometimes she was able to give me valuable information about Terran flora, especially the plants which had either disappeared or been mutated into later forms. I always loved talking with her.

As for our mother, things did not work out quite as well this time and I believe, from what I have seen, that this is not unusual. Somehow, although the first maternal bonding was still there, we were embarrassed by this young woman who had actually given birth to us and for whom we were always, in some sense, children, as we had been, in her time-scale, so lately. I always managed, I think, to make a quick adjustment, but Peachy became embarrassed and rough and probably hurt her more than she let us guess. Talking to my friends, I am sure that this is normal and is one of the almost inevitable social difficulties which sensitive modern living has to cope with. Gradually we became very fond of her, teasing her now and then, though Peachy sometimes got very impatient. Of course what she had to tell us of her space exploration was always interesting, though less so to us than to her colleagues at the Centre.

I didn't tell her much about my cross-time communication ideas. I didn't want her to over-ride them with her own. Though perhaps I was unfair. Probably she could have helped me. But I had not yet worked out exactly what would be needed. Especially of course putting our input into terms understandable by our forebears who lived on Gaia so long ago. And almost destroyed her. But somehow avoided it. Why? How? We keep asking. So our mother left us again. She was hooked, as most of the space explorers are.

Our father visited us too. The first time I was eighteen and — well, I fell in love with him. This isn't unusual. He parried it very skilfully, so that I wasn't really hurt. He came back twelve years later and we could laugh about it and be really good friends. We were both in the middle of other love affairs by then. Sadly his last coming didn't coincide with our mother's, though of course they left constant holograms and videos for one another. He is away now for just one more, or so he says.

And our mother. Well, what was to be her final expedition is now considerably overdue. It is now almost certain that there has been some accident. I only hope there was no pain. Our dear old aunt was being very brave about it; she was more hurt than Peachy and I. But she too knew the probabilities. My aunt is dead now, but our bonding remains.

Lately I have visited the main space centres several times and of course have been to the moon where there are some interesting archives and relics. I am thinking of taking one of the galaxy tours, which mean fairly short space black-outs of the old kind — not disintegration. Only just enough to stop one from being totally bored. But when I visit a space centre I always find it slightly embarrassing. That bright young man — how old is he really? That young woman, what have her clear, un-aged eyes actually seen? Many of their manners, their gestures, take me back to something I have read about or seen on old holovids, or met in a school history book. The older they are, the more they prefer life at one of the centres, among their colleagues with whom they can exchange ideas and memories and the kind of jokes and slang which they can't share with the rest of us.

So we lose touch. Old bondings weaken. And they have lost some of the relationships which are very important for genuine human development. Yes, and for the future. Peachy and I each have a child with whom we have kept continuous contact. For all four of us it has been — very satisfactory.

I have a friend whose parents, like mine, are both space travellers. This has meant that she has a brother who is only a toddler and her mother is in all essential ways a generation younger than she is. Yet it all seems to work out somehow. We humans have spent so many centuries adjusting ourselves, so that it becomes a familiar game, as I am sure you know just as well as we do, though the problems are different.

In fact the odd relationships that develop here usually work out and of course they are a boon for the problem-story producers. There are two or three excellent operas based on this kind of thing, Tristan and Iseult type, all rather naive yet producing genuine beauty and clarifying emotions.

Humans are so delightfully complex, as interesting as any of the other life forms in deep space. Isn't that so, even in your own part of time? Sometimes I wonder whether the days of space travel, as we know it, may not be over. Of course the visitations from other intelligences have been deeply interesting, but have had less effect than one might have expected on our basic moralities or our ways of thinking.

However I have heard mathematicians say that some of the oldest Terran concepts, always taken for granted, have now totally changed. That may well be so, but the impact has not yet come my way. In general, these visitations from elsewhere have not come to much, though we always hope that next time — well, I am not sure whether we and whatever other life forms there may be, are likely to do one another much good and may, perhaps inadvertently, do one another harm, even bring about extinction. This has been considered, in fact is one of the main things that are currently being argued about. Perhaps also by other entities in remote space.

What I have found most exciting, myself, is the feeling and intention behind the artefacts which are sometimes brought back. From time to time there are odd correspondences with objects in the Terran past. In your time. In the centuries of early China or southern America. Understanding, sympathy, is the beginning of communication.

All the same, once there is a problem aching, so to speak, to be worked on, solved, we can't stop, can we? In my own field there have been disappointments and misunderstandings. Inevitably. But we go on. And I feel — well, what is your own opinion. Am I getting through?

What Kind of Lesson?

I REALLY DON'T KNOW WHETHER THESE PARALLEL worlds exist in any sense which we would recognise or whether they have been thought up for some fairly adequate reason which I personally find of little interest. But also it is not my speciality. Communication, yes — but not with something completely unknown. Whether or not these worlds are objectively real, we find ourselves in them and have to make the best of it. Probably you know what I mean. I speak for those who can understand. If you have had a parallel experience, I trust you can look back with equanimity now that it is in the past.

These humanoids then, who inhabited, though sparsely, the world in question, had one main peculiarity: this was the algae in their tissues which kept them going with sufficient photosynthetic energy so long as there was a reasonable amount of sunshine, which there usually was. They ate as well, using apparently normal our-world digestive processes, such funguses, lichens and even occasional ferns as could be found, as well as seaweeds. But these on the whole only gave an illusion of fullness and its pleasures. There was no absolute need to eat and often they went for long periods without doing so. In order to give the maximum exposure for the algae, they had webs between their fingers as well as between their toes, which were longer and more easily separated than those of their human semi-duplicates. In the delicate tissues of these webs the blood circulated near the surface and so it did in the beautiful retractable ear-fans which they unfolded from either side of their faces.

These were their main areas for decoration, with fine designs in what appeared to be gold, although this was something which could not be precisely ascertained, as all individuals were extremely shy of allowing any close inspection, let alone touch where these very delicate organs were concerned. Even a glance of admiration was sometimes enough to set the owner into at least a half-retracted pose.

It appeared to be essential to allow this process of photosynthesis to take place for several hours every day, but in the mild, often completely cloudless conditions of their present planet this was usually possible. It soon became apparent that there were two groups of algae, one green and one brownish red, and that these distinguished two groups of owners who were otherwise much the same. They had a curious kind of aversion from one another, especially when it came to the ear fans which either group would retract if approached by the others.

The weather in this parallel world was exceptionally mild but they had shelters for the occasional storm, luckily always short so that at the end they felt depleted but could recover rapidly as soon as the sun shone again. Often they simply slept through a storm as they normally did at night, only waking at sunrise. These shelters were made with some kind of easily worked metal, usually gold, and a covering of a fabric which was fashioned out of a type of seaweed with a very large spread which could be made to take colours and which was also used for such clothing as they had. It seemed to be durable although often semi-transparent; it could however be made into strips and woven into something rather solider. This weaving always took place outside in full sunlight, as did dyeing and indeed any other pseudo-industrial process. But nobody worked hard; sunshine was free.

The main furnishing was for decoration rather than practical use, though they did have fires and did a little cooking. A few enjoyed the luxury of cushions made from the seaweed material, or screens against the wind. All seemed to take pleasure in designing new patterns for the ear flaps of their friends, or perhaps, mates. They obviously enjoyed making small things while they lay out in the sunshine, feeling the photo-synthetic replenishing going through their bodies. We were given various of these artefacts, but as you know, transfer from one parallel world to another is never very satisfactory. I was sorry not to get good replication of some of the musical instruments, mostly made from shells, and their own long hair. These, combined with very sophisticated part singing, made up a usual background to photosynthesis. But the fine points were beyond me and my colleagues.

Gradually we were able to make contact or at least appear to do so, since we were never completely certain of the external reality of this other world and its inhabitants, who appeared to lead a so unfamiliar life although on a mental and aesthetic level comparable to our own.

Something in the nature of poetry was often being composed among quivering ear fans which, although not very intelligible, probably compared with much in our own world, especially as it was all geared into the music. One cannot of course assume that either our or their mental level was particularly high; we can in fact be moderately certain that somewhere in the cosmos there are other levels far out of our reach. But as I have tried to make clear, after what appeared to be much discussion and experiment, especially by myself, we did make contact. By we I mean the group of colleagues with whom I appeared to be working — but as you know in parallel world conditions there may be curious gaps and omissions and sudden appearances.

What came through from the humanoids on the other side was mainly anxiety about us. They recognised us as fellow beings but felt we were not only ugly but in danger, as we had neither webs nor ear fans, nor was it clear to them whether we were greens or browns. They felt it was most extraordinary when I tried to persuade them that we existed without photosynthesis. In fact they could not really believe this. Their own surrounding fauna, in fact their pets, all depended as they did on algae colonies. Their favourite domesticated animal was a marine mollusc not unlike our own giant clam which, as we all know, normally has a symbiotic relation with algae in its mantle. But our giant clams have never been taught, as these were, not to bite. It was terrifying at first to find our new friends rocking softly on a cushion of mollusc tissue, the sun rays penetrating the shallow water, their ear fans spread and wavering in the mild current above the ferocious grooved shells of their pets, which eagerly snatched up small fishes or other marine life.

Our friends were able, of course, to manage quite well below the surface in shallow water, so long as it let through enough sun to keep their algae occupied in converting the carbon dioxide from their bloodstream and keeping the oxygen supply up. But naturally they could not manage in deep or sunless water any better than we could. However, their beaches all tended to run out over softly shelving pale sand. There was another sea beast, a kind of transparent crab, which I never could get quite to like though I am able to admit that it smelled pleasant: so different from the carnivores that we in our world seem still to prefer as pets. This crab also had a fanlike area in which photosynthesis went on; clearly this mattered aesthetically and even morally in the eyes of all those with whom we were gradually making contact, discovering, for instance, their main pleasure and pain sources.

Sex, we found, was fairly pleasurable and took place in a humanoid fashion, but more publicly than is usual in most this-world cultures even today. Giving birth was distinctly pleasurable, especially, it seemed, the actual moment of expulsion of the small entities, often to an entrancing musical accompaniment. Then there was the excitement of spreading the ear fans and webs of the newborn and watching the first pulsing of the rivulets of lifegiving flow. Sometimes there was an inadequate algae population or the fans and webs had not completely developed. If these did not grow quickly, then death came. This happened sufficiently often to keep the population in balance and affection did not develop until symbiosis was completely established in those who had lately been born. Then it seemed to come with a rush, not only to the mother, but to all the group.

The main unpleasantness in their sunbathed life was cloudy weather, langour and depression. It was at these moments that the adults sometimes died. When this happened, others of the group towed the body further out into deep water. Possibly the giant clams tidied everything up.

To reach this amount of contact between ourselves and them had taken a long time. Or perhaps not. Perhaps it would be inaccurate to speak of time in this connection. Certainly we ourselves and any chronometers which we had appeared to keep curiously diverse notations. This is apt to happen in parallel world exploration (or whatever it is). All one can say is that we appeared to be making contact and that I found myself able to formulate quite elaborate ideas when contacting my small group of red-brown algae adults and children. All wore minimal clothing, sometimes on one part of the body, sometimes on another. They did not appear to have any personal preference, but it was apparent that those with the largest ear fans and finger webs could afford to cover more of the other parts of their bodies in which anyhow the blood vessels lay deeper so that photosynthesis was not very active.

As I have indicated most, if not all, of the humanoid population of this world spent their time along the coastal edges where the sun, about the brightness of our own Mediterranean sun, usually shone. The interior mountains were jagged and bare with nothing but lichens, bright coloured and brittle, until rather further down one came on the occasional bluish or orange fungus or fern. Among them we found a few lizards all equipped with the usual algae and a double crest along their backs which could be spread, as well as a kind of fan-eared mouselike creature with the same kind of development, and various insects in parallel with our own, all adapted to lichen eating combined with photo-synthesis. At first our inland exploration yielded nothing of any apparent new interest or significance.

Naturally we wondered whether the symbiotic relationship which characterised this world had always existed or as nearly as one can ever say 'always'. This question became more acute when some of my colleagues found the remains of what seemed to be a solid building in the interior between two mountain clefts. It appeared to have been made of polished stone though this was now roughened and discoloured by centuries of weather, even the mild weather of this planet. I communicated with the group to which I had become attached and which were usually somewhat concerned about me and my lack of symbiotic equipment. This would come up in some form almost every time we met. Clearly they were surprised to see me apparently alive and well whenever I came near them.

It was the usual sunny day. All lay on a patch of sand, basking. When I was with them I brought a red striped towel which I believe they supposed, or at least affected to suppose, was a genuine anatomical attachment. I always kept it round my shoulders so that it might appear to be attached. Whether or not they really believed this, it was clearly sensible to accept it. I began by saying that we had been in the mountains. They thought we had gone there to eat lichens. I had in fact brought some down as a present. They had been prepared by soaking and heating and the addition of various powders whose names I have been told but whose origins — probably marine — were still obscure. Done like this they were palatable, but only just.

I went on to mention the building and immediately an unease seized the group. They shifted and whispered. Music, which had been playing desultorily in the background, ceased. Three or four folded their ear fans and moved either into the water or on to a further patch of sand. It was difficult to know what was worrying them, but I finally got the communication that this was something which should be forgotten, which never was — or ought to be so considered never to have been. Should I go on? Perhaps not.

Yet it was one of this group who approached me later alone. In humanoid terms Ssessa — the nearest I can get to the name — was a youngish woman of the red-brown algae group. She was much esteemed sexually and had already had three children of whom one had survived and two were forgotten, since they had been born with inadequate fans and webs. She wanted to know more about the building. I communicated to her all I knew and then suddenly she began to ask about our parallel world. This was the first time any of them had deliberately asked questions though we had given them many opportunities. Would Ssessa like to see pictures? She would. I thought of running the machine but then decided that still 3D colour pictures would be less disturbing.

Those of sea and shore which I deliberately chose to show Ssessa at first were not really disturbing, but gradually I moved to others: not yet cities or industrial scenes, but fields and woodland, such as we ourselves admire. And suddenly Ssessa was convulsed with grief, anger, what? I tried to get through to her. At last she used a word I had never heard and saying it, glanced round, then clapped her hand over her mouth. 'Again,' she said — I translate of course and perhaps not accurately. She looked at the pictures hungrily and muttered the word. She stared at a picture of trees, a mixed forest, pine and beech and a few cherries and birch and such along the edge. 'But are they always — green?' she asked.

'Mostly,' I said. It was no time to discuss flower colours.

'Green,' she said, 'like *them*.' There was some disgust in her voice and I knew she must be thinking of the others whose symbiotic relationship was with green algae. She went on: 'And these — things — are with you now, this day, in your world? Now?'

'But with you,' I said, feeling, oh so cautiously, my way, 'they were — when?'

'Long long ago,' she said, 'before we were people — as we are now, as you see.' Tides of feeling washed over her face and neck, her ear fans flushed and faded. 'Tell,' she said. 'Tell what other things you find there —' and she pointed towards the hills.

'Perhaps nothing,' I said soothingly, 'nothing to hurt.'

But she gave me a strange look, more disturbed than anything I had yet seen in that world, and then hurried away back to the sea.

My colleagues and I decided on further exploration. And what we came on shook us, for it was clearly the remains of very ancient wood where lintels and beams long gone to powder had been embedded into the stonework and so survived. Hundreds of years, perhaps thousands in this mainly dry and sunny atmosphere. So what did it mean? What had happened? Why? There were other remains of stonework partly covered with blown earth; it was possible that we might also find artefacts, but some historical clue had to be established.

Ssessa was there, her fans unfolded. A male was trying to interest her, stroking her toe webs rather indecently, or so others seemed to think, to judge by looks and nudges and musical queries — for that was how they sounded. Her webs widened, then contracted. These creamy fans, beaded through by the algal coffee colour, were certainly pretty. Those with the green inlay less so to my eyes and clearly to those of the brown. They were also erotic centres and no doubt would have been an interesting anatomical field of study had there been any opportunity. Ssessa saw me and stood up suddenly, disappointing the male. She questioned: 'You saw?' I had a small piece of crumbled ancient wood which I held out to her. Was it possible she would recognise it? She looked from it to me, raised a finger to touch but could not bring herself to. 'The picture,' she said.

I thought I understood, took out the 3D colour picture of the forest. 'That was once one of these,' I said. One could not say exactly what kind of tree it had been, only that in parallel worlds correspondences are probable.

Ssessa shivered. Then she said very low: 'It is said — I have heard — long long ago —' and broke off. I waited. 'There were — all these —' she pointed to the picture. 'But not green. No. Never green, only a beautiful blue brown.'

Why not after all? We are so used to earth and the chlorophyll in our terran leaves that we have to think again of ungreen trees. But colours of course are in fact secondary though they have so many emotional connotations on all worlds. 'Yes,' I said, 'and people?'

'There were some like us. Partly like us.' She spoke with difficulty. 'So I have heard. In the sad music. Even before the change. They were our parents. They could still live. Not well but enough. Their children did better. Becoming like us.'

'But the change — what was it?' This was the big question.

'Everything died. Those — those big things that spread, that seem to have fans. Those that I see in the pictures of your world. And it is said there were little ones, many colours. Their children. Do you have them?'

'Yes,' I said, 'flowers. Lilies of the field.' But that meant nothing. 'Corn,' I said, 'what we make our food from. Ssessa, we poor things have to eat, often.'

But Ssessa shook her head. It was beyond her to understand about the necessity for eating or, as yet, that these strange things could in any way be food. She spoke again, painfully. 'All died in a short time,' she said, 'how long, you ask how long? We are not told. A hundred years. A thousand. It was the same in the end. Yes, they too had been, it was said, something we lived on. We people. The food of animals also. Big. As big as the biggest fish. But with legs. Do you understand?'

'Yes,' I said. 'Yes, Ssessa, we have those animals still.'

'That must be strange,' she said.

'Like this,' I said and showed her pictures with cows and horses, dogs and elephants. I did not explain that some of these were also eaten by the people of our world. That would have been too strange and probably horrible. For a time Ssessa said nothing. My mind went racing back to the change. It appeared that all phanerogams had just disappeared. Why? How? And then could it happen in the parallel world? Our world? 'How long did it take them to die?' I asked gently.

Ssessa did not answer at first. Then: 'We have only been told that — it happened. They became fewer. Smaller. The colours went away. They did not come again. It is not easy for me to think about it!' and she used a word I had never heard before. Then suddenly her ear fans quivered violently and she cried out: 'No! No! It never happened! It was told to frighten us! Not true, not true!' and she turned and ran back to the others. I watched her go, the fans expanding and contracting. I did not try to follow but hoped that the male would be there to console her.

There happened to be a couple of the green algae group — or was it nation? — close by. They looked after her and laughed, not very pleasantly, cocking forward their green ear fans. How fortunate that the necessity for lying in the sun stopped anything like fighting among the humanoids of the parallel world! But quite clearly I now had a piece of history. But how? Why? Did the phanerogams cease to be able to reproduce? Why did the lichens survive, the mosses, funguses and seaweeds, even the occasional ferns? And how had the remote ancestors who were first able to use even a little photosynthesis mutated? It was an extraordinary jump to have made. And yet the jump which our own giant clams have made is unexplained.

I listened to the dying out of the pleasant music which Ssessa's group had been making. What had she communicated to them? Would I be hated because of it? A harsh sound from the shell instruments seemed to show something worse than unease. Would Ssessa avoid me now? I waited for the questions to stop pounding at me, but I believed that they had reached a peak point. The curve must now in some way return. Both for myself and for them.

This was the cusp, the moment when Ssessa and I collided and parted. As we all know from our own experiences of parallel worlds, the descent from the peak of almost any such experience, tends to disintegrate facts. Certain episodes usually stand out, appear to imprint themselves on our memories. Here, I appear to remember that at some point Ssessa must have communicated warnings against the greens, who, she affirmed, were angry with us and would try to get rid of us, because, in her explanation they thought we were trying to find out — something. But what? Her communication was here blurred by emotions and the music that those called up. We were all somewhat alarmed, but in fact nothing happened and a system of defence which we had set up with some trouble and time wastage proved completely pointless. Probably both the greens and the red-browns felt that our habit of questioning was so alien and unpleasant that they reacted against it. Their world, after all, functioned not through questioning but by taking things as they came; curiosity is a very our-world affliction. Or of course the main point of take-off if that is the mood in which we use it.

There was however one unpleasant experience. We found ourselves encircled by a group of red-browns who all appeared much concerned about us. A rather lengthy attempt at communication ended with a nasty realisation of what they intended. Their concern for us had resulted in a determination to help us by inoculating us with algae while at the same time equipping us with ear-fans and finger webs — they had decided that our toes were so unsatisfactory as not to be worth consideration. To do this they would take flaps of our skin and stretch it onto beautifully designed and constructed golden frames. Our external ears, when gristle, fat and such other useless parts as could be found, had been removed, would stretch quite remarkably, they said. We would find there was most satisfactory elasticity, and of course for adequate ear-fans, the thinner the tissue, the better. Skin from two neighbouring fingers would be joined up and the movement of the fingers would in itself provide considerable traction.

When we expressed our unwillingness to have all this performed on us, they explained carefully that any temporary discomfort would be more than compensated for by the well-being we were about to feel. Something we had never imagined! Could not have. But now, what bliss was coming to us! Hands were on us, Ssessa's and others; many and gentle but decisive, with music backgrounding action. A touch of knife. But you will realise that this is part of the descent from the cusp, quickening as we come nearer to the pull of our own world, our own time. With this rapidity of descent the moment of escape is blurred, as landscape blurs and brightens and blurs again in an earthward drop through cloud layers.

So, what were we to make of it? Or, since the group "we" is now dispersed, what do I make of it? Was it all a lesson? If that is the implication, what is to be learned? First of all, in that world there could have been more exploration, more contact with the other groups, the other colours, but if once our genuine, loving contact had disappeared, as it must have done with the physical threat, our differences could not be halted. We began to distance ourselves whether or not we intended to do so. Reality began to thin out. We could not, perhaps, have survived the knife if it had been entirely real in our dimension.

But you will all be familiar with the process of extrication from another world. First one finds oneself in parallel with one's own. Then the parallel slips. In a way this is sad; one has been offered an experience. This has to be enjoyed if possible and certainly endured. But, as in the experience I have related, it may push us too far. And in the end, always, always, we are left with the unpleasantness, the anxiety, of a lesson put before us by what or whom or why is not known. Nor is it helpful to question or discuss. It must, we suppose, be a lesson intended to lead us further, to teach us something of the utmost importance. But this lesson is in an unknown and unknowable script or speech, and so, whatever our willingness, we cannot learn from it.

One Couldn't Tell the Papers

DR. JEAN MACMURRAY HAD SOFT GREY HAIR, BLUE
eyes and pink lips — pink, not red. As usual she wore a blue velvet
ribbon in her grey hair which almost, but not quite, matched her eyes.
There was a nice untidy bowl of late spring flowers behind her, cow
parsley and bluebells and tall meadow buttercups. They made the
watercolours look even more amateur than they normally did. Somehow
her friend Catherine Crabbe, the wife of the Warden, always thought her
rooms more like an English don's than a biologist's.

Yet there were the famous note books. Wonderful to think that they —
and Jean — had actually been there. This other world.

A polleny buttercup petal dropped and shone on the mahogany of the
book case. 'It's all in the official report,' said Dr. MacMurray, 'In fact I
was working on the proofs this morning.' She leant forward a little: 'But
I didn't like to speak about it at the meeting — or — or — in the Press,
you know. People mightn't think it was nice.' She gulped a little. 'In fact,
it isn't. But so convenient — in a way.'

'I understand,' said Mrs. Crabbe, 'that they are quite evolved. I mean,
in our sense. Civilised. With — with education, and poetry and
something like Universities —'

'Oh yes. There are some remarkable similarities. Mentally, and, yes,
physically except for the reproductive system and what this entails in a
different balance of shape. You see, they took a different evolutionary
line, probably quite a sensible one — forgive me for being so Lamarckian!

· 243 ·

For after all, for the female, this business of being a mammal — as both of us know —' Mrs. Crabbe, mother of five, laughed. 'Yes, eggs. So much more convenient. But egg laying with us is associated with birds and their emotional life: which, you know, Catherine, is reflected in *our* attitude towards *them*. My friends over there —' she tapped on a note book — 'were not particularly emotional. They didn't burst into song any more readily than we do ourselves.'

'Nor does the tortoise. Nor yet the platypus,' said Mrs. Crabbe, then hesitated, 'or does it?'

'No. Nor the lizards. Nor the crocodile and alligator which lay eggs on a considerable scale.'

'They cry, of course.'

'Not at all, Catherine! A literary fallacy. But there was nothing lizardish about my friends. And they certainly had a few somewhat avian characteristics. But once we arrived at an understanding — and that, as we keep on explaining, was entirely John B's doing — one never thought of them except, oh, as being like oneself. They were so — tremendously friendly, dear things!'

'I always thought there was more in John B than meets the eye,' said Catherine, 'but he just isn't the senior common room type.'

'It was partly luck, of course: like most things. But the first steps were thought out very carefully. You have to have a groundwork of hard thinking before the luck can begin to happen. If more people realised that —! But what I want to tell you Catherine, is — well, some of the things I couldn't possibly tell those bold-looking newspaper men! I mean, think of the dreadful headlines they'd have been sure to make.'

She hesitated, again. Mrs. Crabbe passed her a cigarette. 'Come on, Jean. Out with it!'

'Well, you see, all their social customs are based on egg laying. All the songs and stories and — yes, I'm afraid, the jokes, in so far as I could understand them. In fact sometimes — oh dear, they made the kind of jokes that I think are made on certain occasions over here, at least so I understood from John B.'

'Come on, Jean, we've both made jokes in our time!'

'I know. And they are such endearing creatures. But you see, Catherine, it makes a different pattern of courtship. At least I suppose so. Though I'm not quite sure. Here, after all, it's always supposed to be the man chasing the girl, or at least that's how it was in my young days: 'The wolf that follows, the fawn that flies.' You know, I used to think Swinburne so wonderful!'

'That's only what they said. It never was particularly true. Lord, how I chased Tommy! In the twenties that was. And got him.'

'If you'd been one of *them,* dear, you'd have given him one of your eggs.'

'Eh?'

'Yes. An unfertilised egg, naturally! A — a pullet's egg, one might say. Just to make it easier to grasp, although of course in a sense we are — er — ovum producers. But the gift of an egg is the great mark of one's favour, there. Beautiful smooth eggs, with a kind of bloom on them, a lovely irridescence. There were a number of special ways of cooking them.'

'You don't mean the boys *ate* them?'

'Oh dear, I knew you'd be shocked! Yes, you are, Catherine! Well, a little. One enters into the being of the beloved in the most direct way, by the digestive tract. There was a very slight but constant and significant change in the blood sugar after a couple of hours. Why sugar? Catherine, you don't know any chemistry, so an explanation wouldn't help. Some of the more attractive young males would have a dozen eggs in a month from different sources. You could tell by their looks. A sparkle in the eye, good muscular tension, a crispness in the hair. Most of them are fairish, but the egg diet tends to produce red hair and above all red eyebrows.'

'Sounds like John B.'

'Yes. That was the piece of luck. They found him — definitely attractive.'

'Don't tell me John B started eating these — eggs!'

'Of course. You see, Catherine, it would have been a terrible insult to those nice girls if he hadn't. We couldn't have risked that. It might have jeopardised the success of the expedition.'

'And did *you* eat any?'

'Oh no! That would have been — most unnatural. I assure you, Catherine — . Not even in the interests of science.'

'Sorry, Jean! I was only asking. And can a young man refuse?'

'That's the kind of situation they make poems about. Tragic poems. Not that every egg is offered, oh no! You mustn't think they were at all — forward. Alternatively, the eggs might be disposed of tidily: as at school.'

'Isn't that rather wasteful?'

'That isn't how they think of it. They aren't materialists in any sense. Besides, at that stage the eggs are pure white, and — so I am led to understand — comparatively tasteless. It is only later that they get the peculiar bloom which makes them so — so appropriate as love tokens.'

'I see. And what happens after — oh, after one's love has been requited?'

'Oh, then one goes broody. Of course that isn't the word, but it's what it means. Those dear, dear girls with their little clutches of eggs! So reserved and maternal and untidy! Sometimes their hair all falls out and they have to wear sweet little caps. There's a kind of soft, good look about them. And the day the eggs begin to chip, oh the excitement! One couldn't help getting excited oneself.'

'Does all the clutch hatch?'

'Well, that's rather delicate. Not all, usually. And by the end of the brood period there are normally one or two favourite eggs that get better treatment. So you see — . But there is definitely a population problem. However, as we explain in the official account, they have still some space for colonisation. I must tell you, though, Catherine, there are some females nowadays who don't brood their own eggs. Rather shocking, isn't it? Of course not the best type.'

'Actressy ones, you mean, Jean?'

'Yes, yes, quite. They even pretend about their eggs. You see, it would be quite dreadful to give someone a fertilised egg. So they would sometimes obtain the eggs of others. And indeed, cases were known when two or even three eggs in one month were given to different men. So when they compared notes — . But don't misunderstand me, Catherine, this kind of thing is very rare!' Jean MacMurray looked earnestly at her friend, and then away, blushing. 'You see, Catherine, I hardly like telling you, and I couldn't possibly have told that sort of thing to those newspaper people! And it's just exactly what they'd have asked about. Sometimes I despair of the Press!'

'I know. We all do. And yet we go on reading it. But tell me, do they ever eat ordinary eggs — hens' eggs for instance? Or don't they have hens?'

'There aren't any domestic egg-layers. It would be embarrassing, you see, Catherine. But — well, there are certain wild semi-avian species that do lay eggs. And they are eaten. But not just in the ordinary way as you and I might. Though I confess, Catherine, I can't lay a spoon to an egg nowadays without feeling most uncomfortable, even in College! These other eggs, well, an egg meal has a kind of religious significance. They are always eaten very solemnly and with appropriate music. I didn't like their music at first, but one takes to it, yes, one takes to it. You know, Catherine, the egg is the great motive for every form of art, for painting, sculpture, proper names even — .'

'Like Egbert?'

'Well — mutatis mutandis. The egg. And red eye brows in the male. They are so anxious for John B to be sure to come back on the next expedition. We are trying to persuade him. But we shall have to wait until his blood sugar goes down.'

'Speaking as a mammal —' said Mrs. Crabbe abruptly, '— what do you think of the whole thing? Personally? Is it, I mean, a good evolutionary idea?'

'Oh!' said Dr. Jean MacMurray gasping a little, 'Oh, most convenient!

Yes, Catherine, very convenient indeed! So tidy. But of course one couldn't tell the papers that.'

Rat-World

IT IS ODD, PERHAPS UNFORTUNATE, THAT PARTS OF an ancient building can be left still standing while the rest is nothing but a tumble of hard stones with perhaps some kind of other stone-ware, useless. Had those from the remote past — the times which were little more than dreams, terrible, before rat-times — been able to leave death country and re-visit the remains of the British Museum, they might have found here and there small fragments of those things which had been so deeply admired and loved by an earlier intelligence form before its destruction. In the still standing halls — only two or three of them — there were copies of pre-historic human life forms. The student rats who came now joked about them, but mostly thought them a little horrible. The stuff of nightmares. So utterly different from the handsome rats of today!

They were aware of their own history, how after the Great Darkness, which some put down as an attack on the real world from outer space, but most thought was due to men and their terrible inherited need to destroy one another, common to certain insects and perhaps a few still surviving kinds of animals. But out of the Great Darkness came the first changed rats, already with skull-room for more elaborate brains, and with fore-claws becoming more sensitive and able to assist the rest of the body which, inspired by the first changes, grew somewhat. This new sensitivity worked in with the new possibilities of living which were now turning and becoming clear to the new rat populations. And indeed it was still difficult to understand how their ancestors had survived in the thousands, indeed millions, of years before the Great Darkness, when they had so many larger and fiercer enemies, always including men, while their own brains were smaller and less adaptable. The years before the Change, perhaps best forgotten.

Only a few of the young rats took a strong and even questioning interest in pre-history, before rat-time, in the days when the main enemy was not floods or fires but man, who trapped and murdered and tortured, without mercy or understanding. Man who thought he was everything, but who, himself, brought on the Great Darkness, but could not by any adaptation survive it. For man had made a permanent image of himself. He himself broke it. This was all in the deep past, hard to take in or believe, but taught routinely to the young rats, for their perhaps painful edification, often using this building, since within there were stone shapes of what men were, and sometimes probably their females, as well as other animals, like the four-legged, on which, it seemed, men sat.

And in the pre-history world stage, men made their own doom. In the Great Darkness they were not able to find food. They had become born blind, or perhaps sunlight had been so cut off that they became blind. They had almost forgotten, in their curious stage of evolution, how to live by smell and hearing. And often, those of the men and other hominids still killed one another. They had many ways of doing this. Mankind, male or female, was always much occupied in killings, both of themselves and of other life.

Rats were better able to find food, even in the darkness of those days. They ate men or the litters of men which had easy skin to bite through. Many other things they ate, and found which were good and which bad, and for a long time it was dark and cold, yes, for many generations during which the weak died, even as man had died. The great animals died; they could not go underground, as the wise rats did. We have found some of their bones, said the rat demonstrator, so we know what they looked like and how unadaptable they were.

Very many other living things died, both in air and water, as in the roots of the ground. Almost all were food for rats. The big animals died first, in warm air or cold air, even in deep water. But the rats survived. Over the generations rats grew to their promised size and strength, also to increasing brain use and communication, not only by smell and touch, but by the many possibilities of sound and vision. Soon they could communicate well, sometimes in sounds, but not always, as this has its limitations, was indeed a somewhat coarse method often leading to misconstruction. And slowly, very slowly, after years and more generations than we rats can imagine, there was light again, though not totally like the old light. Certain plants began to grow, first in water, then on earth; they were not the same as those before the Great Darkness, but most could be eaten. And so it was that life became easier and longer for the individual rats, so that there was time for communication and thinking about such non-urgent things as the stars.

Sometimes, yes, there was anger and biting, but it was clear that this led to no good, no use. Some even said that it was because of the anger and fighting of the rat world that the Great Dark came, though others thought — perhaps knew — that it was the men and their anger which had made it happen.

The years went on and customs came and went. Once there was light again, the rats began to enjoy the warmth and goodness of colour and began also to carry it about on their persons or make it in the home. There was time now for play and the young ones began to colour themselves, mostly the young males. But the young females would also fight one another over colours, which incited the males to jump onto the winning females and bite them till they squealed with delight and gave birth to strong and clever children, often only one or two to a litter, but hard-boned and active. Nor did the females accept to bear every year, but only when they chose. At that time the females began to decorate themselves, weaving bright things onto neck or tail and using the juices of plants, either to make themselves more wanted by their own males, or to keep strangers away, for it was important to have the best body to make these litters which, through the long years, had become so much fewer but so much cleverer. It was thought well to give birth to ratlings with large and mobile ears. Perhaps it was partly because of this that there began to be music, not only for communication, but for the pleasure of all.

Also they were now beginning to build themselves shelters, not only down the deep ancestral burrow, but, as the years went by, pointing cautiously towards more light, so that their eyes became happily adapted to it, even to bright lights and colours. Now patterns came on the walls, making those in the shelter think of being happy. Hollows were made for washing water and good food. Soon such shelters rose above the ground level, for there were few predators surviving, and these could be destroyed in ways which had been carefully thought out. Even the very large birds began to fear the rats.

But all this was thousands of generations after the Great Dark, but almost as many generations before the wiser rats began to put together the often hideous and terrible history stories. These were told to the young as dire warnings, which held all rats together.

Before that, rats had looked at the tall images of men and asked themselves what had truly happened in the dark world of long ago. So as the generations went by they began to cope with knowledge of the times before the Great Dark, difficult even to think about. This was by now told and taught to the young rats by their elders and where better than among the dead man-shapes which now the rats need never again fear? The shapes could not move, though stories were sometimes made about them, always horrible. Some said that the men had been totally destroyed by the rats, but others said that it was the Great Darkness itself which had killed them.

But only a few of the young rats, male or female, listened to these old stories. They only cared in their hearts for what was happening now. Of course they were also learning the essential rules for living and eating and about certain things which must be avoided, most of all the known places where men had left trails of poison, not perhaps to kill rats, but to kill one another. For they were as wicked as that.

It was hard for the young rats to understand, but it seemed there were certain places where men had built up sky-high walls and had filled them with ways to death. Some indeed remained and still had echoes of poison. Almost all over the great rat-world there were places that carried death, even to the strongest rat. So the young ones looked up at the stone, wordless, unmoving men who still walked the floor of this not yet shattered place. They asked questions, some of which were too difficult to answer or explain. There existed, for instance, places which seemed good and safe, but if a rat were to wander in and stay for long, badness would come on him and he would die. Whose doing was that?

So the young rats were warned of these places. Horrible, they thought; why did mankind do this to the world? Were they all the same? So the teachers pointed at the stone men and said that there had been many different kinds and they could not agree, so they tried to kill one another. 'Yes,' one of the young rats would say, 'but did they not know what would happen?'

'They were warned,' their teachers told them, 'but they would not hear.'

'Why not?' the young rats asked, and they looked at the stone men and their stone horses. There were some with only their feet showing under a thickness which covered part of their bodies. The teachers told them that these were females, so they laughed. 'Even those,' said the teachers, 'had a message for them, to stop killing one another. But they did not listen.'

The young rats looked round at the marble men and their marble horses. They understood that horses might have been like very large rats, but stupid. None had survived the Great Darkness. It was all too difficult to understand for most, too shocking. To think that this world was almost men's. Some of them stopped listening, for none of this old story made any difference to life as it really was. Others joked, looking carefully over the marble men, who were as tall and voiceless as trees. Where were their ears? They could not have been truly loving and thinking with those small, squashed ears. And their hands were too like spiders. And yet they had been living and growing all over the world, and hating one another — but why? Well, the historians had ideas about that, but these jealousies and arguings were so trivial. Surely some must have known of the danger they were making? Had they not, somehow, understood what was so plain? 'Yes,' said the teachers, 'if mankind had remained as the most powerful kind of animal, but not killing one another, even progressing, becoming, perhaps, as conscious of fine sounds and of the thoughts of others as we rats are, where would we be? If mankind had survived where would the rats be, where our thinking, our consideration for one another, our songs, our beauties? Could there have been room in the world for both?'

'But the Great Darkness,' one young rat says, and there is whispering round him. 'Might it have been, without that almost death of the world, and the long twirling of time, would we rats have become what we are?' But the teachers shook their heads. Here were questions which not even the wisest rat amongst all the deeply talented rat historians could answer for certain.